THE QUORUM

THE QUORUM

KIM NEWMAN

TITAN BOOKS

THE QUORUM
Print edition ISBN: 9781781165546
E-book edition ISBN: 9781781165553

Published by Titan Books
A division of Titan Publishing Group Ltd
144 Southwark Street, London SE1 0UP

First edition: October 2013

13 5 7 9 10 8 6 4 2

This is a work of fiction. Names, characters, places, and incidents either are the product of the author's imagination or are used fictitiously, and any resemblance to actual persons, living or dead, business establishments, events, or locales is entirely coincidental. The publisher does not have any control over and does not assume any responsibility for author or third-party websites or their content.

Kim Newman asserts the moral right to be identified as the author of this work.

A CIP catalogue record for this title is available from the British Library.

Printed and bound by CPI Group (UK) Ltd, Croydon, CR0 4YY.

Did you enjoy this book? We love to hear from our readers.
Please email us at readerfeedback@titanemail.com or write to us at
Reader Feedback at the above address.

To receive advance information, news, competitions, and exclusive offers online,
please sign up for the Titan newsletter on our website: www.titanbooks.com

for Cindy

MEPHISTOPHILIS: Hell hath no limits, nor is circumscrib'd
In one self place, but where we are is hell,
And where hell is, there we must ever be;
And, to be short, when all the world dissolves
And every creature shall be purify'd,
All places shall be hell that is not heaven.
FAUSTUS: I think hell's a fable.
MEPHISTOPHILIS: Ay, think so still, till experience change thy mind.

CHRISTOPHER MARLOWE,
The Tragicall History of the Life and Death of Doctor Faustus

PROLOGUE
ORGAN DONORS

She came out of the lift into Reception and heard there'd been another accident outside. Beyond sepia-tinted doors, a crowd gathered. People kneeled, as if pressing someone to the pavement. Heidi was phoning an ambulance. A man crouched over the fallen person, white shirt stained red, head shaking angrily. The picture was silent, a gentle whir of air conditioning like the flicker of a projector. Sally walked to the doors, calmly hugging file folders to her chest. She looked through heavy brown glass.

Without shock, she knew it was Connor. She could only see feet, still kicking in the gutter. White trainers with shrieking purple-and-yellow laces. His furry legs were bare. Tight black cycle shorts ripped up a seam, showing a thin triangle of untanned skin.

A gulp of thought came: at least their where-are-we-going? lunch was off. She choked back relief, tried to unthink it to limbo. Then craziness kicked in. She dropped her folders and waded through paper, pushing apart the doors. Outside in Soho Square, noise fell on her like a flock of pigeons. Everyone shouted, called, talked. A siren whined rhythmically.

A dozen yards away, a van was on its side, a dazed and bloody man being pulled free. The bicycle was a tangle of metal and rubber. In the broken frame, she saw, squashed, the yellow plastic drinks container she'd bought him. A satchel of video tapes lay in the gutter.

'Connor,' she said, '*Connor!*'

'Don't look, love,' someone said, extending an arm across her chest.

People shifted out of her way, parting like stage curtains. Heat burst in her head, violet flashes dotted her vision. Her ankles and knees ceased to work. The ground shifted like a funhouse ride. Connor's head was a lumpy smear on the pavement, tyre track of patterned blood streaking away. She was limp, held up by others. Her head lolled and she saw angry blue sky. Buildings all around were skyscrapers. She was at the bottom of a concrete canyon. Darkness poured in.

At her first interview, Tiny Chiselhurst had been chuffed by her *curriculum vitae*. Like everyone for the last twelve years, he didn't expect a private investigator to look like her. She told him yes, she still had her licence, and no, she didn't own a gun. Not any more.

Her independence was a Recession casualty. She wound up the Sally Rhodes Agency and escaped with no major debts, but there was still the mortgage. None of the big security/investigation firms were hiring, so she was forced to find another job her experience qualified her for. Being a researcher was essentially what she was used to: phoning strangers, asking questions, rushing about in heavy traffic, rummaging through microfiche. There were even seductive improvements: working in television, she could rush about in minicabs and retire her much-worn bus-train-tube pass.

On her first day, she was ushered into the open-plan *Survival Kit* office and given a desk behind one of the strange fluted columns that wound their way up through the Mythwrhn Building. Her work station was next to April Treece, an untidy but well-spoken redhead.

'Don't be surprised if you find miniature bottles in the drawers,' April told her. 'The previous tenant went alky.'

Sally had little to move in. No photographs, no toys, no gun. Just a large desk diary and a contacts book. Her mother had given her a Filofax once, but it was somewhere at home unused.

'Welcome to the TV Trenches,' April said, lighting the next cigarette from the dog-end of the last, 'the business that chews you up and spits you out.'

'Why work here, then?'

'Glamour, dahling,' she said, scattering ash over the nest of post-it notes around her terminal. The other woman was a year or so younger than Sally, in her early thirties. She wore a crushed black velvet hat with a silver arrow pin.

'They put all the new bugs next to me. Like an initiation.'

Their desks were in a kind of recess off the main office, with no window. Sally hadn't yet worked out the building. It seemed a fusion of post-modern neo-brutalism and art deco chintz. In Reception, there was a plaque honouring an award won by Constant Drache for the design. She suspected that, after a while, the place would make her head ache.

'Need protection?' April said, opening the cavernous bottom drawer of her desk. 'We did an item last series and were deluged with samples. Have some Chums.'

She dumped a large carton of condoms on Sally's desk. Under cellophane, Derek Leech, multi-media magnate, was on the pack, safe sex instructions in a speech balloon issuing from his grin.

'Careful,' she warned. 'They rip if you get too excited. We had the brand thoroughly road-tested. The office toy boy was sore for months.'

Sally looked at the carton, unsure how to react. Naturally that was when Tiny Chiselhurst dropped by to welcome her to the team.

* * *

She woke up on a couch in Reception. She saw the painted ceiling, a graffiti nightmare of surreal squiggles and souls in torment. Then she saw April.

'Bender tried loosening your clothes,' she said, referring to the notorious office lech, 'but I stopped him before he got too far.'

April's eye-liner had run but she'd stopped crying.

Sally sat up, swallowing a spasm. Her stomach heaved but settled. April hugged her, quickly, then let her go.

'Do you want a cab? To go home?'

She shook her head. She buttoned up her cardigan and waited for a tidal wave of grief-pain-horror. Nothing hit. She stood, April with her. She looked around Reception. Plants spilled out of the lead rhomboid arrangement that passed as a pot. Framed photographs of Tiny and the other presenters, marked with the logos of their programmes, were arranged behind Heidi's desk.

'Sal?'

She felt fine. The buzz of worry-irritation which usually cluttered her head was washed away. All morning, she'd been picking through viewing statistics. Her impending Connor discussion prevented concentration; she'd had to go through the stats too many times, filling her mind with useless figures.

She remembered everything but didn't feel it. She might have had total amnesia and instantly relearned every detail about her life. Her memory was all there but didn't necessarily have anything to do with her.

'Connor is dead?' She had to ask.

With a nod, April confirmed it. 'Tiny says so long as you're back to work tomorrow afternoon for the off-line, you're free.'

'I don't need time away,' she said.

April was startled. 'Are you sure? You've had a shock, lovie, you're entitled to be a zombie.'

Sally shook her head, certain. 'Maybe later.'

* * *

Although April introduced Connor as the 'office toy boy', it was a joke. He was tall, twenty-one, and trying to earn enough as a bike messenger to go back to college. Like everyone (except Sally), he wanted a career in television. Zipping in and out of Soho gridlock biking memos, sandwiches, video-tape and mysterious parcels between production companies was his way of starting at the bottom. He was one of the lean young people in bright lycra who congregated in Soho Square, ever alert for a walkie-talkie call. He was freelance but Mythwrhn was his major employer. There were a lot like him.

Sally first slept with him on a Friday night, after a party to mark the first transmission of the series. It had been a long time for her and she was flattered by his enthusiasm. Besides he was kind of fun.

As he poked about her flat early next morning like a dog marking territory, she wondered if she'd made a mistake. She hid under the duvet as he wandered, unselfconsciously and interestingly naked, in and out of the room, chattering at her. He said he was 'looking for clues'. April had told everyone Sally used to be a private eye, and the Philippa Marlowe jokes were wearing thin.

She checked the bedside clock and saw it was before seven. Also on the table was the carton of Chums, one corner wrenched open. They'd come in handy after all. It'd have been hard to get aroused if she'd thought of Derek Leech leering off the pack at her. She turned the pack, putting Leech's face to the wall.

Connor jumped on her bed, eager to get to it again but she had to get up to pee. As she left the bedroom, she realised he must be looking at her as she had looked at him. Last night, it had been dark. Putting on a dressing gown would kill the moment, so she went nude into the bathroom. After relieving herself, she looked in the long mirror and wasn't too disappointed. When she was Connor's age, she'd been almost chubby; with the years, she'd exercised and worried away the roundness. April said she envied Sally her cheekbones.

When she got back to the bedroom, Connor had already fit another condom over his swelling penis.

'I started without you,' he said.

Tiny told her she didn't have to come to that week's production meeting, but didn't mean it. Sally was still waiting to wake up an emotional basket case but it hadn't happened yet. She slept through the alarm more often and had stomach troubles, as if suffering from persistent jet-lag, but her thoughts were clear. She even dealt with mental time-bombs like the travelling toothbrush left in her bathroom. Perhaps after all these years, she was used to weirdness. Maybe she couldn't survive without a stream of the unexpected, the tragic, the grotesque.

Networked on ITV at eight on Friday evenings, *Survival Kit* was an aggressive consumer show, proposing that life in the late twentieth century was frighteningly random and unspeakably dangerous. Tiny Chiselhurst was at once editor and presenter, and the show, in its fifth season, was the cash-cow that kept Mythwrhn Productions, a reasonably-successful independent, listed as rising. This series, Sally had helped Tiny, whose sarky humour was what kept viewers watching, expose a crooked modelling agency run on white slavery lines. Now she was switched to something that had little to do with the show itself and so was primarily an ornament at these meetings, called upon to report privately afterwards.

Tiny sat in the best chair at the round table as researchers, assistants, producers, directors and minions found places. He seemed to be made entirely of old orange corduroy, with a shaggy seventies mop and moustache. The meeting room was a windowless inner sanctum, eternally lit by grey lights, a crossbreed of padded cell and A-Bomb shelter. After reviewing last week's programme, doling out few compliments and making Lydia Marks cry again, Tiny asked for updates on items-in-progress. Useless Bruce, fill-in presenter and on-screen reporter, coughed up botulism stats. Tiny told him to keep on the trail. The item hadn't yet taken shape but was promising. What that meant, Sally knew, was that no sexy case – a ten-year-old permanently disabled by fish fingers, say – had come to light. When there was a pathetic human face to go with the story, the item would go ahead.

Finally there was the slot when people were supposed to come up with ideas. This was where performance could be best monitored, since ideas were the currency of television. She'd begun to realise actual execution of an item could be completely botched; what Tiny remembered was who had the idea in the first place. Useless Bruce was well known for ideas that never quite worked.

'I was talking to a bloke at a launch the other night,' said April. Someone said something funny, and she stared them silent. 'He turned out to be a corporate psychiatrist at one of the investment banks, talks people out of jumping off the top floor when they lose a couple of million quid. Anyway, he mentioned this thing, "Sick Building Syndrome", which sounded worth a think.'

Tiny gave her the nod and April gathered notes from a folder.

'There are companies which suffer from problems no one can explain. Lots of days lost due to illness, way above the norm. Also, a high turn-over of staff, nervous breakdowns, personal problems, *sturfe* like that. Even suicides, murders. Other companies in exactly the same business with exactly the same pressures breeze through with *pas de* hassles. It might be down to the buildings they work in, a quirk of architecture that traps ill feelings. You know, bad vibrations.'

Sally noticed Tiny was counterfeiting interest. For some reason, he was against April's idea. But he let her speak.

'If we found one of these places, it might make an item.'

'It's very visual, Ape,' said Bender, an associate producer, enthusiasm blooming. 'We could dress it up with *Poltergeist* effects. Merchant bank built over a plague pit, maybe.'

Tiny shook his head. This was the man who'd stayed up all night with a camera crew waiting for the UFOs to make corn circles.

'No,' he said. 'I don't think that suits us.'

'Completely over-the-top,' Bender said, enthusiasm vanishing. 'We're a serious programme.'

'Thank you, April,' Tiny said. 'But Bender has a point. Maybe last series, we could have done this paranormal hoo-hah…'

'This isn't a spook story,' she protested. 'It's psychology.'

Tiny waved his hand, brushing the idea away. 'Remember the big picture. With the franchise bid, we mustn't do anything to make the ITC look askance. It's up to us to demonstrate that we pass the quality threshold.'

April sat back, bundling now-useless notes. Sally was used to this: it was all down to Tiny and he could be as capricious as any Roman Emperor at the games.

Roger the Replacement, one of the directors, had noticed a dry piece in the *Financial Times* about a travel firm considered a bad investment, which suggested further digging might turn up something filmable. British holidaymakers sent to unbuilt hotels in war zones. Tiny gave him a thumbs-up, and, since April wasn't doing anything, assigned her to work the idea. The meeting was wound up.

In the Ladies, Sally found April gripping a sink with both hands, staring down at the plug, muttering 'I hate him I hate him I hate him hate hate hate hate'.

After her exercise class, they had *al fresco* lunch in Soho Square. In summer, it was a huge picnic area; now, in early autumn, office workers – publishing, film, television, advertising – melted away, leaving the square to tramps and runners. He had sandwiches while she dipped Kettle Chips into cottage cheese and pineapple. Connor always pushed his idea that *Survival Kit* do a week-in-the-life-of-a-wino item, unsubtly pressuring Sally to take it into a production meeting. She'd tried to tell him it'd been done before but his excitement always prevailed. Today he pointed out the 'characters' who pan-handled in Soho, explaining their fierce territoriality.

'You don't notice til you're on the streets, Sal. It's a parallel world.'

On a bench nearby sat two men of roughly the same age, a pony-tail in a Gaultier suit and a crusty with filth-locks and biro tattoos. Each pretended the other didn't exist.

'It's a pyramid. At the bottom, people get crushed.'

He was right but it wasn't *Kit*. Besides, she was irritated: was he interested in her mainly as a conduit to the inner circle? With one of his lightning subject-shifts, Connor made a grab, sticking his ribena-sweetened tongue down her throat. His walkie-talkie chirruped and he broke off the kiss. It was just past two and lunch hour was officially over. He frowned as a voice coughed in his ear.

'It's for you,' he said.

Knowing there'd be trouble, she took the receiver. Tiny had been after her to use a portable phone. She was summoned to the Penthouse. Mairi, Tiny's PA, conveyed the message. Tiny wanted to chat. Sally assumed she was going to be fired and dutifully trudged across the square to Mythwrhn.

She stabbed the top button and the lift jerked up through the building. Tiny had a suite of offices on the top floor which she hadn't visited since her interview. Mairi met her at the lift and offered her decaf, which she refused. She wondered if the girl disapproved of her and Connor. She had the idea it wasn't done to dally out of your age range or income bracket. At least, not if you were a woman. All the young middle-age male production staff had permanent lusts for the fresh-from-school female secretaries, runners and receptionists.

Tiny's all-glass office was a frozen womb. He sat behind his desk, leaning back. She noticed again the figurine on its stand: a bird-headed, winged woman, throat open in a silent screech. It was an old piece, but not as old as some.

'Know what that is?' Tiny asked rhetorically, prepared to explain and demonstrate his erudition.

'It's the Mythwrhn,' she pre-empted. 'An ancient bird goddess-demon, probably Ugric. Something between a harpy and an angel.'

Tiny was astonished. 'You're the first person who came in here knowing that…'

'I had an interesting career.'

'You must tell me about it sometime.'

'I must.'

The last time she'd seen a statuette of the Mythwrhn, she'd been on a nasty case involving black magic and death. It had been one of her few exciting involvements, although the excitement was not something she wished to repeat.

Without being asked, she took a seat. Apart from Tiny's puffily upholstered black leather egg-shape, all the chairs in the office were peculiar assemblages of chrome tubing and squeaky rubber. As Tiny made cat's cradles with his fingers, she was certain he'd fire her.

'I've been thinking about you, Sally,' he said. 'You're an asset but I'm not sure how well-placed you are.'

Her three-month trial wasn't even up, so she wasn't on a contract yet. No redundancy payment. At least the dole office was within walking distance of the flat. The poll tax would be a problem, but she should qualify for housing benefit.

'Your experience is unique.'

Tiny's confrontational, foot-in-the-door interviews with dodgy characters put him in more danger in any one series of *Survival Kit* than she had been in all her years of tracing the heirs of intestate decedents, finding lost cats and body-guarding custody case kids. But he was still impressed by a real life private dick. April said the term was sexist and called her a private clit.

'You know about the franchise auction?'

The independent television franchises, which granted a right to broadcast to the companies that made up the ITV network, were being renegotiated. There was currently much scurrying and scheming in the industry as everyone had to justify their existence or give way to someone else. There was controversy over the system, with criticism of the government decision that franchises be awarded to the highest bidder. The Independent Television Commission, the body with power of life and death over the network, had belatedly instituted a policy of partially assessing bids for quality of service rather than just totting up figures. In the run-up to the auction, battles raged up and down the country, with regional companies assailed by challengers. More money than anyone could believe was being poured into the franchise wars. A worry had been raised that the winners were likely to have spent so much on their bids they'd have nothing left over to spend on the actual programmes.

'Mythwrhn is throwing in its hat,' Tiny said.

For an independent production company, no matter how financially solid, to launch a franchise bid on its own would be like Liechtenstein declaring war on Switzerland.

'We'll be the most visible element of a consortium. Polymer Records have kicked in, and Mausoleum Films.'

Both were like Mythwrhn, small but successful. Polymer used to be an indie label and now had the corner on the heavier metallurgists, notably the 'underground' cult band Loud Shit. Mausoleum distributed French art and American splatter; they were known for the *Where the Bodies Are Buried* series, although Sally knew they'd funnelled some of their video profits into British film production, yielding several high profile movies she, along with vast numbers of other people, hadn't wanted to see.

'Deep pockets,' she commented, 'but not deep enough.'

Tiny snapped all his fingers. 'Very sharp, Sally. We have major financial backing, from a multi-media conglomerate who, for reasons of its own, can't be that open about their support. I'm talking newspapers, films and satellite.'

That narrowed it down considerably. To a face the size of a condom packet, in fact.

'We're contesting London, which puts us up against GLT. So it's not going to be a walk-over.'

Greater London Television was one of the keystones of the ITV net, long-established monolith with three shows in the ratings Top Ten, two quizzes and a soap. In television terms, it was, like its audience, middle-aged verging on early retirement. Mythwrhn had a younger demographic.

'I'd like you to be part of the bid,' Tiny said.

She was surprised. 'I'm not a programmer or an accountant.'

'Your special talents can be useful. We'll need a deal of specialised research. In wrapping our package, it'd be handy to have access to certain information. We need to know GLT's weaknesses to help us place our shots.'

This sounded very like industrial espionage. As a field, IE never appealed to Sally. Too much involved affording the client 'plausible deniability' and being paid off to sit out jail sentences.

'You'll keep your desk and your official credit on *Kit* but we'll gradually divert you to the real work. Interested?'

Thinking of the Muswell Hill DSS, she nodded. Tiny grinned wide and extended a hand, but was distracted by a ringing telephone. It was a red contraption aside from his three normal phones, suggesting a hot-line to the Kremlin or the Batcave.

Tiny scooped up the receiver, and said, 'Derek, good to hear from you…'

'Since the franchise *schmeer*,' April said, a drip of mayonnaise on her chin, 'the whole building has gone batty.'

Sally ate her half-bap in silence. She wasn't the only one diverted from usual duties and hustled off to secret meetings.

'They should put valium dispensers in the loos.'

When the consortium announced their intention to contest

London, GLT replied by issuing a complacent press release. Ronnie Shand, host of GLT's 'whacky' girls' bowling quiz *Up Your Alley*, made a joke about Tiny's ego in his weekly monologue. High-level execs were heaping public praise on programmes made by their direst enemies. The dirty tricks had started when GLT, alone of the ITV net, pre-empted *Survival Kit* for a Royal Family special. As payback, Tiny had ordered Weepy Lydia to inflate a tedious offshore trust story involving several GLT board members into a majorly juicy scandal item. In the meantime, the best he could do was give five pounds to any office minion who called up the ITV duty officer and logged a complaint about a GLT show. It had the feel of a phoney war.

'Bender's wife chucked him out again last night,' April said. 'Found him writing silly letters to Pomme.'

Pomme was an eighteen-year-old PA who looked like a cross between Princess Diana and Julia Roberts. If it weren't for her Liza Doolittle accent, she'd have been easy to hate.

'He kipped in the basement of the building, blind drunk. Must have walked into a wall by the look of his face. I hope he keeps the scars.'

Six months before Sally joined the company, when April was young and naive, she had slept with Bender. It hadn't done either of them any good.

'Are you all right?'

People kept asking her that. Sally nodded vigorously. April touched her cheek, as if it'd enable her to take Sally's emotional temperature.

The funeral had been yesterday. Sally had sent a floral tribute but thought it best not to go. Connor's friends would think she was his aunt or someone. She had never met his parents and didn't especially want to.

From the sandwich shop, Sally saw the square. A knot of messengers hung about the gazebo, all in lycra shorts and squiggly T-shirts. Sprawled on benches, they let long legs dangle as they worked pain out of their knees. Some, unlike Connor, had helmets like plastic colanders. Staff at Charing Cross Hospital had a nickname for Central London cycle messengers: organ donors. Scrapes and spills were an inevitable part of accelerated lives. And so was human wastage. Ironically Connor had carried a donor card: he was buried without corneas and one kidney.

'Come on,' said April, looking at her pink plastic watch, 'back to the front…'

If she had doubts about the identity of the consortium's financial backer, they were dispelled by the front page of the *Comet*, tabloid flagship of Derek Leech's media empire. Ronnie Shand was caught in the glare of flash-bulbs, guiltily emerging from a hotel with a girl in dark glasses. The story, two hundred words of patented *Comet* prose, alleged *Up Your Alley* was fixed. Contestants who put out for Shand (51, married with three children) were far more likely to score a strike and take home a fridge-freezer or a holiday in Barbados. An inset showed Ronnie happy with his family in an obviously posed publicity shot. Inside the paper, the girl, an aspiring model, could be seen without clothes, a sidebar giving details about 'my sizzling nights with TV's family man'. Shand was unavailable for comment but GLT made a statement that *Up Your Alley* would be replaced by repeats of *Benny Hill* while an internal investigation was conducted. Sally wondered whether they'd investigate the allegations or witch-hunt their staff for the traitor who'd tipped off the *Comet*.

Tiny was a bundle of suppressed mirth at their meeting and chuckled to himself as she reported. She'd carried out a thorough, boring check of the finances of GLT's component parts, and discovered profits from hit shows had been severely drained by a couple of disastrous international co-productions, *The Euro-Doctors* and *The Return of Jason King*. The interruption of *Up Your Alley* was a severe embarrassment. GLT must be hurting far more than their bland press releases suggested.

'If it comes to it, we can outspend the bastards,' Tiny said. 'We'll have to make sacrifices. Congratulations, Sally. I judge you well.'

There was something seductive about covert work. Setting aside moral qualms about the franchise system and relegating to a deep basement any idea of serving the viewing public, she could look at the situation and see any number of moves which would be to Mythwrhn's advantage. Taken as a game, it was compulsive. It being television, it was easy to believe no real people at all were affected by any action she might suggest or take.

'I've been looking at *Cowley Mansions*,' she said, referring to GLT's long-running thrice-weekly soap set in a Brixton block of flats. It was said GLT wouldn't lose their franchise because John Major didn't want to go down in history as the Prime Minister who took away the *Mansions*.

Tiny showed interest.

'I've not got paper back-up but I heard a whisper that GLT took a second mortgage to finance *The Euro-Doctors* and put the *Mansions* on the block.'

'Explain.'

'To sucker in the Italians and the French, GLT threw in foreign rights to the *Mansions* with the deal. Also a significant slice of the domestic ad revenues for a fixed period.'

Tiny whistled.

'As you know, TéVéZé, the French co-producer, went bust at the beginning of the year and was picked up for a song by a British-based concern which turns out to be a subsidiary of Derek Leech Enterprises.'

Tiny sat up.

'If I were, say, Derek Leech, and I wanted to gain control of the *Mansions*, I think I could do it by upping my holdings in an Italian cable channel by only two per cent, and by buying, through a third party, the studio and editing facilities GLT have currently put on the market to get fast cash. Years ago, in one of those grand tax write-off gestures, slices of the *Mansions* pie were given in name to those GLT sub-divisions and when they separate from the parent company, the slices go too. Then, all I'd have to do to get a majority ownership would be to approach the production team and the cast and offer to triple salaries in exchange for their continued attachment. I might have to change the name of the programme slightly, say by officially calling it *The Mansions*, to get round GLT's underlying rights.'

Tiny pulled open a drawer and took out a neat bundle of fifty-pound notes. He tossed it across his broad desk and it slid into Sally's lap.

'Buy yourself a frock,' he said.

In the lift, there was something wrong with a connection. The light-strip buzzed and flickered. Sally had a satisfaction high but also an undertone of nervous guilt. It was as if she had just taken part in a blood initiation and was now expected to serve forever the purpose of Kali the Destroyer.

As usual, there was nothing on television. She flicked through the four terrestrial channels: Noel Edmonds, tadpole documentary, Benny Hill (ha ha), putting-up-a-shelf. Like all Mythwrhn employees, she'd been fixed up with a dish *gratis* as a frill of the alliance with Derek Leech, so she zapped through an additional seven Cloud 9 satellite channels: bad new film, bad old film, Russian soccer, softcore in German, car ad, Chums commercial disguised as an AIDS documentary, shopping. After heating risotto, she might watch a *Rockford Files* from the stash she'd taped five years ago. James Garner was the only TV private eye she had time for: the fed-up expression he had whenever anyone got him in trouble was the keynote of her entire life.

The telephone rang. She scooped up the remote, pressing it between shoulder and ear as she manoeuvered around her tiny kitchen.

'Sally Rhodes,' she said. 'No divorce work.'

'Ah, um,' said a tiny voice, 'Miss, um, Ms, Rhodes. This is Eric Glover... Connor's Dad.'

She paused in mid-pour and set down the packet of spicy rice.

'Mr Glover, hello,' she said. 'I'm sorry I couldn't make...'

There was an embarrassed (embarrassing) pause.

'No, that's all right. Thank you for the flowers. They were lovely. I knew you were Connor's friend. He said things about you.'

She had no response.

'It's about the accident,' Eric Glover said. 'You were a witness?'

'No, I was there after.' When he was dead.

'There's a fuss about the insurance.'

'Oh.'

'They can't seem to find the van driver. Or the van.'

'It was overturned, a write-off. The police must have details.'

'Seems there was a mix-up.'

'It was just a delivery van. Sliding doors. I don't know the make.'

She tried to rerun the picture in her mind. She could see the dazed driver crawling out of the door, helped by a young man with a shaved head.

'I didn't suppose you'd know, but I had to ask.'

'Of course. If I remember...'

'No worry.'

There had been a logo on the side of the van. On the door.

'Good-bye now, and thanks again.'

Eric Glover hung up.

It had been a Mythwrhn logo, a prettified bird-woman. Or something similar. She was sure. The driver had been a stranger, but the van was one of the company's small fleet.

Weird. Nobody had mentioned it.

Water boiled over in the rice pan. Sally struggled with the knob of the gas cooker, turning the flame down.

* * *

A couple of calls confirmed what Eric Glover told her. It was most likely the van driver would be taken to Charing Cross, where Connor was declared dead, but the hospital had no record of his admission. It was difficult to find one nameless patient in any day's intake, but the nurse she spoke to remembered Connor without recalling anyone brought in at the same time. Sally had only seen the man for a moment: white male, thirties-forties, stocky-tubby, blood on his face. The production manager said none of the vans had been out that day and, yes, they were all garaged where they were supposed to be, and why are you interested? As she made more calls, checking possible hospitals and trying to find a policeman who'd filed an accident report, she fiddled with a loose strand of cardigan wool, resisting the temptation to tug hard and unravel the whole sleeve.

April had dumped her bag and coat on her chair but was not at her desk. That left Sally alone in her alcove, picking at threads when she should be following through the leads Tiny had given her. She had a stack of individual folders containing neatly-typed allegations and bundles of photocopied 'evidence', all suggesting chinks in the Great Wall of GLT. The presenter of a holiday morning kid's show might have a conviction under another name for 'fondling' little girls. A hairy-chested supporting actor on *The Euro-Doctors*, considered to have 'spin-off potential' even after the failure of the parent series, was allegedly a major player in the Madrid gay bondage scene. And, sacrilegiously, it was suggested the producer of a largely unwatched motoring programme had orchestrated a write-in campaign to save it from cancellation. In case Sally wondered where these tid-bits came from, she'd already found an overlooked sticker with the DLE logo and a 'please return to the files of the *Comet*' message; checking other files, she found dust-and-fluff-covered gluey circles that showed where similar stickers had been peeled off. So, apart from everything else, she was in charge of Tiny's Dirty Tricks Department. She wondered if G. Gordon Liddy had got sick to his stomach. This morning, she had thrown up last night's risotto. She should have learned to cook.

Bender popped his head into the alcove. When he saw only her, his face fell.

'Have you seen Ape?'

'She was here,' Sally told him. 'She must be in the building.'

Bender looked as if he'd pulled a couple of consecutive twenty-four hour shifts.

'No matter,' he said, obviously lying. 'This is for her.'

He gave her a file, which she found room for on her desk.

'She's not really supposed to have this, so don't leave it lying around. Give it to her personally.'

Bender, a tall man, never looked a woman in the face. His eyeline was always directed at her chest. In an awkward pause, Sally arranged her cardigan around her neck to cover any exposed skin. The associate producer was a balding schoolboy.

'We were all sorry about, um, you know...'

Sally thanked him, throat suddenly warm. She didn't know why Bender was loitering. Had April taken up with him again? Considering the vehemence of her comments, it was not likely. Or maybe it was.

'If you see... when you see Ape, tell her...'

There was definitely something weird going down. Bender really looked bad. His usual toadying smoothness was worn away. He had an angry red mark on his ring-finger. It had probably had to be sawn free, and serve him right.

'Tell her to return the files ASAP. It's important.'

When he left, she decided to try work therapy. A minion named Roebuck was reputedly interested in being bribed to let Mythwrhn peek at GLT's post-franchise proposals. He'd contacted Tiny and it was down to her to check his standing. Being suspicious, she guessed Roebuck was her opposite number in GLT's Spook Dept trying to slip the consortium dud information. She only had a name and she wanted an employment history. There were several people she could phone and – since everyone in television had at some point worked for, or at least applied to work for, everyone else – her first obvious choice was Mythwrhn's own personnel manager. If he had Roebuck's CV on file, it might have clues as to his contacts or loyalties.

As she bent over in her chair to reach her internal directory from her bottom drawer, her stomach heaved. Gulping back sick, she hurried to the Ladies.

One loo was occupied but the other was free. Apart from a mid-morning cup of tea, there was nothing to come up but clear fluid. It wasn't much of a spasm and settled down almost immediately. She washed her face clean and started to rebuild her make-up. The lighting in the Ladies was subdued and the decor was ugly, walls covered in wavy lumps like an ice cave. She supposed it had been designed to prevent loitering.

Pomme came in for a pee. She greeted Sally cheerfully, and, after a quick and painless tinkle, chatted as she made a kiss-mouth and retouched her lips.

'That bleedin' door is stuck again,' Pomme said, nodding at the occupied stall. 'Or someone has been in there for a two-hour crap.'

Sally looked at the shut door. There was no gap at the bottom to show feet.

'Have you noticed how that happens in this building?' Pomme said. 'Doors lock when you ain't lookin', or come unlocked. The lifts have lay-overs in the Twilight Zone. Even them security keys don't work most of the time. Must be bleedin' haunted.'

The PA left, her face requiring considerably less help than Sally's. Finally, Sally was satisfied. She put her make-up things back in her bag. Turning to leave, she heard a muttering.

'Hello,' she asked the closed door.

There was a fumbling and the 'occupied' flag changed. The door pulled inwards.

'April,' she said, looking.

The woman lolled on the closed toilet, eyes fluttering. She'd had a bad nosebleed and her man's dress shirt was bloodied. The bottom half of her face was caked with dried blood and flecked with white powder. Sally hadn't known she did coke. Or that things could get so bad with a supposedly 'fun' drug. April tried to speak but could only gargle. She pinched her nose and winced, snorting blood.

Sally wondered if she should get two tampons from the dispenser and shove them up April's nose. Instead, she wet a paper towel and tried to clean April's face. Her friend was as compliant as an exhausted three-year-old. Most of the blood was sticky on the floor of the stall.

'Pressure,' April said, over and over, repeating the word like a mantra. 'Pressure, pressure, pressure...'

Sally wondered how she was going to get April out of the building and home without anyone noticing. She told April to stay while she went and got her coat and bag. When she came back, April was standing and almost coherent.

'Sal,' she said, smiling as if she hadn't seen her for days, 'things are just fine up here. Except for...'

Sally tried to put April's hat on her, but she wasn't comfortable and kept tilting it different ways, examining herself in the mirror. Her shoulders heaved as if she alone could hear music and wanted to dance. Sally settled the coat around April's shoulders and steered her out of the loo.

The lift was on the floor, so she was able to get April straight in. If she could get her down to Reception and out into the square and find a cab, she could say April was taken ill. A nasty gynaecological problem would go unquestioned. Those were mysteries men didn't want to penetrate.

She stabbed the ground floor button and the doors closed. If they got quickly past Heidi, she could limit the damage. But the lift was going up, she realised. To the Penthouse. April was almost writing now, and chanting 'pressure, pressure, pressure' until the word lost all meaning.

She slipped an arm around April's waist and tried to hold her still. April laughed as if tickled and a half-moustache of blood dribbled from one nostril. The doors parted and Tiny got in. He was hunched over in an unfamiliar position of subservience, grinning with desperate sincerity as he looked up to his companion. The other man, a human reptile of indeterminate age and indistinct features, was someone Sally recognised from the front of a condom packet.

'Sally, April,' Tiny said, so overwhelmed by his master's presence that he didn't notice their state, 'have you met Derek?'

Sally prayed to be teleported to Japan. The magnate, who kept going in and out of focus as if it were unwise to look at him with the naked eye, smiled a barracuda smile that seemed to fill the lift. She'd always thought of Derek Leech as a James Bond villain, with a high-tech hide-out in an extinct volcano and a missile silo concealed beneath his glass pyramid HQ in London Docklands. A human spider at the heart of a multi-media web, he sucked unimaginable monies from the millions who bought his papers, watched his television, made love with his protection, voted for his bought-and-paid-for politicians. But in person, he was just another well-groomed suit.

Leech nodded at them. Sally tried a weak smile, and April, snorting back blood and residual traces of nose powder, radiated warmth and love before fainting. She slithered through Sally's grasp and collapsed on the floor, knees bunched up against her breasts.

'That's happened before,' Leech said. 'Embarrassing, really.'

Three days into April's 'leave', Bender went up to the Penthouse while Tiny was out recording an interview about the franchise bid. After voiding his bowels on Tiny's granite-slab desk-top and hurling the Mythwrhn statuette through the picture window, he crawled out through shattered glass and stood on the narrow sill while a crowd gathered below. Then, flapping his arms like the failed Wright Brother, he tried to fly over Soho Square. Ten yards from the persistent smear that marked the site of Connor's death, Bender fell to asphalt, neck broken.

It had not been unexpected, somehow. Sally noticed people were marginally less shocked and surprised by Bender than they'd been by Connor. The office had a wartime feel; the troops kept their heads down and tried not to know too much about their comrades. Everyone secretly looked for jobs somewhere else.

Roger the Replacement went into hospital after a severe angina attack. He was thirty-eight. While he was away, his wife came to clear out his things and told Sally that he now planned to take a year off to consider his career options.

'What's the point,' the woman said. 'If he's dead, he can't spend it.'

'True,' she conceded.

Tiny took to wandering around chewing his moustache, checking and double-checking everyone's work. Still wrapped up 101 per cent in the franchise bid, he suddenly became acutely aware that Mythwrhn's current product would influence the ITC decision. The consequences of being blamed for failure would be unthinkable. Off to one side on 'other projects', she was spared the worst but the *Survival Kit* team suffered badly from the sudden attack of caution. Items toiled on for months were suddenly dropped, wasting hundreds of hours; others, rejected out of hand, were re-activated, forcing researchers to redo work that had been binned. In one case, the company was brought very close to Lawsuit County as a hastily slapped-together exposé of dangerous toys named a blatantly innocent designer rather than the shoddy manufacturer.

'I blame Derek Leech,' Useless Bruce said out loud in the meeting room as they waited for an unconscionably late Tiny.

'Shush,' Lydia Marks said, 'this place is probably bugged.'

'Tiny's completely hung up on the bid and *Kit* is suffering. Plus

Leech has this Mephistopheles effect, you know. I swear reality bends wherever he stands.'

There were mumbles of agreement, including Sally's. There was something else she blamed Derek Leech for, considering the reputation of his products. She thought she was pregnant.

First, her doctor congratulated her in the spirit of female solidarity; then, interpreting her blank expression, she dug out a leaflet and said that at Sally's advanced age, she could probably justify an abortion on health grounds. So it was official: thirty-five was 'advanced'. Also, Sally was unmistakably 'with child'. She wondered if her mother would be pleased. And whether she could stand another upheaval.

There wasn't time to talk with Dr Frazier, since she had to rush from the Women's Clinic to a meet with the GLT Deep Throat. Miraculously, Nick Roebuck seemed to be a genuine defector. He wanted old-fashioned money and a shot at a position with the consortium if and when they took over the franchise. Someone reputedly sharp who knew GLT from the inside was convinced enough the consortium were going to win to gamble his career on it. That should be good news for Mythwrhn.

In the cab, Sally held her belly as if she had a stomach ache, trying to feel the alien lodged in her. A tiny Connor, perhaps, dribbled through a ruptured Chum? Or a little Sally, worm-shaped but an incipient woman? Half the time she thought her body had betrayed her; then she was almost won round by the possibilities. All her contemporaries who were going to have babies had already done so. She'd be the last of her generation to give in.

Roebuck had arranged to meet her at a sawdust-on-the-floor pub in Islington, well off the media beat. The cab cruised Upper Street, looking for the sign.

Sally had seen hard-edged women turn mushy-gooey upon

producing a baby. She wondered if she'd ever even met a child she liked, let alone whether she was a fit mother. She corrected herself: fit single mother. Christ, should she even tell Connor's parents? There was some of their son left after all. Did she want to invite those strangers into her life, give them a part of her baby?

The cab drew up outside the pub and she paid the driver. Inside, a few glum men were absorbed in their pints. It was mid-afternoon and beer was half-price to the unwaged. She supposed they called it 'the miserable hour'. A country and western song on the juke-box proclaimed 'If They Didn't Have Pussy, There'd Be a Bounty on Their Pelts'.

She spotted Roebuck at once, at a corner table. Shiny of suit and face, scalp red and glistening under thin strands of cross-combed blond hair. Apart from the barmaid, Sally was the only woman in the pub. She let Roebuck buy her a Perrier (until she decided what to do about the baby, she was off the gin) and listened to him gibber inconsequentially as he fiddled with the satchel he'd brought the papers in. He was nervous to the point of terror, as if he expected GLT shock troops in black balaclavas to burst in and execute him.

'May I?' she said, reaching for the goods. 'Just a taste.'

Roebuck looked appalled.

'It could be old copies of the *Independent*,' she explained.

Reluctantly, he handed over. The satchel was almost a schoolkid's accessory, not at all like the slimly imposing briefcases common in the business.

'I trust this'll go in my favour,' Roebuck said.

'I'm sure the consortium will do well by you.'

She looked at a few sheets. There were authentic audience figures, with alarmed notes scrawled in the margins. A couple of thick documents marked HIGHLY CONFIDENTIAL outlined proposed changes in GLT production and transmission schedules. Without a close examination, she guessed the purpose was to cut short term production costs to cover the losses GLT would sustain ponying up for a winning bid. She was almost satisfied to find a confidential memo from the board, insisting the company try to buy back its squandered percentages of *Cowley Mansions* before a raider took over completely.

'This seems to be in order,' she said.

Roebuck nodded, face burning. Palpable desperation sweated off the man. He gripped the table to prevent his hands shaking. Sally wondered how low the consortium's unseen campaign would get. Roebuck had looked around throughout the meeting, as if searching for a familiar face.

'It'll stop now,' he said. 'Won't it?'

'I don't know what you mean.'

Disgust bulged through fear for a moment and he got up, barging out of the pub, leaving her with the satchel. A couple of others left almost immediately.

She gathered the papers. She'd win untold brownie points for this coup, but didn't know how much of it was her doing. As she left, she noticed an almost-full pint abandoned on a table by the door. The man who'd sat there had struck her as familiar. Broad, undistinguished, in overalls. With a spine-scrape of fear, she wondered if he might be the van driver.

Out in the street, she couldn't see Roebuck or the nondescript drinker who could have been following him. So much to think about. She looked for another cab.

A man in a suit was dismantling April's desk, sorting through every scrap of paper and odd object in its tardis drawers. April had a system whereby every unwanted freebie and done-with document was shoved into a drawer until it disappeared. Tiny was either overseeing the job or ordered to be present at the dissection. The suit worked like a callous surgeon, calmly incising closed envelopes and packets. Sally wondered if he were from the drug squad.

'This is Mr Quilbert,' Tiny said, 'our new security manager.'

Quilbert smiled and shook her hand limply. She instantly pegged him as a cuckoo slipped into the Mythwrhn nest by Derek Leech. He had one of those close-to-the-skull haircuts that disguise premature baldness with designer style.

'We've lost an important file,' Tiny said. 'Bender might have given it to April.'

'I didn't think they were talking,' she said. 'Well, not recently.'

'Nothing scary,' Quilbert said, 'just stats about the building. There was a security survey in there.'

'We can get a copy from the consultants,' Tiny said, 'but it'd be embarrassing.'

Quilbert slit open a packet and slid out a pornographic magazine in Hungarian.

'That's from one of last year's items,' Tiny said. Quilbert smiled tightly and dumped it on the pile.

'Have you tried asking April?' she suggested.

'A bit tricky,' Tiny said. 'She's had a relapse. They've had to put her under restraint.'

She took the file, which she'd sincerely forgotten about, home, hoping it might help her understand the tangle of mysteries. Besides, an evening poring through arcane security lore seemed more comfortable than an evening phoning her mother and announcing a compromised 'blessed event'.

There was a new security guard, in a black one-piece bodysuit, installed in Reception, presumably on Quilbert's orders. She was sure his X-Ray vision would perceive the documents she was smuggling out but he was too busy trying to cosy up to Heidi. That hardly suggested fearsome efficiency.

She made herself tea and sat on her sofa, television on but with the sound down. The file Bender had given her for April was tied with red ribbon. She let it lie a moment and drank her tea. On the screen, an interracial couple argued their way to a cliffhanging climax on *Cowley Mansions*. The soap's storylines had become increasingly bizarre: Peter, the gay yuppie, was discovered to be 'pregnant', a long-unborn twin developing inside his abdomen; Joko, the cool black wastrel, was revealed to be a white boy with permanently dyed skin, hiding out; and Ell Crenshaw, the cockney matriarch who ruled the top floor, spontaneously combusted the week the actress demanded a vast salary hike. Either the writers saw a Leech take-over as inevitable and were devaluing the property before the new landlord arrived, or GLT had ordered audience-grabbing sensationalism in the run-up to the auction.

After the soap came a commercial for the serialisation of Josef Mengele's Auschwitz diaries in the *Argus*, Leech's heavy paper. Then a caring, sensitive ad for Chums.

Sally undid the ribbon and didn't find a security survey. The first item was familiar: a glossy Mythwrhn press release, dated three years ago, about the redesign of their Soho Square premises. She paged through and found quotes from critics praising the features of the building that now drove people mad. The brochure also profiled Constant Drache, the award-winning architect entrusted with the commission. He'd been an unknown until Derek Leech chose him to construct the DLE pyramid, the black glass creation that now dominated Docklands. In a broody shot, Drache posed in black like the lead singer of a Goth group. A wedge of gibberish about his intentions with the building was printed white on black. It was silly, considering that a lot of Drache's 'severe edges' were now best known for ripping the clothes of passing people, but hardly worth Quilbert's search-and-destroy mission. Drache referred to buildings as 'devices', insisting each have its own purpose and be designed to concentrate 'human energies' towards the fulfilment of that purpose. Cathedrals, for instance, were designed to concentrate prayer upwards. Sally wondered what low ceilings and floor-level lighting were supposed to concentrate you towards, and, before she could stop herself, guessed Bender had probably worked it out.

She zapped to the Leech channel and found a scary scene from one of the *Where the Bodies Are Buried* sequels. A teenager screamed silently as Hackwill, the monster, slashed him with a cake-slice.

Under the brochure was a clipped-together batch of articles from a psychology journal. April hadn't abandoned her 'sick building syndrome' idea, or at least had got Bender to retrieve materials from the files before Tiny pulled the plug. Sally skimmed until her head hurt with jargon. Respectable psychology segued into the *Fortean Times* and even weirder quarters. She found pieces, with significant passages underlined in violet, on 'curses' and 'hauntings'.

The television monster laughed loud enough to be heard even with the sound down. The camera pulled back from a graveyard through which a girl was running to reveal that the tilted tombstones constituted a giant face.

The last items were thin strips of word-processed news copy. A fine print tag at the bottom of each page identified the copy as having been generated for the *Comet*. Sally guessed that for a tabloid these pieces would constitute a heavyweight Sunday section article. She read them through, recognising the style and concerns of the Leech press. Dated a year ago, the article celebrated a major police infiltration of a nest of Satanic Child-Abusers. Naming a few names, the piece was about decadent high society types turning to black magic to advance themselves. A 23-year-old stockbroker was purported to have made a million on Market Tips From Hell. A top model, who'd doubtless have posed nude for the illo, claimed drinking goat blood landed her international assignments.

It was typical *Comet* drivel but had never appeared in the paper. Each strip of prose was individually stamped in red with a large 'NO' design that contained, in tiny letters, the initials 'DL'.

She supposed this was Leech's personal veto. Why hadn't the piece appeared? It seemed a natural for the *Comet*. So, most likely, Leech had an interest in its suppression. She read everything through again and found it. The reference in the copy was to the '£3.5 million modern home' which was the gathering point for the cult. In the margin, in faded pencil that looked as if it had been almost rubbed out, were the words 'Drache Retreat'.

'Where's the goon?' Sally asked Heidi. The security man wasn't at his post.

'Caught his hand in the lift,' the receptionist said. 'Dozens of little bones broken.'

Sally raised an eyebrow. A workman was examining the lift door, screwdrivers laid out on a dustcloth like surgical instruments.

'There was blood all over the floor. Disgusting.'

Carefully, she climbed the stairs, trying to keep her elbows away from Drache's 'severe edges'. If the architect had chosen to inset razor-blades into all the walls, the effect might have been more obvious.

The *Survival Kit* offices were depopulated. Pomme told her everyone was off with a bout of the flu. Pomme's perfect complexion was marred by eruptions.

'Bleedin' worry, I reckon,' she said, scratching her blood-dotted chin.

April's desk had been put together again but was stripped clean. There was a padded envelope on Sally's desk, with her name printed on it. She opened it and found a bundle of £20 notes. There was no 'compliments' slip.

She took a giant-size bag of Kettle Chips out of her case and, after a furtive glance-around, ate them rapidly, one by one. She was eating for two. The cash was for Roebuck's papers, she understood. A bonus, blood money.

She had just scrunched up the crisp packet and buried it in her waste-bin when Pomme slid her head into the alcove.

'Remember Streaky?' she said, referring to the office cat who'd disappeared three months ago.

Sally nodded.

'The lift-repair man just found the bones at the bottom of the shaft. Ugh.'

All the black magicians she knew were dead, which was not something she usually found upsetting. She couldn't ask anyone to explain things to her. Nevertheless, she thought she'd worked it out.

It was possible to climb past the Penthouse and get onto the roof. The original idea had been to make it a party area but Drache insisted on a rubbery-leathery species of covering that made the slight slope dangerously slippery.

Sally sat carefully and looked out at Soho Square, thinking. Her hair was riffled by the slight breeze. She wished she had more crisps. Down in the world, the organ donors were waiting to be sent out. Today, things had ground to a halt in the business. It was an Armistice, a pause before the *putsch* of the franchise auction. Thousands would go under the mud in that armageddon, leaving the map of Media London dotted with crushed corpses.

It was almost peaceful. Above the building, she felt a calm which was elusive inside it. The knot of worry which she'd got used to eased away.

'Chim-chim-a-nee,' she hummed. 'Chim-chim-a-nee, chim-chim-cha-roo…'

She decided she'd have her baby. And she'd leave Mythwrhn. There, two decisions and her life was solved.

Hours might have passed. The sun came out from behind a cloud and the roof heated. Should she give her blood bonus away? She'd been taking tainted money so long, she might as well keep this too. Soon she'd have to buy cribs and baby clothes and nappies. Leech's money was no worse than anyone else's.

A few of the rubberised tiles nearby had been dislodged, and a dull metal was exposed. Beneath was a thick layer of lead, its surface covered in apparently functionless runes. She assumed they were symbolic. She picked free a few further tiles, disclosing more and more lead plates, all etched with hieroglyphs, incantations, invocations.

It confirmed what she had guessed. A cathedral was designed to direct upwards; the Mythwrhn Building was designed to capture and contain. In psychic terms, it was earthed. She hoped she wasn't succumbing to the New Age now life was developing inside her. But for the past few months, she had worked among enough negative energy to blacken anybody's crystal.

No wonder everyone in Mythwrhn was miserable. They were supposed to be. Misery was the cake, she supposed; all the blood was icing. Drache's Design must extend under the pavement into the street, to catch the drippings from Connor. If Bender had jumped from the roof rather than the Penthouse, would he have escaped?

The Device worked like a scale. All the misery weighed one pan down, thrusting the other upwards. She could guess who would be sitting on the other pan. And what the uplift was for.

Under her crossed legs, the building thrummed with pent-up unhappiness. She was above it all. At once, she was centred. In her condition, she had power.

Over the years, she'd collected a library, mainly by ordering from the Amok Bookstore in Los Angeles, which was dedicated to 'extremes of information in print'. She skipped past William B. Moran's *Covert Surveillance and Electronic Penetration*, G.B. Clark's *How to Get Lost and Start All Over Again* and Colonel Rex Applegate's *Kill or Get Killed: For Police and the Military, Last Word on Mob Control*, paused for an amused flick through one of John Minner's seven-volume *How to Kill* series, then selected Kurt Saxon's *The Poor Man's James Bond*.

Saxon, an extreme right-winger and authority on explosives, had authored a guide for the defence of the USA in the event of a Russian invasion, compiling information on sabotage, home-made weaponry and sundry guerilla tactics. Although Saxon declared himself 'very pro-establishment and pro-law enforcement' and that he would 'not knowingly sell his more sensitive books to any left-wing group or individual', given the ever-decreasing likelihood of a Soviet invasion, the only conceivable purpose of his work was as a manual for the criminal.

Along with more conservative texts – Seymour Lecker's *Deadly Brew: Advanced Improvised Explosives*, the CIA's *Field Expedient Methods for Explosives Preparations* – Saxon's book gave Sally a wide variety of recipes to consider. She made a shopping list and went out to the chemist's, a DIY shop, a tobacconist's, Sainsbury's and Rumbelow's to buy the easily available ingredients she now knew how to convert into a functioning infernal device. The most hard-to-obtain items were the steel buckets in which she wanted to place her home-made bombs, to direct the blasts upwards. Everyone had plastic these days.

She was in her kitchen, attempting to distil a quantity of picric acid from ten bottles of aspirin, when her mother telephoned to see how she was getting on.

'I'm cooking, Mum.'

'That's nice, dear. Having a guest for dinner?'

'No, just practising.'

'What's in the buckets?' Heidi asked.

'Live crabs,' she claimed. 'We're doing an item on the crooked pet racket.'

'Ugh.'

'You're telling me.'

The security guard was back at his post, hand mittened with

plaster. Sally held up a bucket and he avoided looking into it.

'Careful,' she warned, 'the little bastards don't half nip.'

She was nodded through. On her lunch-hour she went back to Muswell Hill to fetch the other two buckets from her flat and went through the whole thing again.

That afternoon, there was enough blast-power under her desk to raise the roof. She hoped.

There was a confab going on up in the Penthouse, a long-term post-franchise planning session. Sally would have to wait until everyone left. The idea of detonating some of the consortium along with the building was tempting, but she was more likely to get away with what she intended if no one was hurt. If the roof was blown off the Device, the energy should dissipate. She couldn't bring Connor or Bender back or restore April's mind or Pomme's complexion but she could spoil the nasty little scheme.

As the afternoon dragged on, she pretended to work. She ate three packets of Kettle Chips, shuffled papers around on the desk, phoned people back. She guessed this would be her last day. It'd be a shame to do without the leaving party and the whip-round present. She'd probably have qualified for paid maternity leave, too. Actually, she'd be lucky to stay out of jail.

She had the idea, however, that Leech would not want her talking too much about the motive for her terrorist atrocity. A *Comet* think piece about how pregnancy drives women up the walls wouldn't serve to explain away her loud resignation notice.

The few *Kit* staff around drifted off about tea-time. Pomme invited her out for a drink but Sally said she wanted to get something finished before leaving.

'You look a bit peaky, Sal,' Pomme said. 'You should get a good night's kip.'

Sally agreed.

'You've been driven to smoking?'

There was a packet of cigarettes on her desk. Sally coughed and smiled.

'Your face looks better, Pomme.'

'Fuckin' tell me about it, Sal.'

The girl shrugged and left. Sally realised she'd miss some of the others. Even Useless Bruce. She'd never worked much with people before, and there were nice things about it. From now on, she'd be alone again. Perhaps she would re-start the Agency.

Alone in the office as it got dark outside, she ate more crisps, made herself tea and sat at her desk with a new-bought occult paperback. She gathered the building was a magical pressure cooker and the accumulation of 'melancholy humours' was a species of sacrifice, a way of getting someone else to pay your infernal dues. It was capitalist black magic, getting minions to pay for the spell in suffering while the conjurers got ahead on other people's sweat. Obviously, some people would do *anything* to get a television franchise. Since catching on, she had been noticing more and more things about the Mythwrhn Building: symbols worked into the design like the hidden cows and lions in a 'How Many Animals Can You See in This Picture?' puzzle; spikes and hooks deliberately placed to be hostile to living inhabitants; numerical patterns in steps, windows and corners.

Sally divided the cigarettes into five sets of three. Pinching off the filters, she connected each of the sets into six-inch-long tubes, securing the joins with extra layers of roll-up paper. Then she dripped lighter fluid, letting the flammable liquid seep through the tobacco cores. One test fuse she stood up in a lump of blu-tak and lit. It took over five minutes to burn down completely. Long enough.

At eight o'clock, she put an internal call up to the Penthouse and let it ring. After an age, Tiny's answering machine cut in asking her to leave a message. She double-checked by opening a window in the office and leaning out as far as possible into the well, looking up. No light spilled out of the Penthouse.

The lift was still out of order, so she had to take the works up the stairs. First she went up and circumvented the suite's personal alarm. With some deft fiddling and her electronic key, she got the doors open. The Penthouse was dark and empty. It took three quick trips to get everything into Tiny's office and she arranged it all on his desk, working by the streetlight.

She felt ill. Since realising what was going on, she'd been more sensitive to the gloom trapped within the walls of the Mythwrhn Building. It was a miasma. The water in the pipes smelled like blood.

Had Bender been trying to break the Device when he smashed the windows? If so, he'd made a mistake.

There was a hatch directly above the desk, just where it was indicated on the plans she'd borrowed. Above would be a crawlspace under the lead shield. She put a chair and the now-untenanted statuette stand on the desk, making a rough arrangement of steps, and climbed up to the ceiling. A good thump dislodged the hatch and she stuck her head into smelly dark.

She'd assumed this was where all the energies would gather. The cavity didn't feel any worse than the rest of the building and she had a moment of doubt. Was this really crazy?

After ferrying up the four buckets and the other stuff, she jammed through into the crawlspace. Here she could turn on the bicycle lamp Connor had left in her flat. She shone the beam around. She almost expected to find screaming skeletons and the remains of blood sacrifices, but the cavity was surprisingly clean. Meccano struts shored up the lead shield and criss-crossed the plastered ceiling. There was a slope to the roof, so the crawlspace grew from a two-foot height at the street edge of the building to four feet at the rear. If she placed her buckets near the rear end, the blast should neatly slide off the lead shield and dump it into the square. With luck, not on the heads of innocent passersby.

She crawled carefully but still opened her palm on a protruding nail. The floor was studded with spikes, either one of Drache's devilish frills or a defensive feature. Crouching at the rear of the building, she pushed up, testing the shield. It was unresisting. Prominent bolts were spaced around the walls. With a monkey-wrench, she loosened as many as she could reach. She banged her elbows constantly and skinned her right knuckles. Her hair was stuck to her face by sweat. This was not usually prescribed for expectant mothers.

With enough bolts loosened, she tried to push the shield again. It creaked alarmingly and shifted. Sally found she was shaking. She thought she could almost dislodge the lead without the bombs. But it was best to be safe.

She'd hoped the joists would be wooden, so she could screw in hooks to hang the buckets from. However, the metal struts came equipped with handy holes, so she was able to rig up the hanging bombs with stout wire. In each bucket of packed-down goo, she'd used Sexton's recommended dosage for disabling a Russian tank. She stuck the long cigarettes in each bucket and flicked a flame from her disposable lighter.

Once the fuses were burning, she intended to get down to her desk and alert the skeleton overnight staff. She'd say she'd seen smoke pouring down the stairs. With five minutes, she should be able to evacuate the building.

She lit the four cigarettes and wriggled back towards the hatch. Down in the Penthouse, lights came on and voices exclaimed surprise. Knowing she was dead, she dangled her legs through the hatch and dropped into the office.

'What, no Leech?' she said.

Tiny was between the others, shaking and pale. The Device had been eating at him as much as his employees. Sally guessed he was only in the consortium as a judas goat.

Quilbert was in charge, Drache was along for the ride, and the non-descript man holding Tiny up was the muscle. He was also the van driver who'd knocked down Connor and the balls-squeezer who'd pressured Roebuck. He looked more like a plumber than Satan's Hit Man.

'Ms Rhodes, what are you doing?' Quilbert asked.

'Raising the roof.'

Tiny shook his head and sagged into his chair. Drache strode around the office, examining his handiwork. He had a black leather trenchcoat and showy wings of hair like horns.

'The stand should be here,' he said, pointing to the dust-free spot where it had stood. 'For the proper balance. Everything is supposed to be exact. How often have I told you, the patterns are all-important?'

Quilbert nodded to the muscle, who clambered onto the desk and stuck his head into the crawlspace.

'Smells like she's been smoking,' he said.

'It's a secret,' she said. 'I quit but backslid. I have to take extreme measures to cover up.'

'I think I can see… *buckets*?'

Quilbert looked at Sally as if trying to read her mind. 'What have you done?'

'I've forestalled the Device,' she said. 'It was all wasted.'

Quilbert's clear blue eyes were unreadable.

'Only an innocent can intervene,' Drache said pompously. 'You've taken blooded coin.'

'He's right,' Quilbert said. 'You don't understand at all. Everything has been pre-arranged.'

'Not everything,' she said. 'I'm going to have a baby.'

Drache looked stricken but Quilbert and Tiny didn't get it. She supposed they found it all as hard to believe as she did.

'There's something burning,' a voice mumbled from above. 'In the buckets…'

Drache flew around in a cold rage.

'If she's carrying a child, she's washed clean,' he said, urgently. 'It'll upset the balances.'

'What have you done?' Quilbert asked.

Sally smiled. 'Wouldn't you like to know?'

'Put out the fires,' Quilbert shouted up, 'at once!'

She should tell them not to tamper with the buckets in case the burning fuses fell. For the sake of her child, she couldn't die.

'Careful,' she said...

The ceiling burst and a billow of flame shot into the office, flattening everyone. A dead human shape thumped onto the desk, covered in burning jelly. Sally's ears were hammered by the blast. The stench of evaporating goo was incredible. Metal wrenched and complained. Hot rivets rained onto the fitted carpet. She heard screaming. A raft of steel and plaster bore down on Quilbert and Tiny. The windows had blown out, and the air was full of flying shards, glinting and scratching. She felt a growing power deep inside her and knew she would survive.

The cloud of flame burned away almost instantly, leaving little fires all around. Drache stumbled, a bloody hand stuck to half his face, and sank to his knees, shrieking. Sally was flat on her back, looking up at the ceiling. She saw night sky and felt the updraught as the accumulated misery of months escaped to the Heavens like prayers.

They kept her in hospital for weeks. Not the same one as Drache and Quilbert, who were private, and certainly not in the department that had received the still officially unidentified van driver. She only had superficial injuries, but in her condition the doctors wanted to be careful with her.

She read the media pages every day, following the ripples. In the week before the auction, the consortium fell apart. Mausoleum Pictures, wildly over-extended, went bust, bringing down yet another fifth of the British Film Industry. Tiny promised *Survival Kit* would be back as soon as he was walking, but he'd have to recruit a substantially new staff since almost everyone who had worked in the now-roofless Mythwrhn Building was seeking employment elsewhere. Most wanted to escape from television altogether and find honest work.

The police had interviewed her extensively but she pleaded amnesia, pretending to be confused about what had happened just before the 'accident'. No charges against her were even suggested. Mythwrhn even continued to pay her salary even though she'd given notice. After the baby, she would not be returning.

Derek Leech, never officially involved in the consortium, said nothing and his media juggernaut rolled on unhindered by its lack of a controlling interest in a franchise. GLT, somewhat surprised, scaled down their bid and fought off a feeble challenge at auction time, promising to deliver to the British Public the same tried-and-tested programme formulae in ever-increasing doses. On *Cowley Mansions*, Peter the gay yuppie had a son-brother and, salary dispute over, the ghost of Ell Crenshaw possessed her long-lost sister.

Apart from the van driver and Drache, who lost an eye, nobody had really been punished. But none of them benefited from the Device either. All the gathered misery was loose in the world.

The day before she was due out, April and Pomme visited. April was taking it 'one day at a time' and Pomme had discovered a miracle cure. They brought a card signed by everybody on *Survival Kit* except Tiny.

The women cooed over Sally's swollen stomach and she managed not to be sickened. She felt like a balloon with a head and legs and nothing she owned, except her nightie, fit any more.

She told them she'd have to sell the flat and get a bigger one or a small house. She'd need more living space. That, she had learned, was important.

LEECH

ISLE OF DOGS, 1961

Born of filth, he stood on the river-bed, feet anchored, completely submerged. A lily of hair floated on the surface. His buoyant arms rose like angel wings. Though weak, standing by the dock current streamed at his back. The river worked to uproot him.

He opened his eyes; his first image was green murk, shadows filtering down. Before the murk, there was nothing. He was new-formed. Yet his mind was full: he had language, knowledge, purpose. He had a name: Leech.

For a moment, he hesitated, suspended. The water was warm. It was all he had ever known. To leave would be a peril, an adventure.

A newspaper passed by, sliming his face like a heavy eel. Experimenting with his face, he constructed a tight-lipped smile that grew to be a skull-wide grin.

The adventure began.

He took his first steps, lifting his feet and wading through scratchy silt. His head slowly broke the surface. He blinked away water. A rush of noise poured in: the backwash by the dock, gulls, distant traffic. Nose and mouth clear; he filled his lungs and began, evenly and deliberately, to breathe. He did not gulp or choke.

The Thames coughed him up. Covered in an oily film, he walked. The tug of water passed down his body, pulling at his chest, his groin, his shins. It was the work of minutes to get ashore.

Emerging from the dock's shadow, he stood on a stretch of mudflat at the foot of a grey wall inset with rusty giant rings. Water-smoothed chunks of glass and snapped lengths of clay pipestem pricked the soft soles of his feet.

He wiped sludge from his face. Carefully, before muck could dry on him, he washed. Naked and clean, he squatted by the river. He considered his wavering white reflection a moment, then scattered it with a swirling dip of his fingertips.

The flat was littered with gifts. He collected a pair of empty spectacle frames, a bottleneck with a blade of sharp glass, a stub of pencil, a cellophane crisp packet and a squeaking rubber teddy bear.

A gull alighted on the dock and watched him with disinterest. It beat its wings once. He imitated the movement, shaking his head, straining his shoulder-blades. The bird reached up and flapped into the air. Unblinking, he watched it spiral to the sun.

A ropey twist of cloth, stiff with sewage, unwound into a long overcoat, its pockets exploded, its buttons a memory. He did his best to wring out the dirt and covered his nakedness. He found a length of material, once a school tie, and used it as a belt.

His first meal was a soggy breadcrust with a stone-hard core and a ripe dog turd. He had no taste or smell, but knew his current appearance and habits would give general offence. Soon, he must moderate them. He tore an arm off the bear and chewed it, mouth filling with saliva, sharp teeth grinding. He needed to keep his jaws working, lest his teeth outgrow his mouth.

On top of the wall, something tiny fluttered. It was a pound note, paperweighted with an egg-shaped stone. Using a ring as a foothold, he eased himself up and claimed the prize.

He held up the note and looked through it at the sun. Green light shone through a young woman's face.

* * *

POPLAR, 1961

His first spoken words were 'I want to bet.'

'You got no shoes, mate,' said the man behind the window.

'I want to bet,' Leech repeated, smoothing the note on the formica counter.

'It's your money.'

'Dog Number Six.'

'Twenty to one, mate.'

'Dog Number Six.'

The man shrugged and took the note. He scribbled a ticket and slid it under the grille.

A man in a cap, slouching by the steam radiator pointed and laughed, low-hanging belly shaking. Leech took out his spectacle frames and put them on. Receiving a quick glance, the man stopped laughing.

While he waited for the result, he chewed the severed bear arm. He ignored people who stared at him.

Dog Number Six came in at twenty to one.

'Lucky Jim,' someone said.

Leech told the clerk to let his winnings ride and picked Dog Number Four in the next race.

By closing time, he had nearly £400. Outside, men waited to take his money from him. He put the banknotes into the surviving inside pocket of his coat and took out his treasure trove. In one hand, covered by the long sleeve, he held the bottleneck. In the other, concealed by his palm, the stub of pencil. He left the betting shop and protected his winnings.

SOHO, 1963

He insisted on sprinkling his own *cappuccino*. Without the distraction of taste, he was able to create a perfect image of chocolate-spotted froth.

'You're a connoisseur *signor*,' Mama Gina said. She brought him his pastry. He would crumble it and eat slowly, making it last. He kept food in his mouth to have something to chew.

Leech did business from the rear table in Mama Gina's on Tuesday and Thursday afternoons. His suit had no lapels, his shoes were shined to black mirrors. His hair just grew down over his ears. He wore midnight-black sunglasses and, a distinctive touch, a wide-brimmed hat. They called him 'pilgrim'.

'You're No Good' by the Swinging Blue Jeans came tinnily from the pink plastic radio.

Two girls ventured in and asked for him at the counter: Mama Gina nodded them towards him.

About fourteen: Jackie bands in their hair, white-cream dresses with cassata swirls of colour. Too close in age to be sisters. Best friends.

He took out his wallet.

'We were told,' the more intrepid girl began.

He opened his wallet. It was stuffed with tickets. The Searchers, Gerry & the Pacemakers, The Animals, Dusty Springfield.

'Sold out for weeks, they said at the hall,' the girl lamented.

The Beatles. This year, everyone wanted the Beatles.

'Nothing is ever sold out.'

Nervous smiles.

He named a price. One girl gulped but the other opened a tiny handbag and took out a tinier purse. She unfolded notes and emptied small change on to the table.

'Jan, where d'you get all that?' her friend asked.

'Mum.'

'She know?'

Leech put two tickets on the table.

'My pleasure, girls,' he said.

* * *

CHELSEA, 1967

'You live over the shop?' Tamsin said. 'It's just a box.'

It was a room with a bed. Leech rarely slept.

The bass player and the drummer sat on the bed. Denny Wolfe, the lead guitarist, crouched by the cold grate. Leech and Tamsin stood by the open window. She was the singer.

'Thought you'd have a flash pad,' the drummer said. 'You must be rakin' it in downstairs.'

Downstairs was the original Derek's. Leech started in the King's Road selling militaria, then rented rack-space to local designers. This year, old curtains with armholes would sell as swinging London fashions. There were five Derek's now, dotted over London.

'Money is only a tool,' he said.

The musicians grinned. Boyish in cavalry sideburns and bright shirts. They would have six Top Twenty hits but only Tamsin would have a real career after the break-up. The drummer, now rolling a thin joint, would overdose in a New York hotel within ten years. Wolfe would strike a separate Deal but see little profit from it. The others would fade away.

Leech had had the management contract drawn up. Wolfe made a great show of reading it.

'What's your company called?' Tamsin asked. 'Derek's Discs?'

'Real Records.'

The drummer snorted and lit up. After a heavy toke, he passed the joint to Wolfe. Smoke, odourless to Leech, drifted towards the window.

Leech took out a pack of Wrigley's Spearmint Gum and made a token of offering it round. No one took him up. He unwrapped all five oblongs and put them in his mouth. The ball would last for months.

The girl watched him closely.

'You must love that stuff?'

He shrugged. 'Only way to shut me up.'

Tamsin would marry him and, after three years, walk out claiming never to have known him. By then, she would be an official living legend. And he would still be a coming man.

Now, her face unlined and angular she looked at him. The light from the window hit her face exactly as it would on the first LP cover. She would never stipple her blackheads, but would redefine the word 'beautiful'.

She leaned over and gently removed his sunglasses. He didn't blink as she looked into his eyes.

'Okay,' she said. 'Do you have a pen?'

NORWOOD, 1972

'This top's too effing tight,' the model complained, South London shrill, 'pardon my French.'

Her name was Brenda but she called herself Brie. Blonde hair down to her waist, she knelt in six square-feet of sand. A blue space-hopper lay half-buried in front of a cyclorama of Mediterranean sky.

'Bollocks, dearie,' said Chaz, the photographer. He leaned into the shot to adjust the offending bikini.

'Mind your bleedin' hands, octopus,' Brie said, slapping him away.

She was right. The striped cups squeezed her breasts, the straps bit her shoulders. Angry pink skin plumped around straining edges.

Leech sat in the shadows, champing the ends of a Biro. He wore his hat, brim down, to keep the studio lights out of his eyes. Since his take-over the *Daily Comet* had transformed from dying broadsheet into thriving tabloid. Its image was younger, more daring, more vital; yet offering a return to traditional values. Leech's first great campaign ran under the banner of 'I'm Behind Britain'.

Chaz, irritated with Brie, was nervous with the new boss hanging around. Everything else about the paper had changed, he must think the Beach Beauties were for the chop too.

The *Comet* Beach Beauties had been a national institution since the twenties. From knee-length costumes through to cutaway bikinis, these heroines of garage and barracks had married into titles, rocked governments and becomes hostesses on *The Golden Shot*. Brie, this year's model, had been on television with Benny Hill and was cast in a film where Christopher Lee would suck her blood.

Brie squirmed under the lights and writhed in her top as if it were a hair shirt. Chaz's bald spot was a sorely embarrassed red.

At first rival papers made jokes about the 'with-it' *Comet*. The several fortunes Derek Leech had made in pop music and the rag trade did not qualify him as a latterday Lord Beaverbrook. Within a year of the *Comet*'s relaunch, the competition switched from sneering at his tactics to imitating them.

'I'll do myself a permanent damage,' Brie whined, tugging at the constricting cups. Her pleasant face twisted in discomfort.

Chaz ignored her, muttering into his battery of camera equipment.

'This all right, Mr Leech?' he asked.

Leech walked onto the set and looked the girl over. Her head barely came up to his chest.

'It's agony, luv,' she said.

'Take it off,' he told her.

She undid the clasp and shrugged. Her breasts breathed.

'Take her like this,' Leech told the photographer.

'You can't put tits in the *Comet*,' he protested. 'They'll never stand for it.'

'Let me worry about that.'

Chaz snapped off shots. Brie, suddenly giggly, posed naturally for the first time. She laughed and shaded her eyes, looking into the shadows at him. Leech knew exactly which exposure they would run: thumbnail in mouth, innocent and knowing, sexy but clean.

'Knock out,' Brie said.

* * *

FLEET STREET, 1977

Elizabeth II looked exactly as she did on a pound note, except for the safety-pin through her nose. 'God Save the Queen' was assembled from newsprint like a ransom note.

'It's a strong image,' Leech said, placing the record sleeve on the table. 'You have to admire that.'

Moore, the *Comet*'s notional editor gurgled outrage. He had come with the paper and still loitered nervously.

In the year-end 'Derek Leech Talks Straight' column, he was denouncing the Sex Pistols.

The *Comet,* swathed in the Union Jack throughout Jubilee year would brook no shilly-shallying. *Comet* 'Knock-Outs' had posed as British heroines, climaxing on Jubilee Day with Brie Simon, at twenty-five the *grande dame* of naked breasts, kitted up as Britannia Herself.

1977 would be remembered not for celebration bonfires and patriotic bunting but for gobbing and pogoing. Real Records, buried in the heart of the Derek Leech media portfolio, had ridden the razor-blade along with the rest of the industry.

'Shocking,' Moore said, tapping the poster. 'Some people have no standards.'

'Indeed,' Leech agreed. 'Reproduce it with the column. Give the Queen vampire fangs. It'll be stronger.'

Moore knew better than to object. He scuttled off.

Derek Leech Enterprises had manufactured cardboard Union Jack hats and tin 'Stuff the Jubilee' buttons. Both sold well, sometimes to the same customers.

The current office was not quite suitable. When the *Comet* was rehoused in the pyramid he would put up in London Docklands, things would be better arranged. That was in years to come. Leech already owned the site but the technology that would be housed there had not yet developed. The processes which would destroy the Fleet Street of hot-metal stirred inside the serpent's egg, tentatively poking the shell.

His memory was perfect, from the Isle of Dogs to this moment. The paths of the future were clear, too. Nothing was set in stone but the tendencies were definite.

His jaws worked, grinding. No one remarked on the habit any more. He unlocked the lacquered box on his desk and took out four sets of file cards, lining them up as perfect stacks.

Amphlett, Dixon, Martin, Yeo.

These four – boys of seventeen or eighteen – were his children. If capable of human fondness, he was genuinely attached to them. Already, their lives were complicated and intertwined. Soon, a decision would be made. One must be separated and exalted above the rest. Four sharp, bright little lights. So much potential.

BOOK

1

OFFERINGS

'Capra may have suffered from what would be described in 1978 by psychologists Pauline Clance and Suzanne Imes as "the impostor phenomenon", the fear common to many high achievers that their success is actually based on a fraud. Another psychologist who studied the phenomenon, Joan Harvey, has said that the sufferer also had the "obsessive fear that sooner or later some humiliating failure would reveal his secret and unmask him as a fraud. Some very famous people have suffered from the feeling all their lives, despite their obvious abilities." In such people, "because each success is experienced either as a fluke, or as the result of Herculean efforts, a pattern of self-doubt, rather than self-confidence, develops," and each success actually intensifies those feelings of fraudulence…

"'First-generation professionals are very prone to feeling like impostors," Harvey noted. "When people perceive themselves as having risen above their roots, it can evoke deep anxieties in them about separation. Unconsciously, they equate success with betraying their loyalties to their family."

"'Consciously," she explained, those who suffer from the impostor phenomenon, "fear failure, a fear they keep secret. Unconsciously, they fear success."'

JOSEPH MCBRIDE, *Frank Capra: The Catastrophe of Success*

1

NEW YEAR'S EVE, 1992-1993

She never had luck with this holiday. Over years, she'd dutifully endured disappointing parties and hoarse evenings in open-late pubs. The time she got it together to invite friends round, flu struck; she'd lain down an hour before guests arrived, shuddering uncontrollably in a backless dress, then forced herself to ignore the symptoms until past midnight. Last year, heavily pregnant, she'd stayed in watching TV, her mother plumped next to her on the too-small sofa. Now, here she was again: in the wars.

While Neil Martin was x-rayed, Sally loitered in the hospital corridor still decorated with tinsel and holly. A teenager with cobweb skirts hung on the phone, nibbling a dummy as she explained to an exasperated parent.

Neil probably wasn't badly injured but the nurse wanted him to have a tetanus jab. A skull fracture or even concussion were unlikely; the head x-rays were just to be on the safe side.

Casualty offered all human life. An angry policeman and a merely fed-up lawyer argued over a youth who'd broken an ankle writing-off a stolen car A rave-goer with dental braces and a Mongol scalp-lock had swallowed party pills which her friend said 'looked like smarties'. A fatherly man sat quiet, hand wrapped in a red tea-towel after a mishap with a Christmas present, an electric knife. A bored Asian had been stabbed. Plus there were relatives, witnesses, professional busybodies and hangers-on.

Sally was a professional hanger-on. She'd invoice for time and any expenses. Later she'd compose a note and fax the client a footnote. 'We Never Sleep', she could claim.

The ravette yielded the phone. Taking in Sally's bun-tied hair red cardie and long black skirt, the girl blurted 'Olive Oyl'. Sally had change for coin-ops, cards for cardphones: part of the job. It was nearer three a.m. than two; Mum wouldn't have stayed up even to note the video clock slip silently from 11.59 to 00.00. On the line, her own phone rang. Double-doors opened: a bag lady staggered in, swathed in ratty scarves. Sally wondered what horrible injury she'd sustained, but the weather-beaten virago turned out to be a relief driver come for the joyrider's lawyer. This must be the worst night of the year for minicabs.

'Mum?'

The receiver was fussed with. Mum always got the cordless phone the wrong way up. A baby mewed in the background. The Invader was as likely to wake up screaming without a dead-of-night phone call but Sally still had a guilt-stab.

'You said you'd be home hours ago. Where are you?'

'Casualty,' she said.

Mum groaned silently. Other women's daughters had husbands, careers, settled lives; Maureen Rhodes was stuck with a minimally self-employed single parent who typed reports on Christmas morning.

'I'm not hurt,' she assured Mum. 'A guy at Dolar's party…'

The party was a bus-hop away in Highgate Village. Dolar owned the shop where Neil did odd shifts behind the till. She'd seen him about well before the commission, wizardy in black velvet coat and dragon-badge-ringed hat. They had fringe friends in common but only really met when Sally started on Neil Martin. She'd probably have gone to the party anyway: having been cooped up with Mum and the Invader over the holiday, she could do with talking to someone in her age range and dancing off chocolate and leftover turkey.

The invite said 'come as your favourite comix character'. Fancy dress was a bother. The icy fog that descended before Christmas made Highgate Wood a haunted forest of sparkly frost and witch mist. Imagining Amazon Queen, her childhood heroine, with nipples frozen to knots and acres of goose-pimples between thighboots and brass bra, she decided on Olive Oyl. She pinned a collar to a cardigan, found an ankle-skirt that didn't hobble her, fussed her hair into a ball.

Protective colour, Mummy?

Mind your own business, flesh of my flesh.

'My hero,' she said to her mirror pining for a sailor with forearm elephantiasis. Actually, Olive Oyl was a drip: fecklessly making up to Bluto then yelling to be saved from justifiable date rape. The only cartoon woman worse was Amy McQueen, knock-kneed alter ego of Amazon Queen, but she faked feebleness to stop her boyfriend guessing her double life. Sally did her lipstick. Like Amazon Queen and Dr Shade, she needed a secret identity. Under her cupid's bow, she was Sally Rhodes, Investigator.

After peeking in on the Invader and telling Mum she'd be home before one, she put on a coat and left. It was tenish. The 43 or the 134 would get her from Muswell Hill to Highgate Village in seven minutes. Two and a half hours of party, a walk through the wood, and 1993 would be here, full of chilly promise.

Her year-end report was delivered. Dolar would have invited Neil but she didn't have to pay attention. If anything, she was bored by the man she knew but had never met. The only curiosity was why the client was interested after so many years in so unexceptional a citizen.

Hopping off the bus at the top of the Archway Road, she looked for the address, a garden flat near Planet Janet. A group ten paces ahead was obviously on course: a busty woman in a strategically torn uniform carried a plastic Oddbins bag heavy with bottles; apes with steel helmets, ammo bandoliers and toy weapons.

Sally caught up as they waited on the sunken doorstep, hammering. The flat emanated light and the *Rocky Horror* soundtrack. A door opened; a guy in a green singlet decorated with question marks hugged the marine, then looked over her tooled-up primates.

'*Sergeant Grit and His Gorilla Guerillas*,' said the Riddler, 'ZC Comics, 1942 to 1948, revived 1964. Created by Zack Briscow...'

The platoon struck towards the kitchen, firing spark-guns. Sally was left behind. She didn't know the Riddler by name but recognised him from the shop. She slipped off her coat and waited to be identified.

'No,' the Riddler said, shaking his head. 'Afraid I don't know you.'

'Olive Oyl,' she admitted.

'Not a comic, really. Newspaper strip, *Thimble Theatre*, E.C. Segar.'

She dumped her coat on an overburdened stand. The Riddler moved on to a couple of hairy blokes tarted up as the Fat Slags. Dolar, the Wizard of Id, was hustled past by two eleven-year-old Amazon Queens, to a front room where music throbbed. He tried to stop but the Amazons, black armbands over their toffee-paper-jewelled Circlets of Power, pummelled him until he agreed to demonstrate the Time Warp.

On the wall, cards were strung; snowy demons and bobble-hatted dragons outnumbered robins and Santas. In a nook, Top Cat nodded as a beergutted Green Lantern explained where John Major had gone wrong. Sally didn't know anyone, masked or not, but it didn't matter. Blending in was a speciality.

In the kitchen, she added her Australian red to a bottle forest covering every surface. A trim, prematurely grey woman with a lightning-streak T-shirt over her leotard poured a polystyrene cup of rose. She introduced herself: Janet of Planet Janet fame, mother of the Amazon Queens, significant other of the Wizard of Id.

'I'm Sally,' she said, lost for self-description. 'From the other side of the wood.'

Janet had heard about the Invasion. Sally found herself in one of those Dreaded Baby Conversations that sprang like traps. She didn't want to run through the backstory. At Christmas, Connor's parents, so tactful she was irritated with herself for squirming, had sent a hamper of presents. The DBC died. Janet saw to the Fat Slags. Shunted aside, Sally dipped into Kettle Chips. When pregnant, they had been her craving. Having worked up to a three-bag-a-day habit, she was tapering off.

'Lois Lane?' someone asked.

'Olive Oyl,' she said.

Neil Martin was perched on a tall stool, drinking steadily, bottle of Jack Daniels in his elbow-crook, long legs twisted under him. He was in civilian dress: baggy jumper hanging from wide shoulders, hair flopped over his forehead.

From her usual distance, he was a bear who'd recently been ill and lost weight. Hunched into the wind, knuckly hands shoved into corduroy pockets. His date of birth was July 31, 1959 but she thought of him as pushing forty. Unexpectedly close now, he was younger than she'd perceived. His longish face was unlined, heavy-lidded eyes unsurrounded even by the faint crinkles she increasingly saw in her own face. He looked a bit like one of her earliest crushes, David Warner in *Morgan, A Suitable Case for Treatment.*

'You're not in costume,' she commented, needing something to say.

'Yes I am, child,' he replied. 'I'm Cary Trenton.'

She frowned, missing the reference. These people were so deeply into their world of comics and science fiction and old television.

'The Streak?' he prompted.

Janet was vaguely dressed as the Streak, an American hero from the 1940s who was still running. Literally; he had superspeed.

'Well…' Neil opened his arms and looked down at himself. He'd sloshed Jack on his jumper.

It clicked and Sally couldn't help shivering.

'Cary Trenton,' she remembered. 'The Streak's secret identity.'

Neil made a one-sided grin and tipped whiskey into it.

'Got it in one, Olive.'

No matter how feeble Amy McQueen was, Cary Trenton was a loser she could (and did, when they teamed up in *Dazzling Duo Stories*) look down on. A nerd *avant la lettre*, Cary had unruly hair, bottle glasses, and a habit of falling over that prevented anyone from deducing he was the superconfident and dextrous Streak.

'Superheroes,' Neil sneered. 'Amazon Queen, Popeye, Dr Shade, all of 'em. Flying overhead, getting between us and the sun. Why can't they bloody grow up?'

The stool balanced miraculously against the edge of the counter; he took a gulp and held it in his mouth, letting it seep down his throat. Sally was held, fascinated. What would she think, she wondered, if she didn't know anything about this man?

'Shaggin' Streak,' he said, flapping fingers at Janet. 'I was at school with the bloke who draws the Streak, you know.'

Sally did know.

'Mickey Yeo. Smart biscuit. Wasting himself.'

There were pictures of them all in the file. Dr Marling's Grammar School for Boys, 1970–1973; Ash Grove Comprehensive, 1973–1975; West Somerset College, 1975–1977. In school uniforms, then clothes more antiquated than fashions of the Roaring Twenties. Grouped together, studied in seriousness or goofiness.

'The Streak,' he burped. 'One whoosh and the bastard's gone, gone, gone...'

In the dance room, a TV was on with the sound down. Running up to midnight, Clive James sprinkled wryness between news clips. Derek Leech's face appeared, squeezed between breasts as he introduced the *Comet*'s Knock-Outs of the Year. Dancers paused to hiss; a fanboy complained that since the tabloid tycoon devoured ZC Comics, the stable of superfolk had been reduced. Amazon Queen, Sally was appalled to learn, had been sucked out of existence by a time-warp; not just killed, her whole life revoked.

A 1969 compilation rattled ancient speakers and Sally's teeth. She bopped with the smaller Dr Shade to 'Dizzy' and Tamsin's 'Aquarius'. Dr Shade was another Leech property: a strip in his 'heavy' paper the *Evening Argus*. In her TV researcher days, she once stepped into a life and came face-to-face with Derek Leech. He'd not seemed fiend-like, though she gathered most horror stories about him were, if anything, understated.

Deserted by a temporary hero presumably not speeding off in a Rolls-Royce Shadowshark to combat Forces of Evil, she fended off the Fat Slags, who slam-danced to Thunderclap Newman. She was pleasantly squiffy: the music was loud enough for her not to have to talk; the Invader was at home, love-tentacles slopping out for her heart. Tomorrow, they'd go to Highgate Wood: fairy frosts and frozen trees; ten months wasn't too early to experience the world outside the flat.

1993 approached. 'Israelites' was interrupted; Dolar turned up the TV sound and channel-hopped. As she stopped dancing, Sally felt muscles pop in her legs. Since the Invasion, her exercise class had lapsed. Among celebrities on Channel 4, she glimpsed the client. Was it possible to enjoy a party in front of cameras? Dolar found Big Ben: the preliminary chimes had started. Everyone linked arms and waited for the peals.

'That's it,' a Fat Slag said, 'goodbye Czechoslovakia, hello European Customs' Union.'

Pumping arms, they remembered most of the lyrics of 'Auld Lang Syne'. The song collapsed: Sally was kissing and being kissed by people she barely knew. She broke contact when a gorilla put a hairy glove on her bottom. Party streamers rained in the overpopulated room. The taller Dr Shade, mysterious in wide-brimmed hat and concealing goggles, delicately pressed cold lips to hers. She kept her eyes open: across the room, Neil leaned against a door-jamb, barely supported by an Amazon Queen. Sally shrugged off Dr Shade, who enveloped a Ninja girl with his cape: she considered kissing Neil but he radiated grouchiness even to the Amazon Jailbait who stuck a chaste smacker on his cheek.

Dolar, robes pungent with dope, came from behind and hugged Neil. He wished him a Zappy New Year. Neil managed a chuckle.

Within a quarter of an hour exhaustion set in. Her psychic link with the Invader gently tugged. A deadline-at-dawn, rock-around-the-clock, this-is-much-better-than-what's-in-the-charts-nowadays, who's-been-in-the-bog-for-an-hour?, neighbours-round-to-complain, sick-in-the-street, busted-by-the-police, joints-rolled-on-album-covers, empty-the-fridge party was shaping up. She'd do well to miss the dregs. To 'Goo Goo Barabajagal' she unearthed her coat.

Waving a general goodbye, she slipped out. Neil sat on a low brick wall at the boundary of the front garden, holding his head, radiating the helplessness she associated with the Invader. He lived on her route home: in Cranley Gardens, of mass-murder fame, a large bedsit partitioned into a cramped flat. She'd walked past, attentively, dozens of times.

He looked up at the skies with unfocused eyes. It would be foolish to get to know Neil Martin. He was responsible for her moderate prosperity; that she'd been able to restart her agency so soon was a fluke. Without the client's interest in this befuddled kitchen-sitter, she'd be a single parent queuing at the Department of Social Security.

'Olive,' he said. 'Had your spinach?'

He stood up, limbs not quite synchronised.

'I'm walking down Muswell Hill Road. I'll see you home.'

He'll tumble, Mummy. He'll wonder how you know where he lives. It's suspicious.

Nonsense, darling child. When you're older I'll explain about hangovers. Tomorrow, he won't remember my name.

'You're a heroine, Olive. Not like those supershits.'

'Hurry up. This is a one-time offer.'

Crisp cold air cleared her mind. Neil took a moment to coordinate, a dinosaur with separate brains for knees and elbows. From observation, she knew he was like this even without a pint of Jack in him.

They crossed Archway Road and walked past the steps that led down to Highgate tube. A scattering of people were on the streets, mostly alcohol-fortified. The road, broad and well-lit, curved and dipped slightly as it threaded from Highgate to Muswell Hill, separating the forested patch of Highgate Wood from the smaller Queen's Wood. Sally, confident there were enough huge and threatening forces in her life for her not to be bothered by ordinary dangers, walked at all hours. Dennis Nilsen, the local serial killer, had worked in the DSS, not lurked in the park.

Almost out of the wood, Muswell Hill up ahead, Cranley Gardens a turn to the right: Neil concentrated on making his legs work.

'Got any fags?' someone asked, quickly. Suddenly in front of Neil, standing too close.

Nearby: another young man, ungloved hands not in his pockets. 'Cigs?'

The questioner prodded Neil's jumper. Neil looked puzzled at the pavement. He patted his pockets.

'Smokes?'

The questioner: jutting teeth, shell-suit. Eyes glittered, hostile. His friend: black guy, moustache wisp, oversized flat cap. Neil, half a head taller, looked sad.

'Don't smoke,' he said. 'Sorry.'

The questioner jabbed. Head turning, Neil missed getting a broken nose. He folded against railings, blood blurting from a nostril. The black guy loped forward and tilted on one hip, jabbing a shoe-toe above Neil's ear. He spun and stumbled. Sober and tense, Sally looked into the white man's little face and made fists.

People were coming from behind, interrupting. The black guy

knelt to punch Neil in the side, then pulled his friend's sleeve. They ran off without trying to take anything or touch her. A long dark car cruised by, fanning light on the road. Fleeing shadows became spider-limbed straggles. Dr Shade in pursuit of evil-doers?

She let out steamy breath. Neil gulped porridge into the gutter. People around: Gorilla Guerillas, costumes and make-up half gone. Sergeant Grit waited for Neil to finish being sick and helped him up. A tissue wiped a rope of clear fluid from his mouth.

The gorillas apologised as if it were their fault. Once the Sergeant was sure Neil was okay, she wanted to go home and not be dragged to a cop shop. Who wanted to be detained all night, dressed as a mercenary monkey, not be able to give a decent description, for something not serious?

When the Gorillas trooped off, Sally was left with Neil. She should take him to Fortis Green Hospital. A flappy hand pressed to his face, blood smearing between his fingers, he was pliable. He followed meekly as she led him up towards Woodside Avenue. This was another New Year's Eve she wouldn't look back on fondly.

2

NEW YEAR'S DAY, 1993

'Are we quorate?' Mark asked.

Mickey gave an 'aye' and wrapped thin hands around his coffee mug for warmth. His shoulders shivered in his immobile fringed, white jacket. Despite the log fire, the country cottage froze in winter.

Michael raised a languid hand and eased himself into the best armchair. He wore last night's tuxedo, loose tie-ends on silky lapels. He'd been chubby as a child; sleek now, he still had a fat boy's manner.

'Three of Four,' Mark said, formally. 'Most but not All. We are a Quorum.'

He pulled his forefinger cracking the knuckle. The ring, looser on him than on Michael, felt momentarily strange. As host, Mark was the new Ring. He stood in front of his fire, warmth seeping through the back of his jeans, and looked to the outgoing officer. Michael was Mark's oldest friend; they'd met in September 1970, minutes before Neil came along, a full day before Mickey.

'Open the fuckin' shampoo, mate,' Mickey said. He spoke BBC English to his parents but addressed the rest of the world like Bob Hoskins playing a football hooligan. It came from mixing too much with rock musicians.

'Zhust getting up speed,' Michael said, shaking the magnum. He had trouble with 'J' and 'Y' sounds; thanks to television, it had gone from defect to mannerism to distinguishing mark. The *Spitting Image* impressionist had the trick better than Michael.

Michael eased off the stopper staunching an explosion under a teacloth. He tipped champagne froth into three tankards, then, after bubbles settled, poured overly generous measures.

'Our Absent Friend,' they said, clashing tankards like Musketeer swords.

Mark would have chosen Chateau Pétrus ('82 should be about drinkable), but Moet was classic beyond vulgarity. Michael was the traditionalist, inclined to inherited complacent confidence. Mickey was the anarchist, a vegetarian in a £3000 leather jacket. Self-made Mark balanced the triad, careful, precise and *right*. They'd always been a perfect diagram of the class system; upper (Michael), upper middle (Neil), lower middle (Mickey) and working (Mark). Fortune, the Deal and attempts to rewire social genotypes hadn't made a difference. Neil might be a street away from cardboard city, but their old headmaster, Chimp, would still rate him above a proletarian interloper like Mark.

Settled, Michael knee-perched a slimline briefcase designed to be as much like a high-powered laptop computer as possible for an item of luggage. He tapped out an entry code, the case hissed open. Three red folders were produced, sealed with gold tape and old-fashioned wax.

'Photocopied, sad to report,' Michael said.

Mark rubbed the seal. Imprinted was a stylised Q, descendant of the colophon Mickey designed, one art lesson at Marling's, for their earliest documents. The seal matched the red-gold device inset in black marble on the ring. At the end of the day Michael would hand over the seal and the other instruments of office.

Mickey finger-snapped wax away and riffled through the pages.

'There's a fuckload here,' he commented.

'Ms Rhodes is admirably thorough. One of our more efficacious footsoldiers. I recommend we hold her over for a further zhear'

Mark ummed the suggestion. As Ring, that would be his decision.

'This *ante-meridiem*, Ms Rhodes faxed me. I infer one of zhou will know why...'

Mark had no idea. Mickey tried to shrug, again failing to move his amazing colossal jacket. He scratched the beaded braids that fell from half of his scalp. The other side of his head was shaven, running to stubble after a few days without the razor. Chimp would have popped his pacemaker if anyone showed up at Assembly with a haircut like that.

'I didn't expect her to remain at her post over the vac, but our Ms Rhodes takes commitments seriously. Here...'

He unscrolled a sheet of fax paper from his case. Mark, nearest, took it and read.

January 1, 1993
Between 12.30 and 1.00 a.m., while walking along Muswell Hill Road, Neil Martin was assaulted by two young men. X-rays show no serious injury. After a tetanus jab, he was discharged from Fortis Green Casualty c. 4.00 a.m. The incident was not reported to the police. Martin claims he did not recognise his attackers.

Rhodes

Mark passed the fax to Mickey.

'After midnight,' Michael said, 'the Deal was *technically* in force. Thus far we've abided by informal agreement not to make moves until Twelfth Night. 'Tis a tricky precedent and might well queer whatever Game Plan we decide on.'

'Nada to do with me, mate,' Mickey said.

Michael's eyebrows raised like sideways question marks. His quizzical look was often caricatured.

'Nor me,' Mark said. 'I've always been against actual violence. My reading of the Deal rules it out. Otherwise, we might as well put on ski-masks every year and go after Our Absent Friend with axe-handles. Surely, the point is that, in the end, Neil always does it to himself. We just show him the way and stand back.'

'That's a new reading,' Michael said. 'I quite like it. Might well play in Chingford. Zhes indeedy.'

They were here, but Neil was not. No: they were here, *because* Neil was not. The Quorum could (and had done so, many times) debate the Deal for hours. It was brutally simple in essence, but inordinately intricate if examined in any depth.

Michael retrieved the fax and slipped it into his own folder.

'Act of God then?' he said. 'Improbable, but hardly our first Divine Intervention.'

'More like an Act of Thug,' Mickey commented.

This New Year's Eve had been easier to arrange than the last few. His schedule was more ordered than Michael's or Mickey's; also, he had more space. With Pippa in Edinburgh for Hogmanay, Mark could have either the town flat or the country cottage. He chose the cottage, though it meant driving down late at night after dinner with London friends, a software designer and her art director husband.

The frost on the fields was so heavy it wouldn't completely thaw by nightfall. Thick mist obscured anything more than a dozen yards off. The cottage was clustered with a few others in Herron's Halt, a savage corner of Sussex. His neighbours were a sit-com creator, a theoretical physicist and an ancient who remembered the Halt before it was a Londoners' retreat. Pippa, a senior editor at Real Press, sometimes brought authors here for extensive manuscript autopsies. There was less chance of interruption than in Islington.

Mark got up early to set a fire in the big room. Even so, he managed five hours alone under an antique bedspread in the tiny master's room. The others, on adrenalin or amphetamines, had done without sleep.

Michael had called at his Hampstead address to collect Ms Rhodes' fax but had hardly paused between his television bash and the drive. He'd guested last night on the *Big Breakfast End of the Year Show* on Channel 4, flirting with Zsa Zsa Gabor (whose name he could pronounce superbly). He turned up before Mickey, in a 1950s touring car the length of a yacht, hair as smooth as a twenties' gigolo, bearing the magnum of Moet.

Before the Meet, Michael returned the paper Mark had prepared about Interactive Narrative Technology. He'd match the £100K seed money Mark was putting up. If Mickey came in, the Quorum would buy the ground floor of a tower Mark expected to be a monolith by the twenty-first century. Once zap-the-alien games, *This is Cinerama* remakes and feelie-porno palled, creative applications would multiply exponentially.

'What about Leech?' Michael asked.

'He's in,' Mark confirmed. 'With no limit. In cold cash, he can match us and take us, but I'm locking patents and copyrights in our names. Derek needs us; he's a money mover, he never *created* anything.'

'Except the Deal.'

'That's business, not art.'

Mickey arrived in a red MG with a model, stick-thin but for her chest, famous for an instant *cappuccino* commercial. Mickey, who refused to learn to drive, had persuaded her to chauffeur him to the country and then piss off back to her toy-box without him. Still coasting on last night's buzz, he had been at a ZC party on a Thames pleasure boat.

'They had a funeral for Amazon Twat,' Mickey said. 'Some feminist arsehole gave me stick about totalling the dynamic dyke.'

Mickey's latest comic project was an apocalyptic shake-up of the ZC universe.

'If they thought she had it shitty, wait 'til they see what I've got planned for the Streak,' he cackled.

Mickey hadn't made it to his Camden cave, though he'd hit

a bed for at least an hour. As she left, the Countess of Creamy Coffee contrived to look angry without creasing her perfect and expensive face. The notion of instant *cappuccino* struck Mark as barbaric.

'Our Sponsor made a wham-bam appearance near dawn,' Mickey said, meaning Leech, 'hovered over the river in an assault 'copter wished us 1993 over the PA, then buzzed off to Zurich.'

Three years ago, Leech had taken over Pyramid, a Hollywood studio founded before World War One. Twenty-five subsidiaries down the spread-sheet, this incidentally netted ZC Comics, Mickey's major publisher along with sundry music, hotel, theme park and television interests. He also owned Real Press, a third of Mark's Square Deal Enterprises, the Cloud 9 satellite net, more newspapers than anyone could list, restaurants in twelve capital cities, a once-famous boutique chain on the comeback trail, Chums condoms, and a shape-shifting glob of record companies.

'The whole world is wired up to Derek Leech,' Mark said.

'So whassername – Tanya? – ain't on scene any more?' Mickey said, after a close reading of the report. 'Shame. She was a tasty temptation.'

Having appropriated the biscuit barrel, Mickey chain-nibbled custard creams. At Marling's, the wiry little boy was nick-named the Stomach. During their secondary education, he'd consumed more school dinner than the rest of them put together. As he chewed, he sketched on the flipsides of Sally Rhodes' report pages, roughing out blank identikit faces, scratching in staring eyes and sharp teeth.

Mark sat at the head of his oak table and poured more coffee. Colombian, Strength 7. Refreshments were his duty under the Code Michael, the charter of Rights, Responsibilities and Privileges Michael had drawn up, after full consultation among the Forum, in 1972.

'I'm not altogether certain we turned the Tan-zh... the Tanya situation to our optimum advantage,' Michael said, long cigarette held vertical between his fingers. 'We ultimately gave her enough to cash out. With her influence removed, Our Absent Friend has stabilised in the water.'

'No woman, no cry,' Mickey suggested, feathering spectacular eyebrows onto a harpie.

Tanya Gorse was Neil's on-off girlfriend, a sixties survival with enough personal problems and personality defects to keep a soap opera going for a decade. The most effective way to pull her strings was an occasional anonymous envelope stuffed with £20 notes. Most people get in trouble when they run out of money, but her peculiar gift was to wreak most havoc when she had capital to underwrite her latest whim. Once she bought into a scheme whose collapse stranded Neil in a flat full of bottles of rapidly-perishing Czech beer besieged by angry creditors. She had a knack for picking the most potentially violent partners for the most risk-imperilled ventures. Neil was caught up in Life With Tanya for so long, his own ambitions atrophied. Last March, she'd put a wedge of cash down on a Harley and taken off in search of a revolution.

'Playing *Easy Rider* behind the former Iron Curtain,' Mark noted, 'she'll probably start a world war.'

According to Sally Rhodes, Tanya was currently bouncing in a Bucharest heavy-metal club, den mother to post-Ceausescu bike boys. For Christmas, she'd sent Neil a postcard of a monument to Vlad the Impaler.

'Fucked off in style, though,' Mickey chuckled. 'Signing him up to make the rest of the payments on the bike. The heavies last night were probably from Sick Eddie.'

'Why would anyone engage in a business transaction with a cove whose *friends* call him Sick Eddie?' Michael asked.

'Don't think he gives 'em a choice,' Mickey replied.

Mark tried to imagine Tanya and Neil together. Having never met the woman, his idea of her was formed by photographs and scraps of disjointed information. He had talked with her on the telephone and been surprised by her sweet, Northern voice. She didn't sound like the Mistress of Mindfuck.

'I wouldn't rule out a return,' he said.

Michael pondered. 'Unlikely, Mark. Even Our Absent Friend wouldn't climb back into bed after she dumped his accoutrements…'

To finance her Mission to Moldavia, Tanya sold Neil's stereo and his records. She even unloaded most of his clothes for a fast fifty quid on a stall in Camden Lock.

'…and killed his fuckin' cat,' Mickey added.

While experimenting with Ecstasy, Tanya had tied the animal's collar to her bike and set off, slowly at first, to see if it could keep up.

'It wasn't Neil's cat,' Mark said. 'He was just looking after it.'

'Even fuckin' better mate,' said Mickey, drawing a pancaked pussy with splatted-out eyes. 'With Tibbles a long red smear on the North Circular, it'll be a cold day in my arsehole before his auntie trusts him again. We were worried about her, remember? Too normal, too settled, too calming. Take it from me, that was another beautiful Tanya move.'

In the dossier Mickey assembled on Tanya when he was Ring, there were photos: in a 1961 party-dress hugging the little brother whose eye she'd later put out; serial numbers held up against a cheesecloth blouse during her first dealing arrest, very '68 in a Tamsin hairdo; most recently, leaning in a scuffed jacket against a brick wall outside a pub, grin showing where she was missing teeth. She'd met Neil when he sat in for the drummer of a short-lived pub band she fronted. The group took its name from her signature song, 'Poison Ivy'.

'The girl shat gold,' Mickey said, almost wistfully. 'No way would he have her back.'

Mickey had a fascination crush on Tanya. She was like the girls in the *Skinhead* books he cited as a major literary influence. His dad had managed the Garden Shop where Mark's Mum worked but he had strange ideas about working-class rebellion. He kept up an alternative career torturing keyboard instruments, often guest-appearing with supergroups. He was an unofficial fifth wheel with The Möthers of Pain, who had done the thrash score for his video nasty, *City Hammer.*

'In the past, we've underestimated Our Absent Friend's capacity for embracing the awful,' Mark observed. 'Maybe we should take the trouble to find out exactly where Tanya is? We could always send her a plane ticket.'

Tanya had been a great move and Mark was reluctant to retire her.

'I think she's over and gone,' Michael said. 'Wonderful while she lasted, but out of the equation now.'

'Fuckin' right,' put in Mickey. 'Girl like that comes along once in a lifetime. She was the Ultimate Skag, like a *Blind Date* Terminator. All she does is fuck, eat, sleep and ruin lives.'

Tanya had stuck to Neil through three jobs and five addresses. A normal person would have killed her within six months and thrown himself on the jury's mercy.

'We'll need to replace her,' Mark said. 'Since she cleared out, Neil has drifted along in a species of complacent misery that could easily congeal into normality. Tanya kept the ground shifting.'

'Remember how she fucked his van delivery job?' Mickey grinned. 'Took a load of photocopier paper and laid it out, sheet by sheet, on a field in Norfolk. Girl was an artist.'

He showed a lighting portrait of Tanya with horns and a tail and a sexy pout. They all laughed. Mickey crumpled the picture and tossed it into the fire, where it flared into ash.

'All good things end,' Michael concluded. 'So much for the Gorse Girl. We'll zhust have to be inventive again. 'Tis supposed to be our strength.'

They were all busy, even soon after the holidays. There were always more family and professional commitments, but New Year's Day had been inviolate for twenty years. As he refilled the *cafetiere*, watched by Michael and Mickey, Mark sensed an image overlaid by snapshots. Different kitchens, different drinks, different clothes, but the same faces. Plus or minus facial hair, baby fat, glasses and zits. They'd been doing this since the first day of 1971.

They returned to the table with coffee the Quorum way: midnight black with a swirl of real cream, no sugar. The review of the report – which convinced Mark, at least, that Sally Rhodes was certainly worth holding over – was complete. Documents were spread out on the table, along with the photographs Ms Rhodes provided.

Catching up was like following an annual soap opera. He felt close, not only to Neil but to the supporting cast. In 1992, after Tanya hit the road, Neil worked off and on in a bookshop in Highgate Village. Mickey had done a signing there for *Choke Hold*; he reported Neil had showed up, sheepish in the presence of his superstar old mate, to work the till and talk over ancient history. The squat Tanya found hadn't worked out, thanks to last year's moves. With a reference from the owner of Planet Janet, Neil got into a bedsit near Muswell Hill. He was square with the DSS and his poll-tax fine was nearly paid off.

'No actual progress,' Michael concluded, 'but no disasters either, no backsliding.'

Mark looked at the photos, all taken from a distance, mainly through windows. Neil in Planet Janet, reading a newspaper in the absence of customers. Neil in his dressing-gown in his bedsit, frying eggs. Neil sitting in a pub garden with half of something.

'He has a life,' Mickey said. 'Not much of one, but it's there. He's off the sauce, never really got into the dope, a trickle of earnings, a place to kip. That puts him ahead of where he was last year.'

There had been a point, during the Czech beer fiasco, when it seemed likely Neil would be charged with fraud. With Tanya (herself hospitalised several times for depression and addiction) in his life, custodial mental treatment had always been a possibility.

'I concur,' Michael said, 'Our Absent Friend has not, all considered, had a calamitous twelvemonth. So what are we going to do about it?'

3

NEW YEAR'S DAY, 1993

In dream city, he ran down streets saturated with cold sunlight. Dr Shade's Shadowshark pursued as smoothly as a fin through water. The Streak pumped pavement so fast he could wait in the future for his quarry to catch up. They were heroes. That excused the beating they'd give him. Behind their masks, they were half-familiar. He couldn't remember their secret identities. Dr Shade pinned his arms and held him up like a target. At the top of a hill, the Streak posed, hands on spandex hips, laughing from deep in his gut. He extended a fist and, quicker than a thought, was up close. Four knuckles, one enlarged by a lightning-strike motif, loomed.

The Streak punched Neil Martin out of sleep.

He lay under his duvet, head covered, feet frozen. The room would be a meat locker until he could get to the two-bar fire. A hundred miles across ice-threaded carpet.

One side of his head, from chin to eyebrow, pulsed. He still felt the impact. Probing the tender area, he found engorged swelling. Half his face was bruised. The dab of a fingertip was a prod from a hot pin. His teeth were dots of aching shrapnel. One eye was swollen shut, gummed with sleep-grit. He covered his disfigurement with a hand like the Phantom's mask, an eyehole between fingers.

He wriggled the duvet over numb toes. His face hurt so much, mere cold wouldn't make a difference. His breath frosted in a funnel above the bed. He hadn't drawn the curtains; late-afternoon sun leaked through falling as light as snow on the floor.

He'd only been hit twice, three times at most. It'd taken maybe five seconds. How could boxers stand that kind of punishment for minutes at a time? The pain didn't go away. It wrapped his head like a balaclava. Along with the serious agony in his face, he had the usual knife-thrust of Jack in the back of his skull.

Happy New Year. He hoped the offering would be sufficient to ward off the Norwegian Neil Cullers.

He shut the eye he'd been able to open and thought it away, erasing his memory. Arranging himself in his single bed like a corpse in a coffin, arms crossed on his chest, he used his patented time-travel method.

In the dark of his mind, he pictured the room around him, cataloguing furniture, the placing of bed in relation to door and windows, dingy, ribbed cream wallpaper sink unit next to the two-burner cooker, electricity meter by the fire, five Christmas cards on the mantelpiece.

Then he rearranged the components. Centring on his head, he morphed the space into the higher-ceilinged but smaller configuration of the room he'd shared with Tanya the Terrible in the squat in Colney Hatch. He lay on a square mattress plumped on the floor; it would have to be folded over if he wanted to get up and open the door. There was a damp patch on the ceiling, spotty mould in one corner.

He retreated further, shuffling through a dozen spaces where he had slept: flats, bedsits, shared houses, friends' floors, hall of residence (for a term and a half), a tent at a festival.

At the end of his private time-tunnel was his bedroom. In his parents' old house, the big one they sold when Dad retired from the VAT Office. He wasn't too lanky to fit under the bedclothes. Pre-duvet sheets and blankets so tightly tucked his feet could never escape.

Models hung, slowly revolving in a solemn dogfight that pit a Sopwith Camel and the Pan-Am shuttle from *2001* against a Messerschmitt and Chitty Chitty Bang-Bang. Too old for the models, he was reluctant to deny, by throwing them out, a geologic age spent with stinky glue. He had Airfix soldiers in shoeboxes under the bed, jumbled in time paradox regiments of Afrika Korps, 18th Hussars, 7th Cavalry and Roman Legionaries. Their massed last stand would be on Michael's parents' barbecue area, napalmed with lighter-fluid. Forgotten heroes of outgrown battles deliquescing in a sea of blistering plastic.

Paperbacks were shelved in alphabetical order in a cabinet, mixing sci-fi he read on his own with books he had for English lessons: *At the Mountains of Madness* and *To Kill a Mockingbird*, *Conan the Usurper* and *Under the Greenwood Tree*. *Son of Mad*, *Snappy Answers to Stupid Questions* and *The Portable Mad* had their own section, stacked horizontally. He kept frustratingly incomplete runs of ZC comics in box-files: imported as ballast, they arrived months or even years out of order and any issue resolving a storyline was guaranteed never to cross the Atlantic. *Zowie*, a black and white digest, carried chopped-up reprints ('pounds' and 'lift' lettered over 'dollars' and 'elevator') of the Streak ('faster than sound, faster than light, faster than time!') and Lance Lake, Private Eye (Sir Lancelot reincarnated in Coastal City). He and Mickey Yeo swapped ZCs and shared the revelation that people who wrote and drew comic books had styles as much as book authors or pop groups.

A radiogram as big as a wash-stand stood by the bed; its vast dial promised frequencies for Budapest and Morocco and Hilversum (wherever Hilversum was), but delivered only bursts of static and, zeroed in on the ghosts of the Home Service and the Light Programme, Radio 4 and Radio 1. Only Michael had a TV in his room; the old black and white set, since his parents were the first to switch to colour. He relayed details of programmes on too late for Neil: *Monty Python's Flying Circus*, which Michael could recite word for word as if he were a living book from *Fahrenheit 451*, and *Casanova*, which had tits in every episode. Jon Pertwee was *Dr Who*, Gerry Anderson had forsaken puppets for *UFO* and Mickey wore shirts like Peter Wyngarde's in *Jason King*. Neil and Michael had a theory that the TV weirdness they liked started with the Bear on *The Andy Williams Show*, 'No cookies,' they chanted, 'not *now*, not *ever*, *never*!' Neil's favourite programmes were *Doomwatch* and *Columbo*; his most hated *The Generation Game* and *On the Buses*.

A pinboard was covered by pictures: Brie Simon, pouting voluptuously in *Devil Daughter of Dracula*, shared a pin-up corner with Jane Fonda as *Barbarella*, Madeline Smith, Suzi Quatro and Julie Ege; a map of Middle Earth had the adventurers' route in Neil's planned sequel to *Lord of the Rings* marked by a carefully plotted felt-tip line. A gallery of musicians featured David Bowie, Maria Callas, Tamsin, Alice Cooper and Steeleye Span. On a poster, the Streak grinned in a small whirlwind, masked face clear, costume blurred. A magazine cover showed Armstrong on the surface of the moon, Aldrin reflected in his bulbous gold visor. On the back of the door was the poster Mickey designed for the never-finished 'dramatic extravaganza' the Quorum tried to write for the last day of Grammar School, *Death to Dr Marling*...

If he had that poster today, he could sell it in Planet Janet for a fortune.

For a moment, it was before him. An alternate universe in which he finished *The Revenge of Sauron*, the Quorum did not break up, University worked out. In this real world, Neil Martin was rich and famous and married to a fluffy woman who looked like a young Brie Simon. White planes of sunlight sprinkled the beautiful blue of his swimming pool as his wife broke the surface. Slow droplets fell from her ripe body as she hauled herself out of the water. He sipped a nectar cocktail and felt warmth on his tanned face and chest. Her touch was cool. Strawberry lips fixed to his, warm tongue slipping into his mouth.

His eyes snapped open. A crust broke in his bruise. The rubber band that had connected him to the present snapped back.

A hammer of pain fell on his head.

Universes shifted; Neil was plucked from his poolside palace, whisked across continua to Cranley Gardens, the taste of last night's sick still in the back of his throat.

He'd lived here for seven months. It was officially a basement flat; the sink and cooker were in an alcove that could marginally be considered a separate room. Seven steps down from the hall with a payphone, a draughty toilet and a bathroom which never had hot water, no matter how long before bathing the heater was turned on. There were three other tenants, one of whom received stolen goods and early morning police visits that, being nearest the front door, it fell on Neil to handle.

The pain grew and he sat in bed, holding his head in his hands. His leg was frozen where he had been injected last night. He had pills somewhere. He held the hurt; it was something he owned outright.

'Heartache and pain and misery and suffering,' he hummed, 'that's what we got for fun around here...'

Late afternoon on a public holiday. The road outside was silent, an abandoned city. Apart from him, the house might be empty. The room was an Egyptian burial chamber plundered centuries before by tomb-robbers. The mummy of Neel-Mah-Teen was unknown to history, his offering of pain ignored by the Gods.

In underpants and a T-shirt, Neil walked across the carpet, shock-cold waking him, numb leg dragging. He made it to the alcove and the cupboard over the sink. There was a half-bottle of ketchup, a box of elderly tea-bags and a plastic container of wholegrain flour, along with the fifties utensils that came with the room. He found a pack of paracetamol, two still in the plastic-

and-foil sheet. He dry-gulped them, experiencing no ad-style instant relief.

The fire had been left on when he collapsed last night (early this morning?) but the meter had run out. He had no fresh change but the coin-box had been broken into and not fixed, so he retrieved his much-used fifty-pence piece and fed it through again. He relished the tingy whirr that came from the fire as the current was restored, promising to settle the debt when Mr Azmi's son came round to collect. He owed the tin box about five pounds.

The overhead bulb came on too; it must have been burning when he crashed.

Someone had helped him, he remembered. A kindly, exasperated woman. She guided him from the casualty ward and waited outside the house, in the first dingy light of dawn, as he got inside. Solicitous of his well-being, which was unusual. Molly? Sally? Sally. From the party. Olive Oyl. Some girl Dolar knew. Probably another incipient psychopath. Dolar introduced him to Tanya, and at first she'd been solicitous too, especially when he had some money and she hadn't any. He wondered what Sally would look like with her hair down. She'd had good eyes and a thin, promising mouth.

He thought of venturing out to quest for groceries, then about boiling a saucepan of water for tea. His stomach wasn't in the mood for food or drink and he doubted he could taste anything anyway. He'd have to clean a cup if he wanted tea and he'd been squeezing weak bubbles out of the washing-up liquid bottle for days.

He could think of no real reason not to go back to bed and sleep out 1993. But, after hovering a moment, he began to get dressed.

'Never surrender,' he told himself, unconvinced.

LEECH

CARDINAL WOLSEY STREET, 1993

Darkness was about him like a cloak, taking the shape of a motor car. In the back of his Rolls, Leech sprawled on black leather like a vampire in a coffin. But he did not sleep. Green figures scrolled on one monitor. Another screen showed Cloud 9's twenty-four-hour News. Business must be done. The fax whirred constantly, feeding documents into his hand. He memorised as he read, then slipped paper into the in-car shredder. A part of his mind was always available for the governance of his earthly dominion.

The car prowled through the docklands. He had been born not far from here. When he returned now, it was as an emperor. Through one-way glass, he looked at empty streets. He owned them; if not now, then soon. Many houses were derelict, windows replaced with sheets of corrugated iron, over-full skips parked outside. Some terraces, like geriatric jaws holding their last few teeth, housed one or two elderly sitting-tenants. Bus shelters were demolished, schools abandoned, post offices closed, pubs firebombed. All support had been withdrawn. There was no transport, no commerce, no policing. Street lighting was intermittent. Large properties, once factories or warehouses, were burned-out shells. The district was in its last stages of withering. Even the homeless, sensing with ratwhiskers the terminal sickness, had moved on to other sites.

When this place was dead, Leech would supervise the erection of a dark and shining city. His pyramid, already the dominant shape on the skyline, would be its beating heart. He could already see predictive outlines of the buildings, shadows gathering substance above the roofs. The future would rise like a reef of black coral, structures clustering upon each other, inhabited bubbles spreading across the map, blotting out chalk marks on wet asphalt. Leech's nameless city would be a sprawling cathedral, an act of worship in stone and steel and glass, a culmination that would endure centuries.

On the floor in front of him, in a cage too small for them, a dozen long-tailed mice crawled over each other, squeaking and shitting and gnawing. More servants for the Device, as ignorant and dedicated as the Quorum, as tiny in the scheme, as vital to the working of the purpose.

The approach to the traffic-lights was strewn with rubble and potholes, but the wheels effortlessly bypassed perils that would halt another vehicle. The Rolls braked at lights before turning into Cardinal Wolsey Street. Nobody crossed the road as the light was red. Nobody had crossed here for months. The amber light was smashed, so there was just a filament glow between red and green.

Leech considered a communication from Zurich, confirming matters discussed at the meeting seven hours ago. A sum the size of the GNP of a mid-ranking South American country had just been placed at his disposal. The surplus money was almost an irritation; like most truly rich men, he had no interest whatsoever in cold figures. He gauged success in other measures, some comprehensible in an infants' playground, some beyond explanation.

The lights changed and the car made the turn-off. Entering Cardinal Wolsey Street was like passing from the snows of Tibet into the Valley of Shangri-La. The quality of light changed, the climate became temperate, a street-shaped shaft of sun sliced through cloud cover. Here, it only rained pleasantly between the hours of one and five in the morning, leaving the street clean and the plants watered every dawn.

On one side of the road was a well-kept park, boundaried by shining railings, neatly trimmed green grass shading into blighted wasteland. Families walked on the civilised zone, throwing frisbees with dogs and children. A uniformed keeper spiked leaves with a stick. Near the wrought iron gates, a stall sold eel pies and pickled herrings. A small band clustered in a gazebo, playing a selection of Gilbert & Sullivan to ranks of deckchairs. The tune was taken up and whistled by everyone in earshot. 'The Ghosts' High Noon'.

The residential side was a Victorian terrace of back-to-back, two-up/two-down dwellings, front steps polished to a shine, front gardens postcard perfect, front doors brightly painted, old-fashioned house numbers proudly displayed. A postman cheerfully delivered letters at dusk on a Bank Holiday. Sparkling-clean milk bottles waited by knife-sharp bootscrapers for tomorrow's collection and delivery.

Fast-food containers did not accumulate in the gutter, dogs did not deposit faeces on pavement or park, cars were not abandoned or vandalised, graffiti did not mar red brickwork, the corner shop had no iron shutter.

As the car proceeded down Cardinal Wolsey Street, residents took note. The postman, leaning his bike against a wall, touched fingers to his peaked cap. A black woman wearing a Mother Hubbard, looked up from scrubbing a doorstep and grinned a welcome. A little boy in shorts stopped driving his hoop and gazed in adoration at the Rolls, almost falling on his cleanly scabbed knees to worship the demigod of the road.

There was only one lock-up garage in the street, at the far end, opposite the pub. The Rolls cruised towards it. As the car passed, people turned to wave or bow to its opaque windows. They were deferential, but made a point of not being creepy about it. This was the world as it should be; everyone sure of their place and comfortable in their station.

The garage door slid up into the roof, a maw-like dark opening. Suspension countered the bump as the car rolled up off the road across the pavement. If he had been holding a drink from the wet bar, the miniscus would barely have wobbled.

The garage swallowed the car. He disengaged monitors and punched the door code onto a pad. The Rolls opened with a slight hydraulic breath. Leech set his hat on his head, regarding himself in an ebony mirror to adjust the angle of the brim. Daintily picking up the cage of mice, he got out and stood for an instant, accustoming himself to the different, welcoming dark.

From outside, it was hard to believe the garage could accommodate a monster like the Rolls. Inside, the car was dwarfed in a hangar-like space that stretched thousands of yards. All interior walls and floors had been taken out, leaving a brick and tile shell, roof supported by chimney columns. The structure was shored by iron pillars and struts and spines. The concrete garage area was raised above the level of the rest of the works, which went down to bare, wet earth. Front doors were nailed shut, wire mesh baskets over letterboxes. Hundreds of windows were double-glazed and net curtained. The whole terrace was hollow, an enclosure the shape of Crystal Palace.

The noise of toiling men and machines, inaudible from the street, was overpowering. From others, he understood the smell was equally potent.

'Derek,' a waiting man said, making the horned sign with both hands, 'blessed be...'

'Blessed be,' Leech replied, returning the arcane greeting and gesture.

Drache, his tame architect and acolyte, had a harmless fetish for ritual and ceremony. If black magic helped him understand his Deal, Leech chose to indulge him.

'The auguries are encouraging,' Drache babbled. 'At midnight, the rubies turned black.'

Drache had made his sacrifices. A distinctive half-domino covered his empty eye-socket. The irregular red patch conformed to the contours of his face, outlining one side of his nose and extending from cheekbone to hairline. It matched his thigh-length leather coat.

Ceremonially, Leech handed over the cage of mice.

'For the Device,' he explained. 'Living components.'

The architect accepted the offering solemnly.

'Magic,' he said.

'Take care of them,' Leech warned. 'None must die. The participants in the ritual are all under my protection.'

Drache nodded, serious. He had heard this before, but it bore repeating. The acolyte understood sacrifice, but was sometimes unsubtle.

Above them and extending the length of the hollowed-out terrace, towered the Device. It clanked and screeched, every inch in motion, a crucified iron animal.

Drache took down a brass-nozzled hose that snaked out of the innards of the Device and removed the cap as if it were a speaking tube. He dropped the first mouse into the mouth and squeezed, gently nudging the animal along the rubber intestine into the works.

Glowing smuts pattered down, sprinkling the observation platform. The pain was so thick his senseless nostrils caught the stink. Leech knew now this would be the year. The Device was nearly complete.

BOOK

DEALS

'The face of evil is always the face of total need.'
WILLIAM S. BURROUGHS, *The Naked Lunch*

1

16 SEPTEMBER, 1970

Apart from a fitting in the tailor's recommended by the prospectus, he hadn't worn his uniform before the morning. Walking the length of town from his parents' council house to Dr Marling's Grammar School for Boys, he felt a freak in his blood-coloured cap. The badge on his roomy black blazer was an open wound. He'd never worn a tie; Mum would have to knot it for a further nine months before he got the knack. Estate kids jeered from the bus stop, shouting 'snobby' as Mark quickened his pace.

Two other boys from his year had got into Marling's but he wasn't in their gang. At Edge End Primary, his friends had been girls; any, like Juliet Kinross, who passed the eleven-plus went to the Girls' Grammar. His brother Chris was at Hemphill Secondary Modern, where his sister Sue would go. When Liza, the youngest, finished Edge End, there wouldn't be an eleven-plus exam; all three schools would be combined as Ash Grove Comprehensive.

On the first day of the first term, boys could use the front doors. Just before nine, there was already a bottleneck. For ever after, he'd trudge up the back drive. On his last day, in an unimaginably distant future, Mark would be permitted to leave as he first entered. A school leaver would then traditionally bung his cap in the river. But by that day, there'd be no caps, no Marling's.

Beyond the front doors was the crush hall, antechamber to the assembly hall. Sports trophies shone in cases. High up was a sad-faced portrait, 'Dr Roger Marling, 1768–1809'. A shield bore the school arms, a motto was inscribed on an hour-glass.

'*Tempus fuggit,*' he said out loud.

'*Tempus fugit,*' said a thin master in a black gown. 'Don't you know what that means, boy? You soon will.'

Alarmed to be talked at by so superior a creature, he hurried into Assembly. Despite the smell of polished wood floors, it was like a railway station packed with refugees. Over eighty uniformed new boys milled about. Plaques honoured old boys killed in wars or accepted by universities; the former was considerably longer. The first boy to speak to him was Alan Ward, who thought he knew someone who knew Mark. Wrong, he would exchange no more than a dozen words with Mark over the next seven years.

'He was a clockmaker, zh-you know,' another boy said.

Mark started. The speaker was not fat exactly, but ripe like an apple. His uniform a slightly lighter black, he was taller than nine tenths of the intake.

'Dixon,' he said, extending a hand like a grown-up. 'Michael Dixon.'

Mark shook the boy's hand.

'Mark,' he introduced himself.

'They use surnames here,' Michael explained.

'Uh, oh, Amphlett.'

'Bless you.'

He spelled out his name.

'Acquainted with anyone in this rabble?'

'Not really.'

'Me neither. I'm here 'cause I got booted out of prep school. Smoking. Vile habit. Bit of a blow to the beloved parents.'

Mark goggled at the sophisticated felon. He was like the boys in the Jennings books. When he later mentioned this, Michael told him, patronisingly, it was time he graduated to P.G. Wodehouse.

Masters in academic gowns were stationed at vital points like guards. None wore the mortar-boards he'd been led by the *Beano* to expect. They shushed and the buzz died. 'Caps off,' a master announced. Mark snatched his from his head and folded it into a boomerang. Ranks formed, everyone unsure where they should stand, facing the stage.

A short man with a purple-edged gown stood at a lectern, a foot-tall hour-glass beside him. Mark recognised Brendan Quinlan MA (Cantab) from the early summer evening when Mum had taken him to an introductory talk about the school and its traditions.

'Chimp,' a boy said. For the first time, Mark, who'd been feeling ill, smiled. Mr Quinlan looked a little like a monkey.

The head, who'd never be anything but Chimp until he disappeared apoplectically in the changeover to Comprehensive in 1973, turned the hour-glass. Sand began to trickle.

'He was a clockmaker,' Michael whispered. 'Dr Marling, I read in…'

'You *boy*,' said Chimp, voice a cannon-blast, stubby finger jabbed, '*silence*, or suffer untold *torments*.'

Michael instantly paled; Mark realised he really was a boy, not a grown-up pretending.

'You probably think well of yourselves,' Chimp told the intake, 'because you were *clever* at your last school. Well, being clever at your last school just makes you *ordinary* here…'

As Chimp read off each surname, the intake divided into three forms. He found himself in 1W, taken by Mr Waller who'd taught him to pronounce *tempus fugit* but would be unable to prod much more Latin into him. Mark wouldn't understand for years why the skeletal master was nicknamed Fats. He'd taught at Marling's since the War and been named by boys long since grown up, faded ink names scrawled in the desks their successors now inherited.

Later he realised 1B (Bairstow) and 1U (Unwin) were assigned desks in alphabetical order so responses passed up and down rows as the register was called. Fats marched his form around the quadrangle to their classroom and let them sit where they wanted. Mark and Michael took desks one row from the back, Michael next to the window. Neil, the boy who'd said 'Chimp', was immediately behind Mark. The far corner behind Michael was empty.

After the register, Fats explained the timetable. At Edge End, a class stayed in one room all day; here forms changed each lesson. Mark knew English, history and mathematics from primary school, but science divided into physics, chemistry and biology and he'd do Latin and French. Tagged a 'Roman Candle', he'd take his half-hour of religious education separate from 1W, with a few other Catholics in the year. As an RC, he was supposed to have a head start in Latin, but most of the class swiftly left him standing and he'd drop it after a year. Friday afternoon was for Games, rugby football in winter, cricket in summer.

Having established academic boundaries, Fats explained the judicial system. Minor offences (talking in class, late homework) were recorded in an exercise book: three meant detention, otherwise reserved for major offences (fighting, armed robbery). Three DTs meant a visit to Chimp, six strokes of the cane. In the second year, Mark would come within one minor offence of the cane, escaping only by convincing Fats he'd not been the one running around the bogs pulling the flush chains. Masters could also give lines (the long, hard, dreary sentence) or a slap with the rubber tubing of a Bunsen burner (the short, sharp, exciting sentence).

Another punishment was a copy, a set of the school rules copied out by hand overnight, administered by prefects, identifiable by their tasselled caps, who caught a boy breaking any of dozens of rules: do not eat in the street, do not run in the school corridor, do not appear outside a classroom with cap off, do not appear in a classroom with cap on. In the first week, Hackwill of 5V gave Mark a copy for something he hadn't done, and he wrung his hand into a claw doing the punishment (he told Mum it was homework). Four small print pages, about three thousand words. He later discovered Hackwill, official and universally feared school bully, wasn't a prefect but an offender himself, pressing the chore to a suitable victim.

By dinner, he understood the geography. Like many schools, it was laid out on the Benthamite model used by prisons: a quad (exercise yard) surrounded by rows of classrooms (cell-blocks), admin building towering above. Where Stalag 17 had a mined wasteland, Marling's had playing fields. After three weeks of rugby, Mark decided he'd rather spend muddy Friday afternoons in a minefield.

Instead of queuing in a cafeteria, boys were assigned tables. Mark's table captain was Spit, a freckled fifth-former. When food was on the plates, Chimp would say grace from the stage; Spit always muttered 'bow you heathens'. He had a sidekick, a tubby third-year named Grease who gobbled the leftovers until Spit, at Neil's joke suggestion, put his furious friend on a diet. Spit would chuckle 'it's for your own good, Greasy' and dole out a single roast potato. A devout Tory, Spit was the first politically-active person Mark encountered: Spit and Grease would get wrecked on cider and infiltrate Labour Party events to cause trouble. Mark didn't mention his Dad was a Labour voter.

To draw out the kids (all, apart from Michael, shellshocked), Spit talked about the constant they held in common, television. Mark was vaguely ashamed of having enjoyed kids' programmes, though Neil piped up with embarrassing enthusiasm for *The Wacky Races*. This was the first year of *Monty Python* which, with unprecedented breasts and vomit, Michael and Mark both saw as significant, though Michael pointed out it was *Do Not Adjust Your Set* for grown-ups. In 1983, Mark would write an obit for *Python* in *The Shape*, denouncing the Oxbridge smugness which deemed it automatically absurd for scrubwomen to know about Sartre.

During dinner hour, as Spit and Grease joshed and Michael and Neil joined in, Mark's idea of Marling's changed. In one scale was Latin, hours of homework and scarlet caps, but something he'd had to hide at Edge End (where he was called queer for not caring about football) was freed.

17 SEPTEMBER, 1970

The next day, 1W grew. There were 79 in the intake; in the rush to sort them into equal forms it wasn't noticed that 79 wasn't divisible by three. The school had three lots of 26 with one left over. A lost soul spent the first day shunted from room to room, passing notes of explanation. Chimp had decided to shove him in with 1W. There was an extra desk at the back, seat broken but usable if a boy didn't mind having his bottom pinched. Ushered in like an escapee returned to the prison population, he had longer hair than anyone in the room and would be upbraided for it well into Ash Grove. His large and active hands were multicoloured with ink; Fats judged him instantly, 'I suspect you are artistic, Yeo.'

He took the free desk and the square was complete. Preliminaries over, the rest of their lives began.

'What's your name?' Neil asked.

'Michael,' he explained.

'We've already got a Michael,' Mark said.

'Zh-you be Mickey,' Michael said. ''Twill spare confusion.'

'*Mickey*?' He seemed appalled.

Five years later, Mark would notice Mickey's Dad, by then his Mum's employer, called his son 'Mike'. He had been reborn and renamed forever and his own father had never known.

'Silence at the back,' said Fats. 'Or it'll be a minor offence for the four of you.'

They sat straight and quiet, mortified.

'Two Michaels, a Mark and a Martin. We have a tradition of Ms at Marling's. Not always happy, but a tradition.'

2

2 JANUARY, 1993

Shifting the Invader to another arm, she picked up the phone. The Invader wailed over anything the caller might be saying.

'Hold, please? I have to rescue a baby from a robot-chef.'

She settled the Invader, features screwed together in the centre of its face, on a cushion.

'Gurgle gurgle,' she said, wiping dribble. The beginnings of a smile rewarded her. 'Sorry,' she said into the handset.

'That's quite all right, Ms Rhodes,' replied a voice. Male, youngish, classless, precise.

'Happy New Year'

'Likewise. I'm Mark Amphlett.'

She knew the name.

'Pardon me for bothering. I thought it best this be dealt with sooner.'

On TV, he looked about eighteen. Thin, sharp, penetrating: a stiletto.

'I'm an associate of Michael Dixon's.'

'I saw you together on *Have I Got News For You*. You won...'

'...but he was funnier. I've an interest in the business you pursued for Michael last year. It'd be useful if we met. Could you be available Monday morning?'

'The fourth?'

'Yes. About ten. I have an office in D'Arblay Street. *The Shape*.'

'You've got a date.'

He rang off. The Invader crawled towards the precipitous sofa edge, peering exploratively at the drop.

Several people gave her Amphlett's *The Shape of the Now* one Christmas. She'd never finished the book. She had seen *The Shape* at friends' houses, a heavy square magazine. A few years ago, it was considered essential. 'When in the future people think of the eighties,' he once said, 'I want them to think of *The Shape*.' That must haunt him.

'So, Mummy's Little Millstone,' she said, saving the Invader from an eighteen-inch plunge, 'I'm visiting a Style Guru. What d'you think I should wear?'

4 JANUARY, 1993

She identified herself to a speaker marked with the square logo of *The Shape*. The door buzzed in and she faced an almost vertical staircase. Thankful she'd chosen flats not heels, she carefully climbed. A door opened above her head. Long legs came into view under a short, electric pink skirt.

'Mind your footing,' a voice said.

A black girl with a perfect complexion helped her with the last few steps as if she were a grandmother.

'An accident waiting to happen,' she said, easing Sally through the door. 'I'm Laura-Leigh. Mark will be with you instantly. Filter coffee or herbal tea?'

Ask for proper PG tips, Mummy.

'Rose hip, please.'

Laura-Leigh reminded her of the strange women in sanitary-towel ads who go skydiving or shark-fishing while having their period. And smile about it.

Michael Dixon had interviewed her in a sparsely-populated

office, acres of glass covered by Venetian blinds, in a complex of production companies off Goodge Street. *The Shape* was run from comfortable loft-space in Soho. Drafting tables and computers combined with unfinished wood and original stone, an imposition of modernity upon the past.

She sank into a low couch, insubstantial cushions stuffed into a futon frame, and kept her knees together. She'd chosen a tartan skirt, green blouse and hip-length darker green cardigan. Not striking (if she was noticed on the street, she wasn't doing her job) but not shabby either.

Laura-Leigh returned with tea, an alarming purple brew in a glass beaker with an aluminium handle arrangement.

'Mark won't be but a moment,' she said.

On a low glass-topped table, the last four issues of *The Shape* were laid out like a still life. A fan of brochures for connected enterprises suggested, with technographics, impenetrable mysteries of science.

She sipped her tea (bland at first, but seductive) and picked up the last quarterly number of *The Shape*. Its cover, thick as cardboard, bore an image that might be a face or a tankful of goldfish. A glossy contents page, tiny black type wriggling in a square-metre of creamy space, promised the centenary of the airbrush, sixties ice-lollies, Jim Harrison and Interactive Narrative. She found an obituary for Amazon Queen.

'Ms Rhodes,' he said.

She put down the magazine and stood. He shook her hand and looked at her as she looked at him. Taller than expected: she'd thought Style Gurus likely to be overcompensatory dwarves. Hair cut short, neat bald patch like a tonsure. Four-button, single-breasted suit, dark with subtle silver thread. Button-down collar, skinny keyboard tie. Prominent cheekbones, thin smile, sharp eyes.

'Come into the Inner Sanctum,' he said, sliding away a section of wall to reveal a priests' hole lined with files and thick blankspined books. A desk partitioned the room, a window looked out on the street. He slipped into a swivel chair in a tiny space behind the desk, and offered her either of two matched armchairs, low-slung black leather punchbags strung between chrome tubes.

Still holding her beaker, she sat.

'You do good work,' he said, holding up a red folder.

'I try to be thorough.'

Indeed, over the weekend, she'd researched Mark Amphlett. She finished *The Shape of the Now*, written in his last year at university, 1981. Slimmer than she remembered from her first stab, the book was slyer than its keynote-speech-for-a-decade reputation suggested. The prescient dissection of the yet-to-come extremes of Thatcher Culture struck her as remarkably on-the-nail. Subsequently, he'd written one further non-fiction work (an unambitious *History of Japanese Advertising*) and a single novel, *Envy*. He'd produced and presented *The Science of Seemliness*, a cusp-of-the-nineties aesthetics documentary on Cloud 9, the Leech satellite channel. Though feelers extended into several mutating media, his main interest remained *The Shape*: it had a low circulation but astounding ad revenues, actually picking up in the recession. Available also in electronic format, it had outgrown its boom-and-bust readership to keep an enviable footing.

The part of his history she already knew was shared with Michael Dixon and Neil Martin. Dr Marling's, Ash Grove, West Somerset College, 1970–77. Even celebrities started as kids: Mark Amphlett started in a council house in a town he himself called the Backwater. Early photographs suggested his mother put a German helmet on him and cut off any hair that stuck out. To him, that must be a million years ago. She wondered what his parents made of him.

Something happened then, something which explained now. But that wasn't her business.

'I was impressed with your postscript. Nobody has to work on New Year's Eve.'

She shrugged. 'It was an accident.'

'Nothing is an accident,' he said, quoting the title of the first chapter of *The Shape of the Now*.

He wore an unusual ring, a heavy mock-antique that didn't go with his clothes. He had no other jewellery, not even a watch. Inset in stone was a letter 'Q'.

He was one of those who looked at you all the time, expecting you eventually to look away. In that, he was right; she'd taken in his face quickly and was now more interested in his office. There were fewer toys than she expected. Everything within reach of his desk had a use.

'Michael and I have talked about you. I would like to extend the arrangement you had with him.'

Suddenly, this interview made sense. There'd been a cabinet reshuffle. It happened often in dealings with firms of solicitors, even with the courts. Her old contact was promoted, fired, shifted sideways or otherwise off the case; she had to meet the new man or woman.

'Do I report to you?'

He nodded.

'It's the same job but you'll invoice *The Shape*. Square Deal Enterprises, actually. I'm not in business with Michael or the other party...'

Mickey Yeo, unless she missed her guess.

'...though we have projects in common. I'm taking over this matter.'

'Neil Martin?'

He nodded again.

'You want to continue surveillance?'

'There will be other considerations. The format will change. For the next six weeks or so, we'll need regular, immediate situation reports. Nothing on paper is necessary. One or other of us will be in touch and you can keep us informed.'

'Six weeks?'

'Until the 14th of February.'

'Valentine's Day?'

'We'll need Neil's day-to-day set-up.'

'That can be done, but it's much more work. I imagine the findings will be unutterably dull.'

A sharp smile.

'I doubt that, Sally.'

They were on first names.

'Believe it, Mark. Anybody's day-to-day life is boring.'

And Neil Martin's more than most.

'We don't need to know what brand of cornflakes he has for breakfast. Use your judgement on the detail. You've done well so far.'

'Neil Martin doesn't seem the breakfast type to me. Instant coffee made with hot water from the tap. If he has hot water.'

'Very astute. Your fee will go up. I think we can find you £700 a week. And reasonable expenses.'

Do the sums, Mummy.

Six sevens. £4,200 by the middle of February.

'I have other things current,' she lied.

His smile sharpened.

'I think we can afford first call on your services. Would a non-returnable retainer of 2K above your fee compensate you for lost business?'

'Golly, yes,' she tried not to gulp.

'I'll have Laura-Leigh format a contract. Sally Rhodes Security Services, isn't it?'

He flicked open a box on his desk and toyed with a tiny metal boot, a piece from a *Monopoly* set. He looked away and through the window. A cold new year was creeping on. This was the morning people crawled back, puffy and bone-tired, to offices that hadn't been heated for two weeks.

'You'll excuse me for asking, but...'

'...how did I get into this unusual line of work? A degree in child psychology, no suitable job prospects, receptionist with a security firm, a couple of gigs for them, developed a taste for the chase, out on my own with a business-start loan, a few years snooping and shepherding, saved the world a couple of times, bad ankles and backache from standing about in the cold, near-bankruptcy in the recession, a couple of months as a TV researcher, time off to have a baby, another stab at being my own boss. And here I am.'

'So you are.'

'I like finding things out. Probably a neurotic compulsion.'

Mark pondered her *précis*. She had the speech off by heart and would sometimes deliver it to the mirror. Her mother's version, with snide comments, was much more entertaining.

'You know I was at school with Neil,' Mark said, gripping his boot in a fist.

'Of course.'

'Do you ever wonder why we're... Michael and Mickey and me... why we're so attentive to Our Absent Friend?'

She considered lying but decided against it. 'Yes, naturally.'

For a moment, his look was almost as quizzical as Dixon's. She was being invited to expand on the thought.

'Mark, it's hardly my business. I provide a service. It's legal, it's not really unethical. Most of the time, I don't know *my* motives for doing anything. Why should I try to fathom yours?'

'Fair enough. Just be flexible. What we ask seems weird, I'm aware of that. As I said: nothing is an accident, everything has a purpose. We trust you; please extend the courtesy of returning that trust.'

She touched her forehead. 'Aye aye.'

'Sally, you're not what I imagined a private detective was like.' She shrugged.

'If I wore a trenchcoat and carried a gun, I wouldn't last long.'

'You're more like a... like a child minder.'

'Got it in one. My speciality is custody cases, holing up at the seaside with a mixed-race kid to stop the father whisking it off to Tehran or Oporto. It's always the father. I've also looked after supposedly kidnappable rich brats and, as far as I'm concerned, you can have 'em.'

He dropped his boot back in its box and tipped the lid shut over it.

She said, 'You're the only Style Guru I've met who's kept his favourite *Monopoly* piece.'

3

1971-1977

The Meets started in 1971. Mickey, whose parents had divorced, was with his Mum in London for Christmas, but Michael and Mark, Neil making up the Quorum, were marooned in the Backwater for the duration. Getting together at Michael's on New Year's Day, with Trevor Skelly, the S-Man Out, they played *Monopoly*. Mark was the boot, Michael the top hat, Neil an Airfix Hussar, Skelly the car; Mickey, whom they shuffled poverty-stricken around the board, was represented by a thimble-sized Dalek. Unconcluded after a dusk-til-dawn marathon, the Game lasted three years, mutating to encompass *Campaign* and *Diplomacy*. Financial empires became armed principalities, property wheeler-dealing segued into battlefield conflict. Mickey joined when term started, ruthlessly catching up. Other boys, and Michael's sister Candy, came and went, co-opted for an afternoon or a term, then were destroyed or expelled, sacrificed by major players. Skelly lasted a year, his expansionist dictatorship tumbling when his family moved to Swindon. The power vacuum led to war between Mark and Mickey, a crisis settled only by Neil's diplomatic achievement, the Brink's Café éTreaty, signed after school and witnessed by a puzzled waitress. 'I reckon you talk the most crap ever,' she commented. She looked like Brie Simon, 1973's idea of a sex goddess. In 1981, one of Michael's first TV plays would be *The Game*, a nightmare comedy about superpower arms limitation talks which turn into a boys' bedroom battle.

First they were the Four of 'Em, the Four of M: Michael, Mickey, Martin, Mark. That evolved into *The Forum*, the irregular magazine they put out under the aegis of Ash Grove, then (after the Princess Anne Wedding Special was banned) off their own bat. Mickey produced razor-lined artwork; Mark specialised in collages of found images; Michael formulated cynical essays; Neil contributed 'Neil-Bites', half-pages of prose that weren't quite stories and weren't poetry either. Never printing more than 150 copies, they were usually left with 90 of them; by the nineties, issues would change hands for up to £25.00. They became the Quorum when it was noticed how rare it was to get them all together at the same time. Like the balls which were supposed to roll into dents in the clown's face, only three could be lined up; if the fourth got in, one of the others got loose. Someone was always left out.

Each had outside interests. Having gone from Chopin to Jerry Lee Lewis, Mickey put his piano lessons to use in a succession of bands. Mark was Chess Club King, a spider-like strategist who ruled the boards until the advent of Carole Wolley, the Brain Child whose merciless play made him give up the game. Neil and Michael competed to write novels, sometimes getting fifty pages down before losing momentum. Michael and Mickey went to the Loire with Michael's parents and came back with lies about French girls that made Neil and Mark intensely envious. Neil got a Saturday job in a newsagent's and was briefly rich on seven pounds a week. After an Eisenstein film at the Rat Centre, Michael declared himself a Communist and wrote off to join the Party, prompting Mark to a flirtation with the National Front that ended when he realised his favourite musicians were all black.

* * *

The Game was finally resolved in 1973. With school now comprehensive and co-educational, impressing girls was a higher priority than byzantine death-struggles. Brie Simon, cuddling a fanged Ingrid Pitt in the 'X' films they got into at the Empire, faded out of their consciousness, replaced by the leggy Penny Gaye, who later became a publicist, and the legendary Jacqui Edwardes, who kissed with her tongue. Over the summer, Michael surreptitiously gained a controlling interest in Neil's empire, declaring an intention to reduce him to slavery; the Quorum drew up the Second Brink's Café Treaty, founding an indissoluble secret alliance dedicated to Michael's downfall. One climactic weekend, through the long night when the clocks went back, it ended: Michael was buried under the rubble in his bunker, the other major players reduced to flophouses in the Old Kent Road. Mark would remember more keenly his resentment when Neil casually changed sides during a battle, cutting down Mark's cavalry, than the rift with Michael that came a year later when the fat git got off with Penny Gaye. In 1992, as Michael and Mickey tried to salvage a script from the ruins of Mausoleum Pictures, whose collapse had just taken down another fifth of the British Film Industry, Mickey called a meeting and reduced Michael to helpless laugh-spasms by reviving his old treatment of prisoners-of-war. Mickey straight-facedly suggested of the irresponsible producers who had sunk capital into a disastrous rap musical, *Chillin' London*, 'they should have their fuckin' feet cut off and be told to walk home.'

They saw themselves as leaders of their generation. Neil and Michael alternated being first in English, Mickey was either top or bottom in art depending on how bored he was, Mark scored in history and maths. Aside from specialist subjects, they were academically erratic. At the end of the third year, they planned

Death to Dr Marling's, a historical fantasy about the centuries of suffering which were nearly over. Every evening they went to Michael's and worked, but the school was finished before the script. They later realised they'd never have got Chimp's permission to use the assembly hall for a pageant whose opening scene had Roger Marling singing 'I'm in the Mood for Love' while roasting his first pupil on an open fire. Nevertheless, they were fascinated by performance. Having learned from the show they hadn't got together, they spent terms carrying spears and reciting iambic pentameter in the Youth Theatre. In 1975, Michael persuaded the organiser, Ben Tindall, to let them mount revues as a counterpoint to traditional YT productions. Twice a year; Twelfth Night and Midsummer Night, the Forum took over the Arts Centre (they always called it the Rat Centre) and put on something increasingly more like a party than a play. Their first production was *Twelfth Night '76*, remotely derived from the Shakespeare they'd done straight the year before.

While becoming impresarios, just as they started Sixth Form College, they took serious interest in girls. When Michael announced he was going out with Penny, Mark didn't speak to him for weeks. However, Carole, the first girl he ever really talked to, turned out to be just as screwed-up and interesting as he thought he was. Neil developed a sickening romantic obsession with Victoria Conyer; a year older, she never noticed, so far as anyone knew, whether he was breathing or not. Mickey used his powermouth to overcome a succession of under-age girls he referred to as 'shag-hags'. He launched an extensive campaign to bed Jacqui Edwardes who, after a year, succumbed only to dump him instantly and get engaged to a twenty-five-year-old geriatric who sold drugs. While they were on a residential poetry course, Neil got off (for one night) with a girl from Wells named Clare. Michael and Penny became the college's perfect couple; he was President of the Student Union, she was Social Secretary. Between them, they masterminded every disco, concert, show and party in the Backwater.

* * *

In 1977, for the first and only time, the New Year's Meet was open to consorts. At Michael's grandparents' in Achelzoy, which he looked after when they were away; Michael and Mark brought Penny and Carole, Mickey turned up with a girl called Denise whom they never saw again, and Neil cheated by bringing Michael's sister. While the others found private rooms, Neil and Candy had a day-long talk, imagining what they would all be in ten years: Michael an actor, Mickey a painter, Mark an MP, Penny the editor of *Cosmopolitan*, Carole a Professor of Thinkology, Denise a housewife, Candy a veterinarian, Neil a novelist. Their score was one and a half out of eight: Carole became a lecturer in Social Policy at Liverpool; the half was Denise, who almost certainly got married.

In the evening, also for the first and only time, they had a séance, Scrabble letters arranged in a circle on a table. Hands on a glass that really seemed to move independently, they contacted a spirit who called itself Shad and claimed to have died ('discarnated', Michael said) in 1842. Candy asked about the future. For Michael, Shad spelled PILES but wouldn't confirm whether it meant wealth or haemorrhoids. For Carole, the letters were PHD which was easy. For Neil, the word was DEAL. For Candy, GAS, which upset Denise so much she broke the circle. They were relieved; pathetic fallacy or not, a thunderstorm started as they tampered with the beyond. Mark, rattled but sceptical, suggested that if they picked random words from a dictionary, they'd as easily apply to their lives. To prove his point, he picked 'cephalopod' and invited explanations. Later, the Forum decided to leave women out of Meets. Much later, Candace Dixon became Western Regional Director of British Gas, Carole became a Doctor of Philosophy and Michael did suffer a bad case of haemorrhoids.

* * *

The heavy shadows of *Monty Python* and *Mad* fell on the Quorum's stage work. As early as 1978, Neil and Mark would be embarrassed that, given unprecedented freedom, they'd been so conventional, but Mickey and Michael were recycling material well into the eighties. Michael and Neil wrote approximate scripts, tossing jokes between them as they took turns on Michael's typewriter. Mark, intense and organised, was less director than ringmaster; on any project, there were days when he locked himself in a room and refused to talk to anyone until Neil begged him to come out and get involved again. Whatever band Mickey was in appeared and, with eerie regularity, broke up within weeks of the show. Mickey designed costumes, sets and posters, and recruited footsoldiers; actors, backstage people, ticket-tearers and, most vitally, audience members. Traditionally, by the interval, everyone swore never again to work with the others; but, when the curtains closed, they'd be eager to start again. They were most unified in enthusiasm after *Midsummer Night's Dribbly Fart*, the show that was never restarted after drunken boneheads let off a fire extinguisher during Penny's Tamsin impersonation. 'It wasn't planned,' Michael said at the cast party, 'but it was *theatre*.'

Influenced by rumours of punk and soft drugs, they put on *A Midsummer Night's End* in the summer of 1977, assuming they'd break up in the autumn when Mark and Neil went to Brighton University and Mickey to Art School in Leeds. Michael was taking a year off (to write a novel, he said), but planned on Cambridge in '78. After the show, things changed. All were sorry and found it hard to imagine life without the others, but they were relieved at the same time. In *The Shape of the Now*, Mark would write 'the end of any period, no matter how pleasurable it has been, is a liberation.'

4
MY KIND OF DAY
MICHAEL DIXON

I try to get up before seven and do forty-five minutes grunt-and-strain in the gym. My wife [actress Ginny Moon] sometimes manages to stir her great body and joins me to get in some skipping. She remembers dirty versions of playground rhymes and disrupts our work-outs since we're too busy giggling to get a sweat. We do family brekky with our daughter [Melanie, eight]. I stick to Neal's Yard muesli and fresh orange juice. First thing in the a.m. (don't read this, kitten), Gin is unrecognisable as the glamour-puss from *The Woman Who Did* and looks like an ape, but Melanie is already breaking hearts. I've always been sickeningly lucky with women.

I have days at the word-processor in my study – a posh name for the room I won't let anyone else into. I often pretend to write but actually play computer games. With *Colin Dale* on as a serial and *Ken Sington* in production, I'm doing another in the series, *Mai DaVale*, which should be out this fall (we have American seasons in our house, sadly) and be on telly next year: Colin and Ken are girl-chasing in Book Three because Gin pestered me to write a part for her, and now her agent wants more money than the BBC can pay. I've threatened to hide her precious bubble-bath mix (a family recipe) until she gives in. I do a couple of hours' light tappy-typing in the morning, aiming to get ten pages battered out, revise after lunch and bunk off to watch afternoon telly. I'm addicted to Aussie soaps and clever-clever quiz shows.

On office days, I cruise into the West End, where my production company has exorbitantly expensive premises, and crack-whip over highly-paid runners, assistants, secretaries, researchers and minions. On Mondays, I lock everyone into the boardroom and don't let them out until they've come up with six hours' worth of ideas. Then they beaver away setting them up until Wednesday afternoon, when I jettison things that aren't working. This is accomplished with much bloodletting.

If I'm in town, I usually have lunch meetings with publishers, film people, potential guests or old mates. I have a girlie whose job it is to find new restaurants. My ambition is to eat in every place within a three-mile radius of Goodge Street, and live.

Fridays are hectic panic since the show goes out live in the evening. I can't write, produce, present *and* direct, so someone sits in a box shouting orders at cameramen while I do battle under the lights. But *Dixon's On*, whatever you think about it, is all my own work. I even composed the signature tune. People ask me who my favourite guest was and I have to say Peter Ustinov. I have to because he pays me a retainer, but actually my real ambition-of-a-lifetime was working with Tamsin.

We started with Channel 4 and I'll always be grateful they gave me a chance after the Show We Do Not Name Out Loud, but Cloud 9 offers better facilities and access to international names than any of the terrestrial channels. Some of my mates criticised me at first for working for Derek Leech, but in my experience Derek's done a lot of good in the business.

Most evenings, Gin and I are out at a first night or a movie premiere. Maybe even the same ones at the same time. People suspect we're not just married because the wedding put us on the cover of *Hello*. Sometimes we're so luvvy you could scream. We don't often get a chance to eat out locally and I'm a bit teed-off with a nameless Curry House in Hampstead High Street who put a picture of me and Ginny in their window after we ordered a takeaway from them. Gin cooks like Scott Tracy acts, so I sometimes show off my culinary brilliance by whipping up *ragout a la Michel*.

Some weekends, we pile into one of the cars and boogie off to the country for a ramble. I grew up in a small town in Somerset and that has given me a deep and abiding attachment to Yorkshire.

• Michael Dixon presents *Dixon's On*, Friday Cloud 9 (satellite). *Colin Dale* starts Sunday BBC1.

Radio Times, 9–15 January, 1993

6 JANUARY, 1993

Michael saw his fish-eye reflection in a mug of undiluted caffeine and fought an addict's craving for fry-up. He looked at his Rolex (Christmas present). 8.52 a.m. Middle of the night.

'*My mummy told me*,' a shrill voice sing-songed, '*if I was goody, that she would buy me a rubber johnny...*'

Ginny was being difficult again. He didn't need the distraction. Today wasn't for family. Today was for the Quorum. For Neil.

'*My auntie told her I fucked a soldier...*'

'Give it a rest, Zh-Gin. I had to say something. They phoned when I was mightily pissed up.'

Ginny sat at the other end of the stripped-pine breakfast table. Her clinging floor-length nightie (Christmas present) could pass for a Jean Harlow ballgown. She toyed with a cigarette-sliver of brown toast. Her face was a make-up mask: red lips, dead eyes.

'Ooo-ooo,' she gibboned, folding hands into her armpits and flapping elbows. 'Me Kong, you banana.'

The breakfast room was still Santa's grotto, festooned with Harrod's tinsel. A string of cards had fallen and trailed between the ice-cream machine and the water purifier. The parquet was scattered with needles that had migrated from the drawing room, where a fully-decorated twelve-foot tree loomed over the widescreen TV like a triffid in fancy dress.

'It's Twelfth Night,' he said. 'This lot goes today.'

'Milly-Molly-Melly wants to know why Crimbo can't last longer?'

'Only international arms dealers could afford to reproduce.'

Still on holiday from Rich Kid School, Melanie wasn't up yet. Over Christmas, she'd decided to become anorexic and hadn't eaten anything except brussels sprouts.

'How was your work-out, Arnie?'

He'd rolled out of bed five minutes ago. The trip to the breakfast room hadn't made him break a sweat.

'Fuck off, floozie.'

His wife had inherited her deep, dirty laugh from her mother. God help them all, Ginny's mother was the *Blue Peter* presenter the Quorum placed highly in their 1973 Women We Would Like to Shag Top Ten. Mandy Moon was still a silver fox.

Ginny slipped the toast soldier into her mouth and licked away an almost invisible layer of lime marmalade.

'I don't suppose zhou'd consider oral sex?'

She blew him a kiss in the negative, then bit down on the toast and chewed slowly.

'I try to get it up before seven and do forty-five minutes grunt-and-strain in the bedroom,' she said, in a nastily perfect imitation of his drawl. 'My wife [actress Zh-Ginny Moon] sometimes manages to stir her great body and zh-joins me to get in some knobsucking. I've always been sickeningly lucky with women.'

'Very amusing,' he said. 'Zhou should be an actress.'

'So should you.'

'Cunt.'

'Whore.'

It never failed. His erotic interest in Ginny, always intermittent, pulsed strongest when she was beastly. An erection slipped through his pyjama fly and lifted the lap of his Muji kimono (Christmas present).

'Cocksucker,' he said.

'You wish.'

'You're *disgusting*,' came a voice from the doorway. Melanie stood holding in her tiny tummy to show off a ballet leotard (Christmas present) that outlined alarming, knife-like hipbones. Her hair, piled on one side of her head, was like a burst of lava erupting from Mount St Helens. She'd already mastered the Electric Evil stare unique to the Moon Women.

'Come and join family brekky, Mell,' said Ginny. 'Shall I get you cinnamon toast, poached eggs, croissants and fresh-crushed orange juice?'

'Are there any sprouts left?'

He keyed in the entry code, 2150. Easy to remember: it was the date of the Dalek Invasion of Earth. The inner door shushed open. In the Egyptian-style reception, security cameras swivelled. He did a clumsy tap-step for the video-eye, soliciting applause from the Martian in the control-room. Ayesha, lying in wait, pounced with overnight faxes and ready-opened morning post. Mark confirmed the rehiring of Sally Rhodes; his accountant advised offshore trusts; a producer who'd failed to secure rights to *Colin Dale* admired the finished product, previewed two nights ago at BAFTA; a frequent correspondent from Glasgow threatened to eviscerate Michael's wife and child if he made another joke on air about Emma Thompson.

'Bang him an autographed photo of Gin and Melly,' he told Ayesha. 'And copy his letter to Em.'

Ayesha had a folder from his clippings service, straggling reviews of *Ken Sington* from last year and many mentions of the *Colin Dale* TV tie-in.

'How many Best of the Zhears?'

Ayesha neutrally told him three of the five whose books he picked for *The Independent* and *The Sunday Argus* failed to reciprocate. Two lesser names selected *Ken* for Top Fives and the *Brentford Mail* listed *Colin* as its Christmas paperback choice.

'Arselickers,' he muttered, pleased.

Also, he made one Worst list. In the *Basildon Echo*, a critic named Gary Gaunt called him 'a toothless Tom Sharpe, whingeing into early middle-age with delusions of relevance'.

There was a shift of pain in his stomach. Ayesha soothed him with sales figures. *Ken* was up in the hardback bestsellers; *Colin* had just knocked a hip-thigh-and-groin diet off the top of the paperback charts.

'"Delusions of relevance",' he muttered. 'Photocopy the Best of Zhear mentions, the Ian Hislop rave and the bestseller charts, with titles ringed in red, then dispatch the package to the ghastly Gaunt, care of the piddling *Basildum Void*.'

Ayesha would get on it immediately.

He walked through the open-plan office, stomach settling, nodding mornings to the minions. Most were talking into telephones out of the sides of their mouths.

'How goes it, Michael?' a researcher asked, momentarily diverting herself from a tangle of tasks.

'Globular, Ape,' he replied.

April nodded and resumed her phone conversation. She simultaneously scribbled notes with one hand and leafed through reference material with the other. Presumably her feet worked pedals under her desk.

Safe in his vacuum-sealed private office, he buzzed Ayesha and told her to hold calls and guard his doorway against intruders. His private office was a collection of sharp metal edges in steel-grey and matt black. The Top Hat Productions suite was the work of Constant Drache, best known for the Derek Leech Enterprises' Docklands Pyramid. Ranks of three-yard razorblades strung on piano-wire served as blinds, making samurai music. No distractions today. It fell to the outgoing Ring to make the first moves. The day's business was *dim sum*, tiny treats before the feast.

He touched a concealed device and a framed *Dixon's On* poster slid aside. A fully-stocked bar trundled forwards on hidden wheels. Lit effectively from below, bottles clinked. A curl of dry-ice spilled and dispersed. He twisted the top off a litre of Stoli and poured a measure into a steel-threaded glass. He took a gulp. Perfect. He wanted to savour the day. He put his vodka next to the files on his deskpad and crossed himself upside-down. He sat in his orthopaedic power chair and sipped chilled brainwater. Napoleon a minute before the first salvo. Only Napoleon was a loser.

Sally Rhodes had prepared a rundown of households near Neil's flat, with notes on the degree of intimacy (if any) between Neil and his neighbours. He had few friends in Cranley Gardens and only a scattering of acquaintances. Not surprising. Michael found the entry he'd ticked. The Gregory family. Don (38) and Liz (37): Caucasians, civil servants, homeowners. Children: Jonathan (13), Ellen (11), Stewart (9). As far as Sally knew, no Gregory had ever spoken to Neil. They were civilians. She included only the barest details: name, rank and telephone number.

He punched buttons on the slimline phone. If Don or Liz answered, he'd hang up and try later. It wasn't likely: kids would still be home from school, the parents back at work. After a few rings, a little girl said 'hello.'

'Ellen,' he said. 'Good morning. Might I speak with Jonathan?'

Swallowing the zh-sound his mouth wanted to put in Jonathan, he kept his tic firmly in control. He heard the girl foghorn-yelling, then a clattering. He didn't know what Jonathan looked like: fat or thin, jock or weed, clever or stupid.

''Lo,' came a grunt. 'Who's this then?'

'Jonathan, you don't know me but I sent you a package yesterday. Did you receive it?'

A pause and a gulp. 'Um, yeah… what's this all about?'

He'd posted Jonathan a Swedish magazine. Leaved between explicit pages were a dozen £10 notes: an unimaginable fortune to Michael when he was thirteen, it would even now be enough for top-of-the-line trainers.

'Have you enjoyed your reading, Jonathan?'

Burning silence. If it were just money, the boy would probably tell Don and Liz. The magazine almost certainly meant he'd keep quiet. Michael hoped Jonathan had been alone in his bedroom when he opened the jiffy bag.

'Who are you?'

'You can call me Mr Sington,' Michael said. 'I have another package here, with your name and address on it.'

'Yeah?'

Jonathan sounded like a boy with zits and dandruff. Low brow and fat lower lip. Listens to heavy metal and plays Nintendo, doesn't have much to say to his parents, impatient with his sister and brother.

'Do you play games?'

'Unh?'

'Good wrist action?'

'Wot?'

The boy was slow. All the better: too much thinking, too many questions, could foul this move.

'Jonathan, do you wish me to forward this other package to you?'

'Uh, oh, yeah. I s'pose.'

'Outstanding, my man. There's a service I need performed in your road.'

Jonathan hung on avidly.

'Opposite your home is a large house sub-divided into single-tenant dwellings. The owner is a man named Jamil Azmi.'

'Yeah,' the boy said. 'I know it.'

'Tomorrow, early in the morning, before, say, seven o'clock, you should cross the road, ensuring you aren't seen or at least aren't especially noticed. You are to throw something heavy through the basement windows of the house. Stones, bricks, anything. I'd be best pleased if both panes of both windows were smashed.'

A long quiet. He heard the TV in the Gregory household. *Good Morning with Anne and Nick*. Michael had been a sofa-sitter on the show, tub-thumping *Colin Dale*, cuddling up with Ginny.

'All right,' Jonathan said.

'The package will be in the post by the end of the week, after your mission has been accomplished.'

'Unh.'

'Jonathan, you're a good soldier.'

He hung up and took a swig of vodka. Ice-alcohol hit his stomach and forehead at the same time. Like power like sex: scary and exciting and addictive.

By one o'clock, he'd hit a six or two. Michael worked down the list on his silver-grey notepad. With every call, he drew a line through a number.

He used his best Alf Garnett-Michael Caine voice on Karl Garr, an unemployed black man three doors from Neil who spent his copious free time practising guitar chords. 'You fakkin' coon, why don't you bleedin' shut up so decent bladdy British people can get some kip. I can hear your racket up an' down the whole bladdy street.'

To the North London Music Exchange, he represented himself as Mr K. Garr of Cranley Gardens and requested delivery of the most powerful amplifier in stock. The assistant claimed they had a model whose wall of noise loosened teeth and killed cats. Payment would be biked over in anonymous cash. As an afterthought, he slipped in an order for *How to Begin the Guitar* and *The David Cassidy Song Book*.

In a broad Somerset accent, he telephoned Planet Janet and, calling himself Tosser, asked to speak to Neil, knowing he wasn't there. Told he could leave a message, he dictated a complicated *communiqué* insisting on an urgent call-back. He implied Neil owed Tosser a couple of hundred quid but would be willing to settle the debt for under-the-counter credit.

Using a number not in the Yellow Pages which April had researched for him, he made contact with the Tottenham Command Post of the English Liberation Front. Giving Neil's name and address to the duty officer, who sounded like Corporal Jones of *Dad's Army*, he asked to be signed up as a neo-Nazi in good standing. His subscription would arrive in cash since he didn't trust Jew-controlled banks. Jonesey promised he'd immediately send copies of *Britannia Rules*, the ELF magazine, enclosing details of covert ops.

He phoned Jamil Azmi and used his old headmaster's yell to ask loudly why he'd *again* been woken up by police *raiding* Azmi's property in *Cranley Gardens* and couldn't he *do* anything to curb the *crack dealing* run from the *basement flat*. The landlord said he'd have one of his sons look into it.

To Fortis Green Police Station, he identified himself in a John Major strangled whine as Stewart Gregory. 'I thought I should inform you of a fight I witnessed on New Year's Eve. In Muswell Hill Road. A bloke who lives opposite (Marvin or Melvin his name is). Him and two other blokes were hitting a woman. She popped him one and got away. Bloody disgrace, ganging up on a woman. Hope she put his eye out.' When the policewoman asked him to come in and give a statement, he gurgled and hung up.

For lunch, he had *foie gras* brioche at *Les Amis du Table*, followed with a Mars bar ice-cream bought at a newsagent's. In restaurant and shop, he was recognised and stared at, by a teenager and a paper-buying pensioner with remarkably similar shocks of white hair: one bought, one earned. Then, remembering to arrange a bandit's scarf over his famous face, he visited a post office. He gave Neil's name and address, presenting as proof of identity a BBC remittance slip he'd mocked up while playing with a graphics program. Claiming he was about to move to Northern Ireland, he filled in forms and paid a fee to have his post redirected to a box number in Belfast.

Stepping into the street and loosening his scarf, he was recognised by a brace of girls window-shopping.

'It's Michael Dixon, off the telly,' one said.

He looked quizzically at them.

'I'll be in conference,' he told Ayesha, seriously. 'With Kendra and Gwen,' he added, prompting a further discharge of giggles.

Minions queued outside his office, arguing among themselves, bearing offerings. Ayesha, supernaturally perfect, mentally reordered his schedule, compressing appointments, rearranging deadlines. She told him Derek Leech's office called, selecting the single item of paramount importance from among twenty trivial inquiries. He was reminded about tonight. A car would be sent. Ginny would be picked up on the way.

'By the way, find out who owns the *Basildon Elbow*.'

As he manoeuvred the thrilled girls through the office, Michael made snap decisions. Of two comedians available for Friday's show, he chose the up-and-coming American and back-burnered the newly rehabilitated Brit. He ruled out Sade for the music spot as 'too eighties' and authorised tentative Bosnia gags for the topical monologue, weighing bad taste against the need to prickle.

'We've weeded it down,' April announced, delivering a selection of Big Heart tapes. He loaded Kendra up as if she were a supermarket trolley and promised a decision by four. April, never still, whizzed off to pace and fret until she knew which release forms to pursue.

He gathered Kendra and Gwen into his office, and closed the doors. Sound-proofing cut out chatter and bustle from beyond. The ceiling lightstrips automatically faded on.

'My kingdom,' he announced.

Gwen spun like a top, skirt whirling over black leggings, demonstrating how much space there was. Michael conjured the wet bar and the girls gaped at the gadgetry. They fell upon the coloured bottles, demanding to know what each was. He ignored exotic requests for heavy liquids and took out the half-empty Stoli. He disassembled a Russian doll into a set of tumblers and sloshed generously.

'Everything's something else,' Kendra noticed.

Manipulating the remote control, Michael had a slim screen descend from the ceiling and a multiple-deck video rise from the floor.

Gwen sighed at such wonders.

'Shove those in, would zhou,' he asked Kendra, nodding at the pile of videotapes she hugged to her chest. Fumbling, she managed to get the oblongs in their slots. Tapes were sucked in and the machines whirred.

Gwen took an overly enthusiastic first mouthful and made a balloon-cheeked, red-hot-pepper face.

'If zhou loved me, zhou'd swallow that,' he said.

Gwen gasped a laugh that sprayed vodka through her nostrils. Kendra had minor convulsions.

The screen came to static life. Michael sat on the edge of his desk fast-forwarding four tapes simultaneously on different channels, zapping between them.

'What d'zhou reckon?' he asked Gwen, who had peeled off her blue plastic coat to show a ribbed v-neck jumper.

The Big Heart slot focused on someone ordinary who was heroic, made a true-life sacrifice or pined for a lost loved one. The gimmick was the subject's (victims, they were called in the office) family and friends made the video themselves and submitted it to *Dixon's On*. The production team selected which would air: embarrassingly cheap, inordinately popular.

'I dunno,' said Gwen, whom he noticed was not a brain surgeon of the future. 'Which is which?'

He used the remote to quarter the screen. Each video ran at normal speed in one quadrant. Even with the sound off, Michael gathered the choices: a game granny riding about somewhere rural on a motorbike, a cat staying faithfully by a toddler in a coma, a class of schoolkids rescuing gannets from an oil spill, and a lady lawyer giving it all up to go to Somalia and work in famine relief.

'Look at the poor birdies,' Gwen said, the Voice of the Audience. No matter how the team might mutter about his 'conferences', they were more useful than circular discussions with the overeducated neurotics on his payroll. It was a lesson he'd learned from the master, Derek Leech.

'I like the lawyer,' said Kendra, who would in two years be embarrassed that she'd been best friends with Gwen. 'She's more genuine.'

'Zhou're right,' Michael told her. 'But not for us. There's a difference between zhenuine and real.'

'It's terrible the wildlife that suffers because of tankers,' Gwen said.

Fast-forwarding all four tapes at once, Michael privately decided on the cat. You could take audience research too far. Animals and sick children were surefire: it would be tragically wonderful if the pet-owner recovered, or at least stirred from deep-sleep to blink at her adoring moggy, in time for a follow-up.

He shut off the screen and slipped an arm around Gwen. She looked at her friend, giggled nervously, then cuddled up. She touched the lapel of his Gaultier jacket, drew her fingers away as if she'd had a static shock, then stroked the material.

'It feels funny,' she said.

Kendra had second thoughts. She stood to one side, still in overcoat and woolly hat. She wasn't shocked exactly, more confused. Here on his desk, he could do anything he wanted with Gwen. That made him interested in Kendra. Gwen snuggled against him and licked his neck like a cat. He looked, smiling, at Kendra, and raised his glass in a toast.

'Drink up, it'll warm zhour insides,' he said.

Kendra took a swallow and, slowly, dawdled across the room. He eased Gwen away and put a hand on Kendra's shoulder drawing her close, fixing her eyes. He filled his mouth with vodka and, when it was time to kiss, squirted down her throat. Her open eyes grew wide but she did not choke.

The girls scrawled threatening letters. He said it was a joke on a friend, but they didn't need an explanation. *Lee Harvey, just for a laff, shoot this gun at the President…* The 'we were chust obeyink orders' line of Nuremberg defence was a miscalculation; gas chamber functionaries should have argued that a nonentity's compulsion to do what a celeb tells him was a universal human trait. *What Lee Harvey didn't know is we gave Mr Ruby another gun and this time – tee hee – he's the one who's going to be shot at. So let's see what happened next…* Careers were based on public willingness to suffer intolerable privations so long as they got on telly, on a pretend-equal basis with Jeremy Beadle or Alan Funt.

Grey blotches dotted his vision and his head was pleasantly painful. He diagnosed his condition and prescribed a further course of treatment, washing down red pills with more Stoli.

Kendra squatted, his jacket surprisingly terrific on her, rump peeking out under the backflap, head close to carpet as she laboriously filled in dripping red stains on her death threat. Gwen concentrated on foul language and limited abuse, her most inventive offering being the ancient 'welcome to the AIDS club', but Kendra was interested in design. She decorated her prim little notes ('tonight, you will be killed') with skulls and crossbones, poison daggers and large, staring, mad eyes.

He ran off address labels and stuck them on envelopes (plain, *not* Top Hat stationery) then added leftover Christmas stamps. He made the girls promise to send the letters from their home town (Richmond) at irregular intervals between now and Valentine's Day.

When they were done, Michael had Ayesha give them T-shirts and badges. Twenty minutes after he'd sent the girls on their mission, it hit him, with a headachy surge like a blow from a ballpeen hammer, that their handiwork would be uselessly diverted to a box in Belfast. He'd probably scuppered the ELF membership at the same time.

As he gave yay or nay to the week's line-up, his mind hunted through his bloodstream like Pac-Man, seeking out and blasting vodka particles. The team liked to talk at once to wildly different purposes and protract production meetings into the evening. To cut extraneous noise, he introduced a 6th of January ruling that no one could make a contribution without prefacing his or her statement with 'Mr Whippy-Wobble-Willie of Crab-Apple, Abergavenny says…' on pain of donating a day's salary to Somalia relief.

'What a good idea,' said Roily, office toady and hatchet man. 'Nobody can say we aren't creative.'

'Mr Whippy-Wobble-Willie of Crab-Apple, Abergavenny says… that should be *Mr Whippy-Wobble-Willie of Crab-Apple, Abergavenny says* "what a good idea, etc.", Roily.'

Roily made a goldfish mouth while everyone tried not to laugh.

'Mr Whippy-Wobble-Willie of Crab-Apple, Abergavenny says make the cheque out to Oxfam,' Michael said.

Everyone was keen on Faithful Kitty. April said she'd do what she could on a recovery follow-up.

'It wouldn't even…' she began, amid braying laughter. 'Sorry, Mr Willie-Wobbly-Wonka of Crawfish, Abacadabra says… it wouldn't even have to be permanent. Maybe if they gave her electroshock or an injection we could get a waking moment on tape.'

'Mr Whippy-Wobble-Willie of Crab-Apple, Abergavenny says that's entirely too fondant of you, Ape,' he said, giving her the nod.

The American comedian, Barry Gatlin, was firmed for the stand-up item.

'Mr Whippy-Wobble-Willie of Crab-Apple, Abergavenny says make sure it's the real Bastard Barry not the cleaned-up *Wogan* version,' Michael ordered. 'We're not soggy terrestrial TV. We're supposed to be muckrageous.'

Ayesha had arranged his costume. With the galley slaves still rowing, he retreated to his office and changed.

The padding was from Cloud 9's drama department. It strapped on and inflated like a lifebelt, bulking him to Pavarotti proportions. Ayesha helped him into his boots, tights and puffy britches. The Tudorbethan get-up came complete with cloak, plumed hat, sword and false moustache. There was even a bottle of spirit gum.

As she glue-daubed his upper lip, Ayesha commented that she didn't know Falstaff was in *Twelfth Night*.

'He's not,' Michael said, affixing his moustache, 'Sir Toby Belch is. Shakey wasn't above ripping himself off.'

Michael swirled his cloak and swished his sword, observing himself in the grey mirror of a blank screen.

'Hah, *en garde*,' he said, thrusting.

The palpitating heart of Gary Gaunt was on the point of his blade.

'Lie there and bleed,' he told the vanquished critic.

5

TWELFTH NIGHT, 1978

Here they were in the pit of winter, back in the dressing-room of the Rat Centre. Neil's queasy excitement was tempered with embarrassment, as if Rachael, the blasé girl in the next room at Tadcaster House, were to see through him and picture the gawky fifteen-year-old he used to be, with a rainbow tank-top and shoulder-length curls. He toked on the joint but blow only ratcheted up the tension.

'When we come together,' Michael said, holding smoke in his lungs, 'it's a collision of matter and anti-matter.'

He burped, almost coughed. Making fists, controlling himself, he continued, 'Universe might end but th'explosion be beautiful, *mes braves*.'

In the mirror, Neil saw Mark cringe. His university girlfriend was in the auditorium; he was anxious Pippa would not consider his oldest mates immature clods. An annoying thing about Mark was his over-concern with what outsiders thought.

'I can't believe we're still doing this,' Neil said. 'I thought we'd never live past college.'

'Live *through* college, you mean,' said Mickey, taking the joint.

At Art School Mickey had spiked his hair and pierced his ears. His Buzzcocks T-shirt had ripped-away sleeves; tears in his black drainpipe jeans were sutured with safety pins. For the show, he wore a Dracula cloak fastened with a black and gold Dalek badge.

They faced the long mirror, interacting more with reflections than their real selves. It was cold, despite the slur of the fan heater. Thin snow was settling outside.

'I wish it were Midsummer,' Neil said, not realising how he meant it.

'*Midsummer* is always a shambles,' Michael pointed out, carefully applying a 'tache. 'All our hits are offseason.'

'Are we quorate?' Mark asked.

'More than,' Neil said. 'How long has it been?'

'Forever,' Michael breathed.

For three weeks, until Pippa turned up to claim Mark's attention, they had worked together, ominously not arguing much. The Forum was of an equal mix of altercation and achievement. Now they had separate lives and were less open with each other. The violent arguments came when they felt strongly about what they were doing. This was just a joke. It had only been last summer. How could they be nostalgic about six months ago?

'You sure about Alex?' Mark asked. Alex, a college first-year had been drafted to do the lighting. Neil gathered Michael was going out with her while Penny was at Polytechnic.

'Zh-yeah zh-yeah,' Michael assured. 'She did both town pantomimes. She knows the board.'

'This could be our last stand,' Mickey said. 'Let's go down with all guns blazing.'

'I've heard that before,' Michael said. 'The Forum will never die.'

'You'll just wish it had,' Mark said.

The first thing Mark did with his grant was buy a suit from one of Brighton's many old-clothes shops, a gangsterish pinstripe. Over the term, Neil hadn't seen much of Mark. First they were in different halls of residence, then Mark moved with Pippa into a town flat. They each had new friends. Over the holiday, they'd been together more than in two and a half months away from home.

'We're nineteen, we've *lived*,' said Michael, not without irony. 'We're better now than we used to be.'

They'd all slept with girls (at least once); Neil had hopes (probably unrealistic) for Rachael. They could drink large quantities of bitter and only puke monstrously twice out of three times. For Neil, the crisis came when Michael relayed a message from Mrs Dixon: he was welcome to stay over whenever he wanted, but did he have to be sick every time?

Desmond, an ex-footsoldier whisked out of the audience and drafted backstage, came in with a tray of pints.

'Kill 'em,' he said, leaving the drinks.

Mickey crouched over the heater and sighed in mock orgasm as warm air billowed out his cloak.

Neil gulped his beer. Smoking gave him a thirst. Also, he wasn't sure if he could still go through with all this.

'I thought we agreed this was over,' Mark said. He'd been quiet.

Last Summer, after the end of college, the Forum had staged *Midsummer Night's End* on the assumption they would break up. In an *American Graffiti* end-of-an-era spirit, the entire class of '77 came. Neil was surprised that many girls, and a few blokes, cried as it wound down. A generation, together since eleven (six, for some), split like an iceberg, chunks drifting off to different lives.

''Twas too good to give up,' Michael said.

This post-Christmas bash was on a different scale; just the four of them. There would be music and there would be comedy, but the footsoldiers of earlier years were scattered. Neil understood there was quite a crowd. The deal was the Centre took the bar profits and didn't charge for the use of the hall, so admission was free. A lot of people Neil hadn't seen since summer had come. It was too soon for kids not to spend Christmas with their parents. The girls who'd tearfully said goodbye to best friends were together again, probably wondering why they'd cared so much. Since summer, everything had changed.

'I've missed this,' Michael admitted. He was in full Shakespeare drag, filched from the college drama department. 'I've missed us.'

Neil wasn't sure. The last three months, his first university term, had rearranged his ideas. One night in the kitchen, he'd tried to explain the Forum to new friends, reading extracts from scripts, increasingly aware how childish they were. Only Leo, a dope-head who missed all his lectures, really laughed. Fran, from Neil's Introduction to Marx seminar, said entertainment wasn't enough and waved Brecht at him. He was grateful Rachael knew nothing about this part of his life.

'Who said zh-you can't go home again,' Michael declared.

'Thomas Wolfe,' Mark replied, either missing or making a point.

Mickey finished and extinguished the ceremonial joint. Quiet about his experiences up North, he was least enthusiastic, at first, about the comeback. At some point since September, he'd gained a scar on his chin. He was always the one who most easily got out of control. After *Midsummer Night's End*, he cornered Keith Lanier, who made a point of crashing every gig in town without paying, and pinned him to the floor with a stool, gobbing mightily on his face. 'I thought we'd never see him again,' he explained, 'so I reckoned, it was my last chance to do over the cunt.'

Twelfth Night '78 was all down to Michael. In November, without telling the others, he'd made arrangements with the hippies who ran the Rat Centre. At the start of the vac, he presented them with a *fait accompli*. In three weeks, with the usual day off for Christmas, the Forum would throw together a show. He already had some material written; they'd rely on improvisation and music to get through gaps.

Considering the alternative was coming to terms with Bishop Berkeley, the reunion made sense. Also, he guessed it was important to Michael. Staying in the Backwater hadn't been a good move; he felt he'd lagged behind. Cambridge acceptance or not, he made constant waspish remarks about 'clever students'. He was supposed still to be going out with Penny, but after a few weekends hitching across country to be together they'd provisionally broken up. He was sure she was seeing someone at the Poly.

Michael said he'd written 1000 opening sentences, 100 opening paragraphs and three and a half opening chapters. And binned them all. His planned novel, *Julie Bee*, was an expansion of a *Midsummer Night's End* sketch about punk rockers forced to form a government. Mark said *Julie Bee* was handicapped because no one in Backwater really knew anything (the local idea of a punk band was a Dr Feelgood rip-off). Michael, with a travel agent for a father and an assured Oxbridge place, was hardly best positioned to understand inner-city proletarian nihilism.

'Afterwards,' Michael said, 'I've got the keys to Gramma's house in Achelzoy. We can have the party there.'

Achelzoy was about nine miles out of town, a former island perched on its own hill in the flat expanse of Sedgmoor. After-production parties there were a tradition, since the Forum's revues always coincided with periods Michael's grandparents were away on holiday, innocently leaving it to him to feed their cats.

'I don't know,' Neil said. 'It's snowing steadily.'

'Great, we'll be cut off and get cabin fever and eat each other.'

'I said I'd go for a drink with Pippa and the parents,' Mark said.

'You can do that any time, Marko. This is a Forum party. Attendance is mandatory.'

Mark shrugged.

Desmond returned. 'It's ten minutes past supposed start-time,' he said. 'The crowds are restless.'

They all looked at each other.

'Let's rock and roll,' Michael said.

6

TWELFTH NIGHT, 1993

Derek Leech International squatted in London Docklands, a wedge of dark. The black glass pyramid was often described as a newly landed spaceship; at once, spearhead of an invasion and monument to the defeat of Earth.

In courtier's velvet, Mark strode past ranks of flash cars to the doors. His cardkey parted glass slabs. A liveried guard passed a detector over his doublet and hose. He was ruled admissible, even allowed to keep the sword that came with the costume.

A mannequin with a carved smile checked his invitation against her clipboard. He remembered her from a ballet *Dorian Gray*: she was the portrait, repulsive while her twin remained lithe and perfect, or maybe she'd danced Dorian, and another functionary, greeting at another entrance, had been the picture.

From the atrium, he walked into the ballroom. The building's hollow core was a new gothic silo. Impossible to heat, it was as cold as the wastes outside. Mark was sure he felt a rain-fleck on his numb cheek. Guests in Elizabethan court dress clustered in pools of spotlight. They turned to note his presence then resumed hushed talk, frosted breath clouding. Leech provided the costumes himself, ensuring a consistent look. He was a host who hired a production designer before a caterer.

On a granite dais, a period troupe played 'When That I Was And a Little Tiny Boy'. A performance artist in whiteface stood on a separate plinth, skewered by crossed light beams, repeating the first sentence of *Twelfth Night* in unpunctuated monotone.

'…appetite may sicken and so die if music be the food of love play on give me excess of it that surfeiting the appetite may sicken and so die if music be the food of love play on give me excess of it that…'

'He can do it for hours,' breathed an admirer. 'Hours and hours.'

Mark had a rush of guilt: two years ago, *The Shape* had run a feature on the monotonist. When the time came, that should be worth ten minutes in the Devil's barbecue pit.

'…give me excess of it that surfeiting the appetite may sicken…'

Twelfth Night was also Epiphany, he remembered. But Leech's revel reminded him more of the Masque of the Red Death.

A dignified nude, blue but for a circle in the small of her back, approached with a salver of black and white *hors d'oevres*. The blue lady was a former *Comet* Knock-Out of the Year: a layer of dye prevented her gooseflesh wobbling, lending a peculiarly clothed aspect. He took a roll of black substance that looked like a dolly mixture but tasted of seafood.

'Ho, varlet,' he was hailed.

Michael was red-cheeked, playing it up as Sir Toby, with Ginny Moon as his short-tempered Maria. She must be piqued not to be Viola.

'Shouldn't zhou be Sir Andrew Ague-Cheek?'

'I'm a one-scene wonder,' Mark admitted. 'Gentleman, attending on the Duke.'

'Love the danglies,' Ginny said. 'Are they real?'

Mark's padded jacket was hung with teardrop pearls.

'The way to tell real from false is to roll them between zhour teeth,' Michael told his wife. 'Zhou can spot glass eyes that way as well.'

'Sounds fun,' she said. 'Perhaps Mark would be available later for a consumer test.'

She prodded Mark's breast with a sharp forefinger and tickled a pearl as if it were a nipple.

'Lady, you are the cruel'st she alive,' he quoted.

'We did *Twelfth Night* for "O" level,' Michael explained. 'We did Shakespeare in the Zhouth Theatre, then put on our own version.'

'You *were* Sir Toby,' Mark remembered.

'And zhou were Malvolio.'

'God, yes. Mickey was Sir Andrew, doing Kenneth Williams.'

They both laughed.

'We were terrible.'

'You still are,' Ginny commented.

'Too zhoung for "O" levels,' Michael whispered in exaggerated aside, 'has a GCSE or two, but scant real qualifications.'

Before being cast in Victorian-Edwardian dramas of repressed women, sumptuous costumes and pretty manners, Ginny had been with the RSC. Her Shrew was well spoken of. Now, she was doing a Jackie Collins mini-series, playing an English bitch who loses her lover to Stefanie Powers.

A shape shambled from the darkness, bells tinkling.

'Here comes the fool, i'faith,' Mark quoted.

'How now, my hearts?' Mickey replied, on cue. 'Did you never see the picture of we three?'

He was in a jester's particolour, waving a pig's bladder on a stick. Braids escaped from his three-belled cowl.

'You can't have been Sir Andrew *and* the clown,' Mark said aloud.

'Neil played Feste,' Michael said.

'Neil?' Ginny asked.

'No one,' they all said at once.

'If Neil were here, *he'd* be Malvolio,' Michael said. 'Crossgartered and stitched up.'

It was as if ice-water were dashed in Mark's eyes. Michael was drunk, he knew at once. When drunk, Michael always flirted with the possibility of revelation. He believed most in the Deal and was most its prisoner.

'Such a cruel comedy, *Twelfth Night*,' Michael continued. 'Worthless, rich people torture a middlerank loser.'

Mark and Mickey looked coldly at Michael. Ginny, though involved, was an outsider. It wouldn't do to talk about the Deal, even obscurely, with her. She had the glazed look outsiders always got when the Quorum ganged up. They shared much that was trivial to the rest of the world.

'Take comfort milady,' Mickey said to Ginny. 'Many a good hanging prevents a bad marriage.'

'I marvel zhour ladyship takes delight in such a barren rascal,' Michael struck back, changing instantly from lusty Sir Toby to withering Malvolio.

'I can't believe you remember all this,' Ginny wondered. 'I've forgotten my sides from the *Morse* I did last month, let alone Shakespeare from years ago.'

Michael made a groping lunge at Ginny and she screamed; their way of making up. Mark was grateful Pippa was still off with her parents.

'Isn't it sweet they still can't keep their hands off each other?' Mickey said, head on one side. 'Fuckin' cats in heat.'

'By the way,' Michael said, pausing in mid-assault. 'Sally Rhodes?'

Mark nodded assent. Michael knew what he meant.

'Told zhou so.'

Ginny, momentarily puzzled, was overwhelmed again. Michael grunted like a bear and regurgitated gobbets of Shakespeare.

'How now, my nettle of India,' he said, sorting through her skirts.

'My masters,' Mickey breathed, 'are you mad?'

That was a Malvolio line too. Pidgin Shakespeare was catching.

'Educating us was a very great mistake,' said Mark in a twentieth-century voice. 'It has made us unbearable.'

'Tell me about it, chum,' Ginny said, wrestling Michael upright.

A fanfare filled the vast space with noise. Everyone looked

up to the black canopy. Indoor plants hung from the topmost tiers. Pterodactyls probably nested there. A scenic lift, lit from within, began a slow descent, crawling down the pyramid. The man inside was silhouetted by outward-shining lights. Guests gathered in a semi-circle around the lift-bed; they might indeed be courtiers. A stately and veiled Olivia stood alone.

'Isn't that Tamsin?' Ginny asked.

Michael shushed her; everyone here was Tamsin, or someone else of rank. A junior cabinet minister, a famously carnivorous publisher, a director about to go from *Film on 4* to Hollywood, a scandalous architect, a bestseller-list thriller writer, a reformed rock legend. Even the naked waitresses were stars. Mark tried not to wonder if they all had Deals.

Doors slipped open silently. Derek Leech – Duke Orsino, of course – emerged, posing an instant for flash-photographs, and descended wide steps to be among his people. A thin carpet of phosphorescent mist edged out of the lift and spilled down the stairs, dissipating on engraved tiles.

A woman darted forward to kneel and kiss Leech's gloved hand, tonguing the ruby of his largest ring. In her forties, she fought the planned obsolescence of the human machine, face pulled back as if by Sellotape under her ears, generous body confined by a doublet that lifted and shaped her memorable torso.

'Do you know who that is?' Mark said, nodding. 'Brie Simon.'

Mickey was amazed. '*Devil Daughter of Dracula*? That Brie Simon?'

'She was the first *Comet* Knock-Out,' Michael explained to Ginny, who looked disapproving. She'd gone nude in *The Woman Who Did,* but it was necessary to the plot.

'When I was fourteen, she was the summit of my shagging ambitions,' Mickey said. 'I'm at a party with one of my masturbation fantasies.'

Michael gave out a full-throated Sir Toby Belch laugh, which attracted Leech's attention. He helped Brie up and looked to the

Quorum. As one, they automatically gave courtiers' bows to the Master of the Deal.

'D'you suppose I should try…' Mickey thought out loud.

'Might be like sampling a famous nineteenth-century vintage,' Michael said. 'Gone to vinegar.'

'Don't be sexist,' Ginny criticised, 'or I'll hack off your bollocks and stuff them up your nostrils.'

Mark was struck again by how unchanging, how ordinary, Leech was. Everyone else was obviously important, famous, vital. Without his costume, he'd look like a bank manager on a Monsters of Rock stage. Yet…

'Remember when the allosaurus chewed off Brie Simon's bikini top in *Prehistoric Valley*?' said Mickey. 'Hot fuck, I have to be on a New York flight at three, or I might have fulfilled another teenage dream. Since I killed Amazon Twazzock, there aren't many left.'

Brie Simon put an arm around Leech and leaned forward, allowing a look into her cold deep cleavage.

'If I nail Brie Simon,' Mickey told Ginny, 'there's only your mother left and my life is complete.'

'You can have my mother.'

Michael chuckled at Mickey's tongue-dangling.

'Guess who's thinking of working for me in publicity on the INT front,' Mark said, maliciously. 'Penny Gaye.'

Michael gulped, remembering. Ginny looked perplexed again.

Mark slid off in search of drink. He watched Mickey and Michael pay homage to Leech, chatting and nodding, smiling and pretending.

'Pensive?' a woman asked.

It was Tamsin, oddly unaccompanied. The singer had been married to Leech. She lifted her veil. She had lines but was lovely.

'Have you just seen the bars?'

'The bar's over there,' he said, indicating a low table where body-painted Knock-outs dispensed sparkling, insubstantial wines.

'No, the bars,' she explained, gripping an imaginary cage.

He sipped fizz from a delicate glass flute.

'I used to think it was a menagerie,' she said, taking such elaborate care to pronounce every word that he knew she was drunk. 'Then it was a prison. Now it's a circle of hell.'

'You've had too much,' he was compelled to say.

'The scary thing is he never lied. We knew what we were getting.'

For Christmas, Mark had given Pippa *I Know Where I'm Going*, Tamsin's latest album on CD. It was her best, most mature work. If Billie Holliday had been born white in Egham in 1949, she'd have grown up to be Tamsin.

The legend gargled and tossed her flute into the air. It shattered quietly.

'*I know where I'm going*,' she sang, her voice a claw in the heart, '*and I know who goes with me, I know whom I love, but the De'il knows who I'll marry...*'

Unsure on her feet, she was incapable of less than perfection.

'The De'il knows who I'll marry,' she sighed. 'The De'il.'

'Darling,' interrupted Derek Leech, one word a hand of ice, 'you've met Mark Amphlett.'

'Mark,' she said, eyebrow arched, arm out. Her immense hem gathered and fastened to her wrist, a billow of pale blue falling to the floor. He took her frozen hand and squeezed, unsure if he should kiss her knuckles.

'Mark is a cutting-edge young man. He has seen the future and is making a place for us in it.'

'That's the deal,' Mark admitted.

Gently, without seeming to, Leech held Tamsin up. He chewed, neck muscles undulating his ruff. With serpent elegance, the multimedia magnate steered his ex-wife back to the light.

Mark's lungs hurt. Since Leech spoke he had not exhaled. Choking, he let out breath.

'Too much *vino*?' Mickey asked, belabouring him with his pig's bladder. He held a small scroll of paper. 'Brie Simon's phone number. I'll be back from the Big Apple by the next week. Then...

va-va-*voommm*! As the Bard said, "He that is well-hung in this world need fear no colours."'

"'Hanged", Shakespeare wrote.'

Mickey's pelvic thrust set his bells a-jingling.

'Mickey, you're a clown.'

Mickey did a Jolson kneel, hands outstretched. A grin opened in his face, stretching like a slit throat from ear to ear.

'He's not a clown,' Michael said, having ditched Ginny and slipped away, 'he's positively an Eozoon, simplest lifeform on Earth.'

Mickey laughed and sloshed Michael with his bladder, which prompted Michael to go for his sword.

Mark fingered one of the pearls on his doublet. As far as he could tell, it was real.

'How did we get here from there?' he asked. His friends didn't hear the question. 'We used to hate people like us.'

Michael stood straight to recite. Mickey went for a low hold.

'If these shadows have offended,' Michael yelped, 'fuck off.'

7

TWELFTH NIGHT, 1978

Concentrating on the ground, he sat on the steps of the Rat Centre and hugged his knees. His brain sloshed in its skull-tank of cerebral fluid. Snow fell on his head and hands, tiny lashes of ice. He'd been sick twice and assumed he would be again. Feet passed either side of him and hurried away, leaving slushy tracks on deadly pavement. Snow thickened in the street, as if God wanted to draw a veil over the evening. That'd be quite all right with Michael.

'Ground Control calling,' Mickey said, voice distorting. 'Earth to Planet Dixon.'

'Houston,' Michael gulped, 'we've got a problem…'

A burst of gurgling pain knotted his gut. A string of clear beery fluid hung like an icicle from his mouth. 'Chunderball,' Neil commented. Neil held the Forum's vomit record: seven spasms, one binge. In ancient days, it was Michael handing the bucket and towel to his friend.

Mark, the most nearly sober stood nearby, collar turned up, thin girlfriend waiting, desperate to clear off but unable to leave. Michael's own squeeze might be about somewhere; he thought she'd tootled off with her own crowd.

'It's hard to credit,' he mumbled. 'She's so *stupid*, zh'know. She doesn't understand so much…'

At the safety-pinned height of the biggest cultural revolution since Stravinsky, Alex was into Rod Stewart. Since Christmas, Michael had left six messages with Penny's parents. Home from Poly, she hadn't turned up tonight. He began to think they were seriously finished. When they broke up, he filled notebooks with agonised introspection, always assuming it temporary. Something happened to people who went away. To Penny, to Mark, to the others. Something secret and unshared, an initiation. They were off having the verifiable time of their lives.

He was left behind in the Backwater, forgotten and floundering. Things were sick-makingly desperate.

'This isn't like us,' he said.

Neil shrugged. The lights of the Rat Centre went out.

Other Forum shows had been shambolic disasters but exhilaration and defiance carried them off. *Twelfth Night '78* was the worst flop ever. If it were any more of a dog, it would require a licence. Nothing had really gone wrong, Neil hadn't fallen over, Mickey hadn't savaged the piano with an axe. That might have added spontaneity to the mausoleum on stage. Mark, standing apart from the others, went through it without giving anything of himself. To compensate, Michael overstrained for reaction, any reaction. Heckling and cabbage would have been better than the sussurus of disinterest. The black hole of the auditorium swallowed their efforts. By the interval, much of the audience had drifted to the bar, too involved in their own talk to pay attention. In the last quarter of an hour, Mark joined them, leaving a gap on the stage the others had to revolve around. Every note sounded hollow, every line a stone tossed into a bottomless chasm. It really was kids' stuff.

In olden times, people hung around for invitations to Michael's legendary Achelzoy parties. Half the kids in town lost their virginities at his grandparents' house. Everyone first smoked drugs in the old coal-shed they called the Führer Bunker. Once Desmond had convulsions, writhing across the road in a blue sleeping-bag like a giant worm, causing a milk-float to swerve into a ditch. Tonight, they ducked out early, making apologies about vile weather, pointedly not mentioning the show. It was the end of an Empire.

A car cruised down the road, leaving muddy tyre tracks in the thin snow-blanket. The horn honked and Mark went over: it was Desmond, on his way out to Achelzoy with a couple of die-hards.

'We might be a while,' Mark told him.

Michael was supposed to be driving. His grandparents always left him their car so he could look after the place. They knew about the parties, but he made sure the place was tidied when they got back.

A negotiation was underway. Neil volunteered to go with Desmond and open the house. Michael found keys in his jacket pocket and handed over. Mark convinced Pippa to go with the guys, promising to be along soon.

'I think I'm driving Michael out,' he explained. 'It's my contribution to keeping death off the roads.'

Neither Neil nor Mickey could drive.

Despite everything, a few were going to the party. Michael thought Alex might drag some of her minors along later. And he'd left a message for Penny.

Only the few remained, the loyal rump of the Forum. Mark was patient but superior, a parent. Mickey's eyes burned: Michael might be at the end of his party tether, but Mickey was bottled up, ready to burst. Like the night he finally popped Jacqui Edwardes or the time he duffed up Keith Lanier. Michael's stomach was settling but pain remained in his mind. Tears froze on his cheeks.

Desmond drove off carefully. Falling snow danced in headlights.

The others felt defeat less keenly. They'd started new lives. The disaster confirmed that they should let it go. Mark was so intent on being an adult and Mickey so committed to punk that everything they'd worked on together over seven years was receding into memory. Neil seemed almost middle-aged, as if he'd vaulted into an unimaginable future where he was a travel agent.

A snowdrift accumulated about his shoes. Ice pellets hung in his trouser turn-ups. He was a living ghost, embarrassing friends as he dragged the dead past around on his chains. He wiped his face on his sleeve. Snow-speckles stuck to his eyelashes and nose. Focusing the power of his mighty brain, he made himself sober. He took out his car keys and held them in a fist, gripping cold metal tight enough to break the skin. Physical pain could dispel mental anguish, he had thought.

'Let us depart,' he said, standing carefully. Mark and Mickey followed him to the car.

'I'm perfectly capable of driving,' he insisted. He'd regained his balance. In the cold, he was straight.

Mark looked up at the sky, snow tumbling around him, and spread his hands in martyrdom. 'I could have gone with…'

'Let him be,' Mickey said. 'If the poison ain't out of his system by now it never will be.'

Michael bent into the front seat and belted up. Mickey slid in next to him and, resigned, Mark crawled into the back.

Michael flicked a switch. 'Wipers engaged.'

The windscreen was iced like a cake, thick precipitate furring the lower two-thirds. The wipers cut squeaky slices.

He turned the ignition.

'Contact,' he said.

'Warp Factor Fuck,' Mickey replied, seriously.

The car lurched forwards and Michael manoeuvred out of the parking space. Open road lay ahead. He put on a cassette of the Tom Robinson Band and thumped the wheel to '2–4–6–8 Motorway'.

As they drove out of town, he concentrated on the road. Knowing he was over the limit always made him infuriatingly careful. Mickey and Mark chatted about snow. There'd be a big freeze on the moors. Earth was hard as iron, water like a stone.

Scotland was cut off from civilisation. Radio stations were issuing dire travel warnings: if in doubt stay home, go back now, don't do it, abandon hope. No one mentioned *Twelfth Night '78*, which was more depressing than a gloomy autopsy.

'There's one thing we've got to get, Hayes,' Mickey said.

'What's that?' Mark recited.

'*Out of this business*,' they said together, and laughed.

He'd been making the trip from town to Achelzoy ever since he could remember, first with his parents, then on his own.

The more time his grandparents spent away, the more their house became a second home. He'd lived there for a solid week in November; hammering in frustration at the opening of *Julie Bee*. Alex stayed over three nights in a row. It was unnervingly like being married, or how he imagined being married. He noted the limitations of his fill-in girlfriend's experience and intellect. Maybe it was impossible to follow Penny. He'd shared so much with so few people, it was hard for outsiders to crack the shell.

The Achelzoy road was as familiar as his own house. Michael could make the drive blindfolded, dead drunk and fast asleep.

'This doesn't look right,' Mark said.

They were on a winding road across the moor, twisting from side to side. Slush clogged the wipers. Bowed trees, heavy with snow, lined the way. There was no other traffic.

'We're off the map,' he said. 'Look for signs.'

Mark suggested turnings they might have mistaken. Michael was sure he'd kept the right route. If anything was skewed, it was the road. Proceeding deliberately, he felt the car's grip weakening, and sensed the thin film of black ice beneath snow-frosting. He did not intend to put Gramma's car in a ditch.

A signpost was up ahead, leaning badly. Mickey craned to make it out.

'Shepton Mallet,' he said. 'Two miles.'

'That's not remotely possible,' Michael said. 'We can't be that far off course. We'd have had to motorvate for hours.'

'It feels like fuckin' hours,' Mickey said. 'Fuckin' aeons.'

'It's only about fifteen minutes,' Mark said. 'We should be in Achelzoy.'

'We're out by Shepton Sodding Mallet, boyo,' Mickey insisted. 'We're lost up our arseholes.'

Visibility was terrible. Snow whipped down, hail mixed in, rattling against the car. He took the Shepton Mallet turn.

'We don't want Shepton Mallet,' Mark said.

'No,' Michael said. 'But we know the way to Achelzoy from Shepton Mallet. If lost, no point in getting loster.'

Mark shrugged and slumped in his seat.

'I shouldn't be here,' he said. 'Neil should be here. I should be with Pippa at your Gramma's, waiting for you clods to show up.'

'Don't trust your woman with Captain Makeout Martino?' asked Mickey. 'Neil the Love Machine?'

Mark grunted a laugh. 'Not a problem, I think,' he said. 'And don't let Pippa hear you call her "my woman". She's an independent person.'

Mickey made a face.

'This doesn't feel right,' Michael admitted.

The turn-off was a rutted single-track across moorland. They cut into virgin snow; no other traffic had been through recently. Shepton Mallet passed for a big town, the road to it should be a major artery.

'I don't like the sound of the engine,' Mark commented.

'It probably hates the sound of you,' Mickey said.

The car was coughing and straining. With the heating up full blast, it was almost uncomfortably warm inside. If the engine died, the interior would fridge instantly.

'I spent Jubilee night in this machine,' Mickey commented. 'I don't ever want to do that again.'

That had been at another party, of historic interest: the night

Neil fell into the sea while impersonating Sir Francis Drake.

'We'll be in Achelzoy soon,' Michael insisted. 'Trust me.'

'We trusted you to put on a show,' Mark said. 'Look what happened.'

Stabbed to the heart, Michael gripped the steering wheel. There was quiet in the car, only low music continuing. In a flash, he imagined halting, ordering Mark and Mickey out in the middle of an arctic nowhere, leaving them to the snow, clever student smugness frozen solid.

'I'm solo from now,' Mickey said. 'Or maybe I'll get a band together in Leeds.'

'Zhour mother told mine zhou weren't going back,' Michael said, doling out spite. 'Apparently, zhou haven't done real work since zhou got into Art School.'

Mickey, who'd edged around the subject for weeks, said 'Even if I chuck school, I'm not sliming back to the Backwater. You don't know what it's like in fuckin' reality, Dixon. It's not a Beatles film. We can't live down each other's throats forever.'

The car stalled, caught again, carried on. A huge place-sign was ahead, hanging over the road like a gibbet.

WELCOME TO SUTTON MALLET.

'*Sutton* Mallet,' Mickey said. 'Where the fuck is Sutton Mallet?'

'Nowhere,' Mark breathed. 'We're nowhere.'

Michael had lived in Somerset all his life and never heard of Sutton Mallet.

Dark buildings were around, roofs thick with snow, drifts sandbagged against stone walls. A single streetlamp was stranded at a road fork, its tiny light a candle in an over-arching canopy of dark. The car died. He put on the handbrake. They sat in the middle of nowhere. For a moment, he was tempted to slump asleep against his safety belt, let snow pile up around the car. Eventually a burrow-like hump would form. The Quorum could be buried like Saxon chieftains in their chariot, and rediscovered by archaeologists of the future.

* * *

With the lights on, Mark went through all the maps in the car. Sutton Mallet wasn't obvious on any of them. Michael sat, defeated. Mickey was getting angry, which made him unpredictable.

'Neil should be here,' Mark insisted, 'not me.'

'Fuckin' Sutton Mallet,' Mickey swore.

'It's very small,' Michael said. 'Look.'

There were at most five houses around the junction. None showed a light.

'And they all go to bed early.'

Actually, the buildings, dead and impassive as sarsen stones, were more like barns than houses. Only a few windows, high up on walls. Under snow, the roofs might be thatch.

'I hate Sutton Mallet,' Mickey said, unreasonably. 'All my life, Sutton Malleteers have picked on me, got in my way, stopped me doing things.'

'I swear I've been here before,' Mark said. 'The shapes are familiar.'

Michael tried the choke again. The engine didn't catch. Its cough was drawn-out, asthmatic.

'I don't want to push it,' he said.

'It's getting cold,' Mark said, breath frosting. The lights were on a separate circuit, but it was impossible to keep the heater on if the engine wasn't running.

'Wee bit parky,' Mickey snarled.

Michael had run out of ideas. He watched snowflakes stick to the windscreen, each flake a pointillist dab added to an all-white abstract. It was almost restful.

'Sodomise this for a game of soldiers,' Mickey said, straining his seatbelt. 'I'm going out to get directions. There must be some bloody one up in Nowhere City.'

Mark wasn't sure and began a protest, but Michael, suddenly very tired, didn't intervene. Mickey opened the door and stepped out, hugging his cloak around his thin body.

'Shivering shit,' he said. 'My balls just shrivelled to raisins. I may be some time.'

He slammed the door after him and staggered off into the snow.

'A very gallant gentleman,' Michael said.

'Bone-stupid.'

'That too.'

Mickey was gone instantly, vanished. Michael and Mark sat in growing cold.

'What was that about Mickey dropping out?' Mark asked.

Michael shrugged. 'Mum heard the story, I only had it second hand. He was scrapping again. Apparently, he's lucky not to be up on a charge.'

'You think he'd tell us,' Mark said. 'We're his friends.'

'Some things zhou don't tell zhour friends.'

Like how difficult it really was to write. He had no excuses, no distractions. Michael should be able to fill page after page. He had his outline. He knew what he wanted to say. But words wouldn't come. The zh-curse had seeped into his brain, tripping his thoughts. Michael saw his friends disappearing into shining futures, leaving him stranded in the Backwater. He told them his Cambridge place was set, but actually he had to retake the entrance exam again in spring. Maybe he'd pass, maybe not. There was always Hull, he shuddered.

'How long do zhou think we should give him?'

'How long has it been?'

'Forever.'

'Zhust a few minutes, surely?'

Michael hugged himself. His coat was padded, but cold crept in around his belly and extremities. His face was frozen.

'I'm going after Mickey,' Mark announced.

'We shouldn't leave the car.'

'If you can't move it, who could steal it?'

Mark was right.

'He'll have left footprints. Easy to follow.'

Michael undid his belt and got out into the blizzard. His knees hurt as he unbent his legs. He felt empty. He looked back at Mark, whose hands were deep in his coat pockets.

'Turned out nice again?' he said.

Mickey's prints were fast filling with fresh snow. He'd trailed around the largest of the barn-structures (looking for a door?) and cut off into a field. Here his boots sank deep into unmarred snow, leaving obvious holes.

'Why did he go away from the houses?' Mark asked.

Michael would have shrugged a don't-know, but was shivering too much.

'This is an "I don't like the looks of this" moment,' Mark said.

'Neil should be here, not zhou.'

Three months ago, Michael had been natural leader of the Forum. Now he'd pushed them into a disaster and got them lost and broken them up. He was tired of people asking him what to do. He didn't know what he should do himself.

For a moment, Michael was afraid it was a trick. Mark and Mickey had plotted to lure him out where he could be abandoned to silent snows.

The lamplight was way behind them. Huffing and blundering, they stumped across the snow-carpeted field. There'd be thinly iced ditches buried here, waiting like elephant traps.

"'Often in later life,'" Michael said authorially, "'Neil Martin would remember that night and wonder what had become of his vanished friends…'"

Mark laughed. At the dawn of recorded time, he'd been the first person to understand Michael's humour.

'What's that?' Mark asked.

Ahead were three large lumps.

'I don't know about the one in the middle,' he said, meaning the dark, angular shape, 'but the other two look like snowmen.'

One was a Christmas card Frosty, three bun-shapes on top of each other. When they got close, he saw a face made of a carrot and chips of coal. On the head was an exploded top hat, like his old *Monopoly* piece. The other was a slumped and half-melted pile, stones and sticks poking out. Hard to make it out as anything, it might be a snowsquid.

'Cephalopod,' Mark said. 'At last.'

The shape in the middle was a corrugated iron hut, about the size of a horsebox or an alderman's family vault. Warmth spilled from it. Red light seeped through joints. Near the hut, snow melted.

Mark stepped forward and tripped over something. It was not another snowman.

'Mickey,' he blurted.

Michael and Mark knelt. Mickey was blue and chattering, rivers of snow in the folds of his cloak. They helped him up. He was almost conscious, his skin cold even to their chilled touch.

'He might have the beginnings of exposure,' Michael said.

Mickey muttered, 'Fuck a duck.'

They struggled towards the hut. The iron sheets seemed to have an underglow, as if blowtorches played against them from the inside. Mark held Mickey while Michael fumbled a wire and cork latch with ungloved, senseless hands. The hut was simply sewn together with rings of wire and plumped in the field.

With a nails-down-a-blackboard wrench, the door came open. A small fire burned inside the hut. Clouds of eye-stinging, sweet-smelling smoke billowed out and swept around. Michael coughed but relished the caress of hot air. After minutes of dark, flamelight hurt his eyes.

Behind a smoky pile of burning logs, someone sat crosslegged. He wore dark trousers and shoes, but was naked from the waist up. Soot-streaks crossed his chest like war paint.

Michael, smitten by heat and cold, sank to his knees outside, reaching for fire. He didn't care if he burned his hands, just so long as he was warmed. Mark and Mickey stood behind him, leaning exhausted on each other. The man behind the fire looked at them, chewing. His eyes held fires.

'Gentlemen,' he said, 'welcome.'

The air was different inside the hut. The smoke didn't bother Michael any more. It wasn't dope but it gave him a strange buzz. His head clear, he thought faster, as if he breathed pure electricity. He knew this was one of the key hours of his life.

'Three of the Four,' Leech said, mildly. 'I believe we have a Quorum.'

Mark didn't say Neil should be here instead of him.

'I am here to explain how the world works.'

Michael nodded, understanding. Leech spoke like a careers counsellor, calm and measured, understanding and disinterested. Michael vaguely knew who the man was.

'You have potential, promise,' Leech admitted. 'That is nothing to do with me. I can guarantee absolutely that you will all, even your Absent Friend, live long and healthy lives. None of you will die before the mid-point of the twenty-first century.'

Leech raised a white hand. He spat something into the fire. It hissed like a live thing. The hut rattled with wind and snow. Michael wasn't shivering any more.

'Do you understand sacrifice?' Leech asked.

They all nodded.

'Really *understand*? I doubt it. Nothing is accidental, nothing comes without suffering.'

He lowered his hand into the fire. Flames licked around skin, darting up between outspread fingers. He smiled again, unconcerned.

'You don't have to burn,' he explained. 'Not if you don't want to.'

He took his unmarred hand out of the fire and laid it in his lap.

'For some people, pain is an option.'

If it were a trick, it was a good one.

'First, think of all you want. Imagine a future and fill it.'

Michael understood. It wasn't just wealth and fame and achievement. It was something complete and perfect and eternal. It was as if he saw the first page of his biography, knowing the chapters were filled in every detail. His life was inevitable. Mark and Mickey wound in and out of it, heroes of their own lives. And Neil was intertwined too. He might be the missing corner, but everything would depend on him.

'Here's the Deal,' Leech said. 'You know who I am, you know what I represent…'

In the firelight, his face was red. His teeth shone sharp.

'You will each have the future you deserve but I require sacrifice. Perfect sacrifice.'

'You want our souls?' Mark asked, disbelieving.

'I have no interest in intangible quantities. I do not claim to know what comes after this. My dominion is entirely of the world.'

In the heat, Michael was again cold. A cloud hung under the roof, swirling smoke looking for a way out.

'I want pain, here and now,' Leech explained. 'Lifelong pain. It is the only currency that has any real value.'

'This Deal doesn't seem that hot,' Mickey ventured.

Leech grinned. 'Did I say the pain had to be yours?'

8

7 JANUARY, 1993

Neil dreamed of giant superheroes.

In four ragged colours, the Streak and the Amazon Queen tussled in Muswell Hill Broadway. Sometimes they fought but mainly they fucked. Violent as an earthquake, their sex radiated devastation through North London. Sainsbury's was a flattened mass of rubble and spoiled foodstuffs, Alexandra Palace a spreading fire. Neil ran and panicked with the crowd. Underfoot was a heavy carpet of red velvet, Amazon Queen's cloak draped over pavement and buildings, knee-high wrinkles tripping crowds. With a shift of the lovers, he was trapped between the Midland Bank and a twenty-yard-long thigh. A wall of tanned muscle rolled towards him. He was held for a moment between Amazon Queen's smooth tonnage of flesh and the cash-dispenser, then scraped along the wall. Popped free, he sprawled into a side road. Others ran, but he was fascinated. He looked back at the costumed gargantuas. The Streak pulled out and changed position. Drops of ejaculate burst against rubble like waterbombs. Amazon Queen was on her hands and knees, her great head thumping the bus shelter. Her unbound hair lashed the road like a torrent of whips. The Streak thrust in and out faster than the eye could register. Lightning cracked all around. Amazon Queen made fists and tore at the road, ripping up patches of hot asphalt. An explosive crash broke through the dream, shattering him awake…

Neil woke with a terror-grip on his heart and a burning erection. He'd been sleeping on his front, bruised face into the pillow. The noise made him turn, grinding his duvet under him as he looked up.

He was under attack.

A further crash, the far curtains billowing. A tinkling of glass. Something small and heavy thumped onto the fold-out table, skittered across the surface, swept his reading lamp to the floor.

Pre-dawn light seeped in. Cloaking his duvet around his shoulders, he lifted himself off the bed and called, 'Who's there?'

Another crash. Force spent against a curtain, something slid down. He whisked apart the curtains. The sash window was broken, jagged shards left like broken teeth in the lower frame. In a blur, the upper pane exploded. A fist-sized stone hit his collar-bone. Yelping, he dropped his duvet. A wave of cold draped him. He wore only low-hanging pyjama bottoms, his fast-dwindling penis stuck ridiculously out of the fly.

The stone, a chunk of rough concrete, had bounced onto the bed. Neil, bruised and scraped, wrestled with his old dressing-gown, wriggling into sleeves as he shoved out of the flat. He scrambled up the hall stairs and wrenched open the front door. In 57 varieties of minor pain, Neil stood on the doorstep in the growing dawn.

'Bastards, bastards.'

He looked up and down the road. His windows were completely done for. The assault team must be nearby still, hiding, watching, snickering. The remains of night offered concealing shadows. He looked up and down again, wondering. The houses were the same as ever. An intelligence – vast, cool and unsympathetic –

was directed at him. The Norwegian Neil Cullers.

His rage-flare damped. He shivered. Turning, he found the door had swung shut behind him. He was locked out. Reaching for his keys, he realised they were in his jeans back in the flat.

'Bastard, bastard.'

Making a way by the dustbins, he took a look at the damage. He chose the most definitively broken window, and, with numb fingers, picked the last spikes out of the putty so he could crawl back in. Careful not to gash his hands, he settled bare feet on a carpet of splinters.

At 9.30 a.m., Sally walked down Cranley Gardens, hood of her transparent mac up against the drizzle. She'd loitered in the area for a month last year blending so well she was no more noticed than a lamp-post. Now Neil knew who she was (if he remembered), the job would be trickier.

There was the direct approach: as his saviour of New Year's Eve, she could invite him for a drink and ask how things were going. She didn't know how ethical or sensible that might be, but it was a temptingly easy option. She suspected Neil would take grim delight in telling people just exactly how things had been going, inside and outside his head. But it wouldn't do to be caught between the client and Neil. The intricacies of their relationship weren't her concern; besides, she suspected they were beyond human understanding.

Slowing as she passed Neil's house, she saw his windows were broken. Every pane: either unusual or thorough. And only *his* windows. The other flats had been left alone. His curtains were drawn, a blue wall. It was as if the place had been mortared by insurgents. Sarajevo, N10.

A young-looking middle-aged man parked a Volvo outside the flat. Sally wondered if he were calling on Neil, but he locked his car with an automatic zapper and hurried off determinedly, heavy suitcase on wheels trotting after him like a robot dog.

She kept walking, thinking about the vandalism. It was the sort of thing the client would want reported. First, the New Year's Eve beating, now this.

Neil isn't exactly Mr Lucky, Mummy.

Good point, strange alien being. Maybe he has the knack of making enemies.

At the end of the Gardens, she paused to count to 100, and turned to stroll back. She didn't hang about, partly because she was stranded suspiciously in the middle of a residential nowhere, partly because the cold sank ice needles into her toes.

A long dark car passed, light as a shadow on the road. She'd seen it before. An odd vehicle, its windows so opaque she swore the owner drove by sense of smell: the bonnet was the classic Rolls-Royce sharp-edged box but the rear was streamlined like a 1930s spaceship. Turning into Cranley Gardens, the car barely purred.

She followed as the car prowled through the Gardens, a cool predator with a vanity plate. SHADE 001. Passing Neil's house again, nothing was different. He didn't have a light on behind his curtains. He'd be under a blanket wishing his headache away. Yesterday, she'd scoped him struggling to the supermarket, half his face still a vari-coloured bruise.

SHADE 001 disappeared towards Highgate. It was time to check the Invader. Having a surveillance target within walking distance of the flat was unprecedentedly convenient. Neil didn't own a car; if he took off into town, she could easily follow. Holmes had a magnifying glass, Marlowe a gun; her most useful detection tool was a London Transport bus-train-tube season ticket.

A blast of throttled noise shocked her. In a house nearby, someone with no finger-bones picked out a thrash metal *Dying Swan*. She paused to pity the neighbours. Hurrying on, she wondered if a deadly guitar chord could have shattered Neil's windows.

* * *

The fire was on but the room wasn't warm. He'd gone back to bed for as long as he could stand but hadn't managed to sleep. Arctic gusts poured through empty window-frames. Invisible snow drifts piled around the chairs and against the walls.

When he finally decided to get up, he took off his pyjama bottoms to put on underpants and a vest, then pulled the pyjamas back on, finding the jacket at the bottom of the wardrobe. Over the ensemble, he tugged two pairs of socks (actually, four mismatched individual socks) and his jeans. He augmented the pyjama jacket with a rollneck sweater, a thick woolly jumper and his overcoat. As layered in by clothes as a wino, his crotch and elbows clogged, he was momentarily warm. Armoured, he could face the day.

He worked to extract treacherous ticks of glass from the carpet, his exposed extremities still suffering. His hands froze dead, nails bluish. Cold did more than paracetamol to dull the pain in his face.

Once more, he wondered why the Norwegian Neil Cullers were on his case. If he wasn't sure she was in Romania, he'd suspect Tanya was on one of her crusade crazes. She was not a rational being.

Satisfied the floor was glass-free, he hunted for small change. There weren't even any tens left in the electricity meter. The cupboard was bare. He went upstairs to borrow from Pel, who had the top-floor flat and was some sort of operator. In the forties, he'd have been a spiv.

Pel was on his futon with two girls Neil didn't recognise, posing as a James Bond villain. They were watching a pirate video, a Japanese subtitled Clint Eastwood. A new microwave sat in a scad of foam packaging, cord wedged into a plugboard with matchsticks. The flat was a maze of stacked boxes. Offered a deal on a Korean VCR, Neil didn't have a TV much less money. Pel told him to grab a handful of coins from the jar by the door. Neil thanked him, took the money, and got out. Leaving, he realised how warm Pel's flat was. It smelled of fresh croissants and real coffee.

When he got downstairs, the second post had come. There was nothing for him. Nearby, a Hendrix-possessed maniac murdered a musical instrument with a chainsaw. If Neil were a stone-thrower by disposition, he'd bypass his own place and aim solid chunks at the guitar man's flat.

Fighting the pips to jam enough change into the phone, he got through.

'Neil, what is it?' the landlord answered. 'I'm very busy.'

'My windows, Mr Azmi. They were broken this morning.'

'What did you say?'

'Broken. Someone broke them.'

'You broke windows? Why?'

'Not me. Someone else.'

'Who? Why? How?'

'I don't know.'

Mr Azmi gave a rattling sigh Neil guessed was a swear word in Pakistani. It was the landlord's responsibility to replace the windows. He'd be insured.

'Mr Azmi, it's cold. There's no security. Anyone could get in and steal stuff.'

That didn't impress Mr Azmi.

'They could take the phone, wrench it off the wall, loot the coin-box.'

'I'll send one of my sons.'

'Today?'

'I don't know.'

'The room is like a freezer.'

'I'll send one of my sons over.'

Mr Azmi hung up.

Sonja hadn't been overpowered and reduced to a bag of squishy skin on a broken skeleton, so that was something.

'Gurgle, gurgle,' Sally said to her offspring, who returned in kind. The Invader pretended to be an ordinary baby.

'Such a good little thing,' the childminder said. 'Not like my horror.'

They shared a diet lunch of cream cheese, pineapple and humus. The Invader and Sonja's horror, Francis, took merciful naps. Sonja had taken a message from an Ayesha McPherson, Michael Dixon's PA at Top Hat. When Sally returned the call, she was told Michael would like to make the arrangement for another commission. He was interested in anything she could find about Gary Gaunt, a book reviewer for the *Basildon Echo.* Sally said she'd get on the job. Despite wretched weather and general recession, her financial prospects were cheering. She felt like buying a celebration cardigan but decided to do the sensible thing and went shopping for baby clothes bargains.

Hendrix might be playing 'Paranoid' or 'Carmina Burana' or 'Doodly-Acky Sacky, Want Some Seafood, Mama'. It was impossible to tell. Neil sat hunched over the fire, frozen hands jammed into his armpits, wondering about Norwegian Neil Cullers. It seemed he couldn't make a move without someone aiming a baseball bat at his skull.

The doorbell rang, cutting briefly through the murder rock. Neil jumped. This must be one of Mr Azmi's sons, come about the broken windows. It'd be too much to hope they could get a glazier this afternoon but Neil couldn't take many nights effectively in the open. He'd do anything – report to the police, fill in forms, show investigators around – to help Mr Azmi make his insurance claim.

He went upstairs and opened the door. On the step was a man of about retirement age, erect like a career Army officer, bristly of moustache, weak of chin. The broken-and-mended strap of his shoulder-bag was much too short. Tufts of hair escaped his woolly hat.

'Neil Martin?' he asked.

'Yes.'

'Stan Gull, ELF,' he said confidentially, looking up the street. A big black car dawdling by. Gull waited until it had passed before continuing, as if suspecting directional mikes. 'We spoke on the telephone yesterday. I was in the district so I thought I'd establish contact. I've brought the back numbers of *Britannia Rules* and our membership bumph. Proud to have you on the rolls, Martin. We may be few but, with the rot and rancour, we grow by the hour. I expect you thought you were alone in your feelings...'

'Well, er, I...'

'Fear not, delivery is nigh. No room for slackers in the boats, Martin.'

He dumped his bag on the hall table and produced a large buff envelope which he handed over.

Nodding in Hendrix's direction, Gull observed, 'Fearful racket, what? Coloured, I'll wager. We've their measure, Martin. Yes indeed, no napping on our watch.'

Neil opened the flap and slid out a slickly-produced, badly-designed magazine. It was glossy but felt slimy. The cover painting showed a crowd of heavily negroid faces over-stamped with an official NOT WANTED in blood red. Straplines promised: THE LIE OF THE HOLOCAUST, a Historian Writes; THE HOMO CONSPIRACY EXPOSED, Growing Threat in the Open; PROUD TO BE A RACIST, Decorated Hero Declares! Gull smiled, a pervert sharing a pleasure. He had unbelievably polished false teeth.

'The ELF needs young blood, Martin. Young British blood.'

The world spun out of control again.

'Can I leave you a poster? To put up in the window.'

Gull unrolled a large two-colour poster; red and blue. ENGLISH LIBERATION FRONT written on a flapping Union Jack. 'BEFORE IT'S TOO LATE, END IMIGRATION NOW!' a caption blared.

Neil took the poster, too appalled to think.

'Aren't there two M's in...'

'Come the day,' Gull said, slipping an arm around Neil, 'your children will be rid of the invader.'

A young Asian in a sharp suit came through the front door. Zafir, one of Mr Azmi's sons. He had an attempted moustache and a gold neckchain. Gull couldn't have looked more aghast if he'd opened his eyes to find he was being fellated by a leper.

'Neil,' Zafir said, 'about this damage...'

That dot high up in the sky was a falling piano, aimed directly at his head, growing by the second as it plummeted heavily Neil-wards.

Gull's fingers stretched out to point shakily between Zafir's eyes.

'Put that away,' Zafir said, smiling uneasily. 'It might be loaded.'

'There's one now,' he said. 'A filthy alien...'

It was no use trying to roll up the poster before Zafir saw it. Mr Azmi's son took in everything in a polaroid instant; it would develop in his head for minutes.

'You, coon-features,' Gull said, red in the face and spluttering, 'clear off out of here and scurry back to your own subcontinent. Take your arranged marriages and spicy foods and cattle diseases with you, and give us back our newsagents, our churches...'

'What's all this about crack dealing?' asked Zafir, interrupting. 'Dadiji has gone spare. If it's another scam of Pel's, I can't cover for him much bloody longer...'

Neil felt he had taken another blow to the head. He had to prove to his landlord's son that he was not a Nazi. With righteous coldness, he dropped the copies of *Britannia Rules* on the floor and scraped his shoe on them. Then he held up the poster and, deliberately, ripped it in half.

Gull's eyes grew, his false teeth gnashed.

'Traitor to your race,' he said, cornered. 'What is this? A trap? I'm not afraid of you, alien. Or you, you white nig-nog. The proud blood of King Arthur and St George flows in these veins. It's not afraid to be shed in the cause of England.'

'I want you off the premises,' Zafir said.

Neil's heart congealed, but Zafir was talking to Gull.

'Go on, old man, off out of it...'

'Comes the day,' Gull muttered.

Zafir stood aside to let Gull escape. He bent down, with the painful creak of a man who had done his best to stand up straight for sixty years, and retrieved his magazines, shuffling them tidily, putting them back in his bag.

'Treason will not be forgot,' he said, darkly. 'The ledger is writ in scarlet and stays open so long as the last Englishman's alive.'

Mumbling, he carefully trudged past Zafir and down the steps. Neil watched him go, noticing a rip in the back of his anorak.

'Ought to be reported,' Neil said, too quickly. He had to impress on Zafir that he hadn't invited Gull to present him with nauseating literature.

'He's got a point about arranged marriages,' Zafir shook his head. 'You should see the old dog Dadiji wants to lump on me.'

A buffer who gave off madman vibes marched past on the other side of the road, hugging a shoulder-bag. The guitar hero was still at work, a hazard to passing traffic. Sally quickened pace as she passed Neil's house. He was outside, in the trough between the dustbins and his windows, with a good-looking Asian youth, explaining.

She caught a few snatches.

'...no idea who it could've been...'

'...bloody expensive. Dadiji will have kittens...'

'...colder than Tibet...'

Out of their sight, she stopped and took stock. Someone had broken Neil's windows. He didn't know who. He was trying to get someone (probably his landlord) to have them fixed before he froze solid. Cranley Gardens was at war, evidently.

* * *

In the late afternoon, Neil scrounged cardboard boxes from Pel. They'd originally been for dishwashers, so he could slice out sheets the size of the broken windows. He did his best to jam cardboard into empty frames. It was hardly sufficient but the worst of the wind was excluded. He was supposed to make a statement for the insurance. Zafir said he'd get an estimate for a glazier within a week. Of course, he'd also been promising for three months that 'Dadiji' would replace Neil's missing dustbin.

As he worked, preparing the flat for nuclear attack, Hendrix's guitar atrocities insinuated themselves into his head. While he was taping the last sheet in the last pane, the same pair of legs walked past twice. Nice legs.

This was another day he would write off for experience. All good material for that wryly humorous novel of contemporary urban despair he kept threatening to start. Of course, Michael Dixon had already done a wryly humorous novel of contemporary urban despair, *Colin Dale*. He wondered where Michael was and if he ever thought of his old mate. Last year, when Mickey Yeo had been at the Planet for *Choke Hold*, he mentioned he still saw Michael (and Mark Amphlett) so it was possible he'd told Michael he'd met Neil again.

Finally, the job was done. As he stood back to assess his handiwork, Hendrix's chords rose in a tumultuous crescendo and, at the peak of pain, miraculously fell silent. Either his mother had come home and shot him dead, or he'd ventured out in search of a tuna-and-puke sandwich. A last paracetamol lulled the pain. He touched his bruised face and didn't wince. Slowly, he was healing. Then, spontaneously, a Volvo parked directly outside the flat began to whine. The shrill caress of noise, ground against Neil's mind like a rusty saw. The car alarm didn't shut off until four in the morning; Neil wouldn't stop hearing it for three days.

9

13 FEBRUARY, 1978

With Pippa, a geology major away on a field trip, Mark was free to turn their sea-front flat into a command centre. Mickey insisted on a blackout, curtains drawn tight. It wasn't likely Neil would float past the fourth storey and happen to glance in, but the others treated this as a game. Mark was increasingly aware of the responsibilities he'd have to bear if the Quorum was to fulfil its side of the Deal. In the end, it was down to him.

In a kitchen the size of a phone box, he made tea. According to the Code Michael, the Ring was required to supply provisions but the others had kicked in £10 apiece. This was a tightly budgeted operation and his grant cheque was already overcommitted; if the cost to Mark went above £35, he'd have to crap out. There was half a loaf left in the cupboard and the remains of a fund of biscuits. Last night, Mickey had gone through a whole packet of ginger nuts.

They had from the New Year to Valentine's Day. Mickey thought it foolish to delay the moves until the last specified moment, but Pippa's absence afforded the only possible launch window. No matter how close they'd become in four months, she was an outsider. Even before Sutton Mallet, there were things he hadn't been able to share with her.

He took breakfast to the front and only room, where Mickey and Michael slept in bags either side of the double bed. A male smell (sweat, smoke, curry, beer) permeated the flat. A takeaway food carton had been used as an ashtray, a glut of dogends stubbed in the last of the sauce. Despite the cold, Mark had heaved open the windows.

'We have a Quorum,' he said. 'Wakey, wakey.'

The others stirred; Mickey grumbling and scratching, Michael sitting up straight and stretching. Michael, funding the expedition with Christmas money, had taken a coach to London and a train to Brighton. His parents were relieved to get him out of the house. Mickey had spent Sunday hitching from Yorkshire, a sleeping bag in his backpack, a knife in his boot. He had tales of adventures on icy motorways with psycho lorry drivers. They had met in the fish cafe on the corner and waited for Mark, who was seeing Pippa off at the station, to collect them.

Mark handed out mismatched mugs. Michael pulled on his trousers and made it to the table, but Mickey hopped in his bag and worked his way into a chair. Michael attacked bread, pasting butter and jam on an inch-thick slice, while Mickey rolled up the first cigarette of the day, not saying a word until he had smoke into his lungs.

Michael picked up a library book, Thomas Mann's *Doctor Faustus*, and flipped pages.

'Rather you than me,' he said.

'We're on Marlowe in Tragedy,' Mark explained. 'I'm reading around the subject.'

Clean cold seeped into the flat, deadening last night's fug. Nothing had happened yet. Nothing real. After a long breakfast, Mark convened the Meet. He put the new-cut key on the table.

'As promised, a key to Neil's room.'

'How did zhou get it?'

'I missed the last bus from campus one night and crashed on

his floor. The key was on his desk.'

'They didn't change the locks?'

'No, just gave him a new key and asked for a bigger deposit. To be on the safe side, I had it copied and dropped the old one in his common-room.'

Mickey picked up the key and looked at it as if it were a diamond. 'You done us proud, Marko,' he said. 'We're in.'

It had been surprisingly easy. As they combed the carpet looking for the key, Mark suffered paranoid spasms, but Neil was so irritated – 'I was sure it was here' – he hadn't noticed. When Mark turned up at Tadcaster House, Neil was pleased to help out with floor-space. 'We don't see enough of each other,' he said as Mark left for his lecture. 'We go back too far to lose touch.' He asked after Pippa, whom he'd evidently had a talk with at the party the Quorum never managed to reach.

'I've checked his timetable,' Mark said. 'This afternoon, he has a lecture in the Humanities Block followed by a tutorial in the same building. The last three weeks, he's gone straight from one to the other without nipping back to Tadcaster House. That gives us two hours.'

'What if he needs a book or something?' Michael asked.

'It's a risk,' Mark admitted, 'but it's our best shot. At no other point can we *guarantee* he'll be out of the way for more than an hour.'

'I'm convinced,' Mickey said. '*Vamanos!*'

After midday, they took the bus. From the top deck, Mark pointed out the landmarks in Brighton and on the road to the University. Michael was surprised the campus was so far out of the town.

'It's a village,' Mark explained. 'Like a holiday camp.'

Nearing their stop, Michael got more fidgety, Mickey more controlled. There was a chance Neil might see them walking around. They had a contingency excuse (a surprise visit on

Mark for his birthday) but weren't happy with it. Michael had tried to disguise himself by changing his image, growing a sparse moustache, wearing an Army surplus greatcoat, a woolly hat and dark glasses. Mickey rolled his bus ticket into a tiny cigarette tube, thin lips set, eyes unrevealing. If the Deal fell apart, he'd be the one to explode.

Even Mark, least at risk, was uncomfortable in his stomach. He had no tutorials today but might have to skip a lecture late this afternoon. If anyone from his Tragedy seminar noticed him, the absence would be questioned. Since Twelfth Night, he wore gloves even in the flat, which Pippa said was funny. Most nights, he returned in his dreams to Sutton Mallet and woke up shivering under the continental quilt.

The bus halted and students piled out, late for things, hurrying off across campus. The Quorum sat together until the bus was empty and debarked cautiously. Like a team of undercover assassins, they looked about, wary of venturing into a line of sniper fire. They clustered between the bus and the shelter.

Mark outlined a way of getting to Tadcaster House, Neil's hall of residence, by skirting the campus, staying off the main routes. It was a pleasantly wooded walk, earth-and-grass areas dotted with stubborn pancakes of frozen snow.

They proceeded with exaggerated stealth, like spies they'd seen in films. Mickey darted from tree to tree imitating a cartoon coyote, lagging behind, then catching up. If anyone noticed how prattish they were acting, they didn't get in the way. There were always geeks and misfits on the prowl. Michael had wanted them to get-up in masks and costumes and pose as a rag troupe but Mark explained the Brighton Students Union didn't believe in rag weeks. Charities only encouraged the government to devote less resources to the needy.

Tadcaster House was a red-brick structure, seventy rooms piled around a courtyard. Neil's room was at the end of a corridor, next to a kitchen on the nearside of the first floor.

'See why I moved out?' Mark said.

'It's not so ghastly,' Michael muttered. 'I'll be confined in a medieval college with a curfew and no women.'

They ambled up and grouped against a wall. The sun came out but the light that fell against them was unwarming. Mark checked his watch. Neil's lecture was at two; it was now 1.45 p.m.

'We're a bit early,' he said.

'*Quel signifié ça?*' Michael asked.

'Watch out!'

The doors shoved open and a gaggle of students emerged, talking and walking. Mark's anus turned outside-in as he saw Neil among the crowd, the satchel he'd carried since Ash Grove slung over his back. Michael and Mickey backed around a corner and flattened against the wall. Mark edged with them, eyes on Neil's back. He peeped around the brickwork. Neil tried to keep up with a tall girl: he did a ridiculous lope to get in front of her, half-turning to talk, then getting left behind again. Each time Neil turned, Mark's bowel knotted. Neil's focus was completely on the girl; to him, the Quorum would be background fuzz. He was trying to be funny and sophisticated but coming across as gawky and goonish. It was hard to believe Pippa described him as 'a really nice bloke'.

A minute trudged by like an hour-long lecture on rhythmic patterns in Elizabethan verse. Then Neil disappeared under a bridge, headed for Humanities. Mark's rectum relaxed. He shook his head. The Deal was tougher than he had expected.

Mickey grabbed him by the shirt and jostled him against the wall.

'You fuckin' cretin,' he said, pupils shrunk to furious pinpoints. 'A bit fuckin' early!'

Michael took Mickey's shoulders and eased him off.

'Steady on, old thing. We're all new at this lark. It's not Mark's fault.'

'It fuckin' is,' Mickey said, calming in spite of himself.

'This is really inconspicuous, guys,' Mark told them.

Mickey shook off Michael and adjusted his shoulders in his jacket. When they were twelve Mickey had a fist-fight with Mark over some reversal in the Game. They didn't speak for nearly a month, until Neil negotiated a reconciliation. As a kid, Mickey was too keen to use his skinny knuckles; in too many ways, he was still a kid.

'Are you speeding?' Mark asked.

Mickey shook his head, disgusted. There were chemicals in his head that did the job of most drugs. After a few calming beats, breath clouding around them in white gusts, they advanced around the side of Tadcaster House and strolled into the lobby with shaky confidence.

Mark led them to Neil's corridor. A Nigerian in a thigh-length dressing-gown wandered past from the bathroom, rubbing a towel into wet curls. Michael stared; having lived in the Backwater all his life, he'd probably never seen a half-naked black man before.

'Zhou have coons here?'

'We don't use words like that any more,' Mark said.

Michael shrugged, more surprised than offended. In theory he was a liberal, but had never been called on it. The Nigerian went into his room. It was quiet. Mark could hear distant noises. He led them to Neil's door.

Mark produced the key and held it up. He took a breath, then let it go. Michael guided Mark's hand to the lock. Mickey touched his fingers.

'This is silly,' Mark said.

'Together or not at all,' Michael replied.

It was awkward, but they managed to unlock the door as if with one hand. They jammed into the room and Mark shut the door behind them. His gut wasn't churning now.

'The curtains,' Mickey said.

'What's more suspicious,' Mark asked, 'three kids in a room or drawn curtains in the afternoon?'

Mickey conceded.

Mark was familiar with the room but Michael looked around with interest. Mark noticed his attitude to student life was still torn between envy and intrigue.

'Smells better than zhour place.'

'They have a cleaning staff.'

There was a bed, a washbasin, a chair, a desk and a wardrobe. On the desk, files and papers were stacked either side of a typewriter. Notes, maps, timetables and pictures clipped from magazines covered a corkboard.

Mickey sat on the neatly made single bed and waited for orders. They had discussed what they might find and what they might do.

First, the typewriter. When he left home, Neil's parents gave him a portable. It was common knowledge typed essays were automatically graded higher than handwritten submissions. Michael, the literary expert, took the cover off the machine. He depressed the 'e', and reached into the typewriter's works to grip the key.

'Commonest letter in the language,' he said, twisting.

'Don't break it,' Mark said. 'That's too obvious.'

'Surgical precision,' Michael said, twisting further. He jammed the key back. It grated against the others. He stabbed the 'e' again and the key ground. 'One good "e"-word and it's farewell to legibility.'

'Do the "s",' Mickey said.

'Exaggerating the point, surely?'

'Do the fuckin' "s",' he insisted.

Michael shrugged, and, sheepish, repeated the operation. Smiling at his handiwork, he carefully replaced the cover.

Michael shook his head. 'We vandalise a typewriter and all our dreams come true?'

Suddenly, together, Mickey and Michael laughed. It began as a giggle, then became choking hysteria. Mickey held his abdomen and rolled on the bed. Michael covered his face with his hands.

Mark couldn't laugh.

'Come on, guys. If we do this, we do it properly, right?'

Mickey recovered first. Michael wiped his face with his hat and agreed to go on with due solemnity.

'I'm nineteen. Zhou can't expect me to do anything properly with my raging hormones and lack of experience.'

'That's not an excuse you'll be able to use forever,' Mark said.

'If this doesn't work, Neil is going to piss himself laughing, zh'know.'

'I doubt that,' Mark said, looking at the typewriter. 'Since about thirty seconds ago, Neil isn't our friend any more. You better remember that.'

The hilarity evaporated. Mark realised Michael had lost babyfat in the last four months. He had visible cheekbones.

'Watergate time,' Michael announced, standing away from the desk.

This was Mark's province. He was most familiar with the University, and so best able to identify what was important.

'It's too early for him to have many notes,' Mark said, rifling through the files. 'He's doing two foundation courses this term, one fresh and one continued from last year.'

He found a ring-binder with Introduction to Marx on the cover. It was filled with squiggles that must be lecture notes. There were thirty-eight handwritten pages of notes. Mark detached every fifth sheet. He handed the pages to Michael, who put them in his cavernous inside pocket.

'It'll take a while to notice,' Mark said. 'It won't be crippling until it comes to his assessment.'

'It's only a couple of pages,' Mickey said. 'You sure that's enough?'

'Believe me, we've thrown away three solid weeks' work.'

'You bastards,' Mickey grinned.

'No, *we* bastards.'

Mickey cackled again. He sorted through a mess of notebooks and papers on the bedside table. Michael looked at the shelves. He took a library book, a biography of Engels. A piece of orange sticking-plaster on the spine marked it as a short-term loan. Neil had to get it back within three days or pay a fine. Michael leafed through the book, then slipped it into his pocket.

'There's a computer system. They'll track him down in a week.'

'I wonder if he'll formulate an explanation.'

'This place has a Library Gestapo. They'll grill him for days.'

Mickey looked through an exercise book.

'We've struck gold,' he said, grinning. 'I've found his diary.'

Instantly, Mark ordered, 'Look up Twelfth Night. See what he says about us not showing.'

Mickey turned back a few pages.

'Nothing much. "Production a disaster. Michael sick three times. Party at Achelzoy. Talked with Mark's girlfriend Philippa…"'

'Nobody calls her that.'

'Neil does. There's an illegible bit here. "Michael, drunk, got lost, never made it." Then, nothing. Looks like he didn't have time to write. Once he gets back to University, the entries get longer. They mostly seem to be about someone called Rachael, who lives next door. Rachel with an extra "a". There's a lot of wistful angst.'

'I think that was the girl he was with just now,' Mark said.

Michael whistled. 'Nice.'

'I doubt that,' Mark said.

'Neil likes her,' Mickey said, flipping pages. 'He thinks she likes him but can't be sure. There's a ton of essay notes about her background, tastes, habits. Father's an airline pilot, she's been to America. No visible boyfriend. Long legs. Nothing to suggest the remotest possibility said long legs might ever be wrapped around Neil's neck.'

'It's like he was fifteen,' Mark observed.

'It's Valentine's Day tomorrow,' Mickey said. 'A good time for young love. Ah, but it says here he's decided not to send a card because that would be "trite and childish". Ooo-woo, what an adult.'

Pippa had told Michael not to bother with a card and, after wondering whether she meant it or not, Mark decided to believe her. He still wasn't sure he'd done the right thing.

'We can use this,' Michael said. 'I foresee massive humiliation. Give me paper.'

Mark tore a sheet from a ruled pad. Michael sat at the desk and took the cover off the typewriter. He fed in the paper.

'This will be a challenge,' he said. 'No "e" and no "s".'

'"Dear Rachael" is out, then,' Mickey put in.

Michael nodded and held up a hand for quiet. 'Let me think, let me think... ah, yes, got it...'

DARLING, he typed, TONIGHT, MIDNIGHT, MY ROOM, WAITING FOR YOUR...

'Love? No, it has an "e".'

'Sex,' suggested Mickey.

'An "e" and an "s".'

HOT BODY, he typed.

'Hot body?' Mark said.

'It's the kind of Neily thing she'd expect,' Michael protested. 'It has to be convincing. It's not what *I'd* put in a *billet doux*.'

With his left hand, he signed Neil's name. It was readable, but nothing like a grown-up's handwriting. Mark found an envelope in a desk drawer and Michael popped in the note. Mickey fished out a durex from his wallet.

'Shove this in for that final romantic touch.'

Michael cringed. 'That's appalling.'

He put the condom in with the message from Neil.

'Anything else?'

'Five pounds would be truly insulting,' Mark ventured.

'No,' Mickey said, 'this would be worse...'

He took out a pound note and tore it in half.

'I've always wanted to do that,' he said.

'I don't get it,' Michael said.

'Slip half the note in with the johnny and the letter. Raunchy Rachael gets the rest when she spreads 'em for Mr Suave.'

Michael laughed again.

'This is disgusting,' he said, accepting the half-note. 'Pin the other half to his board. With luck he won't notice it, but *she* will when she comes round to force feed him his wastebasket.'

'She looked like a big girl,' Mickey said. 'Athletic. Probably has a good right hook.'

'It's tragic we won't be here for the fireworks,' Michael said.

Mark checked his watch. They'd been in the room for three-quarters of an hour. There wasn't much more they could accomplish.

'I say we withdraw and come back in to pull the sink stunt when he's at his seminar tomorrow. This Rachael move is too sweet to complicate.'

They agreed. They left the room and locked up. Before they left Tadcaster Hall, Mark slipped the envelope (which Mickey had pencilled a heart on in red) under Rachael's door. The Quorum left the hall. Mark, ahead of schedule, had time to make the last two-thirds of his Marlowe lecture, leaving the others to make their way back into town.

He was working on an essay about masochism in *Dr Faustus*. If his brief omnipotence is followed by an eternity of torment, it's hard to see what's in the Deal for Faustus. After reviewing his undistinguished first term – he'd been too caught up with Pippa and leaving home to do actual work – Brian Ellison, his assessor, admitted Mark had really seized the opportunity of Tragedy.

VALENTINE'S DAY, 1978

The next day, Mark rapped at the door to make sure Neil was out. After sustained knocking, he used the key. The room was different. Neil's bed was unmade and one of the shelves had been ripped off the wall, dumping books over the floor.

Mickey laughed, 'What a woman.'

'Zhou don't suppose she came over and shagged him senseless?'

'I'd doubt that,' Mark said. 'This looks more like the aftermath of a shouting and screaming fit than a night of unbridled passion.'

'Speak for yourself,' Mickey said.

'I think she chucked the typewriter at his head.'

'Amazing, Holmes,' Mickey spluttered. 'How did you deduce that?'

There was a triangular dent in the plasterboard just above the pillow, and the typewriter lay face down on the floor.

Knowing Neil, Mark guessed he was wrung out with embarrassment and confusion. As far as he was concerned, the girl next door whom he fancied, but didn't dare approach, had barged in late at night and attacked him like a fiend. She'd probably have been in no mood to give an explanation.

'This is better than clobbering him on his coursework,' Mickey said. 'Neil could always muddle through by working harder. I think we've found his weakness. Women.'

'Everybody's weakness,' Michael observed.

'Let's hurry up and make our move,' Mickey said. 'One more shot and we're through for a year, remember?'

'Yeah, yeah,' Mark muttered.

Neil's washstand was a mess, squeezed toothpaste tube on the floor, hot tap dripping, towel in a bundle by the bed. The mirror was cracked. Rachael again. Mark found a flannel and jammed it into the plughole as if it had accidentally clogged there. He turned the tap.

'Not too much,' Michael said. 'Zhust a slow trickle.'

Even at its current rate, the level rose. In maybe ten or fifteen minutes the sink would overflow. Within half an hour, water would gush into the room below.

'He won't remember washing his face this morning,' Mickey said. 'He'll be too wound up about Roughhouse Rachael.'

'The tap was dripping. This is a completely believable accident.'

He twisted the tap a smidgen more, the water flowed a tad faster.

10

7 JANUARY, 1993

Crossing the Atlantic, he travelled forwards and backwards at the same time, losing a slice of night. Jet lag was not a problem. His bodyclock came fitted with a temporal gyroscope, he always adjusted instantly. It was a gift: some people were lucky, and he was one of them. Comfortably curled in his Superior Class lounger, lulled by the wine from the party, he snatched four hours' quality sleep. He woke with a clear head as the plane began its descent to JFK. He shared the privileged cabin with Loud Stuff, a shaggy rock group, and a diplomat who gripped an attaché case as if it were handcuffed to his wrist. Miren, Mickey's personal stewardess, offered a jolt of complimentary orange juice. He sloshed it around his mouth, cleaning his teeth. The landing was smooth. It always was in Superior.

He was first off the plane. Miren kissed his cheek as he left. She smelled slightly of citrus fruit. Tangy but refreshing. At the end of the carpeted corridor stood a uniformed hispanic name-tagged 'Raimundo'. He held a sign which spelled out 'Mr Yeo'. Mickey identified himself and was led through a womb-like passage to a sunlit VIP reception lounge. A woman with smooth honey-blonde hair and an orthodontal smile awaited.

'My name is Heather Wilding. I'm with Pyramid and I've been

assigned to you for your personal ease and convenience.'

He couldn't help grinning. Heather wore a tailored business suit: a severe jacket with a short skirt. She was a career magazine cover: hands on hips, jacket wings swept back, chest out-thrust, eyes bright with determined promise.

Loud Stuff trundled in, blaming their road manager for the loss of a case of synthesiser equipment. Mickey shrugged and smiled at Grattan, the lead singer, who peered back through a curtain of hair extensions. Having heard rumours of the *Choke Hold* album project, he'd personally come over to Mickey's lounger to ask to be considered for a slot. Mickey had assured him he was top of the list, keeping to himself that it was the 'Not Now Not Ever NEVER' list.

'Have your people call my people and we'll interface,' Mickey said, his personal slang for 'fuck off'.

The diplomat handed his case over to an American and walked back to reboard the plane for its return flight.

'Mr Yeo's luggage is being processed,' a functionary explained to Heather. 'Would he care for complimentary champagne?'

Heather looked to him.

'Why the hell not?' he said. 'You want a blast?'

'Too early for me, Mr Yeo,' she said.

'Call me Mickey.'

A cork popped, a chilled flute was put in his hand: the party never ended.

'I have your itinerary, Mickey,' Heather said, producing a long envelope. 'But first we'll convey you to the hotel and afford you a freshen-up period.'

Mickey felt the envelope.

'I'm going to be fuckin' busy,' he said.

'We aren't inhuman,' Heather smiled. Her eyes were the same shade of blue-grey as the sky visible through panorama windows. 'We've factored breathing time into your schedule.'

'Ta everso.'

'We don't wish to impact negatively on your health.'

'Too right, John.'

'My name is Heather.'

'Right, Heth.'

Raimundo reported that Mickey's luggage was stowed in the limo, and Heather led him past the queues to Immigration. He gave Loud Stuff the high sign but they were too wrapped up in recriminations to notice. The formalities were accomplished with a wave of a British passport. He almost took his barely sipped champagne through but remembered at the last moment to return the flute to the functionary. Heather had expedited the way, the paperwork was over in an instant. She could get Josef Mengele warmly welcomed into Israel.

'Welcome to the United States, Mr Yeo,' said a gorgeous oriental girl at the Immigration desk. 'May I compliment you on your graphic novel, *Choke Hold*. I'm an enormous admirer of your work.'

'You pay these people, don't you?' Mickey said to Heather, who smiled tolerantly.

Since arriving at Derek Leech's Twelfth Night half a world away, he had been looked after: gently handed from one super-humanly efficient minion to another, eased past queues of fretting and red-eyed footsoldiers, offered complimentary everything, never for a moment allowed to suffer the tiniest inconvenience. It was as if handmaidens preceded him, scattering rose petals in his path. He could feel them crunch beneath his Doc Martens as he walked under the canopy to the limo.

Settled on a backseat the size of a sofa, relishing the leather-and-sandalwood smell, he paid close attention to Heather's legs as she folded herself into the facing seat. She wore sheer hose and running shoes, which she slipped off automatically and replaced with a pair of high heels. She gave an order in Spanish and the limo purred off.

From a sleeve in the door, Heather took a selection of

periodicals and newspapers and offered them. He declined the *New York Times* and the *Wall Street Journal* in favour of yesterday's *Evening Argus* so he could catch up with Dr Shade. Of all the comics characters he hadn't written yet, Dr Shade was the one he most wanted to tackle. After glancing at the three striking panels on the inside back page – the guy who crammed detail into that demented space was Mickey's contemporary hero – he relaxed and enjoyed looking at Heather, who unselfconsciously allowed him his viewing pleasure. Caught smiling in shafts of passing sunlight, she might be wrapped in cellophane, wearing a 'Present from Derek Leech' sash.

The express elevator took them to the Apex Suite, which was one floor above the Presidential Suite and the Royal Suite.

'Derek resides here himself when in New York,' Heather explained. 'He left instructions that your comfort should be a paramount concern.'

Raimundo carried his bags through the panelled entranceway into a penthouse larger than most supermarkets. Heather showed him the rooms, assigning a name and function to each, climaxing with the Sleeping Room, a high-tech grotto with a tinted glass sky-roof. Complimentary floral arrangements were central to each space. A basket of exotic fruits stood on the ten-person dining-table in the Entertainment Room. It was hard to imagine the austere Leech in this place.

In the Reading Room, prepublication copies of spring and summer bestsellers were given prominent shelfspace. A file of synopses gave précis reports of the books, to save the Apex guest the trouble of reading anything longer than three pages. Mickey noticed an American omnibus of Michael's *Colin Dale* and *Ken Sington* (all references to Torchy the Battery Boy and Sky Ray lollies pruned and replaced by jokes about Howdy Doody and Hershey bars) already in its place with the next from Stephen King, Tom Clancy and Umberto Eco.

Heather retreated to the Office Space while Mickey stepped into the Freshen-Up Room. He splashed scented water on his face and assessed his chin to see if his stubble was stubbly enough to merit a trim. Changing clothes, he chose a Wile E. Coyote T-shirt, which outlined his skinny ribs, and complemented it with his favourite ripped jeans, leather jacket and pointy-toed motorcycle boots.

'Heartfucker,' he said to his reflection, passing fingers through the knotty braids sprouting from one side of his half-shaven head.

When he rejoined Heather and Raimundo in the Office Space, which adjoined a spectacular terrace, a fax was churning. It was out that he was in town and requests for interviews, personal appearances and lunch dates were pouring in.

On Park Avenue and 55th Street, Pyramid Plaza was a slimmer variation on DLE London. Both were Constant Drache buildings. Crowded by neighbouring glass towers, the Plaza was ostentatious enough in its forecourt to establish its primacy as toughest skyscraper on the block. From large gold bowls, twin fountains pumped gushes of black water fifty feet into the air. Whenever Mickey called the place the Coming Building, Americans didn't get the joke. It was five blocks from the hotel but Raimundo drove them. It did not do to walk.

The forecourt thronged with banner-waving protesters, kept behind barriers by cops. No matter how many times he came to America, Mickey found it hard not to think their policemen were in fancy dress, toy guns on their hips, cool black jackets for show.

The limo rolled up and the door swung open. This was the nearest he'd got to open air since his arrival in the country. It was even colder than London, but drier, fresher, sharper. Laced with vehicle emissions and amphetamines, the atmosphere tasted potent.

'We're Queer, We're Faggots, We Don't Wanna Be Treated as Maggots,' demonstrators chanted. HITLER WAS STRAIGHT read a placard. Mildly interested, he asked what the fuss was about. Heather explained, gays were picketing because Pyramid Pictures was filming *Pink Swastika*, a bestseller based on the diaries of a homosexual SS officer. The book had been serialised in a Derek Leech paper, the *Sunday Argus*.

Heather walked past the pickets, ignoring them as she would a pan-handling bum or a fire hydrant. A young man with a Queer Nation badge gave pink triangle armbands to people who went into the building. Mickey accepted his and shoved it into his white buckskins.

'Nice jacket,' the protester commented.

Grinning, he entered the foyer of the Plaza. More demonstrators waited among man-sized potted plants. Three women in black leotards and whiteface squatted in a makeshift teepee by the elevator bank, wailing like grieving Apache widows.

Heather made it known to the ice-queen at reception that Mickey Yeo had arrived. She issued a non-transferable security cardkey and gave him a four-digit entrance code which, combined with the card, would gain him access to all but the silver-marked security areas. His number was 1812. 'Like the war,' the receptionist explained.

'What's that about, Heth?' he asked Heather, nodding to the squaws.

'WoFBReIGN.'

'Yer wot?'

'Women For Better Representation In Graphic Narrative. A feminist pressure group.'

He peered again at the women. They all looked like Kathy Bates.

'It's a vigil,' Heather explained. 'They've been there since Amazon Queen died. They say they'll fast until she's brought back.'

He chuckled and, after seriously thinking about it, decided *not* to tell them who he was.

'How did they get in?'

'They have a court order declaring this a public place and upholding their right of lawful assembly. So long as they don't obstruct anyone, they can't be moved.'

'You have a wonderful country.'

'Thank you,' she said, as if she were the ambassador delegated to accept compliments.

Heather escorted him to the ninth floor, the offices of Zenith Comics. She waited in the reception area while Mickey had his meeting.

Two years ago, Timmy Chin had been a nineteen-year-old with the third largest collection of comics in the States; now, with a $500 haircut and a baggy tropical suit, he was vice-president in charge of editorial direction. He had control over the billion-dollar ZC list but, from the red-faced embarrassment he demonstrated when faced with Heather, Mickey assumed Timmy had never met a girl.

They sat in the corner office. Behind Timmy's desk-space was a picture window with a priceless view. Framed in a cabinet were equally priceless comics from the thirties and forties. Also under glass was a two-sheet for the 1946 Republic serial *Adventures of the Streak*, with Clayton Moore. There was no memorabilia from the camp 1966–67 *Amazon Queen* show, which ZC purists despised but Mickey still remembered fondly, if only for Mary Ann Mobley's thighs.

On the desk were the proofs of the next book in Mickey's quality format mini-series, *The Nevergone Void*. The first of the limited-run cross-over title had seen the death of Amazon Queen. Malevolent forces tampering with the ancient past had undone the heroine's fifty-year career sucking her entire history into non-existence. Next up was Mr Mystery, a once-popular occult detective, who was due to be unmasked as the secret collaborator of the Nevergone Conspirators.

'On Book One, we've had our biggest sales ever in this format,' Timmy told him. 'Biggest profits ever period. I've been on *Entertainment Tonight* and *Sally Jessie Raphael*.'

Timmy was less bubbling, his voice a lot less squeaky than usual. He was almost solemn. He was a fanboy first. The vice-president didn't understand the medium had to outgrow steroid cases in tights if it was to hit the twenty-first century on an equal footing with real books. The best way to get all the superslobs out of the way was something apocalyptic.

'This has been coming since that comic there,' Mickey said, pointing to a framed *Dazzling Duo Stories* Issue Number One (June, 1948). 'The Streak and Amazon Queen Together! America's Mightiest Heroes Versus the Red Menace!' 'When Zack Briscow drew that, the ZC Universe was founded. Before, you just had a fuckpile of characters in their own series. When they bumped into each other, it became an epic. And epics have to have a big finish.'

Briscow (a legendary drunk and lecher) left all sorts of logistical problems for his successors. Aside from the truism that heroes from World War Two would be in their eighties if they aged properly, there had been so many interconnecting strands it was now impossible to come up with a plot not strangled with fifty years' worth of labyrinthine backstory. Under pressure from the anti-comics hysterics of the fifties, the Streak and Amazon Queen even got married and settled into tedious respectability for a while. In a pre-*Dallas* stroke, someone rubbed out that by writing off two years of three separate comics as a wish-fulfilment dream on the part of incipiently domestic Amy McQueen, who'd otherwise never be able to get her superindependent hero to the altar. That characters introduced in the dream turned up years later in the real continuity was something no one ever sorted out. Sucking the overbearing virago out of ever having lived was as good a way as any of dealing with narrative tangles.

'There's been flak,' Timmy said. 'The fan press have crucified us.'

This had started with an accountant pondering sales graphs. Comics were like soap operas: weddings or deaths were always boosts. Noticing a projected long-term decline, even if it didn't hit red for fifteen years, a canny bean counter calculated that an ultimate series of weddings and deaths would trigger a burst of sales (taking into account bagged variant collector's editions, trading cards, hardback reprints and attendant merchandising) which would replace long-term decline with a massive gulp of earnings followed by a clean slate.

'For the next-but-one book, I'm bringing back Sergeant Grit and the Gorilla Guerillas. They've not been seen since 'Nam, so they're probably lazing on a beach in Mexico, whiskery old apes with huge beerguts, enormous mental problems and big Harley-Davidsons. Grit was indicted for a Zippo raid. The Nevergone Crisis is a big enough shake-up to get them back in action…'

He wanted to include every character in the ZC Universe, no matter how discontinued or ridiculous, in *The Nevergone Void*. Not just majors like Amazon Queen and the Streak, but all the heroes from all the decades: Teensy Teen, the Shrinking Cheerleader; Lance Lake P.I.; Captain Tomorrow, the Time Tornado; Lynxman; Blubber Boy; Morakk the Barbarian Champion; the Vindicator. And all the villains: Max Multiple, Circe, the Creech, Dead Thing, Mr Bones, Atomic Woman, Boss Bozworth, Headhunter. By the last page of Book Ten, Coastal City would be littered with costumed corpses. The hero of *The Nevergone Void* was Cary Trenton, the Streak's secret identity. Stripped of his powers and his memory, he would end up as the nebbish the world always thought he was. But he'd be alive, defiantly ordinary while all the superendowed show-offs went down in flames.

Timmy liked the Grit idea. He always liked it when a character nobody else remembered came out of retirement.

'Today, Grit would be picketed by animal rights bores,' Mickey said, thinking aloud. 'Tinkering with gorilla brains to make supersoldiers ain't eco-amicable.'

The bean counter had written a memo, and the memo had passed up the corporate pyramid. Ultimately, Mickey assumed, it had been brought to the desk of Derek Leech. Maybe this was the first time Leech realised he owned ZC, having picked the company up as pocket change during a corporate ceasefire agreement. Weighing the memo, Leech would make an instant decision and, discovering who Timmy Chin was, communicate his wish that a course of action be implemented. It was probable that Leech himself suggested Mickey Yeo as Hit Man.

It was hard not to think of *The Nevergone Void* as hack stuff, though he was aware of its historical importance. After this, Mickey wanted to do something serious. He had outlined a graphic novel about a rock singer's mental collapse. That was the project he was saving his arm for.

At the end of the meeting, Timmy tidied the proofs and scripts into a neat package and returned them.

Heather and Timmy took Mickey up to the fourteenth floor, where a luncheon reception was held in his honour. Comics creators bobbed between the canapes and wine, tongue-tied in his presence. Cardboard tombstones marked 'Amy McQueen' decorated the walls; at $5.99 apiece, the souvenirs had netted nearly $20,000 additional profit. Everyone in the room admired his work, but Mickey sensed a certain suspicion floating around.

After *The Nevergone Void*, all bets were off. The bread-and-butter heroes would be out of business and their titles wound up. ZC would have to start again. Exciting projects were in the offing but Mickey guessed a lot of these time-servers, men in early middle-age who'd devoted whole lives to the Vindicator or Dead Thing, would be scrabbling for jobs as commercial artists.

Heather stood close by, making introductions, asking

questions. She was expert at keeping him well-stroked. Often, as she steered someone his way, she would touch his shoulder as he stuck out his hand to be shaken.

An inker, slightly drunk, told him he'd had to break the news to his daughter that his employers were killing off her favourite, Amazon Queen. The kid cried for a week and had nightmares.

'It's not like she was fuckin' real,' Mickey protested. 'Buy your brat a life.'

Heather repelled the inker and he drifted away. If she sensed Mickey was bored, she'd manipulate a change, dismissing a dull person and hauling over a more interesting one. ZC's letters editor told him more readers of both sexes wrote in unprintable communications about him than any other writer-artist, either making athletic sexual propositions or suggesting unhealthy and probably impossible courses of obscene action.

On the nineteenth floor, Heather left him with Dick Karsch, East Coast VP of Real Records. The tape Mickey had made of his *Choke Hold* score had been market-tested and Dick gave the go-ahead to devote serious resources to his rock opera. A cantata about the Boston Strangler, it would be performed by an all-star cast on the video album. Real was talking with Tom Waits' people about the role of Albert DeSalvo. If the product received the predicted positive reception, it would be readied as an off-Broadway show. Mickey promised to design the stage production and at least take a hand in the direction, but he was really holding out to direct the video album, itself a dry-run for an eventual megabudget movie. *City Hammer* – which he'd directed bits of – was fine as far as it went (a video store near you), but he wanted a summer picture next time out, something that would play in Peoria.

'I have a money feeling about this,' said Dick.

On the thirty-second floor, Mickey and Dick met with Eivol Manoogian, a development exec with Pyramid. The *Choke Hold* project had been a movie idea from the outset and Manoogian was its sponsor on the West Coast. Dick made his report and the exec nodded benignly, eyes never leaving Mickey's. Heather stood decoratively in the corner, hugging the spreadsheets.

'I saw Tamsin in London and she didn't say no,' Mickey revealed.

Dick and Eivol became as excited as little boys.

On the forty-seventh floor, Mickey had supper in the revolving restaurant. Still unhappy with anything that wasn't egg and chips, he allowed Heather to select his fare, which was unidentifiable but exciting. She talked to the waiter in French. After a glass and a half of wine, he had heard her autobiography, which was as concise and linear as a studio hand-out. She was twenty-three, a college graduate in physics, had had five serious lovers, was currently in a 'just broken-up' phase, made $45,000 a year as an all-purpose minion, and was preparing for publication a slim book of poems on the subject of 'what it means to be human'.

He told her he'd be interested in reading her poetry. For a microsecond, her poise cracked and she was almost embarrassed. At that very moment, he *was* interested in reading her poetry, if only because it seemed so very unlikely. Then the diamond chips were back in her eyes, and she began to ask subtly flattering questions, drawing him out about his work. As he explained for the quadrillionth time that graphic novels really needed to get rid of their childish image, he knew that it was impossible, given the amount of research she had obviously done on him, that she wasn't as fed up with his line as he was. Her little nods of interest and encouraging smiles suggested she'd taken a course in professional flirting. Impossible as it might seem, this woman was real.

* * *

As they emerged from the elevator in the lobby, the WoFBReIGN squaws hissed at Mickey like angry cats. Someone had told them who he was, or else ZC's publicity department had finally done their job and made his face famous. He gave a friendly wave and was aware Heather had taken a position between him and the protesters. She'd mentioned that she had some martial arts training, and he realised she was, among all other things, his bodyguard.

One of the women scooped up a handful of dirt from a plantpot and flung it at him. He blinked, expecting to be struck in the face, but Heather reached out like an expert and made a fist around the clod. She dropped the squeezed missile and had a tissue in her palm in an instant. As they left the building, he whistled.

'Nice catch,' he said.

'I grew up in the Little League,' she said.

'What are you fuckin' looking at, pissbrain?'

The waiter was shocked out of his deference. Mickey, scenting blood, stood up, fists made.

'I said what are you looking at?'

'Sir, I...'

Heather sat quietly, tinkering with her last lychee, Bitch Goddess of Pudenda. She wore an evening number that had been a distraction throughout three courses. Timmy Chin, having brought them to a restaurant where he was known, flushed scarlet. The Incredible Reddening Editor: in a second, he turns into an embarrassed nerd.

'Are you looking at my sister's tits?'

Of course, the gook had been leaning over Heather's cleavage to pour the wine. And, of course, his glance had been drawn into the deep, speckled valley. Just because he had a white jacket and a dicky-bow didn't mean he'd had his bollocks disconnected.

There was no programmed response in his professional

vocabulary. This had never come up before. The waiter was six inches taller than Mickey, which meant nothing.

Waving a misleading fist at the gook's face, Mickey kneed him in the goolies, biting down on a satisfying squelch. The old magic was still there. It was the move that had put Keith Lanier on the floor in 1977.

A managerial figure hurried over. Big Eyes was bent double, coughing.

'Maurice,' Mickey shouted, having no idea what the newcomer's name was, 'have this dirty beggar dismissed instantly.'

The manager – who looked like a Maurice – skidded to a halt and looked cold into Mickey's eyes, understanding at once.

'Certainly, sir. My profound apologies.'

'Just make sure it don't fuckin' happen again.'

'Of course, sir.'

Maurice helped the waiter away, doubtless totting up the wages owed.

Mickey felt at peak condition. Heather was unfazed, and even Timmy was losing his glow.

'I could do with another helping of pud,' Mickey announced.

8 JANUARY, 1993

The next morning, sunlight pouring through the glass ceiling, Mickey dived under the silk sheets of the circular waterbed, rooting around extensively.

'What are you looking for?' she asked.

'My brains,' he said.

She was poised, head up on one hand, an arm resting to emphasise the long curve from her shoulder to her hip to her ankle.

'Why?'

'You fucked them out last night, Heth.'

Not laughing, she reached and pulled him close, her fingers climbing the ladders of his ribs. She rolled him over on his back and pressed him to the bed. Taking a fresh complimentary condom from the bedside stand, she expertly fitted it.

He looked up as she settled comfortably. She bit her underlip as she engulfed his sheathed erection. Her hair fell perfectly in place as if it were a nylon wig. A golden penumbra haloed her head. When he reached and touched fingertips to her unsupported breasts, she shivered musically. She stroked his braids gently, and made a fist around them, holding his head against a pillow. She pulled enough to give him the delicate beginnings of pain.

'Go ahead, Heth,' he said. 'I'm in your power.'

11

1978-82

Sutton Mallet sat in their memories, unstirring under settling snows. They made no conscious effort to ignore the Deal for ten and a half months of the year but were busy with increasingly challenging, complicated lives.

Mark completed a BA in English and American Studies in 1981, having spent 1979–80 at the University of California in Santa Cruz. In his first year, he started selling pieces to *The New Statesman*, the *New Musical Express* and the *Guardian*. Editors did not realise he was still a student. He directed a student production of *Antigone*, which was a hot ticket at the 1978 Edinburgh Festival. At UCSC (Uncle Charlie's Summer Camp) he wrote a draft of *The Shape of the Now*, a cross-disciplinary study extrapolating from culture and fashion to politics and philosophy. By the time he got his first, he had sold the book to Real Press, where Pippa was now a junior editorial assistant. He learned his way around TV and radio. He drew praise from A.N. and Colin Wilson, and would not have been surprised to be commended by Harold, Jackie and Woodrow. Articles about him were no longer obliged to mention in the first paragraph that he was twenty-one. His parents were proud and puzzled.

Michael did not retake his Cambridge Entrance Examination.

Abandoning *Julie Bee*, he wrote 'Sutton Mallet', a story which took first prize in a *Sunday Argus* competition. On the strength of that, he secured a commission for a book of short stories and left the Backwater for London. The BBC broadcast *Paddy's Will*, his first TV play, in a New Writers' slot in 1980. He combined the half-hour script with two other one-acters for a stage version that was a modest success at the Theatre Upstairs. That year, ITV hired him to do a regular editorial rant on *I Scream*, a late-night freeform programme hailed as an epochal disaster. Singled out from whipped-cream fights and nude rock groups as a redeeming aspect, Michael pinballed from show to show, guesting on celebrity quiz programmes, filling in for older presenters. Officially alternative, one of a generation of angry comics willing to break taste barriers, he was the first man to call a serving cabinet minister a 'snivelling coprophile' to his face on British TV.

Mickey stayed at Art School for a year but was unable to complete his course due to professional commitments. His first sales were album covers, but his name became known when *Krazy Glue*, a fanzine strip, was repackaged by an alternative press. Described as 'a punk Andy Capp', Krazy spun off a merchandising blitz of T-shirts, badges and tattoo transfers. In 1979, Mickey designed and co-directed one of the first rock promos, for a band, The Wankers, who broke up even before their single came out. The next year he self-published a one-shot *British Comic*, interleaving panels of 'Violent War' and 'Mindless Football'. Noticed and well-reviewed in the mainstream, *British Comic* led to offers from overground comics. Turning down an open contract to create a strip for *2000 AD*, he freelanced for ZC, inking an unsuccessful but critically-acclaimed run of *Blubber Boy*. Though he gave interviews condemning the London-centred media and upholding the gritty roughness of life in the provinces, he used money from a never-never film option on *British Comic* to buy a subterranean flat in Camden Town.

All three were listed in a 1981 *Argus* article as Faces of the eighties. They appeared together on television, interviewed by Melvyn Bragg about the coming decade. Even Bragg noticed how pleased the Quorum seemed to be with themselves.

The Pyramid rose in Docklands in an eerie silence, an efficient workforce trooping through pickets every morning to render Constant Drache's radical designs in steel and glass. Derek Leech's face became familiar but few people were interested in him. As the Empire grew, people instinctively flinched from looking too closely into his business. Other magnates were exposed by unauthorised biographies, lampooned by comedians, traduced by ex-wives, investigated by parliamentary committees – but Leech was untouchable. In 1981, with no disrespect to the Queen, he turned down a knighthood. Having consolidated UK interests, he went international. By signing cheques, he had become the publisher of prize-winning books, a backer of box-office hits, proprietor of papers read by 22 per cent of the world's literate population, confidant of heads of state, owner of famous sporting events and teams, mastermind of the most-watched soaps. He supported British foreign policy with thundering headlines and gave ostentatiously to famine charities. He opened union negotiations by offering unprecedented wage increases, claiming to be interested 'in making money not keeping it'. If the eighties were going to be the wild party, Mark Amphlett predicted in *The Shape of the Now*, Derek Leech was the host.

In early 1979, Neil was estranged from his parents: through a never-fathomed misunderstanding, it was thought he had forged cheques in his father's name. In early 1980, while Neil was living with hippies in a cottage in Achelzoy, the only copy of *The Seventies*, his nearly finished novel, was accidentally burned. He abandoned the project and never really tried to write anything again. In early 1981, Neil lost a job at the Arts Centre after a Valentine's rock gig he organised turned into an all-night riot. In early 1982, a reconciliation with his family collapsed when his mother discovered enough heroin in his room to suggest he was dealing. Refused entry to his home, he was told by a friend of his father's that it would be best if he left the Backwater for pastures new.

In 1983, Mickey was the Ring. Michael turned up in Camden Town on New Year's Day for the Meet. Mark, away in Scotland with Pippa, sent wine and apologies. There was no Quorum. Uneasily, Michael and Mickey talked small, edging around the Deal. They had all achieved so much. It was hard to believe they were successful *solely* because Neil was not. Mark obviously was not going to play any more. Without even discussing it, they agreed there would be no moves this year.

'He's on his own,' Michael said of Neil.

'And so are we,' Mickey added.

12

8 JANUARY, 1993

'I had a bad time at university,' Neil admitted. 'Didn't last two terms. It wasn't the work, I just wasn't ready to be on my own. There was weirdness too. It was a crazy spell, the start of the crazy spells. The girl in the next room had an episode. She developed a fixation on me.'

Sally gave an interested look, drawing him out.

'Not *that* kind of fixation,' he smiled. 'That, I could have handled. Believe me. It was a delusional thing. This girl, Rachael, got the idea I was persecuting her. Yeah, me. It was the seventies, drugs all over: just say yummy, you know? One night, she popped her toast and attacked me. It was this insane frenzy. She wrecked the room, screaming abuse at me. It was surreal. For a moment, I thought she was going to shove a pair of scissors into my throat. And she never let up. After that night, it went on for weeks. She got her friends to join in. Would you believe it, they sabotaged my typewriter? And there were other "accidents". She's press secretary for the Greens these days. Rachael Rosen.'

She sipped orange juice. They were in the Tin Woodsman, the pub opposite Planet Janet. She still doubted this was a good idea but had learned more in five minutes of chat than days of walking ridiculously up and down Cranley Gardens. In her bag on the table, a cassette was recording.

'After it got really bad, I walked. At the end of the spring term, we had a takeaway exam. I couldn't make sense of the questions so I went home without saying anything to anyone. There wasn't anyone to say anything to. My parents went spare. All that education gone to waste. God, it was fifteen years ago. I got a part-time job as a hospital porter, but that didn't last.'

He talked about his disasters as if they'd happened to someone else. Probably a denial process, off-loading blame onto external forces.

'I have a degree in child psychology,' said Sally. 'It hasn't done me much good. I left university to be a receptionist.'

Neil shook his head and looked at his empty glass. 'What do you do now?' he asked.

She avoided the question. 'Can I get you another?'

Embarrassed, he patted empty pockets. 'I'd spring for a round, but...'

'It's okay. I'm earning.'

After the briefest hesitation, he accepted a second drink. She got him another pint.

'I need this,' he said, hefting bitter. 'So far, this year has been a nightmare. If I had an income, I'd become an alcoholic.'

Having established that Neil was doing a fill-in day at the Planet, she set up opposite the shop to watch comings and goings. Knowing he'd stay put, she found a phone box and called Ayesha McPherson.

'Not much tale to tell,' she explained. 'I'll have it typed up and fax it later. Gary Gaunt is a twenty-two-year-old trainee reporter. He does book reviews and obits for the *Basildon Echo*, the occasional flower show or 100th birthday. He's a recent graduate in journalism, lives with his parents, straight, but no girlfriend, in good health. White, five-six, slight build. You'd say no distinguishing marks except he's sort of an albino, dead white hair, pinky eyes.'

She was thanked and told a cheque would be in the post. From Michael Dixon's assistant, Sally believed it. Ayesha said Michael might want her to proceed further.

'I don't think there's any further to proceed, unless Mr Dixon has anything specific he wants to know.'

A familiar long dark shape slid past.

On impulse, Sally asked, 'Does a big black car ring bells? A Rolls, but some sort of customised model?'

Ayesha, puzzled, said she couldn't think.

'Just a long shot,' Sally said, watching SHADE 001 dawdle at traffic lights. She imagined the machine growling.

Ayesha said they'd be in touch, and hung up.

So long as no one was queuing, Sally stayed in the box, receiver to her ear, mouthing song lyrics. Watching SHADE 001 slip towards Finchley, she realised why it was familiar: it was a Shadowshark, like the one Dr Shade drove in the newspaper strip. Considering the vanity plate, she guessed the driver must be a fanatical fan. Someone rich enough to have Rolls-Royce make a vehicle to order. As a kid, she'd wanted an Amazon Queen Atom Chariot until she found out the car Mary Ann Mobley drove in the TV series couldn't actually do more than thirty miles per hour. Did the Shadowshark's owner wear a black hat and cape and infra-red goggles, and carry a brace of silver-plated automatics?

Whoever the Dr Shade wannabe was, she bet he was a constant customer at Planet Janet. She looked across the road at the shop. There was a vampire display in the window. A snarling cutout Dracula loomed over a selection of fanged books, videos and comics. Neil's head could just be seen among bobbing rubber bats. It must be a relief not to be stuck in his windowless basement.

Why were Michael Dixon and Mark Amphlett interested in nobodies? A reversal of the Mark Chapman/John Hinckley syndrome? Celebrities obsessed with failures.

It's the latest 'in' craze among the power people, Mummikins. Adopt a nonentity.

A pensioner struggled up the Archway Road towards the phone box. Sally vacated her shelter stepping into blasting winds. The thick scarf she wrapped around her lower face was damp with condensed breath. This sort of job was less unpleasant in June. The Gary Gaunt commission was more comfortable: she'd telephoned him at the *Echo* with a bogus market research questionnaire, getting his personal details as if filling in a form, then asking him what films he'd seen in the last month. He liked *Reservoir Dogs* but wondered why he'd wasted money on *Chaplin*. They chatted for twenty minutes and he tried to impress her with expressions like 'genre' and 'biopic'. By contrast, this was cold and frustrating. She wouldn't count the day a success unless she learned something new. Hanging around purposelessly in sub-zero temperatures was not efficient information-gathering.

Well aware this was a bad precedent, she decided to talk to Neil. Stepping off the kerb to cross the road was like stepping off a bridge.

On the Friday morning, the Planet was underpopulated. Neil was at the front till, chin in his hands, looking disconsolately at a lopsided bat. The young man who'd been the Riddler at Dolar's party was at a desk at the back of the shop, available to field any enquiries. A tiny girl with purple lipstick and filed teeth was three chapters into a hardback vampire novel she wasn't going to buy. A thin-moustached man lurked in the 'adults only' section, breathing heavily on the shrinkwrappers of French *bandes dessinées*.

The Riddler spotted her and waved familiarly, eyes betraying fuzziness about who exactly she was. He had the kind of memory which retained the identity of a special guest villain in the July 1957 issue of *Dazzling Duo Stories*, but was unable to summon the names of real people he'd met last week.

'Neil,' she said, suddenly nervous. 'Hi.'

He looked up, long face blank. His bruise was mostly gone but half his face still didn't match. She realised he'd been dozing.

'Sally, remember? Sally Rhodes? From New Year's Eve? Sigh, my hero?'

He flinched like a dog who assumes any human will beat it, but tried a smile. She guessed from the red in his eyes he'd had a bad night.

'Olive Oyl?'

'How are you feeling?'

He looked briefly up to heaven and made a sad-funny face. 'You don't want to know.'

She shrugged in sympathy. 'I can imagine.'

'Actually, I don't think you can.'

'Try me.'

'You'd think I was the Ancient Mariner. It's a long story. I'm under a curse.'

Not wanting to push it, she pretended to look around. Paperbacks were displayed in separate shelves for science fiction, horror, fantasy, true crime and 'slipstream'; comics were in their own racks. Planet Janet had sections for film stills, posters, hobby kits (*why would anyone want an eighteen-inch Pumpkinhead for £99.99, Mummy?*) and videos.

'What's hot?' she asked the Riddler.

Choke Hold, he said. 'Best graphic novel of the nineties.'

She picked one from a stack on a table. It was a hardback comic like the *TinTin* adventures she read as a child, only five times the price. The writer-artist was Mickey Yeo.

'He did a signing here,' the Riddler added. 'The man's a saint.'

Mickey Yeo was the missing corner of the square. If she met him, she'd have the whole set. She opened *Choke Hold* at random. The pages were fully painted and scratchy, broken into designs less like panel grids, more like cracked mirrors. Mad-eyed people with wild hair throttled each other, ravings scuttling in jagged spaces between the pictures.

'It's about the Boston Strangler,' the Riddler told her. 'Mickey's doing it as a rock opera next.'

Charming. What's the sequel, The Dennis Nilsen Book of Plumbing Tips?

On one page the Strangler, face a crosshatched blotch as if the artist tried to obliterate it, wound a rope around the long neck of a male victim. The purple and red face, with wide eyes and bulging tongue, looked vaguely like Neil.

'There's something sick here,' she said aloud.

'It's not for kids,' the Riddler said. 'It's for adults.'

'I'm not sure adults can handle this stuff,' she said. 'Kids are tougher. Do you have any Hergé?'

Brightening, the Riddler pointed. She decided to buy *The Crab With the Golden Claws* and *The Cigar of the Pharaohs.* Next year, when sentience set in, she'd share them with the Invader. She paid for the *TinTin* books and asked Neil if he'd been back to the hospital. He tried not to answer, a child not wanting to discuss undone homework or uneaten greens.

'You should look after yourself,' she said. 'No one else will.'

'If I'm patched up, I'll only get broken again.'

She could believe that.

After a pause, he said, 'But thank you for getting me to Casualty. I probably didn't say that then. I was, um, ah, you know... incapable?'

He'd just groaned as she steered him home. She was mildly surprised he remembered her.

'You owe me your life, you know,' she said.

He was sheepish, furtive. He didn't seem comfortable talking with people. Or was it just with women?

The Riddler announced it was Neil's lunch hour and came to take over the till.

'I'm going for a drink over the road,' she said, 'want to come?'

* * *

'When I say it's a curse, it's just bad luck,' he said, explaining to himself as much as to her. 'A *phenomenal* run of bad luck. You'd find it hard to believe so many catastrophes could happen to one man in one life. If the rain's gonna fall, it'll fall on me. If the cat's gonna piss, it'll piss on me.'

Strangely, he wasn't bitter, just puzzled. She thought he'd be disappointed to win a lottery. If things were uniformly terrible, his life made some sense.

'Jobs, relationships, houses, anything. I'm a disaster area, me. Those New Year's Eve guys, at least they didn't bullshit before putting the boot in. It was over with quickly, you know. Usually, I get a month or so of unrealistic expectations before anyone buys a knife and works out where my back is.'

She kept quiet. Did her professional commitment to Mark Amphlett and Michael Dixon count as a betrayal of Neil's trust?

'When I first came to London, '81 or '82, there were a couple of months when things almost fell in place. I was working on a magazine. Not much money, but interesting. There was an American girl, Anne. Then, somehow, I lost it…'

As he talked, she studied his face: under the last of his bruising and the tiredness around his eyes, he was still youthful, unformed. All marks on him were temporary, as if his life had never really begun. She felt like telling him to wash his face and get back in the trenches, but, from the dossier she'd compiled, she knew he was more likely to sit here with a pint someone bought for him until he switched from supplementary benefit to state pension.

'Bad things happen to me,' he said. 'If I had talent I could be the greatest blues singer ever to come out of North London.'

'You're too funny to sing the blues. Face it, you just aren't miserable enough.'

'Nope. Not miserable. Just numb.'

His glass was empty and she didn't think buying him another pint was a good idea. If he turned up drunk at the Planet and lost his part-time job, it'd be her fault. As an investigator she subscribed to the Prime Directive non-interference in native cultures. It was her business to report on subjects, not change their lives.

The barman, telephone held to his chest, shouted out, 'Is there a Neil Martin here?'

Neil looked up, surprised.

'Phone call,' the barman said. 'Don't make it a habit.'

From her observations, she knew Neil always had a pub lunch in the Tin Woodsman when he worked in the Planet. She'd noted it in her report last year. But he seemed to think he was difficult to find.

He went to the bar and took the receiver listening intently.

She checked her cassette recorder. It was still running, near the end of a side. She turned the cassette over. After six weeks, she'd be qualified to write *Neil Martin: A Biography of a Nobody.* Maybe that should be subtitled *Bad Things Happen to Me?* It would be a relief to get back to tracing runaway kids and loitering in Boots to deter shoplifters.

Her eye caught by a movement, she looked across the pub. A man in a wide-brimmed black hat and a long black coat was slipping into the Gents, like an angular shadow. The last scrap of his darkness whipped beyond the slamming door. Perhaps it wasn't a coat but a cloak, trailing the floor. A sinister touch.

Shaking his head, Neil came back to the table.

'Anything important?' she asked.

He shrugged. 'Just another Nazi Death Threat.'

She laughed.

'No, seriously. An NF splinter group called the English Liberation Front want to kill me. I think it's a computer error. They've mixed me up with someone who gives a shit.'

He sat down, looking fed up.

'I might know people who could do something about that,' she said.

She still had at least three friends on the police and had shared witness protection with rent-a-muscle from the big agencies. Maybe she could call in favours.

'Best if you stay out of it. People around me run the risk of sustaining severe mental damage.'

'That's an odd way of putting it.'

'No, really. People I know have a habit of cracking up. They discover fiendish malevolence inside them. They become Norwegian Neil Cullers. No matter how big and wet my pleading eyes are, they like nothing better than applying that big old club to the back of my head and seeing what colour my brains are as they squirt out of my nostrils. I don't mean you, of course. Honestly. But it's best to stay safe.'

He looked around the pub. There were a few other late lunch drinkers.

'No one looks an obvious Fascist,' she said.

'Undercover Nazi Zombies. They're the worst kind.'

She looked at her watch. Sonja was supposed to go off duty at two.

'Curses,' she said, gathering her bags and scarf. 'My child minder will kill me.'

He looked at her again, or perhaps for the first time. 'You need a child minder?'

'For a child, funnily enough.'

'You have a child?'

'Obviously. Eighteen monthish. Unplanned. Terribly sweet. Half an orphan. *Don't* ask about the father.'

'I wasn't going to,' he said, worried.

'I bombed a building for him,' she said, knowing he wouldn't take her seriously.

His eyes became guarded, as if she were turning into a Norwegian Neil Culler.

'Don't worry. My arson days are over.'

'I'm relieved to hear it.'

Good. That was the sticky part of any relationship over. Explaining about the Invader had become a chore. She understood Neil's half-ashamed, eager-tentative recital of his lifelong losing streak. After you piled the fifth tragedy onto the others, everything started to come out farce.

'Anyway, must dash,' she said. 'See you around, Neil.'

Dazed, he replied 'See you'.

She left him with his empty glass and, unaccountably excited to have got so much out of the way, hurried off up Muswell Hill Road. It was strange to pass in mundane daylight the spot where the louts beat Neil up. As she passed the last 100 yards to the flat and Sonja and the Invader, she felt a slight stitch. Without really knowing anything new, she felt she had a mental grip on the commission.

13

1983

Mark had skipped the Meet as an experiment. It was their last and only act of rebellion. Despite everything, he was proud he'd been the one to test the Deal, the control subject who exposed himself to the plague *without* taking a miracle cure, proving the drug worked by his horrible death.

In 1983, late on the evening of February the 15th, Mark and Pippa were involved in a road accident on Oxford Street. The incident was entirely the fault of a swerving taxi, but Mark was breathalysed and found to be over the blood-alcohol limit. The taxi driver was beyond reach with brain damage and his insurance company refused to compensate Mark because of the drunk-driving conviction. Pippa's neck was scarred and she had seven operations, which left a quarter of her face nerveless. Mark slipped an intravertebral disc and spent months in and out of hospital. Each time the problem seemed to clear up, further complications were discovered. Impatient with the National Health, both opted for private medical care, which left them teetering near bankruptcy. Pippa lost her job and Mark was unable to fulfil a commitment to a series of TV lectures based on *The Shape of the Now*. Sometimes Mark would visit the institutionalised taxi driver and look into his empty eyes, wondering...

In 1983, Michael finally cleared his decks of chat shows and personal appearances and took four months off, turning down all TV offers to write his long-delayed first novel, a comic nightmare of the near future entitled *A to Z*. After a month of planning and researching, he began writing on February the 1st. He turned out precisely ten pages of prose a day. It was the easiest task he'd ever set himself, like copying something already finished and perfect. On page 151, the book stopped coming. Months passed in a blur; he began every morning by typing 'Chapter 16' and 'page 151' on a fresh sheet of paper and sat for up to seven hours, mentally paralysed, straining for the lost flow. Just as he thought he saw the glimmer of a way past page 151, he was struck with severe piles, a condition far more painful and entirely less hilarious than he'd always imagined. By the time the golfballs of agony ringing his rectum subsided, *A to Z* seemed the work of a stranger. He filed the manuscript in a fire and called his agent so many times the poor woman started to have her assistant allege she was in a meeting at all hours of the day.

In 1983, Mickey tired of spending a week every year adding up figures scrawled on the backs of old envelopes and hired an accountant. A preliminary audit showed irregularities in his income tax returns over the last four years and the government dunned him. An investigation left him liable for tax on monies never received from the merchandising of Krazy Glue, his character. Hunt Sealey, the alternative publisher who'd brought the strip to wider attention, turned out to have an extremely alternative system of bookkeeping, which involved keeping money warm in his personal account and pleading poverty whenever anyone asked him about it. Exorbitant lawyers embroiled Sealey and Mickey in a tangled suit over the question of who precisely owned which rights. The legal wars sapped Mickey's energies and prevented him from meeting a deadline on what would have been a groundbreaking series for ZC, plunging him into career limbo just as Alan Moore and Frank Miller Jr were getting widespread media recognition and everyone started to take comics as seriously as Mickey always said they should. Missing out the kudos that should have been his, he watched others take his ideas and make industries of them. Krazy had a major resurgence when Sealey had other people write and draw the strip. He flooded the market and slapped an injunction on Mickey that he desist from further exploiting his own creation.

It was a cold, unreal year. The Derek Leech International building opened in September. Fleet Street, Wardour Street and Bloomsbury offices closed and companies were removed to a wasteland beyond the river. Late in autumn, after coming out of hospital for the fourth time, Mark ran into Mickey at a book launch. Mickey punched him in the face but was dissuaded from further battering his friend when Mark reminded him, 'You need me next year.' *Private Eye* ran a humorous item about the altercation. Delirious from anal pain and shifting constantly in his seat, Michael spent a weekend motoring around Somerset in search of Sutton Mallet, finding a few signposts but no trace of the village. Several times, he thought himself on the right road only to be disappointed as he drove into Shepton Mallet. Throughout, the Quorum tried to arrange appointments with their sponsor but were unable to penetrate the barrier of personal assistants and vice-presidents surrounding Derek Leech.

By the end of 1983, Neil was more settled than he'd been since school. Moving to London, he'd fallen in with a crowd who were putting out *The Scam*, a fortnightly alternative listings magazine. First, he hung around hellish offices in Holborn doing odd jobs, making bad coffee, running messages, writing picture captions. After proving himself willing by reviewing films and records nobody else wanted to (he became the only person he knew who had seen the sequels to *Porky's* and *Friday the 13th* but not the originals), he began to get journalistic assignments, interviewing

Hackney councillors, following up police cases, profiling indie bands. He also started seeing Anne Nielson, the spiky American news editor of *The Scam*. She was, he realised, the first woman he'd slept with more than five times. Anne had her own problems – an incomprehensible transatlantic family history that matched his catalogue of fluke horrors – but she was funny, tough and surprising. She taught him a bit about writing, patiently going through his copy with a vicious pencil, showing him which priceless words he could do without. They talked about moving in together in the new year but as it was they lived more in the office than in their flats.

It was as if his Wilderness Period was over. For the first time since the Forum broke up, Neil actually enjoyed Christmas. 1984, that science fiction year, arrived.

14

In the first years of *The Shape*, no one left before eight o'clock. When money was tight, everyone pitched in and worked through amphetamine nights. Now, at six on Friday, he was alone in his Inner Sanctum. The outer offices held untenanted quiet. Having Macbethed his way to a swivel-throne, his reward was not guilty madness but a featureless plateau of achievement. Once the moves were out of the way, he'd headhunt a managing editor for the magazine and move on to other projects. Cloud 9 wanted him to produce a documentary about electronic art and he was increasingly taken with the possibilities of INT. He should write another book; a follow-up to *The Shape of the Now* for the Millennium, *The Strength of the Soon*.

Just after six, as she'd done every night since their meeting, Sally Rhodes telephoned to give a preliminary report of her day's work. He put her on the speaker.

'Sally, good evening.'

'Mark, hi. Nothing much new today. I had a drink with Neil at lunchtime.'

He thought about that.

'Good. Excellent initiative.' He leaned back in his chair, imagining Sally in the dark beyond his desklamp's circle of light.

'A name came up. A neo-Nazi group, the ELF. I've hit the press cuttings on them. English Liberation Front. The usual disappointed imperialists and racist skins. They have it in for Neil.'

'Oh?'

'A petty *führer* doorstepped him and was rubbed the wrong way. They've got intelligence on him. They phoned a threat to the pub. It might be serious.'

Michael was stirring that particular pot. Mark assumed any information on Neil funnelled to the ELF came from him.

'Do you want me to find out more? I can call in police favours. They'll have criminal records.'

He hoped Michael was nippy enough to keep out of her way. She could be paid for but not bought. If she went native, she could be a mighty inconvenience.

'Hang fire on that for the moment. If the ELF do anything active, we'll reconsider. In the meantime, concentrate on Neil.'

'Okay.'

Where was she? In a call-box or her flat? He couldn't hear any background noise.

'The other thing is I keep running into Dr Shade.'

'The cartoon character?'

'Yes. Him, or someone who has his car. A Rolls-Royce Shadowshark. Very nifty.'

'Weird,' he commented, suppressing an unbidden shiver.

'Registration SHADE 001. I'm not sure if it's dogging Neil, following me or just cruising Muswell Hill and Highgate. There was a guy in the pub dressed all in black, with a Dr Shade hat. And a couple of Dr Shades at that New Year's party.'

He thought about Dr Shade. A comics connection sounded like Mickey.

'How is Neil bearing up, by the way?' he asked.

'Bearing up?'

'His general attitude? What is it?'

'Hard to say. He describes himself as "numb". I think he

enjoys being gloomy. Like Eeyore.'

'Eeyore?'

'From *Winnie the Pooh*.'

'Of course. The donkey.'

He imagined her holding her breath before slipping in the question bothering her.

'Is there anything I should know?' she asked. 'About Neil?'

'He's not dangerous.'

'No, it's not that. If there's danger, I think Neil is in it.'

She was a conscientious footsoldier, which might be a problem. The more she applied herself, the more likely she was to question. Michael and Mickey preferred stupider tools, but he thought the challenge was precisely to use intelligent people. It was a question of balancing risk and reward.

'Mark, what am I? A spy or a bodyguard?'

He was careful. 'I have no personal feelings against Neil. He is important to me. He wouldn't thank me for taking an interest, but I believe his welfare is my responsibility.'

'Yours.'

'Mine. Ours. You have a past. Everybody does. You must have unfinished business?'

She didn't answer that. He remembered her face. He imagined she was more striking now, with slight hollows in her cheeks, than she'd been when younger and plumper.

'Sally, what do you think of him? Neil?'

A pause. 'I like him. He's funny.'

'Interesting choice of adjective.'

Funny? Michael and Mickey were the funny ones. Mark, as always, was serious.

'But you like him?'

'Yes,' she said. 'He's… ah… he's a survivor.'

Pippa had said he was funny too, the one time they had met. Twelfth Night, 1978. With a cold chill, Mark remembered Sutton Mallet.

'Do you think… um… women would find him attractive?'

'I'm a woman.'

'Yes.'

She spoke rapidly. 'It would depend. That's not something I can really report on. I, ah, well… I don't have much judgement with men.'

'Sally, do you like *me*?'

A pause. A long pause. 'Mark, you're a client.'

'Of course. I understand. I'm sorry. Scrub that.'

'Is there anything else?'

He tapped his teeth with his thumbnail.

'No,' he said, at last. 'Just keep up the good work. In case I haven't told you recently, we're pleased with you.'

'Thanks.'

'I'll talk with you tomorrow.'

'Tomorrow is Saturday.'

'You can reach me at my home number. Town, not country.'

'Fine.'

He cut her off before she could hang up. It was dark in the Inner Sanctum. He only had his desklight on. Through the window, he saw Soho people thronging to short-lived bistros, gaggling outside the jeweller's shops, shivering in fashionably unsuitable clothes.

Funny? Neil, funny?

He called home and got the machine. Pippa wasn't back from Scotland yet. He thought a moment, then didn't leave a message. He fiddled with his ring of office. Since he had been wearing it, his knuckle ached slightly. He hoped it wasn't the beginnings of arthritis or RSI. Pippa would be on a train, reading a manuscript. Sally would be fussing over her baby. Neil would be in his basement, alone.

This was a moment for the Quorum. As Ring, it was up to Mark to arrange the conference call. First he got through to Ayesha at the studio where Michael had just finished the technical rehearsal for tonight's show. He came on the line and banished his PA from the room. He said he was on a mobile phone in the scenery dock, surrounded by canvas castle walls. Then Mark made the call to Mickey's New York hotel. The switchboard put him through to the Apex Suite, where the phone was picked up by an American with a honey voice.

'One moment, please,' she said, summoning Mickey.

'Ta, Heth,' Mickey said, picking up. 'Go down and get me some fags, would you. Marko, Michael?'

'We have a Quorum,' Mark said. 'Are you free to talk?'

'Yeah yeah.'

'Zheah zheah.'

The cost of this call would exceed the total amount the Quorum spent on their moves in 1978. Money made things easier, but also encouraged a certain slackness Mark despised.

'Who was that?' Michael asked Mickey.

'I'll explain later. I think I'm in sex.'

Michael laughed. Mark called the Meet to order.

'Mickey,' he said. 'What can you tell us about Dr Shade?'

Mark could tell Mickey was surprised by the question. 'My favourite British comics character. Guy named Moncrieff created him, using the name Rex Cash. A rip-off of The Shadow, but rougher, nastier. Popular in the thirties and during the War, then disappeared until our sponsor revived him in the *Argus*. Guy named Greg Daniels draws the strip now. What's this about?'

'Sally seems to be haunted by Dr Shade. His car keeps creeping around after her.'

'A Rolls-Royce Shadowshark?'

'Train spotter.'

'This is my fuckin' job, Marko. You're the one who wrote a 2,000 word essay on the centenary of the airbrush.'

'What does Ms Rhodes think of the penumbral interloper?' asked Michael.

'She hasn't really commented. She doesn't strike me as neurotic or paranoid.'

'I don't think Dr Shade is likely to give us any stick,' Mickey said. 'Derek Leech owns him too.'

'We are *not* owned by Derek Leech,' Mark said evenly.

'Tell him that,' Mickey muttered.

'We'd best just watch out then,' Michael said. 'What about the opening moves?'

'My judgement as Ring is the ELF thing seems most promising.'

Michael was pleased. He had nurtured the move in his usual style.

'They've started nagging Our Absent Friend. They phoned him in a pub, just to prove they could find him anywhere.'

'I followed up first contact with a fusillade of drunkenly abusive calls zhesterday. Our man there is a Stan Gull, staunch defender of white virtue.'

'Stan Gull?' Mark prompted, writing down the name. 'I'll have Sally get some background on him.'

'As far as the combatants are concerned, shots have been exchanged. It shouldn't be too difficult to contrive an escalation of the feud into a little war.'

'Nazis,' Mickey said, 'don't you just love 'em!'

'Actually, no,' Mark commented. 'I don't trust stupid people with rigid ideologies.'

'I can stage manage the ELF. Should I get on the shop floor? I could zhoin up with the *fascisti* and prod them towards anti-Neil *blitzkrieg*.'

Michael loved disguises. In the early days of the Deal, he'd delighted in moves which involved dressing up as a vagrant, a postman or a government inspector.

'Your face is too well-known now,' Mark said. 'False whiskers won't work.'

Michael muttered disappointment.

'If we need Nazis, we can buy some,' Mark reassured. 'What I'd like to establish during this Meet is exactly what our priorities are for this year.'

'To stick it to Neil-o, of course,' Mickey put in, voice crackly over the ocean.

'But to what end? As I see it, our options are to concentrate either on getting him kicked out of his flat or losing him his part-time job.'

'Better safe than sodomised,' Mickey said. 'Go for the double.'

Mark wasn't sure. 'Homeless and jobless.'

'And hunted by Nazis,' Michael added. 'Sounds creamy.'

'Take the money, open the box,' Mickey said.

Mark imagined Neil as a rat in a maze, pursued by terriers.

'Sally's been talking with Our Absent Friend. He's in a strange mood. Close to the edge.'

Mickey cackled like static. 'Give 'im a shove, then.'

'Have either of you ever considered how much the Deal depends on Neil?' Mark asked. 'We are happy because he is not, we are successful because he is not...'

Both lines were quiet.

'We all try, but Our Absent Friend fails,' Michael said. 'That's the Deal.'

'What would happen to us if Neil didn't try? Or if there were no Neil?'

'How do zhou mean?'

Michael would understand but Mickey wouldn't. Mark needed to share the thought.

'If Our Absent Friend were to snap, become hopelessly insane, do himself severe damage? Or walk under a bus? Or just sit down in a corner and never get up again? Where would we be without Neil?'

'Game over,' Mickey said. 'And we win, right? That's the Deal.'

'Is it?'

15

VALENTINE'S DAY, 1984

Outside, the skies darkened over Farringdon. Mickey sat at the bar of The Ironmill, stinging his mouth with brandy as if he were back at the Rat Centre a minute before curtain-up. Tonight, the show would have to kill 'em dead. This was the Quorum's most costly move to date. He'd put up the last of his cash, and the others had matched his £1,500. If the Deal was off forever, they were all on the road to the twentieth-century equivalent of debtor's prison anyway. They couldn't be *more* broke.

Regulars might be fucked off to find the pub closed to the public this evening. If anyone gave too much aggro Ken, the quiet lad on the door, was to let them in. The stage was set and staffed but extras wouldn't hurt. Arguments at the door would distract from the main event.

Mark was upstairs by a window, binoculars to his eyes, directing the move, finger on the intercom button, a phone within reach. Mickey reckoned Mark found the Deal a perfect substitute for chess.

He revolved his head, loosening the stiff neck he'd developed hunched over drafting tables. He was dressed to party: tight striped trousers, cowhide jacket with the collar up, black leather Confederate forage cap. He'd even programmed the juke box for the whole evening, non-stop fuck music. The Blues Brothers sang 'Do You Love Me (Now That I Can Dance)'.

Michael had found The Ironmill and hired the pub for the evening. The landlord thought it was a Valentine's party. Over the weekend, Mickey had made enough red crepe hearts to clog a tunnel of love. Footsoldiers, girls with ra-ra skirts and bobbling antennae, had spent a happy afternoon with the staplegun turning the dingy bar into a no-taste romantic's wet dream. They were pulling down fifty pounds each for the evening, with bonuses for rough stuff. He'd recruited the footsoldiers from his pool of shag-hags. They were pleased to be in on something, even if they didn't understand it.

He checked his Timex and slopped down the last of the brandy. The intercom behind the bar buzzed. The signal meant Mark could see Neil's cab in the street.

'Rock and roll,' he said.

Taking a deep breath, he stepped out of the pub into Sekforde Street. As he passed, Ken – an out-of-work actor Michael knew – clapped him on the shoulder and said 'break a leg'.

Neil, a huge art folder under his arm, was on the kerb telling the driver to wait. Mickey hadn't been face to face with him for three years. Neil had changed. From his posture, Mickey could tell he'd developed confidence. He could be drawn with a few pencil strokes, strong lines; the last time Mickey had seen Neil, he'd been floppy and angular, rubbed-out sketch-marks and scribbled stresses.

Mickey stomped along the pavement, eyes on his pointed silver boot-tips. According to intelligence they'd gathered over the last month, *The Scam* was throwing a party tonight to celebrate a year of publication. Because of that, the staff had worked over the weekend so the magazine could go to press on Tuesday evening rather than the crack of Wednesday dawn. Neil was delivering the completed boards (the typeset and laid-out pages of the magazine) to the printer's. His mission concluded, he'd hurry back to Holborn to canoodle with his yank girlie, Anne, and boogie on carefree into the night.

Neil turned to walk to the printer's door. For a moment, he blocked the pavement. Never before had they got so close during a move. This year was serious. At first, Mickey had thought of moves as practical jokes. He wasn't superstitious and the covert stuff was interesting and rewarding in itself. As someone who worked alone, it was a jolt to be with a creative team again. Michael was the one with faith in the Deal, Mark and Mickey went along to see what would happen. Even after Sutton Mallet – whatever had actually gone down that Twelfth Night – he couldn't seriously believe everything he'd made of his life depended on one old friend's perpetual misery. After 1983, he didn't know either way, but had to do something to get out from under. He'd tried everything else – even considered solo moves against Cunt Slimey – and this was his last ditch.

'Mickey,' Neil said. 'Good God, Mickey.'

Mickey stopped walking and looked up, letting out his breath. He grinned, heart racing.

'Neil,' he said. 'Jesus Fuck, Neil *Martin*! It's been…'

Neil shook his head, also grinning, goofily. 'Years, my man,' he said. 'Not since the seventies.'

'Shit on a shovel, but we got old quick.'

'Remember when Jacqui Edwardes got engaged to that twenty-five-year-old guy?'

Mickey did, with a twisting skewer of irritation that would make the rest of the evening a cool pleasure.

'Twenty-five was like a hundred. Now, here we are. Methuselated.'

Dazed to have it brought back, Neil was rooted to the spot. But his body remembered how important his mission was; he twitched sideways towards the printer's. Eugene Reilly (at £400, the second-highest-paid footsoldier of the night) picked up his cue and came out of the printer's. He'd been in the foyer, a bike messenger if anyone asked, ready for action.

'You from *The Scam*, mate?' Eugene asked.

Michael wanted to play the part of 'Man From the Printer's' himself, in a boiler suit and a wig, but the others overruled him. Eugene had been in one of Michael's stage productions but hadn't been on television enough for Neil to recognise him.

'I'm Neil,' Neil said.

'Got the boards?'

Neil held up his burden. 'Where's Joe?'

'Joe's nights,' Eugene said.

Neil handed over the art folder and Eugene held up a clipboard for his signature.

'This a drug deal or something?' Mickey asked, distracting Neil.

'I'm working for *The Scam*. You know, the fortnightly.'

'I've seen it.'

Eugene nipped back into the printer's. He was to wait until Mickey and Neil were in The Ironmill. Neil opened the door of the cab.

'Can I give you a lift anywhere?' he asked.

'I'm just up the road,' Mickey said, thumbing over his shoulder. 'On the piss. Fuck, you gotta stay. Know who I'm meeting? Michael. Michael Dixon, remember?'

Neil's eyes were creepily wide with delight.

'He'd never let me hear the last of it if I let you bugger off without dragging you in for a swift half.'

'Michael?'

'Yeah, Michael, man.'

'The Fat Git?'

'He's lost weight, pal. They call him the Trim Git now.'

Neil was still torn. Mickey had seen pictures of Anne Nielson, and could imagine the trim waiting for Neil at the party.

'What you got will wait,' he told Neil. 'How often do we get a chance to hang out?'

Neil let the cab go, paying the driver and picking up a receipt. They had him. Mickey led Neil to The Ironmill, keeping up a barrage of chat, asking questions to which he knew the answers, disgorging titbits of information. Neil knew roughly what Michael and Mickey were doing and had read *Krazy Glue*.

Ken, at his post by the door, let them in and they went to the bar. The footsoldiers had been sitting in silence waiting for the big entrance and only now started to rhubarb amongst themselves. It was impossible Neil wouldn't notice everyone was faking but he didn't. Mickey kept talking, and ordered two double whiskeys without consultation. Frank, the paid-for bartender provided generous shots. Mickey made sure Neil got the glass with the blue ring. They had debated LSD but decided in the end straight liquor was more effective. The trick was to ensure Mickey got the watered-to-near-innocuousness drinks while Neil downed at least a gallon of the hard stuff.

'Hell and Damnation,' Mickey said, tapping his shot on the bar and downing it in one. After a pause, Neil imitated him.

The hook was in the back of his throat and he was doing his best to swallow it. Neil even ordered refills before Mickey could suggest it. Frank poured.

They talked about their old shared interest, comics. Neil thought the term 'graphic novel' pretentious. Mickey would have agreed but for the marketing fact that a graphic novel sold for ten times as much as the flimsier items they used to call 'giant-size annuals' and thus brought in a much higher royalty for the same work. If you were hard-nosed enough to negotiate a royalty deal with the heart-eating scum who ran the industry.

Neil, into his third drink, started telling Mickey how much he'd like Anne. The shag-hags got rowdy, as pre-arranged. In a dancing space, they ground to soul music. The Ironmill got loud and smoky. In the Ladies, Mama Death, Mickey's dealer was cutting complimentary lines for the extras. Neil didn't note the odd bloke slipping in for a tampon.

'Look at that sweet stuff,' Mickey said, pointing to his favourite rent-a-slut, Ingrid Tell. Her jeans were frayed at knees and buttocks, her top didn't come down to her hip-slung belt. She threw herself about.

'Jailbait,' Neil commented. 'Besides, I'm a married man.'

'Nobody's that fuckin' married,' Mickey said.

Ingrid weaved from side to side, navel winking. She unstuck her sweaty top from her tits and, smiling, fanned air down into the valley. Mickey moaned and shook his head.

'Nipples like top hats.'

Frank lined up more drinks and said, 'Compliments of the lady.'

Mickey waved a thanks and Neil, after a lingering look, turned away.

'It's hot in here,' he said.

'Nahh, it's just cold outside.'

By now, Eugene would have done his business. He was supposed to leave a message with the printer's and then meet Steve, who was waiting by the phone box on the corner to pick up the boards. Eugene was off home to collect his Academy Award and wait for his career to pick up.

Ingrid was dancing with another girl to 'Shotgun', darting her tongue at her partner's nose.

'Both ways, man, fuckin' incredible,' Mickey said, nudging Neil.

Ingrid the Animal wasn't acting. Their best-paid footsoldier at £650, she'd probably do this for free. She hadn't asked for an explanation. The one time Mickey went back to her place to fuck, he'd been surprised to find a neat row of Penguin paperback Sartre on the shelf over her bed.

The intercom buzzed twice and Frank pretended to answer it. Mark was signalling that Eugene was through.

Michael came into the pub and overacted incredulous surprise. More drinks were provided. Neil, spluttering slightly, downed his in one again.

'Zh'know what we've got?' Michael said, eyes alight. 'A *quorum*!'

They all laughed and drank again. Neil moved away from the

bar to go to the toilet. As soon as he was unsupported, he began to sway and put his hand to his forehead.

'Oooh,' he said, 'I can feel that.'

He made it across the room to the Gents. When the door shut behind him, everyone stopped talking and looked to Mickey and Michael.

'Fine, everyone. Keep it up. Zhou're getting an extra tenner apiece.'

There was a boozy cheer.

'The switch at the printer's was perfect,' Mickey told Michael. 'I nearly shat my spinal column, but it was a dream.'

'He's far gone, isn't he?'

'You know Our Absent Friend. Remember when we were kids? How about the college rag day when he sat in the Blake Street Annexe trying to nut himself with a hammer? Guy shouldn't be allowed within a mile of alcohol.'

Neil came back from the bogs, noise picking up as he emerged. Another drink was ready for him.

'I should make this my last,' he said.

'Nonsense, my boy,' Michael said. 'This is *reunion*. Nothing takes precedence over us…'

'There's Anne,' Neil said. 'You could come to the *Scam* party. Anne would love to meet you.'

Mickey leaned out of Neil's eyeline and shook his head at Michael.

'One more libation here,' Michael said. 'Bartender, further liquid dynamite is required.'

Mickey was fed up with the thin taste of whiskied water, but started sipping his next shot as Neil gulped his. A gaggle of Michael's chorus boys, kitted as bikers, mingled with the shaghags, bumping and groping. A tall black guy with a gold earring stripped off his net shirt and started rolling oiled pecs about. He was a model, Mickey knew. Ingrid slithered against his chest and started playing with her own top.

'Get your tits out for the lads,' the pretend-bikers chanted. Ingrid flirted with the idea, chewing a strand of stray hair.

The intercom buzzed three times.

Mickey and Michael clunked glasses. Mark had just placed a telephone call to the *Scam* party, claiming to be from the printer's and wondering where the boards were. There was a slight risk the real printers had already done that, but they were less likely to have the number of the club where the party was.

Steve Dass, an ex-convict who'd written a book about prison edited by Mark's girlfriend, slipped in unnoticed. He had wrapped the boards in a large sheet of brown paper.

Mickey nodded. Ingrid peeled her T-shirt off and held up her skaggy tits. She stole someone's drink and cooled herself off by pouring cider into the hollow of her throat and letting it trickle.

'That zhoung lady's carried away.'

'She ought to be,' Mickey said.

Neil was actually almost the only man whose attention was completely on the act. He was too drunk to notice the oddness. Ingrid begged several of her dancing partners to lick her dry and they tentatively complied.

'Where is this place?' Michael asked Mickey. 'It's wildlife,' he added, redundantly.

Mickey laughed and turned to Frank, easing his body away from the bar to make space between his stool and the footrail. Steve, standing next to him, steadily slipped his bundle onto the rail, sliding it behind Neil. Mickey leaned in close as Steve took away the brown paper. As instructed, he'd unzipped the folder leaving it hanging slightly open. Mickey could see the boards inside.

Ingrid smooched the black guy and quickly pushed him away. She face-fused a girl with antennae and staggered on, obviously intent on tongue-wrestling every man, woman and dog in the pub.

Neil wasn't arguing they should leave. At crucial moments, he always went along with the moves. As ever, he was part of the Forum. Steve edged towards the door. Ingrid caught him and sank fingers into his slickered hair; spiking it as she mouthed the lower half of his face.

Several other shag-hags had divested themselves of outer garments. Peggy Lee sang 'Fever' and the scene, apparently set for an orgy, was ready for a St Valentine's Day massacre.

The intercom buzzed four times. Anne Nielson had turned up, presumably in a state approximating high dudgeon, and barged into the printer's. There, if Eugene had delivered it properly, she'd be given a message that Neil awaited her violent wrath in the pub down the road.

Ingrid had been listening for the signal and, in an instant, swarmed over to Neil and comprehensively rubbed herself against him. He put up a token resistance, drunkenly flapping arms as she tipped his stool against the bar, unzipping his fly and wrenching apart the front of his jeans.

'Baby need some juice,' she muttered.

Mickey and Michael moved aside to give the girl room. Neil held the bar and wriggled, trying to escape. She chewed his T-shirt out of his belt and exposed a lightly hairy belly. Frank pulled a pint and left it for Mickey to tip over gently. Bitter cascaded down the back of Neil's jacket, slopping into the art folder; soaking the boards. Two weeks' work ruined.

The pub doors pushed in. Mickey held his breath.

Neil looked up as Ingrid sucked a mouthful of flesh from his bare stomach and made a chewing motion. His jeans were around his thighs. He couldn't help but laugh, though there was a seam of panic in his tickled giggling. Jerry Lee Lewis sang 'Breathless'.

Anne Nielson had shorter hair than in her pictures. Her face was a blank sheet of fury. Mickey was glad he wasn't the one who'd have to give her an explanation.

Michael hooked with his foot and Neil's stool shot out from under him. He collapsed badly, the art folder breaking his fall, wet boards cracking under his weight. He gargled a scream as Ingrid pressed down like a wrestler, shoving tits into his face.

Michael turned away, unable to look. Mickey sat on his stool, cold sober, watching Anne walk across the room. Ingrid got out of the way and, hugging her chest, squirmed into the background. Neil, surprised again, half sat up and, seeing Anne, closed his eyes to make a wish.

16

'Where would we be without Neil?'

Good point, Michael thought. Trust Mark to think of the really scary question. If the Absent Friend gave up, would everything else in the Deal fall apart? Like Dorian Gray after stabbing the picture?

No time to worry now.

Returning from the scene dock – he'd said he was nipping off for a pee – he was besieged by minions.

Meaghan, the make-up girl, dabbed his face, filling in tiny lines around his eyes. She reshaped his hair and whisked a cloud of spray around his head. As he shut his eyes, April gave him a rundown of technical glitches. The sound man wired a mike into Michael's flowery waistcoat and screwed in his earpiece. He was wired to the control-room. The director buzzed in his ear. Messages were handed to him, signatures were required of him, jokes were passed on.

Quarter of an hour to go.

* * *

Out there in the viewing audience were people he needed to reach. Before talking to them en masse, he had to make direct contact.

He had April bring him a mobile phone and stabbed out the number of the Tottenham Command Post of the English Liberation Front. He found a studio corner and hunched down, keeping outsiders away.

A weak-sounding old lady answered after several rings and he asked to speak with Stan Gull. After a half-minute of enervating – twelve minutes to air time! – doddering, Corporal Jones came on.

'Gull here.'

'You don't know me,' Michael said in a Northern purr, enunciating the 'y' in you, 'but I'm a supporter o' yewer cause.'

'Cause?'

'Keeping them blackies down, laura norder.'

'Good man,' Gull spluttered.

'I'm with t' Muswell Hill Police Station, and I thought you should know there's someone making trouble. I've done my best to bury t' complaints but there's nobbut a little I can do. Ower sergeant is one o' them loony lefties…'

'Vermin,' Gull snapped instinctively.

'Too bloody right. Birching and hanging's too good for 'em.'

Gull grunted approval.

'Any rate, this troublemaker's name is Neil Martin. His address…'

'I know his address,' Gull said, indignant. 'We know all about Mr Neil Martin and his friends.'

'T' lads think he's one o' them journalist pooves, researchin' a big exposé…'

'Journalist? That is a new one. Fear not, the problem will be dealt with. Dealt with, with ruthless efficiency.'

'Good,' said Michael, hanging up. He stood and made April, who had been loitering, jump.

'They want you on set,' she said.

'Coming, coming,' he replied, tossing her the mobile phone.

* * *

He took his throne in the centre of the studio, between a young female politician and an elderly male pop star. The audience, who sat in ranks of raised seats, applauded, but the floor manager waved them quiet, telling them to save their hands for the on-air signal. Four cameras hovered like Daleks.

'Chuffed to have zhou, Denny,' he told the pop star. 'Zhou were the idol of my childhood.'

The singer, shirt open to reveal a mat of dyed chest hair, grinned. Since the sixties, he'd only touched the charts in a duet with an alternative comedian, sending up one of his smouldering kitsch ballads. According to April, who'd researched him, Denny Wolfe had been a good guitarist with Tamsin's first band before he struck out on his own. He had spent the last two months playing Buttons in Bolton.

'And Morag,' he said to the politician, 'great to have zhou back.'

Morag Duff, severe jacket over a feminine dress, smiled exactly as her publicity agent advised. A humourless middle-of-the-road disciplinarian, she had an image problem. Doing *Dixon's On* made her seem more approachable and disposed towards youth. She'd be a pussycat.

The studio clock gave them ninety seconds. The main lights went down, putting everyone in shadow. On a monitor he saw the last of the ads give way to a misleading trail for the late-night adult movie and a station ident as the disembodied continuity announcer (he assumed they were grown in vats in the Derek Leech Pyramid) plugged *What a Grunge!*, a soon-to-debut Cloud 9 series, and read out the lead-in. As the director counted down, Michael nodded along with the numbers.

'Zero, and go...'

The house band played the theme tune – an up-tempo arrangement of Hank Williams' 'I'll Never Get Out of This World Alive' – and the lights came up, spreading warmth across the studio floor; pinning the guests to their chairs. The floor manager waved as if signalling a bomber back to an aircraft carrier and the audience unloosed a burst of clapping. Applause popped in his ears like amyl nitrate in his nose. The you're-on-television rush propelled him out of the seat. Bright light hugged him. He walked up to the camera with the glaring red light and grabbed its attention with a 'hey, look at me' gesture, then read his topical monologue from the autocue.

By the first ad break, Morag had practically wet her seat squealing and giggling. Denny was so floppily laid back it was hard to tell where he left off and his chair began.

They'd got the Big Heart slot out of the way to overwhelming ahhhing and sniffing from the studio audience. While the last lingering shot of the faithful cat mewing at her braindead mistress's bedside was broadcast, he told Morag a filthy joke. When the camera came back to them live in the studio, he had his serious face ready and, as the politician choked on her own laugh, asked her what exactly her policy was on improved care for coma patients. As her face went scarlet, he imagined her publicity agent choking on a vol-au-vent in the Hostilities Suite.

After the ad break, there was a pre-filmed item in which famous women talked (and laughed) about penis size. Nearly seven minutes free.

At the back of the set, mike turned off, he worked the mobile phone again. The audience could see him but wouldn't know what he was doing.

'Gregory Residence,' a woman's voice said. Liz Gregory.

'Might I speak to Jonathan please?'

'Who is this?'

'Tell him Mr Sington.'

There was urping in the background and Jonathan said he'd take it in the hall and it was about school. From the buzz of jinglenoise, he could tell the Gregory household was watching Cloud 9. He tried to remember his Sington voice, hoping it different enough from his own for Jonathan not to make the connection.

The boy came on.

'Got a pen and paper, Jonathan?'

'Uh, what? Yes.'

'Good. You know a shop called Planet Janet? In the Archway Road.'

'Yes, comics and things.'

'Right. I've got another mission for you. The front of Planet Janet. Smash it.'

'Um…'

'This time I want a message around the stone. Get this exactly. Write: Martin, Die You Nazi Filth. Got that?'

'Martin, Die You Nazi Filth.'

'Excellent. Must go now.'

'I'm not sure…'

'I could talk with your parents. You've been getting my packages?'

'Yes. No. No problem with the shop.'

He hung up and got back to his seat. April, as ordered, had provided Denny with a tumbler of vodka. By his slot, he'd be sloshed enough to produce some sort of spectacle.

Barry Gatlin, who had wild eyes and several rows of teeth, did a routine about famous turds. The audience laughed uncomfortably as the vein throbbed in the comedian's forehead. He was a confrontational act. He always picked the most attractive woman in the first row and sexually harangued her.

Tonight, *Dixon's On* was fair-to-good. Nothing to compare with the show last year when Oliver Reed and Alan Bates, fuelled in the Green Room, re-enacted their nude wrestling scene from *Women in Love*. But nothing to be ashamed of either.

Strutting around the studio, insulting the audience, Barry Gatlin prowled in search of a victim-for-the-night. In the end, he ignored the bottle-bleach blonde Michael assumed he'd go for, and picked Morag the MP.

'Darlin', darlin',' he said, teeth click-clacking, tongue darting like an angry lizard, jeans-crotch out-thrust. 'How about a little Private Member's Bill? My *private member* fits your *bill*.'

Appalled, Morag pleaded for help but Michael edged away and let Bastard Barry get into his stroke. After this, anything Michael did would seem reasonable.

In the second ad break, April darted in with the log of phone complaints so far. Barry Gatlin was slipping: only forty-five viewers had been upset enough to call in, and twenty-three of those accused him of political bias rather than the usual appalling taste and crudity.

'I've been pondering North London Nazis,' he told the researcher. 'Get Roily on to them. There might be a good contretemps in it if we had a strike force of skinhead *überfilth* on with Spike Lee next series.'

'Nazis, right?' April queried, unsure.

'English Liberation Front, people like that.'

'Wonderful, lovely, super,' she said. 'Outstanding idea. Admirable content. Quality programming.'

She retreated as the countdown came again.

'Okey-dory so far?' he asked Denny. The singer gulped the last of his third vodka and gave a good-humoured, empty-eyed grin.

'Fantasmashing,' he said. 'Welcome back from the huckstering, beloved viewers. Up next, and I sincerely mean *up*, is Luscious Lola Fogbotham, the Marlene of Macclesfield...'

The special guest was a Northern transvestite rapper plugging his album, *There's Nowt so Queer as Homosexuals*. Then it was time for the star interview. The director said they had five minutes

240   KIM NEWMAN

after the lead-in. The show was running exactly to time.

'Tonight, we're enormously proud and privileged to have as our hot-seat-sitter a man I for one can barely remember, but if zhou wake up Granny I'm sure she can explain zhust exactly who he is. Denny...'

The singer smiled tolerantly, eyes wide and innocent. He was pretty far gone as he rambled weirdly into an almost-revealing interview. Michael chose his most devastating technique, opening with the question, 'Well, whatever happened to you?' and sitting back, eyebrows raised, while the camera fixed itself on the puffy face of the pop singer refusing to budge, as he tried to fill dead air with incoherent sentences.

The audience held their breath as if watching open-heart surgery. Morag tried to butt in, perhaps to take the heat off Denny, but Michael gripped her arm and shut her up. At last, as Denny remembered his detox ordeal, tears sprang out of his eyes and Michael ended the torture. Tomorrow, it would be remembered. Hideous, but good television.

'I had a good deal once,' Denny maundered, 'but I blew it.'

When the agony was over, he announced the week's competition, flashing a doctored photograph of a Royal Personage with his head down a toilet and asking the audience to phone the 0898 number at the bottom of the screen with funny captions.

Before the house band's last number it was time for the What Gets Up My Nose slot. He always did it without a net: no script, no autocue, no nothing.

'Zh'know what's been Getting Up My Nose this week?' he asked the camera. 'Basildon.'

The audience was mainly blank. Someone at the back tittered.

'Zheah, Basildon. I mean: why is it there, what is it for? Who reads their newspaper? Zh'know, *Basildon Echo* was recently voted the Most Boring Local Paper in Britain. Congratulations

Basildonians. Let's take a look at it, shall we?'

He took the paper out from under the desk and unfolded it.

'The big headline feature is about someone from *Department S* opening a supermarket. Remember *Department S*, wrinklies? Pardon me while I hyperventilate. And a cat's been saved from a tree. Major scoop there. Oh, and let's not forget the council's big decision on playgrounds. We've been waiting for that make-or-break moment for six months in our house.'

He tore the paper up and threw it away.

'Basildon, eh? Aren't zhou glad zhou don't live there. Or maybe zhou do. No, let's face it, it's nearly eleven o'clock on a Friday night. In Basildon, that's past anyone's bedtime. Basildon, *wake up!*'

Morag, whose constituency was uncomfortably near Basildon, laughed fit to explode her bladder. The director got in a few cutaways, during the routine.

'Why did the old lady cross Basildon High Street? It's a step in the right direction, away from bloody Basildon. Why does a Basildon fireman wear red braces? Rotten fashion sense. My wife's just been to Basildon. Zhamaica? Bloody had to, mate. What's the difference between a Basildon girl and the *Titanic*? Only 1500 men went down on the *Titanic*. Zhou know, if I owned Hell and Basildon, I'd live in Hell and rent out the Other Place.'

The audience had gone beyond being puzzled and started laughing. The director gave him ten seconds.

'Zhou know what's black and white and crap all over? The *Basildon Echo*.'

Denny, off-camera, had sunk his face into his hands. Tears dripped through his fingers. He had no idea where he was any more or what he'd said five minutes ago.

'This has been *Dixon's On*,' Michael said. 'Dixon's off now. Good night and get lost.'

* * *

In the Green Room, he told everyone it'd been a great show. Bastard Barry tried to get past Morag's hatchet-faced image manager; and the MP's minders closed ranks to protect her. She looked disappointed. Michael wondered if her constituency committee would think deselection.

Denny Wolfe lurched past, supported by the sound man. Michael waved him a good night. He staggered over and breathed a poison cloud.

'Do you have a deal?' Denny asked.

Michael's smile froze.

'I had a deal,' Denny said, tapping his sternum.

Michael shook his cold hand.

'It's been real,' he said.

Denny was taken away and poured into a minicab, sent off alone back to the Where Are They Now? file. He hadn't even plugged his Soul of the '60s tour supporting the Swinging Blue Jeans, which was why he was supposed to be on the show.

He watched the singer go, then turned to his minions, who formed a comforting crowd. April bothered him with more forms to be signed. Meaghan approached with spirits to wipe away his make-up. The director emerged and was thanked for sterling work.

The Hostilities Table was swept clean of crisps and sandwiches as if army ants had swept through. The crew and guests slugged back Moroccan wine Michael wouldn't wash his socks with.

Ginny, who had been invisibly in the audience, swept in ostentatiously and kissed him in public. She must have known there'd be a paparazzo ready to grab a candid. She pressed her cheek to his and spread a smile as the flash popped.

'Wacky one, Gin,' said the photographer; obviously the man from the *Comet*.

She shoved her tongue in his ear. He was dazzled by the lights.

'It's a Day in the Life of a Hyperstar spread, bunnikins,' she told him, posing again.

April had the tapes of the broadcast gathered and ready to be taken back to the office.

'I never knew you had so much against Basildon, darling,' Ginny said.

'Zhust a bit of a laugh. Nothing serious.'

'That's not how it sounded from out there.'

He waved her worries away. 'All make-believe and magic, Gin. We're just flitting shadows across the electronic gulf.'

17

1984-1992

The Quorum prospered.

Mark founded *The Shape*, launching in the summer of 1984 with the strapline 'The future, now!' Start-up capital from Derek Leech enabled the magazine to survive a loss-making five years and establish itself as a cultural presence. Covering politics, technology, fashion, and lifestyle sciences, the magazine became the rallying point of a generation of young thinkers, the beacon of a wider circle of youngish trend-followers. On its say-so, the reputations of designers and artists were made or mangled. Mark produced and presented television shows, asked and answered questions, was profiled by every newspaper, added words to the language. He appeared on as many humorous celebrity quizzes as heavyweight current affairs debates. Pippa returned to Real Press as an editor and worked on Michael's first novels. Together, Mark and Pippa bought the cottage at Herron's Halt. They always assumed they would eventually marry for tax reasons but distractions like a six-month trip to Japan kept intervening. As a 'future consultant', Mark was employed at generous fees by major corporations, suggesting market strategies which would enable them to profit from predicted social changes. Weirdly, by intuition rather than extrapolation, he was more often proved right than anyone could have expected.

Michael was approached by Channel 4 to devise a format for a late night slot on Mondays. *Dixon's On* proved one of the first significant hits of the new station, providing a viewing experience akin to zapping between 100 channels as items jostled each other out of the way accompanied by squiggly graphics and ten-second music stings. In 1984, he met and married Ginny Moon, an actress then winning awards for *The Woman Who Did*, a Film on 4 adaptation of Grant Allen's 1895 novel. Michael and Ginny played a quivering manager and a breathless depositor in a series of popular semi-erotic commercials for a high street bank. When Derek Leech launched Chums condoms, Michael and Ginny advertised them too, even though they had just had a baby, Melanie. In 1988, Leech's Cloud 9 made a record-setting bid and bought *Dixon's On* from Michael's production company, making him the first high-profile defector from terrestrial television. In 1989, *Colin Dale*, Michael's long-in-the-writing first novel, appeared and was an instant bestseller, the TV rights being snapped up at once by a strangely spendthrift BBC. *Colin Dale* was followed by a sequel, *Ken Sington*, in which Colin, the ne'er-do-well everyman protagonist, is contrasted with Ken, one of life's eternal and infuriating winners. Fans wrote in asking when the deserving Colin would finally best the unworthy Ken, but Michael knew the series was infinitely extensible so long as the characters remained as they were.

Mickey spent 1984 working on *Mephistophilis*, a thrash oratorio performed at Castle Donington by The Möthers of Pain, with Lemmy guesting as Helen of Troy. The Möthers's 'Hell and Damnation', with Mickey playing keyboards, became a rare heavy-metal single to break the pop charts. In the summer of 1984, twenty-six-year-old Hunt Sealey suffered a seizure that rendered 10 per cent of his brain inoperative. He lost random slices of his memory and was unable to continue his court battle, ceding ground to his opponent, even covering legal costs.

Mickey responded with *The Only Death of Krazy Glue*, ending the character's career. He returned to ZC by writing and drawing a two-year run of *Circe*, turning the title from moribund loss to market leader. An ambiguous villainess who had knocked about the ZC universe since the 1960s, *Circe* became the most popular female character in comics, the unconventionally sexual protagonist of a dark, scratchy near-future religious conspiracy saga. While in the States, Mickey took a long weekend to write *City Hammer*, a low-budget screenplay about a vigilante cyborg which was picked up by an independent production company. Allan Keyes, a *wunderkind* director, turned it into a midnight movie cult. The soundtrack album, featuring 'Death Tonalities' composed by Mickey, made almost as much as the film. When his score went over 1,000, he stopped counting shag-hags. In 1991, Real Press commissioned a graphic novel, granting him unprecedented control, and he responded with the ground-breaking *Choke Hold*, which pushed back the boundaries of violence in the medium to such an extent that it was praised by *The Times Literary Supplement* and condemned vigorously from the floor of the House of Commons.

In early 1984, Neil Martin parted company from Anne Nielson and *The Scam*. Nearly ten years later, after every other strangeness, he would still wonder what happened…

18

9 JANUARY, 1993

Just past midnight, she was woken by squeals. After changing and settling the Invader, it was hard to get back to sleep. In a too-big bed in a too-small room, she looked at shadows on the ceiling. Living in a front-room on a main road meant getting used to passing lights.

Was there a Shadowshark prowling up and down Fortis Green Road?

The gays in the upstairs flat were partying. Considerate neighbours, they kept their speakers down but Eurodisco rhythms pounded into the floor. The building hummed and throbbed.

Mark Amphlett unnerved her. On the phone earlier, he'd been distant and strained. She missed three-quarters of his meaning but detected in him an impossible envy of Neil. Perhaps the Path Not Taken is always a temptation, no matter how rough? She'd never understand men: their relationships were so exclusive, so intangible. At school, she'd had friends and enemies. Then they disappeared from her life forever. Mark and Neil and Michael were still in each other's pockets after twenty years.

What could have happened?

One day she'd have to explain to the Invader about Connor.

Wouldn't *that* be a delight? *Mummy, why don't I have a Daddy like other children?*

She saw the dressing-gown on the back of her door as a figure. A tall man in black. Dents in the door became piercing eyes. The shadow of the lintel was the brim of a hat.

I do not love thee, Dr Shade.

She turned over and pushed her face into soft pillow, letting her head be half-swallowed. It'd be nice to have an unknown protector: a forgotten schoolfriend willing to pay anonymous money to have her watched over. Or maybe it wouldn't be nice. Maybe it'd be frightening.

Just past midnight (Eastern Standard Time), Mickey was in an Irish bar in the Village. He commandeered an upright piano. Stubbing fingers against yellow keys, he rinky-dinked from Satie to Little Richard. He imagined he was a brutal dentist chiselling eighty-eight teeth out of a willing mouth.

After two days with Heather, he had no more feeling in his crotch. New York was a cyanide gas, but he had anxiety spasms about London. The moves were falling in strange ways. He wasn't sure Michael or Mark could handle it. Both sounded pixilated. Mark was usually the mainstay, cool and calculating; this year, he was in Michael's edge-of-hysteria slot.

Heather, not drunk, leaned against the joanna and stuck her hand into his hair. If there was an emergency in London, he could whip back and sort it. He could take Heather with him; she was for his convenience and comfort. She tilted his head and invaded his mouth.

Before dawn, Mark woke and listened to the quiet of the flat. All his clocks were silent. Thick walls excluded street sounds.

Pippa still wasn't back. She might have gone straight to

Herron's Halt. She'd learned to keep out of the way for the first six weeks of the year. He wondered what she thought the Quorum did in the magic time?

He got out of bed in a grey gloom and padded naked through all eight rooms, practising his slow-breathing. He liked to reclaim his territory every morning, before the sun's light fingers got to it. A pale ghost in the bathroom turned out to be his reflection.

He switched on the brutal light and the extractor fan whirred to life. Without windows and with the unavoidable fan, the bathroom was an isolation chamber. He stared at his young face in the mirror and wondered why he'd started to lose his hair. That hadn't been in the Deal.

They should have asked for more. What eighteen-year-old thinks about going bald? What eighteen-year-old thinks about anything?

He brushed his teeth. Dental hygiene was a fetish of his. He flossed, relishing the bite of sharp cord into his gums. He drew a little blood.

No anomie, no nausea, no fear and loathing. Those should have been the main clauses.

His electric shaver buzzed like an angry hornet.

If they'd asked for happiness, would they have been lobotomised zombies? This was better than that. At its best, the Deal was damned good. From council estate to two homes, from obscurity to – what had Sally called him? – style guru, from geek to *chic*.

He rubbed lotion into his stinging chin and looked at himself. His musculature was well-defined. Physically, he was in better shape than ten years ago. He'd started to take care of himself, to get to the gym once or twice a week. Having the life he'd wished for meant holding on fast.

He left the bathroom and returned to the bedroom. Light slices shone in. He opened the walk-in wardrobe and assessed a rack of suits. Pippa's half was barren of all but a few summer dresses; she travelled like a Victorian lady explorer prepared to attend a formal ball in the Hindu Kush. He selected unobtrusive clothes; jeans and a jacket. He found his old Brighton scarf. It'd be cold out. Smoothing back his hair and feeling skin-skull, he realised he'd need a hat if his pate wasn't to turn blue.

In the middle of the morning, Neil was woken by the glazier, an efficient middle-aged man with tattooed knuckles. He was making a habit of sleeping away half the day. Not that he had anything much to do at night. In the cold of his flat, he made tea for the glazier and coffee for himself; midnight black with a swirl of cream. As the workman measured the wounded windows, Neil got dressed and made toast under the grill. There was nothing for him in the post.

Saturday. The weekend starts here; for everyone else. Neil's whole life was weekend. A long winter Sunday afternoon with nothing on the telly (indeed, no TV) and the threat of icy rain.

He chewed toast. The glazier was on the first pane. Looking through sparkling new glass, Neil realised how dusty the old windows had got. Mr Azmi was supposed to send cleaners round every other month, but no window-washer or hall-sweeper had shown up since autumn.

In the hallway, the phone rang. It would be someone urgently anonymous for Pel. Neil, after waiting out a dozen rings, would venture upstairs and drag his neighbour out from under a woman, to do business. This happened regularly. Neil worried vaguely that taking messages about dodgy deals constituted aiding and abetting a criminal offence.

'Better get that,' the glazier said. 'Maybe you've won the pools.'

Neil grudgingly stepped up into the hall and dragged the phone off its hooks. He recited the house's number.

'Mr Neil Martin?'

Surprised, he stammered a yes. The caller's voice was male, polite, unaccented, bank-managerly.

'Good morning. This is the last day of your active life.'

After coffee, Sally armoured herself for shopping. With Sainsbury's on the corner, less than a minute's walk from the flat, she was theoretically free to nip out at any time, say Tuesday afternoon, and whizz around an almost-deserted supermarket. Without customers, Sainsbury's was exactly the image she had of Her Reward in Heaven. But, as a poor sinner, she always managed to join the Saturday morning crush of nice couples with dual incomes, dawdling around in pastel herds, weighing the virtues of variant pasta sauces, clotting aisles with wonky-wheeled trolleys. If she made it to a blissful afterlife, she'd miss out on the Milk of Ambrosia when a happily cohabiting brace of solicitors grabbed the last economy-size pack to feed their designer cherubim.

Cheery musak played; though she'd have debated the aptness and good taste of narrowcasting 'Suicide is Painless' to shop-happy lemmings. The mix of clattering and conversational buzz echoing about the hangar-shaped building reminded her of a skating rink.

She proudly trundled the Invader forwards, having no compunction about using the flesh of her flesh to ram her way through crowds. Extensively strapped into a stroller-chair and in an oversized blue balaclava, the Invader looked like a Mercury astronaut after a trip through the time barrier. Happy dribble spotted a dinosaur bib. The stroller was subtly armoured, slung with mesh bags that became deadly when filled with snatched cans and frozen meals.

She was still woozy from a night of almost-sleep. At some point, circular thinking had turned into circular dreaming. Reaching for a can of miniature sweetcorns, she was momentarily distracted.

A flurry of dark blotted the eternity-lit brightness of colourfully packaged products and showily dressed shop-in-stylers. A trail of black stealth slipped into the next aisle.

Dragging the stroller as if it were a nine-man chain gang, she pursued the shadow. The aisle was dotted with shoppers who turned like pinball flippers to let a cloaked figure pass into the distance. She didn't know what to call out.

Dr Shade!

She rushed from pastries to preserves, shouldering through like a rugby forward, stroller before her like a runaway lawnmower. Dr Shade turned to wait, cloak spreading. Insect-lensed goggles glittered above a bloodless smile. A black-gloved finger beckoned.

She wanted answers.

Dr Shade stepped aside, whipping away the cloak's curtain like a bullfighter or a conjurer. Two young men were revealed, bent over a freezer, looking at joints of meat.

The shadow was gone and she couldn't curb her momentum.

The meat-gazers turned, eyes and mouths circles, as she bombed towards them. The Invader made fierce turbodrive noises.

A flare of recognition stopped her backpedalling and she put her legs into the charge. A white guy and a black guy. Salt and Pepper. The thugs from New Year's Eve. They even wore the same clothes. Salt's shell-suit bellied out as if he were unnaturally pregnant with something many-spined.

She rammed the stroller against shins. Salt yowled pain and bent double as she whirled around. The stroller's wheels lifted from tiling and the Invader *wheeeed* in delight, laughing as the undercarriage collided with the stomach of the astonished Pepper.

Do that again, Mummy.

With a burst of caution, she set the stroller down gently and pushed it to one side, lining up the chair so the Invader would have a good view of Mother in Action.

Pepper, spurred by panic, hurdled the freezer and sprinted for the nearest checkout lane. He knocked over an undeserving vegetarian and slipped on a *tofu* cube. With exactly the bored voice used for price-checks, a girl put her mouth to a microphone and called for Security at Till Nine.

With Pepper taken care of, Sally turned her attention to Salt. His zip ruptured and a shrinkwrapped chicken burst from his chest like the *Alien* monster. His mean little face showed no understanding. She could almost sympathise.

'Rhodes, Security,' she said, gripping Salt's throat and forcing him back, bending him over the lip of the freezer. She pulled his waistband loose, jogging a large lump of something frozen into his trousers.

At midday, he parked in the Archway Road. He was near enough to Cranley Gardens to make a swift getaway, but far enough off not to be noticed or connected. He wanted to walk, get the feel of the area. It wasn't his beat, too far out of WC1. Highgate, Muswell Hill, Cranley Gardens, Crouch End, Alexandra Park: Neil Martin Country. Also, Sally Rhodes Territory.

High up, over the city, it was cold. The air was cleaner. It was almost not London here. Mark strolled towards Highgate Tube, wanting to pass Planet Janet. According to Sally, Neil wouldn't be there today but it was a significant site. From her reports, he felt he knew the area better than he did.

There was a police car by Planet Janet, and what looked like a drugs bust on the pavement. Uniformed constables stood by a long-haired man who gestured wildly. Interested, Mark slowed his pace to an amble. He sank his chin into his scarf and shoved his hands into his pockets. The only hat he had found was an old tweed cap Pippa liked, which kept his egg warm even if it did nothing for his style.

The shopfront was a *kristallnacht* ruin. A cardboard Dracula, bent at the waist, slopped forwards onto the pavement. A burglar alarm nagged like a headache.

Loitering and listening, he gathered the hippie wasn't the criminal but the victim. He'd be Dolar, owner of Planet Janet, host of the New Year parties, father of two. Someone had attacked his shop. He'd been a witness and was giving a description.

'...it was a kid, man, about thirteen or fourteen. Baseball cap on backwards, blue Möthers T-shirt, red zits, dark hair. Spotty-faced, reverse-cap, metalhead T-shirt, stone-throwing motherfucker if you ask me...'

A constable nodded, taking notes.

'Teenagers today, man,' Dolar moaned. 'All fascist earthlings.'

One of the policemen agreed.

Scenting a Michael move, Mark crossed the road. He wanted to swing by Neil's place then call in on Sally. She'd be off duty and he wanted to talk with her again. He wanted to see where she lived. There was real wisdom in the woman. Somehow, she had explanations he needed. Or if she didn't have them, she could get them.

Real security people – a crew-cut in a brown jacket and his middle-aged female supervisor – converged on the freezer. Salt emitted little squally whines which the Invader found highly entertaining.

'Unnnhgg ahgggg,' the baby said, flapping paws together as if applauding. She was proud her child's first spoken word was an approximation of 'scumbag'.

The security people laughed.

'Who are you, miss?' Brown-jacket asked.

'A concerned customer,' Sally said, squeezing the shoplifter's throat as if she wanted a half-pint of adam's apple juice.

She looked about. Pepper held upright by firm hands, was being steered their way. Dr Shade – or whoever – was nowhere around.

'Rhodes, isn't it?' the security woman said. 'I remember you from the Sunderland Agency.'

She had worked seven months at Sunderland. Her big

assignment was hanging out for weeks in a sporting goods shop where nobody stole anything. Bored enough to exceed instructions and jump from watching to snooping, she'd discovered an employee fiddling the till. Since he was the owner's nephew, it hadn't gone to court. There are eight million excuses in the Naked City; this has been one of them.

'Katie Castle. I was your supervisor.'

'Of course,' Sally said, not really remembering. 'Good to see you.'

'Keeping in practice?'

'I'm on my own now. Sally Rhodes Security Services. Clod-head here has cropped up in an investigation. I'd like to question him. And his friend.'

Brown-jacket wasn't enthusiastic but Katie smoothed it over. For once, a situation was developing to Sally's advantage. If she ever wanted to get back into loitering without intent, she'd be sure of a friendly reception here.

'Five minutes, and no torture,' Katie offered.

Salt tried to wriggle loose. Sally crunched a satisfying heel into his instep.

'Thanks a heap.'

It was nearly lunchtime but Neil wasn't at all hungry. He felt sick in his stomach, with familiar dread. He looked up and down the Gardens, wondering where the attack would come from. This year, he'd made an offering, but the Norwegian Neil Cullers were merciless; their noose was drawing close around his neck.

As long as there were witnesses about, he should be safe. The glazier was fingering putty around the last pane of glass. Zafir Azmi had turned up with an envelope of notes to pay the workman. Even Pel was in the street, nagging Zafir to come in on some scam with discontinued washing machines.

'I've got the last Betamax video in the country thanks to you,' Zafir told Pel.

'It was a better system,' Pel insisted. Zafir, elegantly disgusted, rattled gold bracelets.

'Chance of another cuppa, mate?' the glazier asked.

Neil went back inside. Through his window, he saw the three sets of legs. A long black car cruised past and Zafir whistled. As he filled the kettle, he wondered: could any of the three be secret Norwegian Neil Cullers? He often suspected the enemy had people close to him. Turning off the tap, he wrenched his mental flow to a halt. That way lies paranoia. His only enemy was himself.

A distant church bell sounded one o'clock as he reached the Cranley Gardens turn-off. A sleek machine emerged from the road, crawling towards Muswell Hill. It was Sally's Rolls-Royce. SHADE 001: a dinosaur of the road, deep space black with silver trimmings. The Shadowshark rolled away, its engine was almost silent.

In his pockets, Mark's hands shook. He stopped walking for a moment and drew a deep, lung-chilling breath. Could this be some surprise move of Mickey's? The car was gone but shadow stayed in his eyes: the dancing squiggles of dark negatives of the bright caterpillars you got from looking straight at the sun. He tried to blink them away.

As he set foot into Cranley Gardens, a filthy hand fixed to his elbow.

'I'll no shit ye,' a voice croaked, 'I'm after brass te get pissed out o' me head.'

He shook off the wino.

'Ah sorr,' he said, brogue thicker, 'just ten mingy pence fer a snort o' mother's ruin.'

The vagrant had a child's duffel coat stretched around his big body, hood as tight about his head as Batman's cowl. His thick glasses were fixed at the bridge with a wodge of Sellotape. To get rid of the pest, Mark fished out coins.

'Zhou'll never regret it, sorr,' the wino burped.

'Michael,' he said, wearily. 'Is the accent supposed to be Scots or Irish?'

The wino straightened, assuming exaggerated dignity, and spat out the joke teeth. 'My boy, I am an ack-tor!'

Mark began to put his money back.

'I earned that,' Michael said, snatching the coins. Mark let them go and looked his friend up and down. The disguise was complete visually and odorifically.

'And what have you got against Basildon?' Mark asked.

The police would be there inside five minutes, which didn't give her long with Salt and Pepper. Katie let her use a stockroom and even agreed to watch over the Invader. The Shoplift Twins sat on cardboard boxes of canned spinach.

'New Year's Eve,' she reminded, 'after midnight but before one. Muswell Hill Road.'

'The nutter,' Pepper said, remembering. 'You were his girl.'

'Not quite,' she snapped.

'Fucking weird, sister,' Pepper shook his head, dazed and embarrassed. He would like to be a professional. Salt was just a stack of humiliated resentment. Katie had stripped off his shell-suit in public and hauled a frozen steak out of his shorts.

'What kind of neon slime has nothing better to do on New Year's Eve than beat up strangers?'

'Weren't no stranger,' Pepper said.

'Shut up,' Salt put in. 'Just shut up.'

'Neil wasn't a stranger?'

'Neil?'

'The nutter you call him. The man you thumped.'

'His name was Neil?' Pepper asked.

'Fucking nutter,' Salt said.

'Where do you know him from?'

'Tin Woodsman.'

'The pub?'

'Yeah. Met him in there pissing it up on New Year's Eve. Bought us drinks, gave us money, bought us off.'

'And you beat him up? You guys are liquid filth.'

'He paid us,' Pepper insisted.

A dizzying chasm yawned. Her mind stood on the edge, looking over. Miles below, jagged rocks waited, washed by foamy tide.

'He paid you to beat him up?'

'Shut the fuck up, Bendy,' Salt said. 'She's Old Bill.'

'Your name is Bendy?' she asked Pepper. 'I'm a private detective. I don't give Shit One about Sainsbury's. The prices are extortion, anyway. I'm interested in New Year's Eve.'

Pepper tried to explain. 'This bloke you call Neil. The nutter. He paid us to put a bloke in hospital. Told us where, told us when, told us what the target would be wearing...'

'He had on the same kit in the Woodsman,' Salt said, joining in. 'Only we never noticed. Fucking nutter, John.'

'We took his drinks and his dosh and did the job. When we twigged, we scarpered. He paid us for more than a couple of bops and a lick, but we didn't want no more of it. In the Woodsman, he said the blowlamp he wanted done over was picking on him, screwing him over all the time. He told jinx stories, about losing gaffs, having his melts nicked. Broke your heart.'

'You're sentimental, Bendy.'

'Fuck you, sister.'

'You wish,' she said, pouting a kiss-mouth. Katie let two policemen in to make the formal arrest.

Sally watched Pepper and Salt get read their rights. She had plea-bargained with Katie, getting out of making a statement. The supermarket had enough evidence to make a case without her. One of the policemen already knew both parties and greeted them like old friends.

He paid you to beat him up. She felt she'd been sent back to Go and robbed of her £200.

* * *

Michael had been in his vile tramp suit for hours. He'd made £1.87 from hassling passersby. Whenever a police car zoomed down Muswell Hill Road, he did his best to chameleon with the grimy park railings.

Mark, annoyed to be fooled, buttoned up completely. From their corner, they could see the house where Neil dwelled. A glazier was at work. Michael said he deserved a commission for drumming up business. Mark gave a little sneery snort that was worse than not laughing.

'Know who lives there?' Michael said, pointing to a biggish semi-detached. 'The Gregorys. A fine family. Typical and average.'

A boy he took to be Jonathan Gregory had come out of the house earlier and pedalled past on a BMX, spotty face into the wind over the handlebars, pert bottom bobbing up and down as he pumped his legs.

'Your move with the windows,' Mark said. 'You did it again, didn't you? At the science fiction shop?'

Michael had a fart of warm pride. 'The Good Soldier Strikes. Things are really working out this year, don't zhou think?'

'What about Sally's Dr Shade?'

'It's *Sally* now, is it?'

'The black Rolls-Royce. Did you see it?'

Michael remembered the car. It took longer to pass than the QE II. A wonderful beast.

'I want one, I've decided. I'll nag Zhin to get me a pressie with her Zhackie Collins loot.'

Mark's brow cracked in a frown. He was worrying himself to premature senescence.

'It's zhust some local loon, *mon brave*. We're not the only crazies in North London.'

A sturdy little cyclist popped out of a side road and zigzagged past. Michael gave Jonathan an unseen salute. The kid was puffing. He must have taken a roundabout getaway route.

'Home is the Window Breaker, Home from the Vandalism,' he said. Jonathan let his bike collapse on the thin carpet of lawn outside the house and ran round the back. 'It's so peaceful and sit-com Saturday, isn't it? Tykes on bikes, window-workmen whistling, dinner in the oven, sport on telly.'

Mark mentioned that this was where Britain's most notorious postwar serial killer had lived.

Neil had a tray of teas together. He took them into the street. It was cold for standing about.

'It's only teabag tea,' he apologised.

'Warm and wet is what counts,' the glazier said.

They all drank.

'Any idea who broke the windows?' Pel asked.

Neil shrugged. Zafir looked furtive.

'Your Old Man hasn't been messing about with the Pakki mafia? I hear ragheads chop off your fingers.'

'That's the Japs,' Zafir said. 'If Dadiji's ticked off anyone, it'll be the uncles. 'kin mental, the uncles. They're planning to assassinate Salman Rushdie.'

'I didn't know your family was into Islamic Death Jihad Jazz,' Pel said.

'They're just after the reward,' Zafir said, shaking his head. 'They spend more time working out how to get Rushdie's head from High Barnet to Tehran than they do thinking about where the government has him stashed.'

A burst of barely-competent death-metal exploded from two doors down. Neil and Pel, familiar with Hendrix's frenzied and endless solo abortions, exchanged a look of resigned disgust.

'Who is that?' Zafir asked. 'Sounds worse than fucking *bhangra*.'

* * *

After seconds of guitar holocaust, Mark jammed fingers in his ears. Even Mickey had never made a noise that horrible.

'That's Mr Karl Garr,' Michael said, proudly. 'Those speakers are my contribution to endowment of the arts. Loud, aren't they?'

There was no denying how imaginative Michael's moves were. He still had a kid's enthusiasm for pouring vinegar into wounds.

'I wonder if Mr Garr has a comrade who needs a drum kit?' Michael thought out loud.

'Sometimes I think we go too far,' said Mark.

At two, Sonja came back from the hairdresser's and was able to take the Invader off her hands.

'It's an emergency,' Sally swore. 'Code red.'

Sonja didn't ask questions.

The Invader had been hyper ever since the trip through space and the crashlanding on Bendy's stomach. She could tell the baby enjoyed the flight. Her child would grow up to be the first Briton on Mars.

Her maternal responsibility discharged, she was free to wander the Broadway in horrorstruck panic.

Neil had arranged his own mugging. He must have had to save up for months. She hadn't found out how much he'd paid Salt and Pepper.

From a call box, she phoned Mark and got the machine. She wanted to talk over this development. Something truly sick was happening and she was part of it. She hadn't been told enough to understand. It was time Neil's friends stepped down from their lofty observation platforms and *did* something.

She said some of the words she'd been trying only to think in front of the Invader. Shoppers gave her a wide berth, politely not staring at the insane person.

* * *

The clock woke him at seven. Light scratches stung on his back. It felt as if the edges had curled. The sheets were a tangle around his ankles and he lay naked on the waterbed, looking at his reflection hanging in the glass roof. He was still wearing the last of the night's condoms. A jet passed, sliding through his body like a winged knife.

'You have a nine o'clock with *Newsweek*,' Heather told him. She sat, nude but for power spectacles, on the rim of the bed, reading from a clipboard. 'The journalist's name is Leonard Scheuer. He's a friendly, but objected to the "mythologising of serial murder" in *Choke Hold*. It'd be best to slant his profile to your work-in-progress, since Scheuer likes to feel he's cutting-edge. He needs to know everything first. Then, at eleven, you're signing in the Marching Morons Bookstore in TriBeCa...'

'The Marching Morons?'

'It's named from a short story by Cyril M. Kornbluth.'

'How could I forget?'

She continued, 'The manager's name is Buddy and his girlfriend is a big fan of yours, Cherill.'

'Cheryl?'

'Cherill.'

'I bet they weigh a half-ton each and wear bib-overalls.'

'It doesn't say. In her fanzine, Cherill writes that you're "greater than Neil Gaiman".'

He tried to sit up but his back wouldn't work. 'Score one for Choosy Cherill, then.'

'You'll lunch in the limo, then at three Dick and Eivol will meet you for drinks at High Rollers with Irwin.'

'The District Attorney from *Hill Street Blues*?'

'Irwin Jenevein. He's interested in producing *Choke Hold*. His *Ballet Dancers With AIDS* mini-series took three Emmies and he needs a prestige first-feature project. Major enough to meet but no A-list player. Dick thinks he has a line with Bruckheimer-Simpson, so hang fire. At five, you're debating the Death of

Amazon Queen with Nancy Lucey Kunst of WoFBReIGN on Cloud 9's *Big Apple*. Kunst has an unattractive vocal mannerism which will leave you sounding reasonable. When she gets annoyed, she stutters; best to irritate her before you get on air.'

Mickey managed to get fingertips to Heather's thigh. Velvety skin dimpled.

'At 6.30, Timmy Chin has a buffet at the Plaza. All the creators, happy flacks, sundry cheerleaders. You press flesh and make small talk. Try not to cripple a waiter. At 9.15, I've reserved a room in the Pyramid and we'll have forty-five minutes for sex. At ten, the limo will pick you up for the Mayor's reception...'

After half an hour of loitering, Mark was cold and bored. Nothing seemed about to happen. He wanted to get on and find Sally. Michael, insulated in his tramp costume, was obviously enjoying himself. He even derived some pleasure from Garr's tortured axe solos.

'Hello,' Michael said, 'visitors.'

A 2CV parked behind the glazier's van and leaked exhaust into the gutter.

'Enter Dolar,' Mark said. 'Neil's boss.'

'He of the smashed shopfront?'

'The very same.'

'This should be of considerable interest, coz. I'm going to lurch along the road a ways and hie myself within earshot.'

'Neil will recognise you instantly.'

'Zhou didn't.'

'I'm not paranoid.'

'That's not what Pippa says.'

'When did you talk to her?'

Grinning, Michael said, 'See, zhou are paranoid too.'

Michael was in one of his under-your-skin-and-itching moods. Usually, they meant he was having a bad time at home.

Mark was pleased to let him go off on his own. He'd found a niche in some park railings, a semicircular dent which once harboured a wastebin, and was using it for concealment and protection from the elements. He wished he'd thought to bring a Thermos. Michael hammed it up again for Mark's benefit, shambling drunkenly between precise footsteps. Charlie Chaplin in Hell.

Dolar hammered on the door of Neil's house. Then he was talking with the Asian man who was overseeing the glazier. A minibus ground its way into Cranley Gardens, stuffed with football fans. There was a plastic soccer ball on the roof like an ice-cream van's luminous lolly. Michael found a position by the low wall that boundaried the Gregory front garden and slumped. Neil opened his front door and stood on the doorstep, looking out at Dolar. The football van got in the way and stalled. Mark couldn't see anything.

Kick-off would have been at 2.30. The football supporters must be late and lost. The bus was between Michael and Neil's house, but he still heard incoherent ranting.

Dolar, who might have done well to smoke a calming joint, was angry in a mellow sort of way, and unable to tell Neil about the note wrapped around the rock tossed through his shopfront.

By peering through the driver's-side window of the bus and focusing on the far-side window, ignoring the fuzzy bulk of the driver and his mate, who had themselves swivelled their heads to look, Michael could still see Neil's open, puzzled face.

'Are you homeless?' a clear voice asked.

A little girl, her face a lot like Jonathan Gregory *sans* spots, stood by her brother's abandoned BMX, looking over the wall at him.

'We're doing a project on the homeless,' she announced. 'Once being a tramp wasn't so bad. They were called Gentlemen of the Road.'

He dredged the girl's name from memory: Ellen.

'Nowadays, Miss Young says being homeless is a social problem.'

The driver's-side door of the bus wrenched back, and the driver clambered out. He wore a green combat jacket, a football scarf and a black balaclava. Like a jousting knight carrying a lady's favour, he had a Union Jack tied around his upper arm.

'Are you alcoholic as well as homeless? That's very common, Miss Young says.'

'Didn't zhour mother ever tell ye not to talk with strange men?'

More football fans piled out into the street. One wore a white bedsheet tabard like a waistcoat over his jacket, a red crusader's cross emblazoned on his chest. His ski-mask looked like chain mail.

'Excuse me,' the driver asked Dolar and Neil, in a distinctly non-proletarian accent, 'but would one of you be a Mr Neil Martin?'

A moment later, Mark was startled as Sally walked by. Intent on craning to see what was going on in Cranley Gardens, he hadn't been watching his back. She wore a bottle-green coat and check trousers, a beret and flat heels. He recognised her at once but she didn't notice him. From her straight back and swift stride, he saw she was determined. The intelligent thing would be to walk away now. But that might mean never knowing what happened next.

Again, the man in the black balaclava asked, 'Would one of you be a Mr Neil Martin?'

Neil was wary. But Dolar, pausing in mid-harangue, pointed at him and said, 'He's Neil.'

The back of the bus opened and Balaclava's friends gathered around to pull things out like workmen picking their tools. Neil saw an axe-handle, a baseball bat, a length of chain.

'Any rate, Neil,' Dolar resumed, 'this is too heavy for me, man.

This window gig, you know. There's insurance, but…'

'Need windows done, mate?' interrupted the glazier, who was packing up. 'I'll give you a card.'

'Neil Martin,' Balaclava called, issuing a challenge. He stood in the middle of the road, hefting a foot-long screwdriver from hand to hand. Its point twinkled sharp.

'You'll have to shift that bus if I'm to get out,' the glazier said to Balaclava. 'You're blocking the way.'

Balaclava slashed. His eyes were fixed on Neil. The glazier cried out more in surprise than pain. Blood dripped onto his overalls from his open cheek.

'Bloody Nora.'

'Neil Martin, I am Retribution,' Balaclava said, stepping forwards. 'Fear me.'

'Heavy,' Dolar commented.

Neil should have stepped back and barricaded the door but stood frozen on the steps.

Balaclava's boys unleashed a fusillade. New windows burst, imploding glass into the house. A missile dug a chunk out of the wood of the front door and fell onto the step. It was a solid metal bolt, a couple of inches across.

The glazier looked at his ruined work and climbed into his van, locking the door. He sat, watching, holding a wool glove to his gashed face.

Neil was fascinated by the shining point of Balaclava's sharpened screwdriver. He imagined he'd feel almost nothing as it slid in; the pain would come when it was pulled out.

For the middle of a Saturday afternoon, Cranley Gardens was overpopulated. Surplus vehicles blocked the road to motor traffic. Sally saw Neil on his doorstep, paused like a panicked public speaker. Expectant people – she recognised only Dolar – gathered around the gate and the short concrete path to the steps.

She coasted on anger, slipping through a crowd of wide white youths in combat gear, nodding a hello to Dolar. Neil, intent on the big man a few steps below him, didn't see her for a moment.

'Neil, I want to talk with you,' she said. 'I want answers.'

She sounded like an outraged wife. In a sense, she did feel she'd been cheated on. She'd wasted half a night looking after a man who paid to have himself beaten up.

An arm yanked her out of determination, grabbing her around the waist, pulling her tight. She smelled beer breath. An ice sliver came to the corner of her eye.

'Come out, Neil Martin,' a loud voice said.

Remembering a long-ago self-defence course, she let her body relax completely, not resisting. She was close to someone, her whole body held to his side. With disgust and indignation, she realised the lump stuck in her hip was an erection. She couldn't turn her head to see the man. She recalled a broad green back. A black balaclava. A flag was tied around one arm. Heavy boots edged with metal. He'd been holding something sharp, something now too near her eye. She blinked reflex tears.

Neil's face was empty of all expression.

'Step down or the lady wears a patch,' the man said.

Neil extended his arms, showing he had nothing up his sleeves.

'Hold on,' he said, gulping, 'don't do anything you'll regret...'

A nasty laugh caught in her ear. The sharp point shivered.

'Look at the man and the lady,' Ellen said.

Michael was already looking. His guess was the big man holding Sally Rhodes hostage was the Tottenham Enforcer of the ELF. This was his move. He was entitled to watch. A shame about Ms Rhodes, but you couldn't make an omelette without breaking eggs.

* * *

It was as if Neil had got his wish. For almost everyone, time stopped cold. Dolar, Sally, Balaclava's Boys: all stood like wax figures, open-mouthed in surprise. Zafir and Pel were behind him, in the hall, also frozen.

Only Neil could move. And Balaclava.

And Hendrix: the Unknown Guitar picked out a first recognisable tune, 'Istanbul, Not Constantinople'. Each note was a jolt to a dental nerve.

For a calm moment, Neil felt he had command of his life.

'You stand accused of treachery to your British blood, Neil Martin. You have collaborated with the urine-skinned oppressor.'

Balaclava's screwdriver was aimed at Sally's temple, as if she were an android with a fliptop cranium. An angry tear shone on her cheek.

Balaclava said, 'I've always wanted to screw a gash's brains out.'

He angled the screwdriver and held it horizontal to Sally's head, pressing.

Mark was out of his alcove, drawn towards Neil's house. He still couldn't make out what was happening. The road was blocked by the bus and a crowd. A car was next to him, idling. Its way was barred but the driver didn't hit the horn.

Michael's Guitar Man serenaded the Damned.

One foot in front of the other, Mark was tugged along the road. He saw Michael, standing with a little girl, watching. Sally was in the crush on the doorsteps.

He missed his footing on the kerb and leaned, knowing the idling car would break his fall. His wrist jarred. His palm stickily froze, as if he'd pressed it to the inside of a deep freeze. A shock shot up his arm. Turning and cringing away from the car, he recognised its midnight black window. He had no feeling at all in his arm, as if bones had dissolved the instant he touched the Shadowshark. He found himself on his knees in the gutter, gripping his floppy wrist. As he clambered to his feet, there was a hiss of expelled air and an almost-damped electrical whine. A tinted window opened a crack.

He looked away, afraid the car was stuffed with fissionable anti-matter, sucking all light into its black-hole interior. If he was drawn to the window, he'd be stretched out of reality and vacuumed into eternal night. His shoulder numbed.

What would Amazon Queen do in a situation like this? Nothing: she didn't exist, not even in the comics. So, what would *Sally Rhodes* do in a situation like this? Turn into Jellyfish Girl, usually.

Why don't you have two eyes like all the other Mummies!

The textbook first move – she'd used it 100 years ago in Sainsbury's – was to stamp on the assailant's foot. This hulk wore boots she probably couldn't dent with her heel. She had to find somewhere soft and stick something hard into it.

'Neil,' she said, evenly, 'there are some questions about your life I'd like you to answer...'

'What are you saying?' Balaclava asked. Neil could tell he was puzzled by Sally's question.

The Nazi might have relaxed his grip. Sally bent forward from the waist, angling her right shoulder out, then jabbed back with her elbow. She caught Balaclava at the belt buckle, jamming a large tin eagle into his rubbery gut.

The screwdriver stabbed but her head wasn't next to it.

She bent down and sprang up, sinking her shoulder into Balaclava's crotch, lifting him off the step. He shouted, arms and legs flailing, and over-balanced, tumbling on his back. Balaclava's head smacked concrete.

The screwdriver rolled between dustbins.

Neil was amazed. He hadn't thought of Sally as the Emma Peel type.

Sally, face tight with pain, shoved Neil through the door and followed inside the house. Pel was standing, appalled, by the hall table. Zafir was on the phone, gabbling in a foreign language.

Sally slammed the door and the lock caught. There were painted-over bolts. She wrestled the bottom one home and shouted for help. Pel used his hands as hammer and chisel to thump the top bolt into place. The front door jarred as someone heavy rammed it. Through glass side-panels, Neil saw Balaclava's Boyos streaming up the steps.

They were shouting wordlessly, emitting a tribal battle cry. 'Oi oi oi…'

'Where's the back way out?' Sally asked.

'There isn't one,' Neil said.

The side-panels were smashed in. Hands twisted through, scrabbling for the lock. Sally thumped away any that got close, squashing flesh against the jagged edges of the broken panels. Battle cries mixed with pain cries.

'Haven't you heard of fire regulations?' she asked.

Neil and Pel looked at their landlord's son. Zafir, calmer now, was speaking a mix of Pakistani and English.

'Yes, right, Dadiji,' he said, and hung up.

'Well?' Pel asked.

'Dadiji says we should throw them Neil.'

He couldn't stand. He couldn't lift his head. Half his field of vision was occupied by asphalt. Road grit bit his cheek. Painfully turning, he saw the bottom curve of the Rolls-Royce tyre, shining silver wheelspokes. A bottle-top near his face was a huge pop art object, detailed and clear; the noisy people by Neil's house were blurry distant toys. His cap lay upturned in the gutter, faded lining exposed.

He shivered; not with cold but as if struck by an allergic reaction. Limbs he couldn't feel twitched and kicked. Lack of sensation spread through his chest and head, tendrils of dead nothing reaching for his heart and brain. This wasn't in the Deal. They wouldn't die: it had been *promised*.

A shadow passed over his face and he heard the non-squeak of a metal door smoothly opening. If he could raise his head, it'd bump on the underside of the car door jibing across him. More cold cascaded from the Shadowshark's interior and pooled like invisible mist. His sinuses clogged with soft ice, his chilled eyeballs shocked his eyelids. Getting out of the car, the driver stepped over him. A trailing curtain dragged, briefly covering his face, then whipping away. A cloak.

A polished boot was close by his face. In the black leather curve, his stricken face reflected. From this angle, his bald patch was disturbingly blatant. There was slush in his throat. He coughed it out. It was an effort to keep breathing. The driver stood by his car, watching. Mark tried to roll over to look up, but his body was useless. His mind prowled, trapped.

The Tottenham *Fascisti* battered Neil's house with axe-handles, chanting 'Oi oi oi'. Karl Garr provided counterpoint cacophony. Michael sat and watched with Ellen. Being a vagrant rendered you invisible to anyone of wage-earning age.

The stormtrooper Sally Rhodes had tossed off the steps was by the bus, feeling his back for broken bones. His comrades kept up the attack. People had come out of nearby houses to watch or join in. Michael was aware of more standees on the Gregory front lawn. Turning, he smiled at Jonathan Gregory, who didn't notice him.

The glazier, wounded early, emerged from his van with a blowtorch. Its tiny blue flame was wind-whisped. He tapped the stormtrooper on the shoulder with Oliver Hardy daintiness. The rip on his cheek still oozed. The ELF man turned and the glazier stubbed the torch against his chest like a cigarette. The stormtrooper yelled, a smouldering circle on his sternum.

Michael wondered if Mark had retreated. He looked to check

and saw only that freak Roller parked at the end of the street. Nearer was Dolar, stunned and dazed by the pace of events. The shop owner had been demoted to onlooker by the White Knights of Tottenham. He looked around, eyes sharp, and seemed to stare directly at Michael.

No, he was looking behind Michael. At Jonathan. The hippie's placid expression shapeshifted. He became a snarling cossack werewolf, a mouthful of sharp teeth in a face-covering tangle that mixed eyebrow and beard.

'You,' he shouted, pointing at the Good Soldier, '*earthling!*'

'Out of the question,' Sally told the Asian, Zafir.

She could tell Neil was relieved she wouldn't let them throw him to the Nazis.

'It's between him and them,' Zafir said. 'It's not fair Dadiji's property should suffer.'

From upstairs there was a crash as a window smashed.

'Now their bloodlust is up, you reckon they'll stop at doing Neil over? Think about it; if you were a white supremacist, whose face would stand out in this crowd?'

Zafir nodded, taking the point on board.

The door of Neil's flat burst open. A couple of yobs – skinheads whose short jeans had Union Jack ankle extensions – jammed through. They'd got into the house through Neil's broken windows.

Neil, moving fast for once, wrenched up the hall table – a wrought-iron stand – and ploughed it into the charging skins, knocking them back into his flat. He pulled the door to with one hand and dug out his keys, stabbing the lock with them.

Sally stepped in and held the door handle. There was a tugging from inside the flat. Neil's key turned and broke. The door was locked forever. It was much easier to batter a door in than out, but if they had tools, they could pick at the hinges.

'We have to go out the front,' she said. No one looked happy.

'...graphic violence is a part of art,' he said, 'and has been since Fred Flintstone bragged about spilling the brains of an endangered Mastodon.'

Leonard Scheuer tutted, thinking of snide comments, Mickey was sure.

'I'm an enemy of censorship, I believe in pushing back barriers. The publishers wimped out over the panels in *Choke Hold* where the whore gets fucked with the pneumatic drill, but I say that's life...'

'Actually, isn't that death?'

'Fuckin' red, raw and dripping. That's how I draw things, that's how I see things. And if anyone don't like it, they can suck exhaust pipe and expire, all right?'

He darted a look at Heather, sure she'd step in and pinch Scheuer's neck with a Personal Assistant's Death Grip if it became necessary.

Beyond Heather, by the door where the waiters congregated, he saw a man-shaped shadow. Then he didn't.

'Mr Yeo?' the interviewer asked, concerned. 'Are you all right?'

He shook off the shadow feeling.

'Yeah, sorry. Half my head is in London. Sorry. Anyway, so far as critics are concerned, they're just tossing off. Everyone loves a juicy car accident, let's face it. Me, I love a juicy car accident involving a critic.'

'I'll open the door,' Sally said, 'and we make a run for it, scattering. The police must be on their way by now.'

Neil wasn't sure the police weren't part of it.

The door to his flat was shaking as Norwegian Neil Cullers battered. They'd smash what was left of his stuff. For a second, he was grateful to Tanya; he'd much rather his records went to good homes than got trampled by bovver boots.

'Does anyone smell smoke?' Pel asked.

Zafir shook his head.

'I've got five grand's-worth of top-of-the-line microwaves upstairs,' Pel protested.

'*Five grand*,' Zafir shouted, 'you said three!'

Pel shook his head, unwilling to give up the ship.

Someone opened the letterbox and piss-stream shot in, jetting onto the rucked carpet.

'Pick up the table,' Sally ordered.

Neil hefted the heavy table.

'When I open up, you throw it,' she said.

She eased bolts loose. The stream kept up, incredibly. This was a seven-pint piddle. She turned the latch and set it. The door was unlocked. Nodding and standing out of the way, she let the door swing open.

An unconcerned yob was on the doorstep, fly open, dick in his hands, whistling as he let spray. His face was an aghast picture as Neil hurled the table at him.

When the pisser was flat on his back on the steps, howling under the table, Sally grabbed Neil's hand and ran out of the door. By instinct, he tried not to tread on the skinhead, though it would serve him right if he got stomped.

Cranley Gardens was a war zone.

He looked at his own distorted face in the boot-leather mirror. His mouth was slack and leaking. The rest of him wasn't even cold now.

He could hear what was happening, but it was like a TV with the sound down as far as it would go. There were shouts and crashes and explosions and guitar chords, but they were faint and distant.

The shadowman shifted and unblocked light fell like fiery rain. Not for the first time, Mark wanted out of the Deal.

As Michael watched, Dolar slammed Jonathan against his BMX, snarling abuse at the startled kid. Ellen clapped as the funny man assaulted her brother.

'Why, earthling, why?' Dolar asked, big hands loose around Jonathan's spotty neck.

Dolar grabbed a handful of Jonathan's T-shirt and shook the terrified kid, roaring deathfire into his face.

The mob continued to attack Neil's house. There was a break in the siege. The front door flew open and defenders rushed out, shoving through the ELF forces. Sally Rhodes was first, dragging Neil like a furious mother hauling a child away from playing in the traffic.

'Look, pretty,' Ellen said, pointing.

Licks of fire came from one of the broken upper storey windows. After years of mending, the glazier had finally succumbed to the lure of breaking and tossed his blowtorch like a grenade.

Sally and Neil ran past. For a moment, Neil looked at him. Really *looked*, not taking a vagrant for a dustbin or a bush. If there was recognition, it was ripped away at once.

There was no one between them and the end of the Gardens. She held Neil's hand and ran. At the top of the road was the black car. Someone lay in the gutter by it. Over him stood a man-shaped shadow. The light was behind him, he was a spreading silhouette. A stitch shot through Sally's chest as if the thug had jabbed her with his screwdriver.

Michael said goodbye to Ellen and began to walk away. Now was the time to go home and peel off the disguise, have a long bath, and spend quality time with Ginny and Melanie.

'What's up, man?' asked someone.

He looked. On a porch was a very short black man, under four feet, with skinny arms and legs. He wore large shorts and a Michael Jackson T-shirt and had a guitar slung around his neck like a kid dressing up as a rock star. Michael was shocked: he had imagined a giant, determined against odds to make his music heard.

'It's a street party, Karl,' he said.

Karl Garr grinned, enthusiastic in an instant.

'I'll get my amp,' he said.

Michael walked off down a side road. He heard large crumping noises that might be explosions.

Broken glass and brick shards rained into the street. Neil realised the gas main must have blown.

He was homeless.

On a lawn, an enraged Dolar was piling into the kid who lived opposite.

He was jobless.

Sally had stopped pulling his hand. They stood, caught between dreadful past and unthinkable future.

The minibus lurched past, yobs leaning out of the open windows and thumping the side of the vehicle.

'Oi oi oi…'

He was hopeless.

She watched as the bus swerved around the Shadowshark. She memorised its licence plate, for what it was worth. The ELF yobs were gone but people still fought. In a scuffle on a nearby lawn, she saw Dolar throttling a teenager: Pel and Zafir were making a punchbag of a child-sized black man.

Dark, thick curls of smoke crawled along the road. Another window blew out. Glass pattered on parked cars. The glazier stood in the shower, ignoring any hurt, a mad smile on his face.

Ahead was Dr Shade. Waiting.

'That's it,' Neil said. 'I give up.'

He gently extricated his hand from hers and sat down in the middle of the road, cross-legged, arms folded.

'What?' she shouted.

'I give up. I'm dropping out of the human race. Go, stay, whatever. The road can swallow me.'

'Neil?'

'There is no Neil. Just a bump in the tarmac.'

'We've got to get out of here.'

He smiled sadly, eyes shining with useless wisdom. 'No, I don't. I really don't.'

She turned away for a moment, not to abandon him but to consider her options. Dr Shade stood in front of her; a real person, not an apparition. His mouth was expressionless.

Up close for the first time, she recognised him. She had been close to him once before, in a lift.

'Derek Leech,' she said, her place lost completely.

Individual fights coalesced into riot. Houses all along the road had broken windows. Flames rose from fires. Lawn sprinklers gushed ice water jets. Everyone shouted at once, a Ragnarok rattle. Overturned cars leaked petrol trails into the gutters, begging for the spark.

Dr Shade/Derek Leech stood there, solidified dark.

'We must get him into the car' he said.

She looked at Neil. He sat, looking down, an empty glove puppet. A snake of petrol slithered around his crossed legs, dabbing at his jeans.

'Yes,' she agreed.

LEECH

CARDINAL WOLSEY STREET, 1993

Crane-like iron limbs battered the walls and roof. Bursts of steam and belches of flame emitted irregularly, scalding and scorching. Each day, dislodged tiles and bricks had to be replaced. Those who tended the Device made sacrifice. The illusion of Cardinal Wolsey Street must be preserved a little longer.

'Why are you letting us see this?' Rhodes asked.

She was a sharp little spring, tinily buried in the workings of the Device. If snapped, she would be hard to replace.

'You aren't seeing it,' he explained, 'you are part of it.'

Leech had seen the Device grow from a cold stove in an abandoned kitchen. It was interesting to discover how it struck those who hadn't lived with it for years. Through Rhodes, he saw the Device anew. A vivisected dinosaur: colossal, magnificent, dreadful.

Martin was disappointing. He had allowed himself to be brought here, but displayed no awareness, no recognition. Leech had thought he might throw himself into the grinding gears, each atom of his flesh spread and smeared throughout the mechanism.

Martin was the furnace at the heart of the Device.

Drache hovered, red robes matching his face-patch. Visitors excited the architect. He longed to conduct a tour of the Device, explaining its every nuance. Oddly, Drache believed *he* had built the Device. Truly, that honour belonged to Martin. If it was anything real, it was a model of his suffering.

'This is pain,' Drache told Rhodes. 'Rendered from the abstract into the real.'

The Deal was struck over a fire. After the Quorum left, the fire dwindled to embers. He found a glowing lump in the ashes and, nourishing it in a fist, carried it from Sutton Mallet to Cardinal Wolsey Street. Fifteen years ago, there was only one derelict house in the terrace. He broke in and found the stove. Breathing on the ember, he rekindled the flame. He broke an abandoned chair to stickwood and fed the fire. Over years, the burning heart buried itself in metal and wood and oil and flesh. Walls and floors and ceilings were taken out to accommodate its spurts of growth. The street was eaten hollow.

The practicalities were enormous: he had to buy properties, remove residents, hire machinists, authorise expenses. The Device was as hard to conceal on the books as it was in the world. Drache supervised building and demolition, brilliantly meeting the challenge of preserving the skin of Cardinal Wolsey Street as the Device grew inside.

'That's a cow, isn't it?' Rhodes asked.

'A steer actually,' Drache corrected.

The animal was held by leather straps and canvas sleeves, nourished and drained through clear plastic tubes. It was trephined, electrodes fixed to its exposed brain. A perspex bowl protected cranial matter from the flies that buzzed around its eyes.

Leech understood the smell was as awesome as the noise.

'It's disgusting,' she said.

Above, a transformation began. Mechanical limbs extended, hydraulic fluid dripping from joints, and claws fixed into crossbeams. A bulky component that was once a newspaper printing press extruded from the body of the Device and nestled among the arms, reshaping. Hot nuts and bolts sloughed like fragments of dead skin, hissing as they plopped into a muddy stretch near a coolant outlet. The press gnashed and squirted. Foil-thin sheets of metal were imprinted with filigree designs. Inside, neon pillars glowed and revolved, casting streaks of light all about, barring the walls with bright colours.

'Blessed be,' Drache breathed, bowing in wonderment. 'Hail Sathanas, Ba'alberith, Jibbenainosay...'

Leech was tolerant of Drache's diabolism. Only with Rhodes and Martin present, did he find it embarrassing.

'It's me,' Martin said, recognising.

In his dark, Leech felt a stirring. To be so close to the Perfect Sacrifice was exhilarating. Ever since the river, his options had been narrowing. He laid a hand on Martin's shoulder, easing him forwards, draping him with his cloak. Firelight illuminated Martin's tired face, gave a red shine to his eyes.

'He said the magic words,' Leech explained.

'I give up,' Martin confirmed.

The girl watched, disgust in her mind. She'd never have given up; not, in this case, a survival trait. Those who refuse to yield lock themselves into fruitless, destructive patterns.

Leech and Martin walked in the shadow of the Device. Its heat and sweat engulfed them. Components meshed and ground, waste products spurted, fuel was consumed.

'All I had to do was give up?'

Leech nodded.

Martin slipped out of Leech's cloak and walked alone to the Device. Leech respected his new determination. Rhodes called to Martin. Leech raised a hand and Drache held her wrists from behind. The communion would not be interrupted.

A siren shrilled near Martin, making him jump and laugh. The noise set the steer mooing. Martin tentatively touched a metal wall, finger-tracing a jagged weld-scar. He laid a side of his face to the Device, hugging a barrel that supported a screen. Fractals wove on the monitor.

Leech returned to the others. He had Drache release Rhodes.

'Martin built this,' he explained. 'It is *his*.'

She didn't understand. How could she?

'Who are you?' Rhodes asked.

'Leech,' he replied.

'Dr Shade?'

He was a little embarrassed by his costume. 'An aspect. A melodramatic convenience. It is hard to live without toys and games.'

'Very mature.'

He ignored her taunt.

'You're what he calls the Norwegian Neil Cullers, right? You've persecuted him for years. I don't know how or why, but you've systematically wrecked everything he ever tried to make of himself.'

Leech said nothing.

'Do you know what he did this year? He collaborated, paid to have himself beaten. He thought if he hurt himself, you'd hold off hurting him worse.'

She understood Martin. Better if truth be said, than he did. But she had the Deal and the Device mixed up.

'His friends were on to you. I guess they all tie in to you somewhere. You own a part of everything. They hired me to watch over him. That's why it's all off, isn't it? His unknown enemy has a face, a name. The toys and games are over.'

'Miss Rhodes, you are a very clever woman, but not, in truth, much of a detective. I am a neutral component. I don't do anything, I'm just here. I did nothing to Martin. I never have and never would. The Device has accepted his offerings gratefully.'

Her jaw flexed.

'It was his friends. Anything that was done to Martin was done by your employers.'

With that puzzle-piece, she could disassemble her wonky theory and put it back together perfectly.

He spelled it out. 'Dixon, Amphlett, Yeo. They call themselves the Quorum. I showed them the Deal but I did not coerce them.

Indeed, I've been consistently surprised by their invention. To me, this is not personal.'

She looked across the floor to Martin. A chairlift contraption had lowered for him. A hairdrier helmet descended around his head. Safety belts criss-crossed his chest.

'People like you,' Leech said, pointing, 'they call footsoldiers. Ever since they could afford it, they've employed people like you.'

She was thinking, trying to negotiate a way around guilt. 'You rewarded them, though. He was a sacrifice. You made them… what? Rich, successful, famous?'

On rails, Martin's chair trundled upwards and into the Device. Gates opened and closed for him. A shower of sparks fell from an arc. A steam whistle fanfare celebrated his ascendance.

'What's the Deal?'

'A great man once asked us what if there was no Heaven, no Hell,' Drache said, 'well, imagine… the freedom that gives us. The freedom to do anything, to be anything.'

'Everything is answerable,' Rhodes said.

'Where have you been living this century?' the architect asked, unkindly. 'Nothing is answerable. Everything is possible. We have opened up a whole world of possible rewards.'

'Isn't it hard to be an architect without a sense of perspective?' she asked. 'You don't see many two-dimensional buildings.'

Drache touched his half-mask, and smiled. 'I didn't say anything was free. I've made sacrifice, as must we all. The universe is a capitalist system. The things we want we must pay for. If pain is the only valid currency, then we must acquire pain. No one man could suffer enough to earn the things I want, so I need the pain of others.'

'No one man,' she said. 'I know a man who has certainly tried to suffer enough.'

Rhodes and Drache faced each other off, her grim frown against his easy smile. She broke the staring contest by winking first one eye, then the other. The architect swallowed disgust.

'He's your footsoldier, isn't he?' she asked, nodding at Drache.
'More fancy dress.'

'Miss Rhodes, I have no wish to upset you further,' Leech said.
'You've conducted yourself with unusual integrity. You and I
are the only honest players in this game. Your loyalty had to be
earned, not bought. If the Quorum had tried to use you to harm
Martin, you'd have balked. Amphlett had already realised that.
He is strangely keen on you.'

'What about him?' she said, nodding at Martin, still visible
inside the Device. 'Isn't he innocent? Isn't that the point?'

He admired her adaptability. She had been plucked from the
world she always imagined, the world without rules where people
muddled along and did their best. Exposed to the secret workings
of the universe, she was still capable of debating moral points.

'Innocent, who can say? They didn't choose him, he chose
himself. Do you know why he's here? He wanted to chat up his
best friend's girlfriend. There's no real difference between him
and the others. It could as easily have been any of them. You don't
know the circumstances. The decision was entirely random. I
took no part in it. Martin wasn't even the most likely choice. That
was your friend, Amphlett.'

'He's not my friend,' she said, vehemently.

'If it'd been Amphlett,' Leech posited, 'the working-class
Catholic, the serious scholar, the premature adult… if Amphlett
had been on the outside and Martin one of the Quorum, do you
think Martin would have acted any differently? They all came
from the same pot.'

'If it had been me,' she began.

'Not a relevant argument. You never cared enough about
anyone to do for them what the Quorum have done for Martin.
Never cared enough either way.'

That stung her.

'Until now,' he added, soothing. 'You care for your child. I
don't doubt that.'

Martin was inside the Device. It calmed, its heart secure.

'Being a mother has given you strength,' he told her, spreading his arms. 'By my own rules, I can't hurt you. There are rules, you know.'

'Who...'

'Who am I?' he anticipated, mocking. 'Who am I really? Drache thinks I'm the devil...'

Drache was on his knees, forehead pressed to bare earth. On the back of his robes was picked out in gold thread a five-pointed star containing the horned face of a goat.

'The Quorum call me their Sponsor. You thought I was a comic strip come to life. The government either want to give me a knighthood or put me in jail. Martin can't help but see me as his deliverer. My former wife said I was the Blues Walking Like a Man. None of that matters. I can be whoever and whatever people want of me. That's my gift.'

From nowhere, she laughed. A single, astonished bark of laughter. She looked away from his dark glasses, then looked back.

'What do you want me to be?' he asked.

'Better.'

'Miss Rhodes, even if, to take the worst case scenario, I'm what Drache thinks I am, if I'm the Prince of Fire and Darkness, then I'm still not as terrible as all that. For instance, I'm not as bad as the Quorum. I am incapable of the kind of quixotic malice they have shown. I can't feel like that. And, make no mistake, the Quorum are no worse than the general run of people. If anything, they're a little above average. In their public lives, they entertain and stimulate more people than they annoy and bore. Otherwise, they don't kill people, they are reasonably honest. You alone have seen only the worst of them. These are not unredeemed monsters.'

'They do a lot of work for charity, right?'

'Mickey Yeo was on the bill at Live Aid.'

She shook her head. For a moment, Leech thought he missed

something. Then, it was over. Whatever either could derive from the interview had come and gone.

'Martin must stay for a while,' he explained. 'He'll be looked after. It may seem disturbing from the outside but you have my word he won't be further hurt. The Device will cherish him. It can hardly do otherwise.'

'Thank you,' she said.

'You'll be driven wherever you wish. If money would help, call my executive secretary.'

Together, they walked back to Drache, to the car. The Device rejoiced with fire and music.

For a long while, Rhodes thought.

'Bastards,' she said finally, with feeling.

'Which do you mean?' Leech asked, interested.

'Take your pick,' she said, eyes hard, 'take your pick.'

BOOK

3

DEVICES

'Life is short, but long enough to get what's coming to you.'

JOHN ALTON, *Painting With Light*

1

11 JANUARY, 1993

A sledgehammer woke him. He felt his skull shattering as he groped the bedside clock. Four-thirty in New York City. He'd been in bed two hours, asleep for ninety minutes. Next to him, Heather breathed heavily (only the unchivalrous would say snoring). It was past nine a.m. in London. His mental gyroscope had faltered. For the first time in his ocean-hopping life, Mickey was jet-lagged. He tried to squeeze the fog from his brain. Thumbs of ache pushed the hammer wound, pressing broken bone plates into grey matter.

Unbelievably, he was completely awake. Too tired to sleep, he lay on the bed. Water wobbled under thin plastic. The silk sheet was slippery. Above him, through the skylight, he saw no stars. Grit had worked its way behind his eyes. He found a remote control and turned on the large-screen TV. A pale glow preceded the picture.

He remembered being in a TV studio yesterday or the day before, demolishing a humourless feminist. Nancy Lucey Kunst stammered terribly, leaving him to toss in snappy replies, to work the studio audience. She'd burbled about the need for positive role models. His base line was that 'Amazon Queen ain't exactly Hedda Gabler.'

He zapped through dozens of channels. As a kid, he'd imagined American all-night TV a wonderland of the movies the BBC never showed: Italian musclemen, the Bowery Boys, Hells' Angels, Japanese monsters. All he found now was news in Esperanto, shopping for fake jewellery, *The Dukes of Hazzard* in Spanish and public access transvestite gossip. He settled for Cloud 9, which he could get in Camden Town.

He caught the tail-end of British news. John Major was dithering over Maastricht and there'd been a riot in North London. About fuckin' time. He was astonished Brits put up with so much before shooting policemen, liberating electrical goods and burning down cornershops. Americans were more combustible: *You want a riot, sir? Jeepers, what a marvy idea! Let's have the riot RIGHT HERE!*

Heather murmured in her sleep and turned, curtaining her face with hair that still looked as if someone else had spent two hours on it. She had a sister working in London and might visit. Something in him stirred at the idea of two Wildings, working together for his personal ease and convenience. But something else reminded him he was only in town for a few more days. Shag-hags never last. After a while, they cross the line and become fuck-pigs. Then, there's only the long walk to the door.

Coming next on Cloud 9, according to the announcer was 'the sci-fi classic, *City Hammer*'. He owned his film on video cassette, laser disc, computer game, comic tie-in, soundtrack album on vinyl and CD, novelisation and bound original script autographed by the entire cast and crew. But the pre-credits sequence always worked for him. Dentata, warrior queen of the wasteland, ground Cameron Mitchell under the spiked wheels of her Chevvy chariot.

As he watched, for maybe the fiftieth time, he noticed a continuity error between the first and second shots. Dentata's scorpion armlet changed from her right to left arm. Funny nobody had ever mentioned it. Too many lines of nose candy in the edit suite. After a burst of ultra-violence, The Möthers of Pain delivered a crash of thrash and opening titles ripped across the screen in red. 'Scream queen' Breeze Brasselle, who had given him one of the five best blow jobs of his life, froze in the frame as her credit came up. She played Dentata, a career step between X-rated cheerleaders and daytime soaps.

The print was worn and splicy, unusual on Cloud 9. A few frames were missing every couple of seconds, so individual credits came and went faster than the eye could scan. When it came to 'Story and Screenplay by Mickey Yeo', there was a lurch; his own credit was swallowed completely. He felt like telephoning a complaint to the duty officer. It had been a long weekend, turning out the script.

Then the final credit exploded in letters of molten steel. 'Written and Directed by Allan Keyes'. A nail of rage shot into his brain. *Allan Keyes!* Mickey had, without credit, directed any sequences of *City Hammer* not involving exploding cars. Confronted with Breeze in leather thongs and keloid nipples, the film school wanker flushed scarlet and went off to play with miniatures. Only charity, and an uneasy feeling the project was doomed to the 'ex-rental tapes from £2.99' bin, prompted Mickey to let Keyes take solo credit.

'*Written* and Directed...' He wanted to wake Heather and have her arrange the termination of Allan Keyes. He shouldn't be difficult to find; after the fluke success of a franchise horror film, *Where the Bodies Are Buried*, he had nosedived with a ruinously expensive fairy tale cop movie, *Pixie Patrol*. Keyes was probably doing episodic TV or scrabbling to direct a *Friday the 13th* sequel. On how many prints had Keyes usurped his credit?

The film ground on. Then, as Breeze established telepathic contact with her unborn mutant, the scene shifted to a cardboard space station where a fat comedian with green antennae made wise-ass jokes.

'Great movie, huh?' he said to the camera, addressing Mickey directly. 'NOUGHT!'

An ident crawl gave the name of the show. *Melvin the Martian's Tube Trash Theater.*

'If this flick sucked any more you could use it as a vacuum cleaner,' the Martian ranted. 'Let's face it, this specimen is the sort of motion picture you'd walk out if it were playing as an in-flight movie. What about that snappy script? Did you catch "suck my sump, you mutoid filth-breather!" No wonder William Faulkner didn't want to take that additional dialogue credit...'

Mickey was appalled. Hadn't *City Hammer* been registered with the Museum of Modern Art to preserve it from this sort of idiocy? If *High Noon* was protected from colourisation, wasn't he protected from asinine interruption? Only this wasn't his. It was *un film de Allan Keyes.*

'And Breeze Brasselle, eh? What an actress! I bet Meryl Streep has nightmares about her around Academy Awards time. NOUGHT! I understand she's a graduate of the Producer's Girlfriend School of Dramatic Arts. For that scene where she gets raped with a broomstick, she studied with Lee Strasberg so she wouldn't be upstaged by her co-star. It was a great injustice that the stick walked off with all the reviews.'

The comedian's face shrank, matted into a screen within the frame of the film. *City Hammer* continued where it had left off, with Dentata kidnapped by the Eco-Fascists of Futuria. Mickey put his hand on Heather's warm shoulder and shook. He had to stick something to someone or explode. For the first time, she refused to be roused from sleep. Heather buried her face in a pillow and went comatose, even when his fingers squeezed her ass hard enough to leave marks.

Breeze stuck out her tongue in close-up and bore down on Brock Daves, the surfer hunk she'd later kill and eat. Daves was as queer as a nine-bob note but Breeze prevailed on him to give a natural performance in the sweatbox sex scene. Irrevocably awake and pissed off, Mickey watched the movie, gritting his teeth against the next unavoidable interruption by Melvin the Martian. Tomorrow, he'd find out which fuckwit sold the rights to *Tube Trash Theater* and have them disemployed.

Next morning, Raimundo was driving a different car: a perfectly adequate four-door sedan, but not a limousine. The back seat stank vaguely, as if the last passenger had been a chain smoker.

There were even more picketing fudge-packers in the Pyramid Plaza forecourt than there had been last week. The S&M community was well-represented; Mickey saw a protester in a PVC and leather reproduction of the Streak's skintight leotard. *Pink Swastika* premiered on 1,000 screens across the country this Friday.

'Urgh,' he said, 'WoFBReIGN.'

'Pardon?' Heather said.

'This is the first time I've run the lobby gauntlet since I did for Nancy Loose Cunt. Her groupies will have sharp sticks and pots of paint.'

'You intuit physical danger?' Heather was concerned. 'I'll reconnoitre.'

She decided it'd be best to drop Mickey off and go ahead to the Plaza then come back for him.

Finding himself at liberty outside a large bookstore, he went in and searched out graphic novels. They didn't have *Choke Hold* or any of his stuff. Not even *The Nevergone Void*, for which there was a poster of a disappearing Amazon Queen. There was a tall stack of new Alan Moore and more Neil Gaiman than the human mind could stand. He looked at the *Nevergone* poster and noticed his name was mispelled 'Mickey Yo'.

'Yo Yeo,' he thought. 'Yo-yo.'

Wandering back to the entrance, he came out in time to be

picked up by Raimundo. Without explanation, he was ferried to the Plaza. Crowds parted to let him through.

Heather waited just inside the lobby. The WoFBReIGN teepee was gone.

'They packed up over the weekend,' Heather explained. 'There's a rumour Marvel are doing a lesbian serial killer storyline in *The Fantastic Four* and they've gone to protest that.'

He felt light-headed, disoriented. The absence of protesters should have been pleasant, but he kind of missed them. It'd been nice to know he had an effect. Everyone else in the building rolled over and let him do what he wanted; only the WoFBReIGN Wimmin even tried to fight back. Didn't anybody care any more?

Timmy Chin was in a meeting and they had to wait. Heather posed on a chair and said nothing, a switched-off robot waiting to be reactivated. Mickey sat with a cup of cooling coffee (last week, he'd rated real espresso – with a swirl of cream – now he got instant muck) and looked about. His night of weariness crept up and anchored him to a couch. He looked around the reception area.

He would have sworn his first *Circe* cover was among the framed classics displayed behind the receptionist's desk. It seemed to have been replaced. He couldn't tell with what. He thought he remembered the *Sergeant Grit*, the *Vindicator* and the *Teensy Teen*. Some of the comics now valued in hundreds of dollars he'd bought for nine old pence when he was first reading ZCs. He remembered buying a missing *Dazzling Duo Stories* from Neil Martin for twenty pence in 1972. Who'd have thought then he'd be the one to kill Amazon Queen?

The Vindicator, a Vietnam vet cyborg created as a villain in the late seventies, who grew to be ZC's most popular character in the eighties, never seemed as real as the forties stalwarts. Vin came along after he had stopped reading comics, and was an established usurper when he returned to the field. The Nevergonners were going to alter the past and make sure the grunts who fragged the cybernazi in the first place did a better job of it.

His mind was crammed with ZC factoids. Neil and he had debated them for years. He couldn't have written *The Nevergone Void* if he hadn't cared deeply about the four-colour, two-dimensional characters. For him, the game was to destroy the ZC Universe while being true to its trivia. He remembered Teensy Teen was Blubber Boy's cousin; their secret identities were high-schoolers Carrie Kilian and Bubby Boyd. Why nobody guessed Bubby Boyd was Blubber Boy was one of those questions even eleven-year-olds ask.

Amazon Queen had a sister. What was her name? She was on the wall in a clean-lined fifties cover, menaced by Max Multiple. Amazon Queen's sister? In his mind there was a small blank space where the name should be written. He scrolled through a ton of adjacent information. His New Year's Eve shag-hag in 1978 was called Denise Brierly. The entry code to Michael's London office was 2150. In the TV series, Catwoman was played by Julie Newmar and Eartha Kitt, but in the movie she was Lee Meriwether (Michelle Pfeiffer didn't count). Loud Stuff's breakthrough album was *Pusher X*.

And Amazon Queen's sister was...?

The tiny white gap gave him a headache. He tried not to think about it, sure it would spring to him automatically as soon as he forgot it. He tried to think of something else entirely. He wondered about this year's moves. Should he call Michael or Mark?

Persephone? No.

It was like trying to pick up a pin with boxing gloves.

Proserpina? Pandora? Philomena? Penelope? Pippa?

Pippa? Where did she come from? It was ages since he'd seen Mark's toffee-twat girlfriend. She disapproved of the Quorum.

He looked up at the ceiling, memories leaking through a

pinprick in the back of his head. Soon he would forget who Cary Trenton was...

Timmy's office door opened and Timmy appeared, showing out a young black man with an Egyptian eye shaved into his hackles. He carried an art-folder. Timmy was excited, hovering close to the kid – he must be only about twenty-one – restraining himself from touching.

'Mickey,' Timmy said, finally noticing, not apologising, 'this is Farhad Z-Rowe. He's going to be big.'

Z-Rowe looked at him, obviously knowing who he was, and kept his free hand in his baseball jacket pocket.

'He's the new you,' Timmy said, grinning.

Z-Rowe showed perfect white teeth. His eyes narrowed to slits.

'Yo Yeo,' he said. 'Yo-yo.'

'You've got to see his stuff,' Timmy enthused. 'We're giving him his own book. It'll be a breakthrough.'

Z-Rowe nodded. He was small but his shoulders were broad. Under his jacket he wore a T-shirt stretched taut over muscles. His stance said he could break Mickey in two.

'You used to be hot shit,' Z-Rowe said, and left.

Heather was expressionless. He wondered if she were meditating.

'I can only spare you five minutes,' Timmy said. 'I've got an interview. There's nothing much we have to talk through, is there?'

The *maitre d'* at Chiodo's had no reservation in the names of Karsch or Manoogian, and neither Dick nor Eivol had got to the restaurant before them. Heather negotiated. A table was found in the leper colony by the kitchen door.

'You will be four?' the *maitre d'* confirmed. Two could be seated with much less agony.

Heather told the functionary others were expected. After twenty minutes, neither Dick nor Eivol had shown and, on the fifth imperious pass, a waiter was snagged to take their order. He could do with a pile of egg and chips but was forced to have a crispy ring of spinach garnished with bitter red sauce.

Heather, who'd said very little today, ran out of conversation. If anything she looked more perfect than usual but the motor inside was running down.

'That Z-Rowe geezer,' he asked, 'have you glommed him?'

She hadn't.

He could imagine: young, ethnic, brilliant. The new Mickey Yeo. Sorry, the new Mickey Yo.

He would be Hot Shit.

'What was the name of Amazon Queen's sister?'

'Priscilla.'

Even before she said it, he remembered. His mind was whole again. The scrap had been the keystone of his memory.

'Fuckin' right. Priscilla.'

They finished their appetiser and main course. Heather slipped off to make a call to Dick Karsch's office to be sure there was no mistake. Dick had picked the restaurant and given precise instructions. Left alone, Mickey sagged in his chair. It was one o'clock in the afternoon in Manhattan, six o'clock in the evening in Camden Town, and hours past midnight in his brain.

Looking across Chiodo's, he saw Eivol Manoogian with a group of six or seven men and women. He was cracking open and consuming a crab, laughing at something that was being said. The *maitre d'* had fouled up completely and, with a vicious determination, he vowed to have the poltroon's job for it.

He got up to cross to Eivol's table and Heather returned.

'I couldn't get through. Everyone is out to lunch, including Dick. I'm to try again.'

'There's that Manoogian fucker over there,' he said. 'We've been exiled to fuckin' Siberia.'

Eivol's table was surrounded by an almost mystic glow. It wasn't in a bow window, exposed to the gawp of passersby, but golden light fell around it. At that table, people dined with the angels.

He made a move, but Heather held his arm, almost fearful.

'No mistake,' she said.

His brows clenched. 'What's up, Heth?'

Heather wouldn't let him move.

'Let's do dessert,' she said, with brittle sweetness.

Eivol laughed again, lustily. His portion was huge, delicious steam rising from it.

'Knickerbocker glory,' Heather suggested.

The afternoon interview was scheduled at the hotel. They checked at the front desk and found the journalist had cancelled, leaving no explanation. He was probably crawling up Farhad Z-Rowe's arse, or having venison fritters with Eivol Manoogian.

Heather made a call from the desk, to discover whether the interview was to be rescheduled. Mickey wandered about the cavernous lobby in a special orange twilight. In a far corner, surrounded by a fortification of suitcases and instruments, he found Grattan of Loud Stuff, drooling slightly, eyes as red as Dracula's.

'Hey, Grat,' he said, 'fuckin' yanks, eh?'

'Fuck yes,' the musician said, head rolling up with his eyes, 'fucking *fucking* yanks.'

An eleven-year-old dressed like a hooker pounced on Grat with an autograph book. He made a huge effort and talked to her, running wearily lecherous eyes up her long, bare legs. Excluded, Mickey drifted back to the desk. Heather was gone.

A twinge of panic came and went.

'The Ms said she'd wait for you upstairs, sir,' the desk clerk said. 'In her suite. 1908.'

He had no idea Heather had a suite in the hotel. The clerk handed over a cardkey and directed him to the nineteenth floor. Limbs heavy, he dragged himself to the elevator bank.

At the end of an unfamiliar corridor, he found 1908. The key opened the door, and he stepped in. It wasn't the Apex, but it was luxurious enough. The curtains were drawn, sunlight penetrating the weave. Water was running in the bathroom.

'Having a soak, Heth?' he asked, tempted to join her.

He was shagged out. Looking at the four-poster bed, his first thought was to get a good eight hours' kip and wake up to sausage and bacon and fried bread with brown sauce and a mug of creosote tea. His scalp itched under his braids.

Shucking off his jacket, he sat on the bed. Bending at the knees, he lay down as if on a guillotine, looking up at the blade of the canopy.

Amazon Queen's sister was called Priscilla. His mind was still there.

He kicked off his boots, undid his belt and wriggled backwards out of his jeans. An afternoon of sleep was what he needed, followed perhaps by a refreshing blow job about teatime.

Heather came out of the bathroom. He heard her and couldn't work up the strength to lift his head. Fuck, he was shattered. She leaned over him, hair tickling his face, and he opened his eyes. She wore a black and yellow domino mask and red lipstick.

He eased himself up on his elbows, pain rippling down his spine between his shoulder-blades. Heather had changed her clothes. Besides the mask, she wore a one-piece yellow swimsuit cut high on her thighs and low in front, with missing panels showing circles of tanned skin. A leatherwork whip dangled from a six-inch black leather belt. She had matching spike-heeled thighboots and elbow-length gloves. A yellow cape was fastened around her neck by a jewel cameo.

'Amazon Queen,' he said, unbelieving.

She slapped him lightly, a backhand that bumped his skull off the headboard. She laughed self-consciously and apologised.

Then, solemn, she uncurled the whip and flicked his inner thighs with its point. She'd not become skilled enough to do that without a lot of practice.

'You never were,' he said.

She kissed him, gloved fingers working up his body from thigh to armpit then pushed herself away and laid a stroke across his stomach. It stung like a bastard.

'Heth,' he said, 'sorry love, but I'm just about dead on my feet. Couldn't this wait?'

The next stroke hurt more.

'This'll teach you to kill me,' she said.

He tried to sit up again but all the strength had gone out of his arms and back.

Afterwards, he escaped. Bruised and tingling, remembering real pain and pretend pleasure, he staggered alone to the elevator. Heather, changing, agreed to leave him be for a few hours. Having gone through the charade, she was almost embarrassed. In the end, despite a burst of willing on his part, she'd finished herself off with the whip-handle. It was hard for mortals to keep up with superheroines.

He leaned against the wall of the Apex elevator and chanted the name Priscilla over and over. If everything else went, he would remember Amazon Queen's sister.

Did all Pyramid employees get their own superhero costumes?

The Apex elevator halted and the doors opened. In the antechamber he fumbled his own cardkey out of his jeans and passed it through the slot. Nothing happened. He tried again, experimenting with different sides of the card. Still, the inner door wouldn't open.

Fuck.

He turned to the elevator to find it had gone down. Private for the Apex Suite, it was no use to anyone else. He stabbed the button, but it didn't return. His knees felt like giving out. He tried the cardkey again. He ran it through the slot several times rapidly, as if trying to strike a damp match. No joy.

A tiny cut on his back was dribbling into his shirt, sticking the fabric to his skin. Heather getting enthusiastic.

He tried the elevator button again. The indicator which could only indicate the first floor – the ground floor in English – and the Apex Suite, said the cage had descended to the lobby. It was staying there for the foreseeable future.

There were stairs. He could go down a floor to the Presidential Suite and grab one of their elevators, or go down even further and find Heather. Maybe this time she'd let him sleep in her bed.

He tried the door once more. *Bastard!*

Incredibly, the Apex Suite had a private staircase too, winding infinitely, never connecting with the rest of the hotel. He staggered, hand weakly on the banister, down through numberless, featureless levels.

His ankles ached in his boots. Cold seminal fluid scabbed inside his foreskin. Drawing pins behind his eyes jammed into the sockets. Down and down he went. This Monday was different.

Finally he came out of the staircase in a sub-basement bowel and had to make his way past deserted function rooms and a disused kitchen. Wandering into a sunken ballroom that listed strangely as if on the *Titanic*, he thought he saw a man in black by the orchestra dais. The shadow turned out to be a long fold of curtain trapped on a music stand. The ballroom was as cold inside as a fridge and he left quickly, looking for stairs.

He emerged into the lobby. Musak tinkled in the gloom. Grattan was gone, luggage and groupie with him. Late afternoon sun spilled in from the revolving doors but was squashed after a dozen feet.

There was a new desk clerk, another efficient young man in a blue blazer. Before he took his problem to the clerk, he'd sit down on one of the couches for a few minutes and get his breath back.

Maybe he could subtly take his boots off.

Grattan had looked like a wino and nobody had bothered him, except the pre-pube shag-hag. He took the rocker's old post and sank into slightly warm upholstery. He did not fall asleep exactly, just switched off.

2

11 JANUARY, 1993

She hadn't left the flat in two days. She regularly fed the Invader but not herself. She slept in spells of a couple of hours, mainly with the baby. For the first time since the hospital, she couldn't bear to let her child go. The warm unquestioning loving bundle fit perfectly against her body. Together, they stayed in her bed.

It was possible she'd cracked up.

The telephone rang and her own voice – younger, brighter, stupider – told the caller to leave a message. It was Ayesha McPherson, asking her to call Top Hat. She shuddered, cold. Just now, she never wanted any more to do with any of them. The Quorum. Neil. Leech.

The Invader gurgled warm fluid over her neck. With her left hand, she extracted a man-size kleenex from the bedside dispenser. After easing the baby aside, she wiped herself off. Then she applied a spit-damped tissue corner to the soft, tiny face. It'd be walking soon. Then the long, slippery slope that leads to leaving.

'Mother, I feel it's my duty as a citizen to report you to the Secret Police...'

How would she feel when her baby grew up and joined the English Liberation Front? Or was responsible for the repopularising of Barry Manilow? Or struck a Deal with whoever Derek Leech was in the next century? Maybe next time, he'd ask someone to make a Perfect Sacrifice of their mother, their child...

She shook with hatred.

The Invader bawled and she was overcome with a rush of guilty love. Cooing and humming, she jollied the baby back to sleep. The offspring was sensitive to Mummy's Moods.

The telephone rang again.

'Ms Rhodes, this is Michael Dixon. Could you call me, at the office or at home? It's the Gary Gaunt situation. I'd like to take action.'

He didn't sound different. He didn't sound like a man who'd spent fifteen years wrecking a friend's life.

Outside, darkness was accumulating. Upstairs, music was playing. She had a cramp from so much lying in bed. Her dressing-gown was starting to smell of more than baby-sick.

Neil Martin had collaborated, then given up. There was no reason for her not to go along with him.

Mummy, are there really monsters?

She'd always known creatures like Leech were in the world. She'd met them. She could hardly even pretend to be surprised or disgusted. In person, he embodied a dark purity that could even seem admirable.

It was the Quorum. She tried to stretch her mind around what they'd done. It was disturbingly easy to imagine, a fascinating game. So many details of Neil Martin's life, puzzle-knots she'd combed against, now made sense. And so many things she'd picked up from her meetings with Mark and Michael. All the clues had been there.

The Deal must have been an enormous challenge, especially at first, when they were students. If it could be done with no financial resources and few contacts, how much easier was it for the men they became? Men with influence and power and friends and money. She'd done her time as a footsoldier. How many moves had been prompted or abetted by her reports?

Then you worked it out, Mummy? Like a proper detective?

She'd been hired between New Year's Eve and Valentine's Day. The dates bounded the Deal. The Quorum had only six weeks to make moves. Time enough. In under two weeks, the persecution had achieved its ultimate end.

Was it over? Had the Quorum won?

If Neil was out of the game, where did that leave the others? Where did it leave her?

Another person might turn on her masters, undo the Device, pull the Deal apart. See cosmic justice done. She half-thought Leech wanted that of her. But if serving the Quorum left her wrung-dry and dead, how would she feel if she became Leech's footsoldier?

She held her baby.

What did you do next, Mummy?

Good question, kid.

3

9-11 JANUARY, 1993

'I've got a plate in my skull,' Dolar said, for the twelfth time, 'a silver plate from like Vietnam, only I got it coming off a bike at Reading. I get interference from secret government stations. It's why I'm here, man. I'm locked up cause I like know too much. It's Mars. They're all going to Mars, the pigs, the Royal Family, the gunmint. We're like left gasping when the Earth's air farts away through the ozone layer, but they're gonna terraform this alien world and make it Earth II. There're no aliens, like extraterrestrials, in UFOs, they're gunmint spies, setting up this Exodus of the Establishment. It's been coming a long time. Lenin knew all about the ecosphere, that's why they killed him. The Nazis were part of it, and Aleister Crowley. Kennedy said he'd get to the bottom of it before Castro had him shot.'

'And Elvis?' Mark said, pointedly. The cell was a ten-foot cube; sharing it with Dolar was like being buried alive with a hyperactive stoat.

'Elvis?' the hippie said. 'What's Elvis got to do with anything? We're into important issues like the survival of humanity, and you're talking rock 'n' roll icons.'

Mark didn't know where they were and no one, not even kindly WPC Cotterill, would deign to tell him. There'd been an overflow in Muswell Hill (not enough cells for the 'rioters') and some were bussed out to other holding facilities. Since he was lumped with Dolar, who addressed constables as 'Earthling Pig', not much sympathy was directed his way.

In the next cell, ELF bruisers struck up an 'oi' chant of 'Rule Britannia, Britannia Kicks Coon Arse' as a black policeman walked by. Mark understood the Metropolitan Police underrepresented minorities; he suspected they'd drafted in a token black face to wander the cell corridor and irritate the arrested Neo-Nazis.

He'd been in his clothes for what seemed a week. His chin was sandpapery when he twitched his lower lip across it. There was a toilet but he wasn't able to use it in comfort when Dolar was awake. Several times, he'd unzipped and pointed, desperate to empty his strained bladder, but found himself unable to get a flow started. It was not pleasant.

'The world, man,' Dolar said. 'It's gone. Welcome to the Planet Shit.'

Lying face-up in the road, he was sure his arm was under the front wheel of the Rolls-Royce. When it drove off, his elbow would be crushed. If he sat up, he'd leave his forearm and hand stuck to the asphalt. But the car shifted its shadow, exposing him to the light, and he was unharmed. At least, unharmed by wheels.

He could blink and breathe but nothing else. He was a passenger in his own body. It was as if he'd been injected with ice. People ran past. Someone trod on his hand. He heard glass breaking, shouts, sirens. The white sky blurred, black smoke drifting across it.

Hands gripped him roughly and rolled him over. His face bumped the kerb. He felt his back pocket ripping away. That was his wallet gone. Seven credit cards and some cash. A picture of Pippa.

A bruise was coming on his forehead. The shock of pain gave

him back some control. He propped himself up. Cranley Gardens was burning. A thick cloud of stinging smoke wafted past him.

He got slowly to his feet. He looked around for Sally but couldn't see her. Michael was gone. Neil was lost in the melee. He was half-possessed, an inept *dybbuk* in his mental driving seat. He was still in control but had to issue irritatingly literal orders to himself, as if dealing with a primitive computer.

Walk, don't run. Leave.

Police vans poured into the road. Constables in hastily assembled combat gear piled out, huddled behind shields, brandishing batons. They charged.

He found railings and clung to them, still feeling as if he'd been zapped in the heart with a stungun. His train of thought kept dissolving in bursts of mental static.

The house where Neil lived was seriously on fire. Distant fire engines clanged.

Where was Sally?

It was important he find the private detective.

'You,' a policeman said, 'on your knees.'

'Pardon,' Mark thought, fuddled. 'Fuck off,' the *dybbuk* controlling his mouth said aloud, tentative but audible. 'Fuck off and die?'

A baton lashed his kneecaps and he sank in a prayer of agony. More hands grasped and patted him.

'Clear,' a policeman said.

'Bin 'im.'

He was wrestled along the pavement. Two policemen had him jammed in a wedge of perspex shields. He was shoved towards the open back of a van.

Without a wallet, he had no identification. He gave WPC Cotterill, the policewoman who was processing him, numbers for the town house and the country cottage. She tried – he was there as she made the calls – and got only machines. Pippa was either not back or out. There wouldn't be anyone at *The Shape* until Monday morning, so no one there could identify him. She said they'd have to check the electoral roll, to prove he was who he said he was and lived where he said he did. Stupid people still give false names to the police though every record could be accessed by computers. He didn't say anything but had a horrible feeling he wasn't on the roll: at the last election he'd turned up at the polling station to find Pippa had erroneously filled in a form, disenfranchising him at both addresses. WPC Cotterill didn't treat him – as did her Gestapo riot squad colleagues – as if he were solely responsible for the affray and arson in Cranley Gardens. Her approach was that his arrest was probably a mistake and she'd do her best to sort it out. In the meantime, he had to be photographed and fingerprinted. The ink would not wash off easily.

They took his belt, scarf and bootlaces and stuck him in with Dolar, owner of Planet Janet. Their cell had a tiny, unattainable window-slit near the ceiling and was tiled, floor and ceiling as well as walls, like a shower bath. There was a bunk bed. Dolar greeted him as if he were a comrade from the barricades.

After a couple of hours, it came out that Mark was the author of *The Shape of the Now*. In his chapter on 'Bad Influences', he was highly critical of William S. Burroughs, whom Dolar regarded as the premier creative genius of the century. Ten years on, Mark hated debating anything in *The Shape of the Now*. That book was so closely argued and thoroughly thought-through that nothing anyone could say would make him concede a point. Unless someone had been through the process of researching and writing the book, they weren't even qualified to enter the debate. Anyone who tried, always turned out to be the kind of addled half-clever kook he was stuck with now.

Dolar's three-hour harangue operated from a premise Mark

could not accept: that Burroughs was worth more than the footnote he'd given him. At the end of the rant, he did revise his personal literary pantheon, out of spite. That niche where he'd once placed Burroughs, in the Gallery of the Hippie Hold-Outs between Vonnegut and Salinger, now seemed about right for Enid Blyton.

Eventually, Dolar wound down and went to sleep. He rasped like a chainsaw. This was not the sort of thing that happened to Mark Amphlett. This, he realised with a profound coldness, was the sort of thing that happened to Neil Martin.

He woke in the night, and took a moment to remember where he was, to realise this was not a further nightmare. Someone else was in the cell, crouched by the sink, a shaft of light brushing his head. He was balding and bearded, dressed in what was once, a million years ago, a suit.

Mark hadn't woken up. He was dreaming still.

Leaning into the light, the new prisoner showed his face. It was Mark's own, obscured by a fuzz of beard, forehead and cheeks deeply creased. He held a pair of broken glasses.

'I let Michael drive,' the other Mark said, Somerset accent absurdly thick. 'Neil and Mickey could handle 'en, I knew that. Wanted to clear off, with Pippa, I did.'

His own voice sounded different. Not the difference he heard when watching himself on TV. This was a stranger with his vocal cords. There was tiredness in every word.

'I lost thic place. Noth'n ever come out right for I.'

The other Mark tried to fit his glasses together on his face but they kept falling apart.

'I's like they bloke in Neil's books,' he said, an idiotic sad smile appearing. 'The Eternal Loser.'

From the shadows of the lower berth, Mark looked at himself. A crack of panic appeared in his dream, and he gripped the edges of the bunk, determined not to scream.

'Neil done well for hisself, though,' the other Mark said, with a horribly pathetic smile. 'He deserves 'en, all the work he done.'

The other Mark's neck was scrawny, dirt in the lines under his ears. His fingernails were blueing and broken.

'Michael and Mickey too. Real talents, they.'

They couldn't keep him in this cell much longer. He must go free soon.

Musing, the other Mark said, 'Wonder whatever happened to thic Pippa?'

In the morning, he was woken by gargling. Dolar turned to Mark and looked seriously, disapprovingly. He stood hairily naked at the wash-basin.

'I really think you should like reconsider your statements on Bill Burroughs…'

Mark turned his face to the wall. He considered praying. It had been a long time. They said Catholicism put a brand on your soul in infancy. He hadn't thought much of his alleged religion since school. His sister Liza, pregnant and married at sixteen, had turned religious the way some people become drug addicts, and her occasional ill-spelled postcards – always asking for something – were full of 'God's Will'.

'Burroughs really *understands* the way the world is put together, man. He knows all about the fish police from Jupiter.'

Mark looked up at the bottom of the upper berth and tried to construct Sally Rhodes's face in his mind. He never had connected with her. Perhaps that was when it'd all begun to fall apart.

'I'm afraid we can't find you on the electoral register and all the numbers you gave us are unlisted.'

WPC Cotterill, who had the sort of face usually found

advertising frozen foods, was apologetic. She understood he was an innocent passerby who had the misfortune to be involved in a riot. It was unspoken that they would forget him insulting a police officer if he forget the baton across his knees. Last night the Chief Constable of Greater London had made a law and order speech, promising the instigators of the Cranley Gardens Troubles would be duly punished. Stiff sentences were expected.

Mark recognised justice. In the end, he *was* guilty. If not for the Quorum, there wouldn't have been a riot.

He hadn't been charged so they'd have to let him go soon, he thought. WPC Cotterill kindly told him the Chief Constable was claiming the Prevention of Terrorism Act ought to apply, which meant the police could keep hold of suspects for weeks without making any formal case.

'Terrorism?'

'The English Liberation Front are a political faction.'

'They looked like a bunch of obnoxious yobs to me.'

She asked him if he'd been fed properly. Would he like a cup of tea? Something to read?

'I could do with a cell without a hot and cold running hippie.'

She smiled sympathetically and told him he was well off. Among the other arrestees were a vanload of ELF stormtroopers who embarrassingly bumped into a panda car fleeing the scene of the crime. He could be in with them.

'You could phone Pippa's parents. They live in Scotland. The number was in my wallet but I can't remember it offhand. It's in Edinburgh. 031 something…'

'What's his surname?'

His heart plunged. 'McDonald.'

'Anything more than Edinburgh?'

'No. Sorry. Everyone calls Pippa's Dad Jock, but I don't think that's his real name. It's what they called him in the Army.'

She tried to look bright. 'Not much use, I'm afraid. But we'll try!'

* * *

Sure Dolar was asleep, he tiptoed to the toilet. Blissfully, his bladder let go of fifteen cups of police tea. He directed the stream at the porcelain rather than the water. The quiet swish didn't wake his cellmate.

A low moan sounded out. Mark's stream backed up, a crawl of urine clogging his urethra with a needle of pain.

He turned and saw himself huddled by the sink. Moonlight shone like a shaky halo around the battered figure. The black streaks on the other Mark's face were blood. One eye was bruised shut, a network of barely scabbed cuts cobwebbing his cheek. His suit was ripped along its seams. Black splotches of blood marred the lapels. Tonight he didn't speak, just keened like an animal and hugged his knees, rocking back and forth.

Mark sat on the cold floor and looked at himself.

'Looks like we're in the same boat,' he said.

'I tried the magazine you mentioned,' WPC Cotterill said on Monday morning, 'The Shape?'

It was obvious she had never heard of it. He'd have to do something about market penetration.

'Thank God. Did you talk with Laura-Leigh?'

She was puzzled. 'They weren't very helpful, I'm afraid. The girl thought I was asking for Mark Amphlett and said he wasn't available.'

She was trying not to say they doubted he was who he said he was.

On Monday afternoon they let Dolar out. A patient woman – Janet of Planet Janet fame – came to collect him and ease him through the station, calming his outbursts, signing papers as if picking up a sheep worrier from the dog-pound.

'Remember Bill Burroughs,' Dolar shouted as a parting shot.

'He's the man who knows...'

Mark was left alone with his cold thoughts.

He imagined how many quadrillion McDonalds were listed in the Edinburgh area. He fantasised his saintly WPC calling all their numbers and asking for 'Jock'.

The corridor outside the cells was quieter than it had been. On Saturday, ELF goons and looters had shouted and taunted each other. Now Mark was one of the last remaining arrestees in custody.

He couldn't shake the cold out of his bones. The black ink on his fingertips seemed to have turned sticky. His knuckle ached under the weight of the Quorum Ring.

When a constable came round with tea and a slice of bread and butter, he gave him a message to relay to WPC Cotterill, asking her to call Sally Rhodes Security Services. As his employee, Sally could identify him and get him out of here. At last, he felt he had done something positive.

4

11 JANUARY, 1993

With Ginny returning Melanie to the rich kiddery, he was alone in the house, pretending to tidy his desk, when the papers came. The regular deliverer, a sprightly and conscientious pensioner on a slave-wage from his newsagent son, rang the bell. He dawdled to the door

'There's prob'ly been a mistake,' the pensioner said, holding up a *Basildon Echo*. 'I've never even *seen* this one before.'

'No,' Michael said, 'that's right. I put in a special order.'

The paper man looked at him askew. It was inconceivable anyone should forsake the *Ham and High* for a Basildon paper. Michael didn't have to explain himself to a tradesman. Today, the *Echo* should run his letter of comment. That should settle the hash for good.

He had spent a full day drafting and redrafting a rebuttal of the infamous Gary Gaunt slurs. He'd read and reread Gaunt's original review (much more detailed and waffle-headed than his Worst of Year mention) and could answer it on every point. He'd culled testimonial quotes from real newspapers. To the accusation that he was a 'toothless Tom Sharpe', he had an ultimate counter: an approving write-up *by* Tom Sharpe, from one of the Sunday heavies. He'd been tempted to photostat his dental records. Nothing wrong with his choppers.

The *Echo* lay on his desk. Its front page headline declared 'School Teacher Retires'. Hardly a circulation-grabber. 'Inside: Full Jumble Sale Details'. His lip curled in a practised sneer.

He wanted to savour the moment. In the kitchen, he made himself a Quorum coffee. Midnight black with a swirl of cream. Mark invented it on New Year's Day in 1975, experimenting with Michael's parents' percolator. They'd vowed to standardise their coffee-drinking habits. Before, Michael had taken instant with milk and sugar and liked it.

As he returned to the study, the long-case clock chimed half past ten. By now, he should be three and a quarter pages into a day's work. He hadn't even touched the computer. Last week, with the moves and the fading gasp of holiday chaos, he'd only managed a few hours (four pages). Later, he could catch up. If needs be, he could amphetamine through the night.

After a swallow of caffeine, he looked through the *Echo*. Dull as day-old dishwater. Gardening, charity, weddings, funerals. When a Basildonian died, an obit could be headed 'Another One Gone, And a Good Job Too'.

After last week's show, there'd been a gaggle of whine-ins from the Basildon area. Satire? We don't do that here, guv.

At last: Letters to the Editor.

'Letter of the Week' was from S.M. Charles, who was disturbed by 'our slide towards a godless society in our attitude to the monarchy'. For that, No Sex Charles got the editor's weekly basket of fruit, from Constantinou's High Street Grocer. Next up was a platitudinous screed from a retired colonel with a drastic solution to the crisis in the former Yugoslavia. Yup, bomb the blighters!

For a moment, he thought the *Echo* hadn't printed his letter. Then, crammed between a stack of ads for lawnmowers and fanbelts, he found it. Headlined 'I'm Not Crap, Author Writes', his letter was reduced to 'Dear Sir, while Gary Gaunt is entitled to his opinion of my novel *Ken Sington* (Real Press, £17.99), I should like to point out it has been enjoyed by many. Sincerely, Michael Dixon.' His original had been three pages of close argument.

'*Our Reviewer replies,*' the paper continued in italics, '*Bestsellers are a funny breed. Mike (Friend of Basildon) Dixon regularly tops charts but have you met anyone who admitted to reading his books? He sells because he's on telly, especially around Christmas when people buy books they don't have to read themselves. As a critic, I did have to read Ken Sington. Anything I do to spare others undue suffering is worthwhile.*'

Michael hated being called 'Mike'.

Fuming, he prowled through the house. For Christmas, his sister had given the family a set of six 'unbreakable' mugs. Now, he decided, was the time to put them to the test.

They bounced cheerily off the tile kitchen floor with no ill effects. He went upstairs and pitched one out of the window, aiming for the wall at the end of the garden. The mug ricocheted intact into Ginny's roses. Venturing outside, he unlocked the shed and selected tools.

He took out his workbench and, after anchoring its legs with bricks, put a mug in the vice. He spun the handle and the vice exerted its grip. He imagined Gary Gaunt's albino toad head in it. His wrist hurt, but after as many turns as he could manage the mug still wasn't cracked. With a hammer, he battered. The handle snapped but the main body of the utensil would not be breached. Blows resounded.

Finally, he took out the heavy firewood axe. He swung it and missed. The blade caromed off the iron lip of the vice. With his second try, he scored a direct hit. The *faux* unbreakable mug crunched into fragments. He hadn't even had to use the chainsaw.

If Candace still had the receipt, she could get a refund.

* * *

After five phone calls, he obtained a number for Tom Sharpe. Newspapers, publishers and agents were all willing to help Michael Dixon. It was one of the advantages of being well-known.

As he stabbed out the number, he felt a crescendo of triumph. He was really achieving something. To his frustration, a machine answered. He left a long message, humbly asking Tom to put his thoughts on *Ken Sington* in a letter and send them to the *Basildon Echo* to counter vile slanders issued by said nauseating rag. He didn't assume to put words in the mouth of an accomplished wit, but ventured to suggest a few choice phrases that came to mind.

Though the machine beeped and cut him off before he'd quite finished, he felt satisfied. Gaunt could hardly argue with his idol, Tom Dickens-of-the-Day Sharpe. That should settle his smug little bunny-eyed hash. Yes indeedy. And it's a big goodnight from Al Bino.

Actually, Sharpe was over-rated. The comparison kept coming up and Michael resented it. If he weren't a familiar TV face, he'd be reviewed better. If he were just a novelist, he'd be held as at least Sharpe's equal. The cosy critical community that ruled the literary world had a prejudice against television, a greater prejudice against anything popular or successful. In Britain, they hate people who are too bloody clever. Doing one thing well was bad enough, but doing two or three was showoffy. Liliputian intellects like Gary Gaunt always gathered to pull down giants.

He must press on, show them all up, put them in their place. The next book, *Mai DaVale*, would show them all.

After lunch, he turned on the PC. As the disc drive hummed, ideas surged. Prose was backed up, ready to come out. His characters had been waiting in the dark of his head, frozen where he'd left them, eager to get on with their lives. He looked at the last page he'd written. Like Graham Greene, he always left off in the middle of a sentence.

Maybe in this book Colin Dale, world's greatest loser, should get a job on the *Basildon Echo*? Perhaps he'd wake up one morning and find his hair turned white overnight?

He chuckled.

Then he had a thought. He exited the novel file and opened one with his letterhead template. He should bang off a reply to the *Echo* himself. This shouldn't be dropped. They'd be flattened by Tom Sharpe, but in case Sharpe was out of the country, a back-up wouldn't go amiss. No siree-bob.

It was a delicate thing of wit and bile. Deliberately, he misspelled his nemesis's name: Gray Gaunt. It sounded better that way. A gray gaunt presence: stifling and deadening, a walking dead thing, hideously ancient and withered. After a few terse sentences, he printed out.

Having faxed his perfectly polished sting to the *Echo*, he smashed another supposed unbreakable mug. This time, he set the mug on a flagstone and bashed it with a hammer. China shards sprayed, stinging his legs. The flagstone itself cracked into four irregular pieces. He imagined it was Gary Gaunt's chalky face.

Back in the house, he left a message on Sally Rhodes's machine. He wanted to delve further into Gary Gaunt. He sniffed a conspiracy. Behind the grey gauntness was a faceless committee. All those who denied him prizes and accolades were involved. Even the critics who doled out grudging praise probably subscribed. They were lulling him, trying to seduce him with less than he merited in the hope he wouldn't notice what was being withheld.

They met monthly in a dank dungeon, masked and robed, chortling over their deliberate and malicious suppression of all that was Michael Dixon's due. He had offended the Great British

Mediocracy, and was marked for marginalisation. The worst thing was that they *knew* he was deserving, brilliant, audacious. By lying consistently, they created the fiction that he was derivative, second-rate, competent. It was all envy, poisonous bile chewing at their white livers. The public was stupid: if enough reviewers told them tea was coffee, they'd believe it.

How many times had he shook hands with members of the Gray Gaunt Conspiracy? How many smiles concealed razor-edged malice and murderous glee?

It couldn't just be one pathetic nobody. It had to be a national – nay, international – affair. Gray, Gaunt and Ghastly.

There were four mugs left. And the chainsaw was still unused.

'Dixon's here,' he snarled into the telephone, answering a call.

It was Richard Pierpoint from the BBC, producer of the *Colin Dale* serial. The last episode would be transmitted next Sunday, and they were planning a testimonial dinner that evening.

'There's something the whole cast and crew would like to give you, so keep your diary free.'

He made a space. His peers at least recognised his worth.

'A car will be sent. It'll be a bash.'

After chat, he thanked Richard and hung up.

If the *Echo* ever held a testimonial dinner for Gary Gaunt, it'd be with takeout from the local chippie and cans of perished lager.

He spared the remaining mugs and returned to the word processor.

In the book, Ken Sington was receiving an award for saving Mai Da Vale from an escaped tiger. Actually, Colin Dale had rescued the girl, but, as usual, Ken took credit for Colin's efforts.

Everybody misunderstood the series, so he planned an explicit passage. The reason Ken prospered while his friend foundered was that he was more deserving; his amorality and charm were at least honest, his eye for opportunity marked him as a survivor.

Colin was so hung up on what others thought, so timid and meek in a disgustingly British manner. He represented every whingeing thing Michael detested about Britain. At the end, Mai would marry Ken. In his Best Man speech, Colin would acknowledge he had lost to the real best man. The Mediocracy would be cast down and shat upon.

Colin was scoring high in the TV ratings. Richard was already well into pre-production on *Ken* and talking as if *Mai* was a sure thing. The gray gaunts could do nothing to inhibit the steamroller of genius.

His agent called to report several hard film offers for the first two books. The scripts would be altered for Hollywood, set in New York rather than London. Less dialogue and more physical comedy.

'We're holding out until Eddie Murphy's people get back to us.'

The news warmed him. He returned to the screen. The award scene continued. At best, it really was as if books wrote themselves. For a moment, he forgot the name of the tiger. He'd have to look back and check. A print-out was on his desk somewhere. He lifted the *Echo* and something hooked his eye.

In a box on the back page called 'Snippets', listing which famous people were born today and other trivial facts, was a snide item. 'Has anyone else noticed Michael (My Heart Belongs to Basildon) Dixon is so busy counting profits that he's been getting sloppy? In *Colin Dale*, his character Ken Sington is clearly described as green-eyed, but in the sequel *Ken Sington*, Ken's eyes have mysteriously turned blue-grey. Tut Tut.'

The 'Snippets' column was unsigned. But that didn't fool him. The compiler could only be Gary Gaunt.

Rage boiled. He turned his attention to the WP and exited the current file. Accidentally, he punched 'Abandon Edit' rather than 'Finish Edit', losing the work he'd done in the last hour. It didn't matter. He was bleeding from a mental wound. He'd have to return fire. Immediately.

* * *

It was not medically impossible for eye-colouring to change spontaneously, he thought. He had no reference books to hand and the high-street optician he telephoned with the query rang off in rude bewilderment. He looked up a Harley Street eye specialist but when he made it clear to a secretary that he wasn't booking an expensive consultation, he was put on hold and played light classical music.

After hanging up, he calmed down. With amusement, he realised he'd been tricked. He'd believed something he read in the *Basildon Echo*. Even Colin Dale wasn't that gullible.

Such a major howler could not escape the team of loyal copy-editors at Real Press. Pippa, Mark's girlfriend, had been through both manuscripts and come up with a list of minor queries. Most had been useless quibbles which he ignored, but at least she was paying attention.

He took down hardback first editions of both books. Paging through *Colin*, he sought out references to the colour of Ken's eyes. On page eighty-seven, 'Ken's glance flashed green'. Turning to *Ken*, he found a passage on page 308 mentioning 'the steely grey flecks in Ken's piercing azure orbs'.

He thought of his chainsaw and the remaining mugs, but that was a distraction.

Forcing himself to be cool, he considered options. Perhaps he could drop in *Mai* a reference to an unprecedented medical phenomenon. It had little to do with the story, but was the sort of bizarre thing that happened in his books. It would balance Colin's turning albino if Ken miraculously grew handsomer. But why hadn't it been mentioned in *Ken*? If it had already happened, why wasn't it already explained in detail? Why, why, why?

He called Pippa but she wasn't in the office today. He called her at home but got Mark's answering machine.

A headache started in his temples and spread through the rest of his skull.

Somewhere, an albino was laughing. His terrible chortles resounded through the vaults. Mockingly, Gary Gaunt sang 'Don't It Make My Pink Eyes Green?'

Michael could alter the blue-grey eyes to green in the paperback of the second book, but the first edition hardback would never disappear from library shelves.

Pain settled in the back of his neck. His own eyes ached, and he saw dancing red dots.

He returned to the novels and reread. On page eighty-seven of *Colin*, Ken was being seduced by Barbi Can, the saintly social worker Colin idolised in silence. Under Ken's influence, she turned out to be somewhat less saintly than Colin believed. It was a funny scene, badly muffed in the TV version. Josie Lawrence was all wrong for the part.

It occurred to him that the phrase 'Ken's glance flashed green' was ambiguous. It mightn't refer to his eye colour, but simply mean he gave a 'go' signal, like a traffic light, to Barbi. He practised an expression, using his screen as a mirror. A slight narrowing of the eyes, a tiny downward look and an almost subliminal nod: that could easily be a non-verbal green light.

It wasn't ambiguous. It was obviously what he had meant. He remembered now, with a clarity that made him angry with himself for ever having forgotten, for ever having succumbed to the wiles of the gray gaunts. Ken's eyes had been blue-grey from the very first. It was established, he was sure. He formulated another blistering fax and printed it out. He would make the pestilential *Echo* print a grovelling retraction or else sue the shitbags into the Stone Age.

5

15 JANUARY, 1993

It was hard to believe this was the Mark Amphlett she'd last seen secure in his Soho office. The face was the same but something was broken. A weekend in the cells will do that.

After formally identifying the prisoner and signing him out on her recognisance, she escorted him out into the street. The police would be in touch if charges were preferred. Had he done anything for which he could be prosecuted? In Cardinal Wolsey Street, the Deal had seemed on a level so far beyond human law as to be actionable only in terms of forces of nature or destiny.

They were in Tottenham Lane, a nebulous area between Hornsey and Crouch End. A prosaic, remote location; it could have been a street in any provincial town. An off-licence, a gone-out-of-business video shop, fish and chips, a bicycle business. Only a passing red bus identified it as London.

Mark blinked in the cold daylight. He had an earthworm pallor and his unshaven face was grimy. He held his belt and bootlaces but had no idea how to put them on. His loose shoes flopped as he walked down the steps.

'I'm here against my better judgement,' she told him.

She was lying. When the policewoman called and asked her to collect him, she hadn't hesitated. Knowing what she knew, she needed to look him in the face again.

'It wouldn't break my heart to leave you in prison.'

In her imagination, she delivered a stinging speech, puncturing his inhumanity, stripping him of his hypocrisy. At the end, he was left skinless and sobbing in the gutter.

Only this morning he was too pitiful. The spine had gone out of him, leaving a dizzy, lost soul. Nothing she could say would make things worse. Just as nothing she could say to Neil would make things better.

'I'm giving notice. As of now, I don't work for your Quorum. You can pay me for what I've done or not. It doesn't matter. The two grand I'm keeping. You specified non-returnable, so I'm not returning it.'

He shook his head as if he didn't believe her. She thought he hadn't heard. At this moment, he looked like the one who had been sacrificed.

'Understand?'

She should leave him to make his own way home. Only he didn't have any money. The WPC with his paperwork told her he claimed his wallet had been stolen. He had car keys but must have parked miles away. It was possible his car had been clamped or towed away over the weekend.

Mark was breathing slowly, tasting freedom. He slid his belt through the hoops of his jeans and did up the buckle.

Putting pieces together, Sally realised Mark had been in Cranley Gardens when everything went up in flames. She'd concentrated so much on the screwdriver in the corner of her eye that she missed a lot. Saturday seemed as long ago for her as it must for him. Over the weekend, they'd both been forced to reassess their relationship to the real world.

'Leech told me about your Deal,' she said.

'The Deal?' He shook his head, disbelieving.

'You bastards.'

With his hair untidy, his premature baldness was more

obvious. If he had a hat, he'd lost it days ago.

'Sally?'

He looked at her forehead. His eyes were empty. They had almost no colour.

'Thank you,' he said at last.

She wished there were villains and heroes. This ambiguity was confusing and hurtful. Leech said it could as easily have been Mark as Neil. Would she then be working up warmth for Mark the victim and despising Neil the monster?

In this picture, who exactly is the victim?

He reached out and let his hands fall lightly on her shoulders. She flinched. His touch was cold through the wool of her cardigan and the cotton of her shirt. He might have been about to collapse but she didn't put her hands on his hips or ribs to hold him up.

'Sally?'

'Are you ill?'

He shook his head but it was hard not to think he meant yes. His eyes wouldn't focus.

'I'm cold,' he said.

Her back was against the brickwork of the police station. He lightly pinned her there. She cringed, holding her body away from his. Looking down, she saw his belt was threaded backwards and upside-down.

If she bunched her fingers into a point and jabbed him below the adam's apple, he'd leave her alone.

'Cold.'

She couldn't give him sympathy. Not after what she knew. Not after what he had made of Neil's life. Yet something invisible was leaking out of Mark. He'd been as seriously hurt by the Deal as Neil. It was possible the others suffered too.

Leech had sold them all ashes.

Mark was on the point of crumpling. His body bent sideways and his head loomed close to her face. Her jaw and neck muscles contracted, as if threatened with an injection. Cold lips brushed hers. She kept her mouth firmly shut and her eyes wide open, wishing him away.

He withdrew and turned his back. His shoulders were shaking. When he couldn't see, she wiped her mouth with the back of her hand. She hadn't worn lipstick. A strange taste was in her mouth. Sweet and sour. She tried to lick it out onto the back of her hand.

Mark's head was hung, almost below the level of his shoulders. His scarf fell away loose from the back of his neck. She saw his hackles, once neatly shaved and now stubbled. There was a point she could strike which would cut his strings and drop him on the pavement.

She had made a fist and pressed it under her breasts, close to her heart. Her nails indented her palm.

One blow. A blow for Neil. For all the footsoldiers. Against the Quorum.

She did not strike.

When he turned back, she felt nothing. She gave him money and told him to go home.

Then she left.

You're good at that, Mummy, the familiar voice said inside her head. *Leaving.*

6

12 JANUARY, 1993

'It is not permitted to sleep in the lobby.'

Mickey jerked awake. A Mormon in a blue blazer was shaking him vigorously. He coughed and swallowed phlegm. Even after three throat-stretching yawns, the pressure in his ears wouldn't equalise.

'Sir, I must request that you leave.'

He didn't understand. The pain in his head was exploding. The grip on his arm suggested years with a muscle-building squeezeball. Mickey was firmly eased upright. His ears popped; something warm seeped inside his skull.

'Are you awaiting a guest?'

'What time is it?'

'Five minutes shy of one in the a.m., sir. I repeat, are you awaiting...'

'I am a guest, sunshine.'

The Mormon's tanned face didn't register surprise, embarrassment or interest.

'In that case, perhaps the best course of action would be to sleep in your room.'

'Good point, john,' Mickey barked. 'I'd be in my room if I could get in, but the fuckin' card won't go in the slot.'

'There has been some malfunction?'

The Mormon's eyebrow-raise was copied from Mr Spock. Also his deferential, sly way of talking to people as if they were arsehole human beings and the sentient universe would be better off without them.

'Too right.'

Mickey dug out his gold cardkey and handed it over. Morman looked at it with one serious eye. Now the Mormon knew he was in the Apex Suite, he should transform instantly into Johnny Smarm and lay down a carpet of tongue to be walked over. Without comment, the Mormon put the cardkey in his top pocket.

'If you would remain here, I'll see to this immediately,' he said.

'I won't go anywhere.'

The Mormon walked off, footfalls padded by thick carpet. There were pools of light in the lobby, but beyond the glass doors the streets were dark. Mickey had slept the evening away. An empty hunger bit in his stomach. His head still buzzed.

No one else was in sight. He felt as if he were recovering from a bad bout of flu, having been through the gallons-running-out-of-the-nose stage and entered the sinus-plugged-with-drying-concrete phase. He shook his brain and wondered what had happened.

In his head, there was another silent thundercrack. Mickey felt a *frisson* as if an invisible jet had just passed. An abandoned newspaper whisked off the couch and was tugged across the lobby as if hooked by a fishing line. His vision was fuzzy; he thought he saw a streak of smoking footprints on the carpet.

The Mormon didn't come back. A Nevergone Void had opened up and swallowed him from history.

After an unreasonable passage of time, Mickey trekked the hundred yards. Two burnished copper half-cones protruded from the wall either side of the front desk, which was lit up like a mirage. A toothy young woman in a blazer, a perfect Marie to the vanisher's Donny, looked up. Her name-tag identified her as Shirley.

'What happened about the Apex cardkey?'

'I beg your pardon, sir?'

'Your mate said he'd get it sorted.'

'I'm unmarried, sir.'

He wasn't surprised.

'The bloke who was here just now took my cardkey. Handsome guy if you like the type. My cardkey wasn't working.'

'That's not likely, sir.'

'Likely or not, that's the way it is.'

'If you say so, sir.'

It was like talking to a faulty cash dispenser. The responses didn't correspond with the inputs.

'Can you get me another key, love?'

'Not without authorisation from my supervisor, Mr Candy.'

'In that case, I suggest you trouble yourself a jot and get authorisation.'

'No need to be testy, sir. Mr Candy comes on duty at seven a.m.'

'What am I supposed to do till then?'

She had no answer.

'Can I check into another room?' He had a wad of cash in his wallet. ZC were picking up his bills and would recompense him.

Shirley tapped a few keys on a discreet computer terminal and told him 'We're fully booked, sir.'

'Even the Presidential Suite? I reckoned Bill Clinton would be busy in Washington this month, what with the inauguration and all that hoop-la.'

Her eyes were downcast.

'I'm not authorised to access information on the Presidential Suite, sir. It's a matter of national security.'

'Go on, love,' he cooed, making irresistible eyes.

'That would be a federal offence, sir.'

He thought of another tack.

'Can I use this?' he asked, reaching for a slimline telephone. Her hand, as strong as the Mormon's, descended.

'The telephone is for the use of staff and residents only.'

'I'm a resident.'

'Of course. May I see your cardkey, sir?'

It was hard to keep his temper. 'I gave my key to your mate.'

'As I said, sir...'

'Yeah, yeah, yeah. Could you make a call for me. To Miss Wilding. Heather Wilding. She's on the nineteenth floor.'

Shirley's eyes narrowed. To her, this was highly irregular. Just now, he understood how serial killers felt about women. If he were drawing *Choke Hold* over again, the Strangler's victims would look like her.

'Ms Wilding?'

He nodded. She tapped more keys. He stretched but could not see her screen from his side of the desk.

'Ah, yes, *a* Ms H. Wilding is registered. Is she, ah, your fiancée?'

He was infuriated.

'No, Miss Wilding is *not* my fiancée. She happens to be a gorgeous hag I've been thoroughly shagging for the last three days, if you must know. I've taken enormous delight in porking her up against walls, in the bath, on floors, even in beds.'

He heard himself and realised he was losing it. Aches in his ribs reminded him of the alloyed pleasure he'd shared with Heather when she got out her fancy-dress and whip.

Shirley reddened. 'Sir, you misunderstand me. Your private affairs, and Ms Wilding's, are entirely your own and not the concern of this hotel. However, Ms Wilding has left instructions that no calls be put through before her 6.30 wake-up unless they are from her fiancé. Do you wish to leave a message?'

'Fuck me,' he breathed.

She wrote it down.

'How do you want that signed, sir?'

While he talked with Shirley, discreet security guards appeared from their holes. Two of them: brown uniforms stretched over superhero pecs, matching mirrorshades. They made no threatening gestures but it was clear he was required to leave the lobby.

'Why would anyone wear sunglasses at two in the morning?' he asked.

'It's so you can't see their eyes, sir,' Shirley helpfully explained. 'It's supposed to be intimidating.'

Two sets of thin lips bent almost imperceptibly into sneery smiles. Mickey could have drawn the expression with a contemptuous pencil-flick. It was a subtlety reserved for those so powerful they didn't need to make a show of violence.

He moved involuntarily towards the doors. The guards deliberately advanced on him. Doors automatically hissed open. Night air reached in like an ice hand. A distant police siren whined, the inescapable sound effect of Urban America. Cars with searchlight headlamps prowled past. There was nothing for it but to find an all-night bar. He stumbled into a velvet dark punctured by pools of lost light.

Within seconds, he understood the secret meaning of cold. Turning up the collar of his leather jacket didn't help. A layer of ice formed between his skin and his clothes. Wind cut his face like a flail.

He walked a block and, in an instant, everything shifted. A gust of crosswind slashed his face and he shut his eyes.

He opened them again and was blinded by daylight. A warm breeze blew. His body still shivered but his mind adjusted. It was an early summer day. The streets were thickly populated. People noise crashed in on him. Car horns beeped. Everything was unnaturally bright and shining. A shop-front caught the sun and flashed back unbearable light. He shut his eyes and felt the warmth ooze about him. He was jostled and shoved against the glass.

This time, he opened his eyes slowly, blinking. A big red truck was passing. Its red was solid and arresting, the reddest red imaginable. Fire engine red. He looked up. The sky was seaside blue, with perfect scuds of cloud in the distance. High up, birds flew. They looked like the eyebrow curves children drew in holiday pictures.

Mickey walked on, cautious and dazed. The city had no shades, just blocks of primary colour.

At an intersection, a twelve-year-old in an oversized flat cap hawked newspapers.

'Extry, extry,' he yelled. 'Max Multiple Convicted!'

The news vendor was holding up the *Coastal City Mercury*.

Mickey looked at the simple, clean-lined passersby. The men wore hats and had square jaws, the women had perfect helmets of hair and tiny waists.

'Look,' someone said nearby, pointing up. 'Faster than sound, faster than light, faster than *time*...'

Mickey's eyes were drawn skyward. Above the buildings, in the clear blue, a white streak shot across the sky.

Mickey looked again. The Streak was gone. With a lurch, blue turned black and he was in New York.

Hours had passed. Dawn was close. Mickey worried he'd been slipped a new drug. He couldn't remember anything like this from his acid days.

A police car, armoured like something out of *City Hammer*, cruised by. A burst of rap music escaped through a crack in the windows, and he saw two black officers nodding heads to the rhythm of the rant.

Instinctively guilty, he cringed into a shadow. The covering dark disappeared...

Chaos in Coastal City. Traffic jammed streets, automobiles abandoned. Chunks of fallen masonry dotted sidewalks. People ran, men losing hats, women trotting on heels. In the near distance, gunfire chattered. The ground shook.

Without provocation, a fleeing citizen turned to Mickey, who was shoved into an alcove between stores, and explained 'Streak and Vindicator are fighting Dead Thing and Mr Bones in the Plaza!'

The ground rocked again, a minor earthquake. He slipped, concrete shifting beneath him.

Fuckin' heroes!

A nearby explosion lifted three or four cars out of the pack. He saw a panicked child's face behind a windscreen, then a blossom of unreal flame. His ears were assaulted by the boom. A distinct wall of fire cut across the road.

A seven-foot manshape walked out of the curtain of conflagration, flames licking charred overalls. His long-dead face was impassive. His heavy bootfalls were cannonshots.

Something shot out of the fire, so swift as to seem invisible. It wheeled in the air and struck the zombie in the chest, driving him back into the inferno. Mickey recognised Dead Thing and the Streak. He'd redesigned DT himself, ditching his faintly campy green leotard in favour of a raggedy-man outfit.

The Streak hugged a child in one arm. Slowing to visibility, he gently set down the kid he'd rescued from the exploding car. Then he returned to the fray.

Mickey watched a fight he'd drawn several times. If he fixed his eyes on the action, he could see the Streak as a succession of unblurred still pictures, dynamically posed. It was hard to get DT's snarl right, and the zombie's face shifted from one frozen expression to the next.

'This could be The End,' an innocent bystander shrieked.

* * *

It was mid-morning in New York and he could still hear explosions in Coastal City. He felt the heat of the fire on his face.

He had to get help.

He was outside the bookstore he'd been in yesterday. A flow of people carried him in. Without thinking, he made his way to the comics section. They had new stock in. Crowds of young people in bad clothes fought towards the racks, bearing off bagged goodies.

The next issue of *The Nevergone Void* was due out. Perhaps it had arrived here early. He needed to hold something of his own. It would anchor him to his reality. He eased through the fanboy throng.

Up on the wall, where there'd been a poster for *The Nevergone Void* was a new one-sheet. Amazon Queen, not fading but vivid, stood over the Coastal City skyline, costume redesigned for the nineties, tougher look drawn on her face. A lightning stroke lashed behind her. 'I am Woman,' read a caption, 'Feel My Power!'

Mickey's ribs twinged. Had Heather cracked one yesterday?

A strip under the poster proclaimed: '*Amazon Queen: Born Anew!*, a NEW monthly series by Farhad Z-Rowe, debuts from ZC February.' This AQ looked like Heather down to the speckles in her cleavage.

There was an excitement among the comic buyers. They clamoured for *Born Anew*.

But Amazon Queen was dead. *No*, Amazon Queen had never existed. The Nevergonners had taken back her life, sucked her out of the ZC Universe. *Mickey* had revoked her entire career.

He checked his watch. It was the 12th of January. Everything was speeding up. It was impossible for ZC to commission and publish a new title overnight. It must have been planned for months. Timmy Chin should have kept him informed. *The Nevergone Void* wasn't even concluded and its plot developments were already compromised.

The February debut of *Amazon Queen* was already on sale,

stocked in depth. A special rack was given over to variant editions, sealed in plastic bags for collectors. Mickey looked for *The Nevergone Void* or *Choke Hold*. No luck. Edged out by the sudden explosion of Farhad Z-Rowe, it was as if he had never existed.

He made it on foot to Pyramid Plaza, without suffering the Effect again. Competing furies boiled.

It was a long while since he'd walked anywhere. His feet hurt inside his boots. The streets felt different from outside a limousine. People got in the way, shouting at him about the imminent arrival of a prophet, offering suspiciously generous terms on the instant purchase of video equipment or doing choreographed solo begging routines as they held out McDonald's cups for small change.

Finally, he achieved the Plaza. He paused for breath by the fountains and felt faint spray. Inside was safety and a raft of explanation. The chanting of the Queer Nation protesters was somehow comforting. He walked through the crowd and made it to the front doors just as riot police appeared from nowhere and let off teargas. White bursts disgorged clouds of stinging smoke.

Coughing from his lungs, he collided with the revolving door, went round twice, and was shot out into the foyer. Water streaming from his eyes and slime from his nose, he was received by guards and wrestled down to the parquet.

He tried to tell them he wasn't a protesting shirt-lifter.

'My constitutional rights have been abridged,' shouted a strident youth in a lemon-yellow T-shirt. 'I claim my lawful right of assembly...'

There were scuffles throughout the lobby. Transvestites in Brazilian carnival costumes jammed into the revolving doors. Plumage pressed against the glass, orange and red frills squashing flat.

Mickey, still choking, tried to explain who he was. Mercifully, a receptionist recognised him and called off the goons.

'Mr Yo, we deeply regret this mistake,' she explained.

'Yeo,' he gasped.

'Thank you, sir.'

His nostrils stung as if packed with nettles. She handed him a fistful of paper tissues and he unslimed his face. He saw through tears as if through a rain-lashed window.

The revolving door burst open and gorgeously coloured creatures invaded the Plaza, shrieking like angry parrots, laying about with placards.

The Effect struck…

The mural, a Mexican desertscape, exploded as melon-sized bullet-holes stitched across the wall. Fragments of coloured pottery pattered like hailstones around the reception area.

Mickey was barricaded behind an overturned desk.

The Vindicator, snarling scarred hate, hefted a complicated weapon which fit over his entire arm. A belt of ammo was sucked into a slot; bullets spurted out of the barrel.

Mr Bones, an elegant skull-face above perfect evening dress, conjured a flock of bats. They swirled and clustered around the cyborg, nipping at the joins between flesh and machine.

Mickey's ears burst in agony with each shot. The Vindicator was firing at the ceiling now. Clouds of dust and clods of brickwork fell. The sprinkler system was set off…

Indoor rain drenched the transvestites, turning them into bedraggled hags, make-up running in streams.

The receptionist manoeuvered Mickey into the safety of the elevator.

'You're my heroine,' he told her as the doors shuttered.

The elevator cage, a comforting coffin, rose.

* * *

It ground to a sudden halt. Mickey stumbled over his aching feet and sat down on the deep-pile carpet. It had happened again.

The doors were wrenched open by chubby fingers. The cage had stopped about three feet short of a floor. Instead of hauling Mickey out, the door-opener popped into the elevator.

'Phew,' he said, face flushed red.

The boy was an American Billy Bunter: a round-cheeked, big-bellied mid-teenager with a crew-cut, thick glasses and freckles. He wore a bow tie and a high school jacket like something out of *Archie*.

'Don't tell anyone about this, mister,' the boy said timidly, whipping off his glasses to reveal unusually determined eyes.

Mickey was confused.

The boy had two pinky rings, each with a Greek letter. He rubbed them together and muttered magic words. A painful violet light surrounded him and he transformed, his clothes shrunk into a skintight costume with a 'BB' chest motif. His body swelled, becoming almost spherical, and glowed with purple power.

'You are sworn to silence to protect my secret identity,' Blubber Boy told Mickey, his voice deep and resonant.

He flowed through the six-inch gap between the elevator doors and was off to combat the forces of evil. The doors closed with a clang and the elevator resumed its ascent.

He used his card at the entrance to the ZC office suite, and punched in his code number, 1812. Like the war, he remembered. The doors didn't open, and his card was sucked into a slit-mouth. He rattled the locked doors, and a bike messenger on his way out let him in.

The ZC receptionist recognised him with a tiny smile of

impatience and picked up her internal phone.

She poised in mid-number and looked at him. 'I'm sorry, but what was your name again?'

'Mickey Yeo,' he said, heart petrifying.

'Of course,' she said. Then, into the phone, 'Mr Yo is here again.' She nodded, listening, 'Uh huh.'

A framed *Newsweek* cover showed a scowling Farhad Z-Rowe ripping in half an eighties issue of *Circe*. The headline read 'Comics Get Serious'.

The receptionist hung up. 'If you'd wait, Mr Yo. Mr Chin's assistant will be out soon.'

He knew what would come next but had to go through it. He even had a sort of understanding of what had happened. In the comic, he'd been wrong about the Nevergone Void. It didn't suck people out of existence, it just revoked everything they'd ever done with their lives, leaving them stranded out of time, unrooted to reality.

He wasn't even angry any more.

A plump catamite who could have been Blubber Boy's older brother emerged and introduced himself as Timmy's assistant. Mickey remembered him from the reception last week. The gunsel had wrung his hand for a full minute while gushing about his genius.

'Mr Yo,' he began, 'is that an Asian-American name?'

Mickey shook his head and grumbled 'British.'

'Oh well, never mind,' the assistant continued. 'I'm afraid Timmy can't see you without an appointment. He's ultra busy with the new Amazon Queen. There's scads of media interest. It's been real exciting. If you want to leave samples of your work, we will get in touch with you. I can't promise you when, but Timmy's real conscientious. Hey, you can never tell where the next Farhad Z-Rowe is coming from.'

7

13 JANUARY, 1993

Within the Device, Neil relived every moment of his life. Only this time, it turned out better. This time, even his dreams were happier. His lives multiplied, following myriad forking paths. In some lives, he wasn't even Neil. It wasn't real, but that didn't matter. Reality was a poor second.

The Device allowed him simultaneously an infinity of experience. He enjoyed one-night stands, affairs, relationships, marriages, lives. With all the women: Victoria, Clare, Candy, Penny, Rachael, Pippa, Anne, Janet, Tanya, Sally. He found fulfilling careers. A writer, a businessman, an actor, a musician, a scientist, an explorer, a celebrity, a genius. He fathered adoring children. He created works of lasting merit. He amassed harmless fortunes. He commanded the destinies of nations. He stood by his friends. He ruined his enemies utterly. He made things better. He was rewarded for his suffering.

Part of him still knew his actual situation. It wasn't without its own interest. People swarmed around the Device, tending to its – to *his* – needs, repairing its ruptures, greasing its gears, making offerings on its altars. A prosaic tile roof kept out the rain. A rank of net-curtained windows admitted shafts of grey light by day.

His consciousness explored the contraption with which he had become one. He had an idea of its size and purpose. He sensed the accumulated power and recognised it as his own. For years, it had been channelled into the machine and stored. An original ember had grown into a furnace.

The Device harboured other fires. Faintly surprised by his intuition, Neil recognised Mark, Michael and Mickey. In this contraption, they had more than a Quorum. His friends' fires differed from his own; they were smaller, more concentrated, brighter. Filaments flaring for a last time. If he were not beyond feeling, he'd have worried about his friends, sensing a danger in the darkness encroaching on their bright lights.

All along, he'd known, even as he looked up from his rut at the shining paths of the others, that the four of them were bound together forever. Marling's put a mark on the boys for life.

There were still aspects he didn't understand. He'd run through so many bright and equally real alternative lives, the dull original was fading. He knew how he had been transported from Cranley Gardens. He even knew he was physically somewhere in Docklands. Before that, the years blurred together a succession of fragments which might have been real or imagined.

The Device was, among many other purposes, a puzzle. It broke and reformed in new configurations, each part fitting insidiously and surprisingly into the whole.

Neil remembered saying 'I give up'. More, he remembered meaning the words. It was as if he'd given the right answer on a quiz programme. A million pounds fluttered down from the eaves while brass bands struck up show tunes and a dozen spangled dancers high-kicked around him. All the prizes were his.

He should have given up years ago. At any time, he could have ended the curse. He could have seen off the Norwegian Neil Cullers. But who knew capitulation was the just course? His whole culture told him to keep on keeping on, never to give up the ship, to try and try again.

If at first you don't succeed...

...then the Hell with it.

But did the Streak ever give up? Did Robert the Bruce? Did Horatio Nelson? Did Nelson Mandela? Did Jesus H. Christ? Even now, it was hard not to feel surrender was shameful. He might enjoy temporary raptures, but he would suffer later.

The Device reassured him with visions of endless contentment. He enjoyed irreconcilable happy unions with all his women, pursued vastly different but joyous lives.

He had had a real chance with Anne before he fucked it up. And if he had handled Tanya better, they could have helped each other. With any of the others he could have made a life, but Anne and Tanya had been his best bets. Before Sally.

The Device grew around him, cocooning his body with foam-rubber, feeding him intravenously, painlessly disposing of his bodily wastes.

He thought of Sally. She had come here with him and left. She was part of most of his lives.

His dreams continued, spiralling and expanding.

8

13 JANUARY, 1993

He hadn't slept since leaving the police station. Periodic lapses into torpor replaced actual slumber. Mark couldn't stop thinking. Always, his thoughts continued a low-level buzz. After two days, he wasn't exactly exhausted. Mentally, he was as clear as adventurous, as on the coffee-and-benzedrine nights of *The Shape of the Now*. However, he noticed an increasing ineptitude with minor domestic tasks like opening cans or shutting the fridge door. If he could keep together for a few more days, he might achieve conceptual breakthrough, true knowledge.

He returned to *Dr Faustus*. One of his university books, the yellowing and crack-spined Methuen paperback, had lain in wait, dirt rind sealing its pages, on his shelves since the seventies. The dust irritated his eyes. It was hard to focus. Had his eyesight deteriorated recently?

Faustus's Deal was for knowledge. 'What a world of profit and delight, of power, of honour, of omnipotence, is promis'd to the studious artisan.' At eighteen, when considerably stupider, Mark understood that with a fiery certainty. 'Had I as many souls as there be stars, I'd give them all for Mephistophilis.' He'd ended an essay 'In Defence of Damnation'. At thirty-three – having lived four years longer than Christopher Marlowe managed before someone daggered his eye – he was, for the first time, forced to take seriously the last act. Brimstone and evisceration. Eternal torment. Suffering beyond imagining.

As Ring, he was supposed to look out for the others. After days of trying, he finally got through to Michael.

'Hello,' the distant voice said, guarded, defensive. Mark guessed Michael was afflicted too.

'Michael,' he said, 'it's Mark.'

There was a pause. He wondered if Michael's mind were affected. Mark had been struck with an intense awareness of everything; possibly, Michael was taken the other way, smitten with forgetfulness.

'Mark,' the voice repeated. 'Yes.'

'What's been happening?' Mark asked.

'Tumultuous business. This Gary Gaunt impossibility. It's required a shitload of attention. All else is back-burnered.'

If Mark had ever heard of Gary Gaunt, he had forgotten.

'I may be forced to go to blighted Basildon in person, Gods help me. It may come to zh-zhust that.'

Michael's zh-zh shrilled down the phone line, worse than it had been since school.

'Is the Deal off?'

'The Deal?'

'Michael, how bad is it?'

There was a long, drawn-out silence.

'Pretty bad,' Michael admitted.

'I thought so.'

Michael hung up.

Among the people he'd been unable to reach were Leech in Docklands, Pippa in Scotland and Mickey in New York. His entire address book was inoperative. He'd left more than enough machine messages for Sally to phone him.

Damnation and Sally were his major concerns. Sally loomed enormously in his mind. He wasn't sure if he loved or hated her. He wasn't sure if he loved or hated himself. He used to be good at making up his mind. That was how you became a style guru, by making decisions and sticking by them.

He sat in his dressing-gown in his living-room, not sure which of his suits to wear. They all had points worth considering.

Sally? Why Sally?

It was hard to say. Of all the people he knew, Sally was the only one who seemed outside the Deal.

Seemed.

He was unable to impute base motives to the woman. She alone had the clarity of vision. She had made Mark see his life from the outside, and he was still suffering from the aftershocks.

If she could be persuaded…

If she could forgive him, might he not be redeemed?

He found himself saying her name at odd moments, like an invocation, like a prayer.

Sally, Sally, Sally.

Je vous salue, Sally…

She was out there somewhere, judging him. He had to plead his case with her. He had to give her an explanation.

The office hadn't tried to get in touch, so *The Shape* must be getting by without him. He should have let Laura-Leigh run the magazine months ago. He would have called, but he didn't think he was in any condition to have anything to contribute. Besides, Laura-Leigh had (deliberately?) let him rot in jail. There might have been an editorial coup.

Should he have the main light on or off? It was dim in the room but not too dark to see. The central heating had failed, or been turned off and neglected. He was used to cold. It was his constant companion. He considered he deserved it.

A thin blank spine stood out on his bookshelves. Its whiteness – a negative gleam that would delight Melville – attracted his eye from across the room and he got up, tripping on the edge of a coffee-table, to examine the artefact. He hauled the volume free and discovered a white-covered book of empty pages. Scrawled in fading ink across a bare first page was a personal dedication from Mickey.

'This word "damnation" terrifies not him…'

He sorted through his CD racks and found, still in its cellophane, a Möthers of Pain LP Mickey had performed on. The *City Hammer* soundtrack album. Mark had never played it. After several scrabbling attempts to slit the shrinkwrap with a blunt thumbnail, he stripped the outer layer and shoved the disc into the player.

It was horrible, of course. He didn't know the first track – 'And the Horse You Rode In On' – well enough to be precise, but something was missing. For a start, it was an instrumental and he was sure it had been recorded as a song. Mickey's droning death-head lyrics should have resounded. No matter how he played with the balance of the speakers, the sound was lopsided. The guitars kept fading, making room for keyboards that were no longer in the mix.

He couldn't find Mickey's name on the cover. A credits block for the film described it as 'Written and Directed by Allan Keyes'. There was a photograph of the band dressed as postholocaust warriors, grouped around an empty space where no one stood. The final track – 'Look Upon My Works, Ye Wankheads, And Despair' – was entirely blank.

Mark could imagine Mickey's situation. His own predicament was more subtly terrible. It was hard to articulate just what was wrong, even to himself. But things had changed forever.

* * *

He telephoned Sally again. This time, she answered. He found he had nothing to say.

'Hello,' she said, 'hello…'

He held the receiver close, imagining her at the other end, face puzzled. His voice wouldn't work. Nothing physically wrong with him beyond fatigue and a lack of appetite, but he was unable to speak.

'Is this Mark Amphlett?' she asked, disapproving.

He made a noise between a croak and a hiccough.

'Mark?'

What inflexion did her voice have? Contempt? Pity?

'Help me,' he said, simply.

'No.'

The connection was cut.

It could have been a fault on the line. She might not have hung up. With the buzzing phone in one hand, she would be paging through an address book. Maybe she'd memorised his number – something a detective should be good at – and didn't need to look it up.

He recited his own number in his mind, imagining Sally pushing buttons on her phone. He calculated the time it should take for the connection to be made and put out his hand to answer.

His telephone didn't ring.

Perhaps his number was written on a scrap of paper not easy to find on her untidy desk. He thought again of his number slowly this time. She could be finding the paper and making the return call. The phone should start ringing… now.

She did not call. She was not calling. She would not call.

He waited minutes, then snatched the phone and pressed the redial button. Sally's number was connected. Her phone rang once and a machine cut in.

'Sally,' he said, interrupting her polite, cheerful message. Alarmed by the feeble sound of his own voice, he cleared his throat and waited. At the beep, he began again, 'Sally, it's Mark...'

She would pick up when she heard it was him. There must be things she wanted to talk about. Even if she could never forgive him, there were aspects of the Deal she must ache to understand. He knew her well enough to appreciate her need to know. She said that was why she was a detective.

'Sally, please pick up...'

She could have left the house. She could have been on her way out when he called the first time. She could...

There was a jiggle and the connection was cut. The dial tone sounded. It could be a fault. Another fault. More likely, the same fault. A faulty connection, always cutting off after a half-minute. Sally had not necessarily cut him off.

He pressed redial again. An engaged tone. She was calling him back. He hung up and waited for the phone to ring.

After half an hour he called the operator and reported a fault on Sally's line. He was informed that it was at her end. The party must have left the phone off the hook. He was thanked for his concern. Implicitly, he was called an interfering loon and told to fuck off.

Uncaring, he dressed. If his clothes matched, he didn't notice. Even a newly cleaned and pressed suit felt as if it had been worn for days and slept in.

He couldn't remember sleep.

He called Pippa in Edinburgh. Now it didn't matter, he had the number easily to hand. Her mother answered, surprised to hear from him, and asked how he had been. He hung up.

Where *was* Pippa?

He called Mickey's New York hotel and was told there was no Mr Yeo registered. He had to spell out the name.

He called Derek Leech's emergency number. A private line

only a handful of intimates were granted access to, a portable phone always by Leech's hand. A recorded message told him the number was discontinued.

He called Sally again. Still engaged.

Engaged.

It occurred to him he knew little about Sally. She might be married with kids. She was in her mid-thirties, he judged. If anything, a little older than him. It was impossible to get that far in life without forming attachments. The first time she talked with him on the phone, there'd been a child. A baby.

No, in her line of work, she was on her own. Divorced, maybe. She had agreed she was like a child minder. The baby might not be her own.

Could she be gay? No.

He called again. Still engaged.

Should he go around and see her? He didn't want another scene. Maybe he should leave her alone for a few days.

He had to explain himself to her. If she could forgive him, he might have a chance.

A chance for what?

Pain cut through his open-eyed doze. Either his knuckle had expanded or the ring of office had shrunk. A cheesewire noose of hot agony constricted around his finger, needles transfixing the bone, tiny explosions rupturing the joint.

He slipped the ring off easily. The pain stayed in his finger. There was no apparent swelling or abrasion. The hurt was inside, nestled and entrenched.

He put the ring in a drawer.

Over and over, he reread Faustus's final soliloquy, like a contract lawyer looking for a loophole. But... 'the stars move still, time runs, the clock will strike. The Devil will come and Faustus *must be damned*.'

At the very end, Faustus tries to go back on the Deal. 'Ugly hell, gape out! Come not, Lucifer; I'll burn my books…'

The gentle Goethe gets Faust out of the Deal – 'if a man makes continuous efforts, we can save him' – but the merciless Marlowe goes through with the bloody business of perdition.

'O, help us, heaven! See, here are Faustus's limbs, all torn asunder by the hand of death. The devils have torn him thus.'

'Ugly Hell' claims the scholar and 'cut is the branch that might have grown full straight… Faustus is gone: regard his hellish fall, whose fiendish fortune may exhort the wise only to wonder at unlawful things whose deepness doth entice such forward wits to practice more than heavenly power permits.'

It was necessary, Mark now believed, to come to terms with the concept of Damnation.

'I'd like to talk with a priest,' he said.

The kid slipped off his earphones – Tamsin tinnily sang 'I Know Where I'm Going' – and said, 'I'm a priest.'

The kid – well, he was younger than Mark, late twenties, maybe thirty, but in shape, face unlined – wore jeans, a rollneck jumper and a windbreaker. He'd been doing a subconscious shimmy as he raked twigs and crisp packets from a patch of grass.

'I'm Father Menzies,' the kid said. 'Will I do, or would you like someone older?'

He couldn't let Menzies think he was prejudiced. Enough older people took Mark seriously when he was in his twenties. Why shouldn't he be as open-minded? But he was so far from the church his only experience was with Bing Crosby or Max Von Sydow. If he was taking this seriously, he wanted the collar and the black suit.

'You'll do.'

'Beezer,' Menzies said. 'Let's get inside, where it's warmer.'

The church was modern, a local government office with stained-glass windows. It was in a quiet residential patch where Sunday seemed to last through the week.

Menzies took Mark into a cluttered office. A framed poster for *Saturday Night Fever* hung behind his desk.

'That changed my life,' Menzies said.

'You wanted to be a disco dancer?'

'No, a priest. Travolta's brother is a priest in the picture. He lapses...'

Now he was here, Mark was embarrassed. He hoped nobody he knew would find out. He'd picked a church out of the Thomson Local Directory. He hadn't telephoned ahead. He wasn't having good fortune with phones.

'Sit down,' Menzies said, shifting box files off a wonky chair. 'Coffee?'

'Thank you. Black with a swirl of cream.'

'Top of the milk?'

'That's fine.'

Menzies busied himself with a kettle.

'Father...?'

'Call me Kevin. And you're...?'

'Mark,' he admitted. 'Amphlett.'

The worst that could have happened did. Menzies turned and looked at him again, eyes penetrating.

'*The Shape of the Now*? That Mark Amphlett?'

Mark nodded, ashamed.

'I read that when I was in the seminary. We had some great arguments about it. I wasn't always on your side. Brilliant stuff, though.'

Menzies handed over a cup of instant with blobs of congealed milk floating in it.

'Sorry about the vile brew. I wish Sister Chantal were here. She's a fan of yours.'

This wasn't going to work. Perhaps he should ask for the sacrament of confession and give Father Menzies the whole Deal. No, that would take hours. And the shame might be too much. He remembered Sally's eyes. One glance like that was enough for one life.

'Are you writing another book?'

Mark saw a way. 'Yes. That's why I'm here.'

'You rather played down religion in *The Shape of the Now*,' Menzies said, not meaning a reproach. 'Though the chapter about style spirituality is dead-on. Some of the kids who come through here, with three-month crazes for saintliness, should be forced to memorise it like a catechism.'

It was just his luck to get a chatty priest.

'There are some concepts I'd like the Catholic viewpoint on, and I was wondering if you'd mind if I asked you some questions…'

Menzies grinned. 'It'd be an honour. I'm not exactly the Pope, though. I can't speak for all of us.'

'You'd get an acknowledgement.'

'No need,' he said, shrugging skyward. 'By the way, were you born in the church?'

'I didn't realise it was obvious.'

Menzies smiled, congratulating himself. 'I can spot one from one hundred paces. Some people are the same about gays. Me, I used to think Liberace was just a bit overfond of his mother. But a Roman Candle, that's unmistakable.'

'I haven't heard that since school.'

'What, about Liberace being gay?'

'No, Roman Candle. They used to call us that.'

'It's harmless. I did a sermon on it once. I like the implication. You know, a bright, burning, wonderful light.'

'I'm interested in Salvation.'

Menzies chuckled. 'That's what they all say.'

'No, not like that…'

'I'm sorry. Just my feeble wit. I use humour as a protective mechanism. Chan never lets me get away with it. She's a real nun.'

'The concept of Salvation. What does it mean? Today, what's the church's teaching?'

'Salvation? Our reward in Heaven. A spiritual state. Not something you win – don't trust people who shout "I am saved and you're not" – but something you have to accept.'

Mark thought Max Von Sydow would tear this kid apart. But he pressed on.

'And Damnation?'

Menzies wrestled with the idea, tried his best to be serious. He wasn't comfortable. He probably didn't know many good Damnation jokes.

Mark persisted. 'What do you think of Damnation in the nineties?'

'We're past the lake of burning fire and toasting forks and eternal agony, I hope. Now, we're talking about Perdition, the state of being lost. When we say we're lost, it's literal. We've strayed beyond the Love of God. It's not His fault. It's ours.'

'Denied the Love of God?'

'They used to say the worst punishment of the Damned was knowing they'd never see the face of God.'

Mark tried to think.

'So Hell is a place we enter of our own will.'

'That's a good, concise description. Can I use that?'

'Feel free.'

Menzies continued. 'The idea that's hard to get your head around is that God made you and everything you are, then gave you free will. Which means you're on your own. He wants to love you, but it's up to you to return the calls.'

Mark thought of Sally. There was no deceiving himself: she had hung up, set the answering machine to avoid him, cut the connection when he called the machine, left the phone off the hook. Whatever their relationship was, she did not want to continue it.

'God made us and God loves us,' Mark said, 'but it's not God's fault if we're damned?'

'Certainly not. God still loves the Damned. It's just that the Damned turn away. Love exists between two parties, a compact. It's impossible for God not to love me, but I can, in my error, not love Him, which leaves me in the dark.'

Mark tried to imagine, tried to picture the dark. It was disturbingly easy. It was disturbingly like an empty dialling tone.

'So you don't have to get an afterlife to be Damned?'

'Strictly, you do. But now you mention it, there's no reason why we can't reap our reward, whatever it is, on Earth as in Heaven.'

Mark focused. He didn't think this had helped at all.

'This is interesting,' Menzies said. 'I haven't got into any of this since the seminary. Most of the faithful want to talk about their sciatica or whinge because they got pregnant before they could do their GCSEs. I spend more time playing ping-pong than taking confession.'

'What about the Devil? Where does he fit in?'

'I'm not at all sure there's an actual literal Satan with horns and a tail. Unless you count Derek Leech.'

Cold terror sweated through Mark's forehead.

'Sorry,' Menzies said, 'another bad joke.'

9

None of his cards were accepted, but he still had cold cash. His reserves dwindled quickly but he had gelt for a 42nd Street hell-hotel. He gave up and registered as M. Yo. It wasn't like the Apex Suite. Someone had used the sink as a toilet bowl.

On the second night, a white guy with a tattooed neck shoved in and stole Mickey's jacket and boots. The thief stood over the bed and held a knife to Mickey's throat, eyes jittering around the room, scoping for valuables. He snatched bills from the nightstand but most of the cash was safe, hidden in a sock jammed into a hollow bedpost.

As a parting gesture, the guest took out his penis and masturbated at superspeed, ejaculating onto Mickey's legs.

The *Basildon Echo* printed his faxes in full, inserting sarky little *sic* italics after words he'd supposedly misspelled. The paper ran an old, out-of-focus picture from *I Scream* along with his letters. In the still, Michael was fat, shouting and unhappy.

'*Gary Gaunt Replies: Don't you think there's something a wee bit obsessive about this, Mikey?*'

Pink-eyed bastard! If there was anything he hated more than

being called Mike, it was being called Mikey. It made him sound like Mickey.

He was composing a letter to finish the correspondence once and for all. He kept writing and rewriting. It had to be perfect, answering the upstart's every pernicious point. He'd filled thirteen pages. His plan was to take out a full-page advertisement in the *Echo*. It was the only way to be sure his Open Letter to Gary Gaunt was run in full.

A journo from the *Argus* telephoned to inquire about his 'on-going feud' with Gary Gaunt. Discovering the reptile had talked with Gaunt first, Michael refused to comment. Treacherous vermin! They were all in league with the arch-conspirator. As he left another message on Ms Rhodes's machine, it came to him that Gary Gaunt might have seduced her to his cause. After all, she'd actually talked with the milk-haired filth. He'd possibly wormed and squirmed around her, turning her against her masters. There was no loyalty any more.

He should warn Mark. This could have repercussions.

At night, he dreamed of boxing with Gary Gaunt, landing brutal blows in ultra-close-up, pummelling him into screaming submission. Ranks of howling literary critics bayed for blood. As the final bell sounded like an alarm, Michael strutted around the ring, gory gloves raised in triumph, accepting the justifiable applause. Then, a mantrap grip bit into his leg. He looked down. An albino alligator chewed on his leg, jaws clamped around his knee, teeth grinding bone.

He awoke in terror. Ginny grumbled beside him and stuck her face deeper into a pillow. His heart hammered. He still felt dream pain in his real knee.

Guests were required to be out of the rooms in the day. Mickey figured the management rented the same beds, unchanged, to night workers. His legs were still warm where come had sprayed.

But the rest of him was carved from ice. Without a jacket, he shivered uncontrollably. People mistook him for a crack addict.

After a street odyssey, avoiding perilous pan-handlers and five-dollar sirens, he made it uptown to his real hotel. His thick-socked feet were grunge-grey and bleeding; he could no longer pretend this was some beyond-moccasin fashion statement.

'*Cut their feet off and make them walk home*,' he remembered.

The broad steps up to the automatic glass doors were more agonising than the regular sidewalk. He stumped up, one step at a time, gritting his teeth against six-inch pain prongs that skewered his feet. Two Security Nazis (new faces, not the pair from nights ago) converged in front of him, firmly barring his way.

In the exaggeratedly posh English voice that usually worked on Americans, he explained that the hotel had his passport in the safe and he was stranded without it. He didn't mention his clothes, assuming they were a forlorn hope.

They grinned at him outright.

One said, 'So you'd like to have a peek in our safe?'

He casually prodded Mickey's Wile E. Coyote T-shirt, flicking him back into the street.

Brightly, the security thug said, 'Have a shitty day, you hear.'

At the breakfast table, he picked the *Basildon Echo* apart page by page, combing car boot sales and school sport scores for snide references. He was sure there were coded messages from Gary Gaunt to his confederates.

Ginny, her face a cold cream mask, trephined her egg with a Ninja implement.

The *Echo*'s centre page pull-out ran complete TV listings for the upcoming weekend. In the Cloud 9 column for Friday, was a note by the entry for *Dixon's On*. '*Last of series. After this, Dixon's Off*.' The alligator-grip came again, now around his heart. On Sunday evening, BBC 1, *Colin Dale* merited '*Comedy-Drama, last of three*.'

'What's up, doc?' Ginny asked. 'You're grinding your teeth again.'

He showed her.

'So.'

'Dixon's off! Hah! They're trying to get me, Zh-Gin. They're saying I've gone off…'

'You say "Dixon's off" at the end of every show. Before you say "goodnight and get lost". It's your catchphrase.'

'But I don't mean it in the weasel way the ghastly Gaunt does. It's in the intonation. This is life and death. They're out to finish me.'

Ginny's face was blank.

'Darling, I'm getting worried about this.'

He snarled at his wife.

'Zh-you too, Zh-Gin? What are zh-you being given to throw in with Gary Gaunt?'

'I don't have to listen to this.'

She folded her napkin over her plate and stood up. She was in one of her grown-up moods.

'Michael, get help.'

'I don't need help, I need zh-zhustice.'

The Effect had settled down. Coastal City was an occasional four-colour glimpse of a ravaged block or a darting cloak. Mostly, he inhabited a three-dimensional New York.

He searched for himself. In used record stalls, in regular bookshops, in specialist comics stores. He saved his best hope for last: The Marching Morons. Barely three days earlier, he'd sat in the store – a queue of fans stretching into the street and around the block – and signed *Choke Hold* and *The Nevergone Void* until his fingers seized up. He had signed old comics, softcover collections, Möthers albums, *City Hammer* videos, biker jackets, girls' cleavage.

Now the store manager – a fat guy with a beard – scratched his head when Mickey asked if they had anything by Mickey Yeo. Last time Mickey was here, Buddy – Fat Guy's secret identity –

would have crawled over broken glass to kiss his arse. Now he scratched his beard amiably and got out a reference book.

'Miki Yo, you say? Is that a Japanese name? We have a *manga* section upstairs.'

Buddy Fat Guy at least didn't reckon Mickey looked or smelled weirder than most MM customers. He made no comment about the mud-and-blood stiff socks and even let him look at the reference book. The page where there should have been an article on him, with a photograph, was blank.

'Look at that, huh,' Fat Guy said. 'Printing error. Probably makes it valuable.'

'If useless.'

'Yeah, that too.'

There was a queue of excited buyers for *Amazon Queen: Born Anew*.

'Have you got into Farhad Z-Rowe's stuff?' Fat Guy asked. 'He's signing Saturday. It'll be a bonanza.'

Mickey imagined he was sinking fingers into Fat Guy's gut and rooting around until he squished entrails. As he imagined, his hands reached out, and jabbed belly. A couple of staff members hauled him off the manager and ejected him into the street.

No one had written to the *Echo* in his defence, despite all the messages he had left. Not even Melvyn Bragg. Michael decided to remedy the omission. He'd only write what others would have if Gary Gaunt hadn't got to them first.

Setting aside his own master-letter for the moment, he wrote a note from Tom Sharpe, commending *Colin Dale* as more important than anything in his own pitiful bibliography. The unworthy Sharpe was flattered by comparison with Dixon and hoped he could, in future, live up to the high standard his friendly rival had set.

He printed out the note and signed Tom Sharpe's name. He'd

stamp and address it later. Then he wrote a letter from an eye specialist, pointing out that not only could ocular colouration spontaneously change but that the reference to eyes flashing green in *Colin Dale* was an obvious metaphor. As a humorous postscript, he offered Gary Gaunt a complimentary eye test in the hope it would improve his critical faculties.

He laughed for a full half-hour before entrusting the letters to the post.

'Yo,' someone shouted. 'Yo, yo!'

Instinctively, Mickey turned.

'How yo' hangin',' asked a black guy in a superfly hat. He was standing in a doorway, half-hidden by the door.

Mickey shivered.

'Chillin', huh?'

Mickey laughed bitterly.

'Wanna jacket? Cheap? Fi' dollar?'

'Is it warm?'

'Ain't warm, homeboy. Is *hot*.'

Superfly beckoned, opening the door more. He showed a ratty-looking padded jacket, patches of bare fluff leaking out. Whatever state it was in, it was better than freezing his nipples to stones.

'That Coyote, man,' Superfly said. 'What a mofo.'

Mickey looked down at his dirty Wile E. T-shirt.

'Five dollars?'

'Yo.'

Mickey took the wad out of his side jeans pocket.

'They's a handlin' charge,' Superfly said.

Wary, Mickey asked, 'How much?'

'Much you got?'

Superfly whisked Mickey inside the doorway and shoved him onto the greasy linoleum floor. There was a flight of stairs going up. A grey-faced child sat on the landing, watching with huge eyes.

Mickey lost his cash but Superfly insisted he take the jacket. With it wrapped around his shoulders like a waist-length cloak, he was pushed back onto the street.

'Word, man,' Superfly said in farewell.

He put his arms in armholes and found it was a child's coat. The drainpipe sleeves barely reached his elbows. A Streak decal was sewn onto the chest; no matter how much he picked at the stitches, it wouldn't come off.

Ayesha telephoned to ask if he would be in the office today. He realised he'd skipped the regular Tuesday meeting. He told her he hoped to drop by sometime in the afternoon. He had important business.

His magnum letter was up to twenty-one pages. Devastating stuff, scorching, blistering…

Ayesha put April on; she outlined the guests and items lined up for the last *Dixon's On* of the current series.

Current. That was the word the *Echo* had maliciously excluded from its listing. Last of the *current* series. Not last of series. The show was recommissioned and would return in eight weeks. He scrolled to the end of the document as April wittered on, and typed out a postscript on the correct use of the word 'current' in relation to the word 'series' when writing of *Dixon's On*.

'Cloud 9 have asked us to have Pris Wilding on.'

'Pris Who?'

'Some Americano. She's presenter-producing a show called *What a Grunge!* It's in our slot for the next two months. A funny version of *This is Your Life*, they say.'

'Gelatinous by me.'

'Sure?'

'Sure.'

April had tried a follow-up on the coma-sitting cat but the family of the sick little girl had withdrawn co-operation.

'By the terms of their original waiver we should have unlimited access. We can get an injunction, but it'll not look pretty, forcing our way into a hospital room with cameras.'

'Who got to them, Ape? Was it Gary Gaunt?'

April said nothing. In her silence, Michael read fearful confirmation. He thought he could still trust April – she wasn't speaking out loud because people might be listening – but it was obvious the gray gaunts had infiltrated Top Hat. They might have anyone: Roily, Ayesha, the director, the runners?

'Ape, listen very carefully,' he began.

'Yes, Michael.'

'Remember Mr Whippy-Wobble-Willie?'

'Of Crab-Apple, Abergavenny?'

'The self-same. Don't accept any orders not prefaced by a request from Mr Whippy-Wobble-Willie of Crab-Apple, Abergavenny. It's a security measure. A state of war exists.'

Silence. Good girl. She wasn't giving anything away to the traitors in the office.

'Ape, we shall prevail.'

New York was the best city in the world to be a success in. And the worst to be penniless.

Now he had nothing left to lose, predators let him pass unhindered. He could probably go to ground in Central Park and watch the wildlife struggle for survival. Better still, he remembered passing a primordial patch in the Village, thickly-wooded behind railings. The size of a small city block, it was an Environmental Sculpture, maintained in the state the island of Manhattan had been in the fifteenth century, before the coming of the Europeans. Mickey thought he should seek it out and move in, then lose himself in the forest tall like Davy Crockett.

Maybe there were wino Indians in the depths.

Lunch was five chips – sorry, fries – and the grey corner of a Big Mac patty, salvaged from an abandoned McDonald's carton. For dessert, he ate the carton.

Every time he tried mentally to retrace his steps to work out how he had reached this career stage, he was struck with a buzzing, paralysing headache.

He found a subway grate which regularly provided updraughts of hot air and plonked himself down on it in a prime position. His soles had toughened and melded with what was left of his socks, forming a seamy new skin.

Up in the sky, he saw a streak.

10

15 JANUARY, 1993

Nearly a week after Cardinal Wolsey Street, it was hard to imagine the Device as a literal thing. She still believed she'd seen Neil swallowed by a living machine the size of an ocean liner. But doubts accrued around the experience. That must be how miracles were assimilated. Witnesses delude themselves. In another week, she would not believe.

She sat in a 100-yard square of ashes and rubble, on a park bench without a park. The Invader was bundled and happy, grateful for the occasional jog of movement as the stroller rolled six inches back-and-forth. Sally couldn't presume on (or afford) Sonja much longer and so was going through a nurturing, responsible phase.

Mummy, what are we looking for?

Answers, dearhart.

The only prominent vertical feature between here and the river was the Derek Leech International Building. It stood among levelled ruins like an image from a seventies album cover. No matter which turns she took in the maze of Docklands, she always came back to the black pyramid. It was in sight from the end of every derelict road.

This was her second day of searching for Cardinal Wolsey

Street. It wasn't listed in the *A to Z* and none of the few remaining locals she'd questioned – mainly elderly Londoners or nervous immigrants – had more than a vague memory of the name. No one would admit to never having heard of the place; they all had strong ideas of how to get there, and she'd followed insubstantial directions for hours at a time, always abandoning hope as the familiar black triangle hove into view.

At least she had the stroller to lean on. Handy Gadget: doubles as a baby carriage and a Zimmer frame.

A gap opened in overhanging cloud and a shaft of sunlight struck the face of the pyramid. The Invader gurgled with delight and said something that might have meant 'pretty bright'. Sally, eyes assaulted by a painful flash, looked away and saw movement in the rubble. Something straggled towards her. Her first thought was rats but it turned out to be Mark Amphlett.

Because of the Quorum, she'd had to leave her phone off the hook for days. If Mum or a prospective client or an ardent suitor wanted to get hold of her, that was tough luck. She couldn't even leave the machine on: Mark and Michael filled the message tape with unbearable maunderings.

Mark walked carefully towards her, a man in a minefield. His long coat flapped in the wind.

Scary man, Mummy?

She wanted to avoid this. Enough to risk the probable alienation of her parent or the loss of serious work.

She watched Mark move across the wasteland. Since his spell in prison, he'd aged. He looked balder; the fly-away hair around his patch was wilder, ragged. His jacket and trousers came from irreconcilable suits. The shine was off his shoes.

'Grow up like that and you're disinherited,' she told her baby.

* * *

He sat on the bench and got back his wind. Condensation plumed from his mouth and nose.

'Don't ask me to feel sorry for you,' she said, pre-emptively.

He had no answer.

She was still angry with him, with the Quorum. She looked at him but saw Neil.

'I tried,' Mark said.

The Invader waved non-judgemental arms at Mark, delighted by a new person.

Funny man, Mummy?

'To get out of the Deal,' Mark said. 'I was the one who tried.'

She wasn't impressed.

'At first, the Deal was just… well, not a joke… but, you have to understand, an extension of the moves we'd always made. Three in, one out. Two sets of two. We had every permutation. A lot of times, it was me against the rest. I'd sit in my room and chant hatred, then someone – Neil, usually – would coax me out.'

He wasn't talking to himself. For some desperate reason, he was compelled to explain to her. Mark seemed to think it in her power to give him absolution.

'We're still tied together, Neil as much as anyone. The Deal depends on him. Depended. In the end, we'd have brought him out of the cold. We had to.'

Sally could imagine how awful that would have been. Neil hadn't struck her as the type to be grateful for charity.

Mark saw her unvoiced objection. 'We wouldn't have been blatant, Sally. We could have made moves. He'd never have known it was us. He still doesn't know it is us.'

'Doesn't he?'

Panic slapped his face. Sally didn't know either way but Mark took the suggestion seriously.

'He can't. We got too good at it. Anything we tried, we got good at.'

She shrugged. He was probably right.

'We didn't really understand the Deal. That's how it works. You sign away something you don't know you have.'

'You sacrificed Neil.'

He shook his head, impassioned. 'No, that's the sting. We thought we sacrificed Neil. But we sacrificed ourselves. We are the Perfect Sacrifices.'

'Perfect?'

'We've been elevated. Look at us. We have everything. And we're losing it. How much greater is our sacrifice.'

'You sound like a Jehovah's Witness.'

A painful twitch of a smile acknowledged her point. 'Biblical language is all we've got. Salvation, Damnation, Sacrifice. Heaven, Hell.'

'You should write a book,' she said, snidely. '*Damned in the '90s*.'

'I'll never write again,' he said, swiftly. 'I've lost that. I can't share anything in my skull. That's my reward. I can't share anything.'

He was shaking, impassioned. He was right. She really couldn't understand what he was talking about. The Great Communicator mumbled to himself.

'Why is it so much worse for me, Sally?' Mark asked. 'So much worse than for Mickey and Michael?'

Without knowing much, Sally assumed both of the others would say exactly the same thing.

But she had an answer for Mark. 'Because you knew what you were doing.'

Mark nodded to himself, accepting the judgement. He looked up at the clouds and howled. It was an animal noise, older than speech, older than communication. It was private and meaningless.

Sally flinched and the Invader jammed mittens over rudimentary ears. There was nothing for an echo to resound off. The howl rose and dissipated and was lost. The sky swallowed Mark's agony and ignored it.

He reached for her. Without thinking, she jumped away, sliding off the end of the bench.

'Mark,' she said, firmly, 'no.'

She saw his ungloved hand hover in the air. Blue veins stood out like wool threads. Slowly, he made a fist and took it back, holding it against his coat.

His watery eyes looked up. Inside her, disgust squirmed. And resentment. This was something she had been made to feel.

Without especial intonation, he said, 'Sally, I love you.'

Razors of ice scraped her bones.

She shook her head, annoyed, horrified. The Leech Pyramid shone black in its wilderness.

'Sally…?'

Inescapably, she was a component of the Device. Leech had included her in the design from the first. She was the instrument of Mark's punishment.

'No,' she said.

The anger fell from her. Without it, she was naked. She was not above this situation, she was trapped inside it. She felt sorry for everyone. Including herself.

'Kid,' she said to the Invader, 'we're getting out of here.'

She left Mark alone on the bench and trundled the stroller across the uneven ground.

11

15-17 JANUARY, 1993

On Broadway, surrounded by strangled Noo Yawk whines, he listened for accents. Nationality was his last redoubt. Young Americans purposefully strode along the sidewalk, jaws like bumpers, bags like weapons, eyes hard and glittering.

Yank bastards.

A brace of British girls goggled at theatre facades and glossy porno stores. Their voices were Northern. Mancunian, maybe. Flimsy polka-dot skirts over black wool leggings; hip-slung paisley trousers with flare extensions. Americans outpaced them, streaming around either side.

'You English?' he called out.

The girls saw him. Before speaking, he'd been invisible. Tinier than Teensy Teen. Just another shred of street garbage.

'Ignore him,' one girl said to her friend. 'He's a street person.'

'No,' Mickey protested. 'I'm English.'

A week ago, he could have had both shag-hags. At the same time. A bit of flannel and a grin and a line cut with an Apex Suite cardkey. They'd have popped, and been pleased...

Now, it was, 'Well, good luck to you,' and fuck off.

Without hope, he leaned against a poster for *Jelly's Last Jam* and watched the girls wander along Broadway. For them, America was a youth musical; for him, a neon *noir* nightmare.

Thirty pages. Twelve thousand words. Michael's Open Letter to His Garygauntness was growing. He'd been at his word processor for five hours, since well before dawn. His kidneys ached. Still, he typed and corrected, typed and corrected. As new points came to mind, he interpolated them into the text, adding more evidence, supporting his case.

Working on the Open Letter, he came better to understand his struggle. He was exploring the nature of Gary Gaunt. He no longer believed the albino was human. There was a cold alien malevolence there. Gary Gaunt, he had decided, was a philosophical condition, a pink-eyed worm in the apple of the universe.

Today's *Echo* hadn't printed the letter from Tom Sharpe. How could a pissy local paper ignore a missive from the second-best comic novelist in the country? Michael chuckled. He knew Sharpe would be furious when he discovered how little his words counted in Basildon.

There was nothing about Michael in the whole paper. They were getting perilously close to lawsuit territory. Michael had left messages with his lawyers. Once the Open Letter was published, he'd see about the judicial moves. He had the resources. In the end, only one man would walk out of the courtroom vindicated and he wouldn't be a rabbit-eyed scribble.

In reading the *Echo* from cover to cover, he discovered the nastiest of its strategems, a calculated attempt to set Michael against the staunchest of his allies. In tiny print, along with the register of infamy that was the paper's masthead, was written 'A Derek Leech Newspaper'. When the Sponsor discovered the putridity perpetrated in his name, his wrath would be devastating. His lawyers would join with Michael's in smiting the *Basildon Echo*, indeed Basildon itself, off the map of the earth.

Alleluya! He typed, invoking the name of Derek Leech. Each

word was a tiny missile. Each sentence a salvo.

Shocks shot from his palms through his wrists up to his shoulders. It was as if the muscles had been cut. He ignored pain and kept typing. Nothing would sway him from his purpose.

Around Neil, the Device was frenzied in motion. Gears ground, flame spurted, molten metal poured, valves pumped, furnaces roared. Energy was unconfined. He shared the exultation of the Device.

Mark pressed redial, listened to clicks, let the engaged tone sound for long seconds, broke the connection, pressed redial, listened to clicks, let the engaged tone sound for long seconds, broke the connection, pressed redial, listened to clicks, let the engaged tone sound for long seconds, broke the connection, pressed redial, listened to clicks, let the engaged tone sound for long seconds, broke the connection, pressed redial, listened to clicks, let the engaged tone sound for long seconds, broke the connection, pressed redial, listened to clicks, let the engaged tone sound for long seconds, broke the connection, pressed redial...

'You English?'

'Fuck a baboon, buddy.'

Pris Wilding was an American with hair like white flame and matching lipstick. She had a red bunny bow in her hair and a larger one around her throat. Her voice was stridently perky, like a sexy cartoon animal. As she talked to camera, ignoring his eyeline completely, she seemed to be chewing.

Michael asked her about Basildon and she insisted on talking about her cursed show. Through his earpiece, the wimp-out director told him to 'drop Basildon' because it was well past its laff-by date. Nobody even bothered to phone complaints any more.

'Haven't you ever watched *This is Your Life* and wished they'd haul out someone from a celebright's past who *really* loathed the smug slime? A schoolkid he used to bully, an old girlfriend he knocked up and dumped, a work partner who got the royal shaft. Nobody gets a life worth showing on TV without treading on people, and on *What a Grunge!* we give the treadees the window to shout out of, to cry out "look at me, I'm a person too, I have worth". If Mother Theresa made a porno flick early in her career we'd find out. The message is that famousoids deserve everything they get.'

As Pris spoke, a cute but fanatical gleam behind her tinted contacts, Michael was fascinated. She wore a filmy top that went transparent under lights. Her brassiere was an intriguing work of engineering, restraining breasts the size of small planets. Fifty-one per cent of the viewing public would hate her but she was going to be very, very popular. There was no doubt she was a woman, but she talked and gestured like a transvestite.

'We see ourselves as messengers from God, wagging the flexible finger at those naughty-naughties who abuse position, sticking the thermometer of truth into the armpit of deceit. Pervo politicians, beware! Rapacious rock stars, look out! Mendacious movie brats, shudder! Be on your best behaviour, lest you take the *Grunge Plunge!*'

He asked the question that had nibbled at him since April presented Pris to him in the Green Room.

'Lover-doll,' he said, 'are zhou an albino?'

Mark pressed redial, listened to clicks, let the engaged tone sound for long seconds, broke the connection, pressed redial, listened to clicks, let the engaged tone sound for long seconds, broke the connection, pressed redial, listened to clicks, let the engaged tone sound for long seconds, broke the connection…

Before he could touch the redial button, the phone rang. He was startled. The bell was louder than he remembered. Louder than was possible.

Sally!

The receiver was in his hand. 'Hello,' he gasped, 'Ss…'

'Mark?'

It was another woman's voice. Not Sally, but familiar…

'Mark, it's Pippa.'

'P-p-p…'

'Mam says you've been hassling her.'

He tried to remember Pippa. It wasn't easy. There was something about her: Scots girl. Editor. Geology major. She said Neil *was a really nice bloke.*

'It's been months, Mark.'

'Pip…'

She was all right, he supposed. If you liked the type. But she wasn't Sally Rhodes.

'I want you to stop. I want you to grow up and stop.'

'Pippa?'

'Just let it go, Mark. Just let go.'

A dozen slates shot off the roof, jets of steam escaping. They clattered and smashed in the street. Life flickered through his mind. Moments stuck and repeated. Random moments.

He looked at two unfamiliar boys in the assembly hall, indicated the man at the lectern, and said 'Chimp'.

People pressed around a rupture in the Device, ignoring steam that lobstered their faces, and fixed plates over a fissure.

He stood on stage in the Rat Centre, dressed as a jester, and recited 'and thus the whirligig of time brings in his revenges'.

The Device's fires poured together a ball of inferno.

He sat in the kitchen at Michael's Gramma's, talking with Mark's girlfriend, wondering where the others were. Surprisingly, Philippa leaned over and stuck her tongue down his throat.

Girders wove around the fire.

He sat up in bed as Rachael broke the door down. This wasn't how he'd fantasised the moment. His typewriter bounced off his headboard, grazing his cheek, falling on the floor. Rachael's mouth was a circle of fury, her hands bird talons.

The Device was nearly finished.

'Lois Lane?' he asked. 'Olive Oyl,' she said.

On the monitors, he saw Leech. Impassive but approving. His one-eyed familiar was excited, raving at the success. But Leech expected no less.

He stood on his doorstep and faced the Nazi who put the screwdriver to Sally's eye. He gave up.

A rain of sparks fell past his face.

A living pool outside the Fershluggenheim Museum gathered, extended arms to streetlamps and pulled itself into human shape. Blubber Boy shook off amorphousness. The Creech, Dead Thing and Circe had combined forces to defeat him, but he'd win. In Coastal City, good guys always won. A tiny sprite chirruped from a nook in the sidewalk. Mickey waded through the dispersing glop of the hero's sloughed-off mass, the last of Blubber Boy pulling at his knees. Circe's Enchantment of Bewilder made it hard to coordinate. The whole city stumbled.

The Effect passed and he was back in a New York night, somewhere near the Guggenheim.

'Yo,' someone said.

He assumed a fighting stance as a preparation for getting the shit kicked out of him again.

'Yo,' someone else confirmed.

A man in uniform approached cautiously, as if expecting Mickey to turn feral.

'It's him,' the uniform said.

He recognised Raimundo, the Pyramid chauffeur. And clocked Raimundo's supervisor. She stood by a small van, arms folded, watching.

'Heth?'

He didn't say anything else. Raimundo grabbed his arm and forced his wrist up between his shoulder-blades.

'Careful,' Heather warned. 'He might be rabid.'

Something hot bit into his lower back. His brain frazzled and he heard and smelled the singing *zzzztt* of something electric. Pain came and went and his last strength vanished.

Raimundo shoved him towards the van. When Heather looked down at her clipboard, a curtain of hair shadowed her face.

'Get him into the light,' she ordered.

He gave no resistance. Heather compared his face with a photostrip on the clipboard.

'Check, get him into the compartment.'

She went round to the back of the van and opened a door. The interior was a windowless box, hardly big enough to hold a man. Raimundo helped him up and showed him how to bend his useless limbs to fit the space. There was a light in the ceiling but, like the one inside a fridge, it went out when the door was closed.

He sat in the dark, rocked by aftershocks. The container was soundproofed. The van began to move.

The end-of-run party was noisy. He could tell from the rapid, hollow cheer of their patter which of his staff were with the gray gaunts. He found a spot where he got his back to a real wall and watched traitors conspire against him.

The *Dixon's On* set was crowded with Top Hat staff and Cloud 9 brass, picking at canapés he'd paid for, sloshing his wine. They clowned with the cameras. The house band blundered through numbers. His minions, freed of the shackles of the series, danced in a strobe-lit pit.

He saw a length of white hair whipping, burning his retinas. Ayesha had dyed her hair a very, very light blonde. Everyone said it was striking, but Michael got the real message. They could get so close to him he would never suspect.

Little did the gray gaunts know just how vigilant Michael Dixon could be, how ruthless. They had badly underestimated his character when they set out to ruin him.

A ruptured beer-barrel sprayed the Cloud 9 Vice-President of Light Entertainment and everyone cheered. The bigwig stood, Armani dripping froth, and laughed like a drain. Roily, a toady in search of a patron, handed over a towel.

April was drinking profusely, snorting relieved cackles, hugging people she'd see in eight weeks as if they were to be parted forever. He'd thought her reliable but now wasn't sure. She was loyal but weak. She could be bought.

'Mr Whippy-Wobble-Willie of Crab-Apple, Abergavenny says you're all sacked,' he muttered.

He wondered if Gary Gaunt himself were here, somewhere. A hat and some glasses and he could pass for normal. Hair dye and contact lenses, even.

There were many faces he didn't recognise. Even those he knew well were not ruled out of suspicion. The albino might have spent years getting into place, preparing for the final assault.

Gary Gaunt could be anyone. Anyone anywhere.

'Mikey,' said a big scene-shifter smiling, arms spread, 'what can I say...'

The scene-shifter stuck a quick fist into Michael's gut. Air shot out of his lungs in a gasp.

'That's with love from Basildon.'

He replayed the conversation, certain of what he should have said, imagining how her reactions would have differed.

'Don't ask me to feel sorry for you.'

'I tried to get out of the Deal. I was the one who tried.'

She half-turned, listening.

'It could have been me, not Neil. It could have been any of us. We're all victims.'

She saw the depth of his suffering, and got closer to him on the bench. Her clear eyes were forgiving.

'We didn't really understand. We were tricked. We were just kids.'

'You sacrificed Neil?'

'No, we sacrificed ourselves. We are the Perfect Sacrifices.'

'Perfect?'

'Like Aztecs elevated above the tribe for a year, granted their every wish, honoured and loved. They lie willingly on the altar as the priests cut out their hearts.'

She was shaking, moved.

'Why is it so much worse for me? So much worse than for Mickey and Michael?'

'Because you understand.'

She was right.

He reached for her.

'Sally, I love you.'

'Mark,' she said, softly, 'no.'

He went back to the beginning, and thought it through again, taking more care, thinking out what he wanted to say. Eventually, it must work out.

The door opened and he was hauled out of his compartment. Raimundo made a face. Mickey realised he must smell awful.

'Remove him from his clothes,' Heather said.

Raimundo attacked with a pair of tailor's shears, snipping his kiddie coat and Wile E. Coyote T-shirt into removable sections. There was a light drizzle, icy but not clean.

Adjusting to the blobby light, he realised he was in a carpark at an airport. Queues of travellers with baggage watched without interest as he was stripped.

When Raimundo dug the shears into his waistband, he capitulated. Indicating that the chauffeur should back off, he undid his fly and unpeeled jean-legs.

In happier times, he'd left his underpants in Heather's bed. Now, she looked at his skinny, shrivelled nakedness with unconcealed distaste.

'Shame we can't clean him up,' she said, sliding a tartan bag across the tarmac. 'Have him get into these.'

Raimundo unzipped the bag. There were clothes inside. Warm, clean clothes. His luck was changing. He was almost fully-dressed before he realised he was wearing a bank clerk's turquoise suit from the early seventies. Lapels wider than the shoulders and flares like crinolines.

'I'll look a dildonian,' he complained.

Raimundo raised a device that looked like a high-tech stapler, and a tiny arc crackled.

'Fine by me,' Mickey conceded.

He was allowed to keep his once-yellow socks – they'd have to be surgically removed along with 90 per cent of the skin – but was given a pair of stack-heeled platforms a size too small, which he painfully hauled on.

'Satisfied?' he asked.

Heather ventured close and examined him thoroughly. Her eyes were dispassionate and dangerous. She'd either forgotten or was deliberately ignoring whatever had passed between them.

Raimundo gave her the shears. She took his braids in her fist and neatly snipped off the lot.

'That's better,' she said. 'Now, let's get this package out of the country.'

* * *

'It's been dayglo dream, Mikey,' Pris said. Her smile made dimples deep enough to lose a coin in. 'We'll do our bestest to keep your slot warm for when you come back in September...'

September!

'...I'm sure we'll work together again. Bye-now, kiss-kiss, love-love.'

Pris made a puckermouth at the air, gave a cheery little paw-wave, and sashayed out of the party. Five silent minders, who'd been blending with the minions, took note and followed her, looking back for assassins.

His stomach still hurt. He looked around for the VP/LE – who'd told him *Dixon's On* would return in March – and saw the beer-soaked exec bopping with April and Ayesha in the pit.

Ignoring grinding pain, he made his way to the pit and shouted at the VP/LE. Eventually, he penetrated the man's head.

'When are we on again?' he yelled.

'Pardon,' the VP/LE shouted, tugging his ear.

'When is *Dixon's On* back?'

The VP/LE heard this time.

'Can't we schedule an interface next week?'

He wondered if he was ruptured. Nearby, Ginny grind-danced with Roily. April leaned against the side of the pit, holding her head. Ayesha listened quietly, glowing white hair falling half-way down her chest, eyes flashing red.

'Tell me now,' he insisted.

The VP/LE tried to seem sober. Stinking stains spread on his shoulders and lapels.

'Cloud 9 wonder if we shouldn't rest the format. Devise something more relevant to the nineties.'

'Like *What a Fucking Grunge?*'

'Demographics on *Grunge* are highly positive, Michael. Advertiser response is startling. We see a 35 per cent improvement on slot profitability even *before* the first of the run.'

He saw the hand of the gray gaunts in this.

'Mr Whippy-Wobble-Willie of Crab-Apple, Abergavenny says... stitch that!'

Michael headbutted the VP/LE.

In the dark, he thought back further. By his talk with Sally in Docklands, everything was lost. Nothing could have been changed.

It was 1983. That was the turning point. Mark should have coralled the others, forced them to endure the setbacks. Simply not turning up at the Meet wasn't enough; he should have gone, and taken the others through the argument.

When they all crawled back to the Deal, they drew dotted lines across their own throats and said 'cut here'.

If he had explained to Mickey and Michael, 1983 would have been a short-term disaster. By now, they would all be better. Not great, but good.

Michael would have written a few decent books, cult successes. Mickey would be drawing the Dr Shade strip in the Argus. *Neil would be assistant editor of* The Shape. *Mark would be engaged to Sally Rhodes.*

None of them would have any complaints. Though maybe they'd all be haunted by possibilities.

Mark thought of other paths not taken.

In the bathroom mirror, if he turned the lights out, he could see the sub-Mark who might have been if he had gone directly to Achelzoy on Twelfth Night. The Mark who had suffered, but would be redeemed. In his eyes, Mark saw a repellent righteousness.

Twelfth Night is also Epiphany. The night Christ manifested Himself to the Three Wise Men. The night Leech manifested himself to the Three Stupid Boys.

Stupid, stupid, stupid...

If they had said no, they would have been heroes. Obscure, perhaps, but heroes.

But their courses were set even before Sutton Mallet.

His ring finger had no feeling at all. He could only bend it with an extreme act of will.

He thought over and over the first days at Marling's. He could have made friends with Alan Ward, the first boy who talked to him. He could have ignored his first-form peers and hung around third years, becoming Spit's jester. He could have tried harder and been in the rugby team.

He didn't have to be part of the Forum. He didn't have to be a geek and a freak.

He could have failed his eleven-plus and gone to Hemphill. No one really expected anything else of him. His brother had gone to the Secondary Modern and left school at sixteen to work in a garage. Now, Christian had a recession-proof motor parts business in the Backwater. Like Mark's sisters, he was married, had kids, a mortgage, an accent. They all had lunch with the parents every Sunday.

He hadn't had to do anything.

At the security check, they made him take off most of his clothes again. There were useless bands of metal inside his lapels. Every time he walked through the magic door, a ping sounded. On the other side of the barrier, Heather gave Raimundo a packet containing Mickey's passport, deportation papers and boarding pass. The airport was impressed with Heather.

'Do you work for the government?' an official asked.

'I'm with Pyramid,' she said. 'Ease and Convenience.'

The official's back straightened.

'I'll be glad when this one's terminated,' Heather said.

Mickey was further prodded and poked and conveyed to the departure lounge. A crowd of students and tourists waited, surrounded by mountains of carry-on luggage, red-eyed already for the overnight flight.

Raimundo and a steward took his arms in a firm grip and guided him through the tube into the airliner.

'Look,' said a student, 'they always take the scum on first.'

Saturday's *Basildon Echo* had nothing about Michael at all. He wasn't fooled. The campaign had gone underground.

He worked on his Open Letter for ten hours, not getting up to eat or drink or use the toilet. He had his priorities. This must get finished.

Ginny was off with Melanie. They'd probably gone over to the gray gaunts.

His keyboard was dotted with bloody fingerprints.

Raimundo slept in the next seat and snored, sprawling into his personal space, invading his nose with strong aftershave.

Heather was up in Superior. They were at the back of the plane, by the bogs. Mickey's seat didn't recline. His spine, still prickling from stun-shock, wouldn't bend to fit the contours.

The in-flight movie starred Dudley Moore and Patsy Kensit. Supper was a packet of peanuts and a thimble of orange extract laced with washing-up liquid. Cheek frozen against the cold of the window, he managed flickers of sleep. Cruel dawn woke him.

The Device settled, stabilised. Power thrummed in every strut and rivet. Metal roots burrowed into earth, reaching down for wet warmth.

He looked down at Leech. He wore a dark suit and a hat. Drache, the disciple, was prostrated in the mud, praying to the Device. Neil and Leech knew better.

At last, he was empty. Soon, he'd be free.

* * *

In the dark, Mark sat and did nothing. He tried to think nothing.
Tried.

At Heathrow, he had to queue for two and a half hours. Raimundo, impassive and uncaring, stood with him. The musak loop came round five times. When he was finally processed, an official confiscated his passport and cut it in half like a credit card.

'Your right of international travel has been revoked,' he was told.

Finally, he was ejected from the airport. Heather and Raimundo stood by the main doors and watched him venture out into the cold day. Mickey had no money for a cab, a bus or a tube.

'Michael,' Ginny said, 'the car will be here in an hour. You must get dressed.'

'Not zhust now,' he said.

On the screen, he had Gary Gaunt staked out in the sun, eyes skinned, ants swarming over honeyed wounds. The albino would not survive the Open Letter.

It had grown in the computer memory, eating up space, edging the *Mai DaVale* files into limbo. It took precedence. He was writing for his life.

'Michael,' Ginny said, determined. 'Look at me.'

He swivelled. His knees, locked in place after another day at the WP, cracked.

Ginny wore an evening gown and a matching turban.

'It's *your* testimonial,' she said. 'You can't not go.'

Melanie peeked around her mother's skirts. She was dressed as a miniature Ginny.

'All your friends will be there.'

'What friends?'

* * *

Contacts were broken. With mechanical whirs, the supports were withdrawn. Neil stood shakily on the platform. He had lost track of time inside the Device.

He felt newly awake, as if he had dreamed pleasantly for a year.

Several people stood at the foot of a spiral staircase, ready to start up and help him.

'No,' Leech said. 'He can get down on his own two feet.'

'I'm fine,' Neil reassured.

Carefully, he climbed out of the Device.

A Ford Escort stopped and the driver called over, 'Wanna lift, mate?'

Mickey stepped from grassed verge to damp asphalt.

'Fab gear, pal,' the driver said, chuckling. 'Who does your hair, Stevie Wonder?'

He trudged to the door and put a hand to the handle.

'Hahhahhahhah,' the driver laughed, and drove off.

The next car stopped and the door was opened for Mickey to get in. The driver told him to belt up.

'Michael Yo?'

Alone in the back of the cab that had been sent, Mark was tense. He didn't like to be away from the telephone. Sally might call. The machine was on but she might not want to leave a message. Many people didn't like to pour out their souls to machines.

He had to talk with Sally. He had to explain. In the end, it had been Sally. She was the keystone.

'Sally, I love you.'

'Mark,' she said, softly, 'yes.'

The cab drove through empty streets. It was Sunday evening in winter. Everyone else was indoors. He might have been all alone in the city.

Where was Sally? He thought of her face, trying to interpret every feature, every expression. She must understand.

'Darling,' Ginny said, 'you should see your face.'

Michael had no speech. Inside, he burned.

The Pyramid ballroom was crowded. He recognised most faces. Some had worked on *Colin Dale*. Others were familiar from earlier projects. He saw the producer of *I Scream*, even.

'Zh-you,' he said to his wife, 'zh-you were a collaborator.'

'Of course, dear,' she giggled. 'We've been creeping around for weeks. It's been such fun.'

Melanie asked if there were any sprouts.

'Even Melly helped.'

His daughter gave him a gap-toothed grin.

'But it's been worth it,' Ginny said.

One in five of the guests had dyed (or real?) white hair. Ginny took off her turban to reveal a milky fuzz-cut.

'Do you like it?' she said. 'I've decided to go natural.'

Melanie mimicked her mother. She had the same hair.

'Look at this,' Ginny said, popping her contacts. She opened pink eyes and snorted like a rabbit.

Melanie followed suit.

In the foyer of the Pyramid, Mickey ran into another of the walking dead. They didn't recognise each other for moments. They were both too weary to conceal their shock.

Mark's bald blotch had spread. His face was deeply grooved with pain. His clothes were assembled at random.

'Don't tell me,' Mark said. 'I can imagine.'

So could Mickey.

Attendants helped them through into the ballroom. They both looked for the third ravaged face.

Michael, lost like a child dressed in his father's dinner suit, was standing a little way from his wife and daughter.

In the crowd, they were alone.

They were seated together at a strange table shaped, Mickey realised, like a Q. They had nothing to say to each other.

Neil, comfortable in the clothes provided, followed Leech along the corridor to the lift-cage.

It was as if he'd dozed off in 1978 and dreamed a life that didn't matter.

The doors hissed open and they stepped in.

The glass lift, suspended under the roof of the Pyramid, was a balcony in the sky. Below, in a sea of light and darkness, swam hundreds.

'From up here, they look like one beast,' Leech said. 'So many, with one purpose.'

'Me?' Neil asked.

Leech said, 'This is your night, Neil. Enjoy it.'

Was Sally here?

Mark looked around. He recognised many of the guests. There was his cellmate Dolar, with Janet of the Planet and two young girls. A woman with a striking white dash in her black hair was Anne Nielson of *The Scam*, ten years on. There was a table flagged with a Union Jack for the ELF, who sat with stiff backs as if stranded in enemy territory. Next to them were a couple of black guys, one with an absurd 1972 hat, and a white guy in a shell-suit, all wondering what they'd done to get here. Michael told him a nervous-looking family group were the Gregorys of Cranley Gardens. The guitarists in the house band were Denny Wolfe and Karl Garr, the singers were Grattan and Tamsin.

'Where did they get all these people?' he asked.

At a table alone, Tanya Gorse chain-smoked. Pippa gaggled with a cluster of Mickey's shag-hags, avoiding Mark's eyeline. Others: Hunt Sealey and Allan Keyes, Penny Gaye and Brie Simon, Kendra and Gwen, Farhad Z-Rowe and Timmy Chin, Ayesha McPherson and Laura-Leigh, April Treece and Richard Pierpoint, Trevor Skelly and Fats Waller, Raimundo and Father Menzies, Desmond Dennett and Candy Dixon, Carole Wolley and the aged remains of Chimp, Dick Karsch and Eivol Manoogian, Morag Duff and Barry Gatlin, Eugene Reilly and Steve Dass, Zafir Azmi and Pel, Rachael Rosen and Ingrid Tell, Constant Drache and Heather Wilding. A fancy-dress corner was packed with heroes and villains: Amazon Queen, the Streak, Blubber Boy, the Riddler, a smaller Dr Shade, Max Multiple, Dead Thing, some Gorilla Guerillas.

At one quiet table was an elderly couple it took Mark a full minute to recognise as Neil's parents. The actors who played Colin Dale and Ken Sington were in their telly costumes, chatting up Ginny Moon and her mother. There were others: footsoldiers, minions, bystanders, associates, victims, celebrities, lords and ladies.

Sally, alone, wasn't here. That made the evening meaningless.

The scenic lift began its slow crawl down the inside of the Leech Pyramid. Inside, Mark saw two figures, faces in darkness.

The lift landed like a space capsule and opened. Derek Leech and Neil Martin emerged. Balloons went up and sparkle-dust flew into the air.

Michael noticed TV cameras perched around the ballroom like machine gun nests. There was no escaping.

Gary Gaunt was in charge. The world was lost. The conspiracy prevailed.

Red dots glowed on the cameras. It was all live. The house band performed a Nina Simone number, 'You'll Go to Hell'.

Pris Wilding wound through hushed crowds, carrying a remote mike. Spotlights followed her course. Her hair, under a pearl-dotted mantilla, shone whiter than the sun. She wore nouveau Elizabethan costume, with a breathstopping bodice and taste-gagging flamenco sleeves.

Looking to camera, she smiled...

'Hello, lovelies everywhere. Tonight, we have a very special triple edition of the show everyone's gabbing about. Taking the Grunge Plunge are three young men who've been together for many, many years. Ahhhhh. They thought they were gathering here for a testimonial, but we knew different.'

She worked her way to the 'Q' table.

'We've gone back further than you'd believe into the pasts of these pesky personalities, and some of the slimy sleaze our daring dirt-diggers have surreptitiously unshovelled will make your hair go white as a nun's conscience. Everyone has a teensy-tiny smidgen of sordid sin in their deepest past that shames them to the quivering core of their being. But these famousoid fellers don't seem to have anything *but* shame on their collective CV.'

Mark looked at Michael and Mickey. Finally, they understood the Deal. Truly, they had presented themselves as Perfect Sacrifices.

'It's us,' Mark said. 'Not Neil.'

'How long?' Michael asked.

'Leech said we'd all live past ninety.'

He saw a future stretching past the middle of the twenty-first century.

'Sally,' he said to himself. The name no longer meant anything. It was not attached to a person but to a condition, an absence in himself. He wound down.

'Lovelies, lovelies,' the strange American woman gasped. On a monitor, her breasts were positioned behind Michael's head like Mickey Mouse ears.

Between them, the Quorum had the whole story. Michael made angry fists, while Mickey was slumped in resignation.

'Hold this moment,' Mark told them. 'This may be the last time we understand anything. Tomorrow, it's back to the trenches.'

Mark looked up at the American. He was ready to take his medicine.

'Tonight,' Pris Wilding said, 'we look at Michael Dixon, Mark Amphlett and Mickey Yeo, celebright cephalopods who have achieved so much in so many fields. Tonight we look at these three and say...'

Everyone in the room shouted.

'...*What a Grunge!*'

The show continued without Leech. He had no appetite for it. The Device was earthed, the fires feeding into the ground. Its purpose was fulfilled. Nothing forced him to watch the knives descend.

He walked away from the Pyramid. Just out of sight, Cardinal Wolsey Street was evacuated. The Device would go its own way. Tonight, its accumulated power was directed into the earth. By tomorrow's dawn, the machine would be useless metal and decaying meat. The fires it contained would seed the ground.

If he looked from the right angle through his dark lenses, he saw hard bubbles in the night sky, the outlines which would be filled by the city's bulk. Winged shapes flew between the minarets, talons dangling, beaks agape.

The Perfect Sacrifices would continue. Tonight had seen the turn of the cards for only three of innumerable Deals. Their lifelong acts of devotion would feed the new city.

He walked across the rubble-strewn wasteland as if it were smooth as still water.

The cycle had been interesting. Many movements of the Device surprised him. He learned there were some people – infinitely rare – he couldn't touch. His city would be walled against them.

In the distance, Cardinal Wolsey Street shook. Its hollow shell collapsed quietly around the final throes of the Device. Its last glow lit the sky.

He walked onto the old dock, its timbers briefly crimsoned. This would be cleared soon, like everything else, swept into the river and borne away. He heard the current running. For the first time, he was allowed to smell the water, the mud, the sewage.

His foot strayed into a mulchy depression in the wood. He bent down and cupped water from the puddle in his gloved palm, then sucked the liquid into his mouth. His tongue exploded.

Taste!

Rewarded, he stood and turned. The Derek Leech International Building was illuminated from inside by the rite of sacrifice. Black facets took colourful tints as light-beams struck up into the skies. His Pyramid was a jewel in the night.

VALENTINE'S DAY, 1993

'You missed the party,' Neil said. 'It was massive. You'd never believe who was there.'

'I was invited,' she said. 'Leech even sent a car. But I didn't have anything to wear.'

They were in the garden of the Tin Woodsman. He'd sent a note asking her out to Sunday lunch. Sally had been glad to hear from him. He had answers for her and she had pieces for him.

'I missed you,' he said, touching her wrist. 'It wasn't complete without you. Mark said as much.'

She could imagine.

'I don't have luck with parties. I met Connor at a party.'

'Who?'

'The father,' she said, thumbing at the Invader. 'He's not around any more.'

'In town?'

'On Earth.'

'You met me at a party,' he said. 'Remember?'

'I rest my case.'

He grinned. It was an easy, un-neurotic grin. Now he was willing to stand up straight, Neil seemed taller.

They were the only souls hardy enough to be outside. As they drank, Neil trundled the stroller back and forth over a little hump in the grass, exciting the baby to produce delighted gurgles.

'Good kid,' he commented.

'Sometimes. Mainly a darling nuisance, though.'

Wrapped in a coat and hood, the Invader mumbled. Occasional words were recognisable. Steps had been known. A little personality was coalescing.

'No, this is really a good kid. What's her name.'

'It's a he,' she said. 'Jerome.'

She was glad to be out in the cold. She didn't want to be in the flat with long-past-comprehensible Valentines pouring from her fax. She'd changed her phone number at great inconvenience, but forgotten the fax line.

She was working steadily if unspectacularly. At a discount, she'd surveyed the wrecked Planet Janet for Dolar and suggested features to improve security. She was making a speciality of protecting small businesses from pilfering and vandalism. And a Community Action Group in Tottenham had her teaching a course, training bar and door staff to run social events resistant to attacks by racist groups. The night would come when one of her graduates would dole out lumps to the ELF thug with the screwdriver.

'Did you even see the show?'

She shook her head. She'd had Cloud 9 disconnected. With Jerome in the flat, she wanted to minimise TV. With the money she saved on cable, she bought books. *TinTin*, *Asterix*, dinosaurs, *Winnie the Pooh*.

'What went out was strange. It must have been impossible to follow if you didn't know the backstory. *What a Grunge!* is a cringingly embarrassing programme. That's probably why it's such a hit.'

'Can *you* follow the backstory now?'

'Oh yes,' he said, 'most of it. Strange, I used to think I had friends and enemies. Now, it looks as though I only had a conspiracy.'

She was surprised at his even tone. 'Aren't you angry?'

'I *was*. Believe me, in that contraption, I went through anger.

And fear and awe and Epiphany and holocaust and a whole lot else. I'd wasted so much paranoia on Norwegian Neil Cullers, certain I was fantasising and rationalising my own inadequacies, that it was a facer to find out the worst dream was not only true but an underestimation. But I get off easy. Nothing was my fault. Nothing at all.'

'Leech said you got picked because you wanted to chat up Mark's girlfriend.'

'Philippa? Other way round, I think. It's so long ago, I can't remember.'

That was an evasion, but she let it pass. There was no point in being entirely truthful. She didn't want to talk about Connor, so she'd let him off Pippa.

'If it hadn't been you, if you'd been one of the Quorum, what do you think you'd have done?'

He sat for a while, hand around a pint he'd paid for and shook his head.

'That's not a question anyone should have to answer,' he said.

She'd asked it of herself many times.

'I think I'd have gone along with the Deal,' she said now. 'If it had been me, I'd have done it. Up to a point.'

'What point?'

She shrugged. 'Some point. I wouldn't have gone as far as they did. I hope.'

'I think it got more and more difficult to pull out. One year Mark tried, apparently.'

'"Tried".'

Neil disapproved of her tone of moral superiority, she could tell. She must look like a witch-burner.

'Sally, I don't resent or hate them. We go back too far for that. In the beginning, we were all just kids. I went through a break-their-fucking-necks phase, but we always had those. There was a time with Mickey, just when we went Comprehensive, when I wanted to strangle him with his guts. Ancient history.'

'I don't believe you.'

'You don't have to.'

She wanted to talk about something else.

'Where are you living?'

He grinned again. 'Not in Cranley Gardens. I stayed with my parents for a few weeks. I can't tell you how much that means, to be back in touch with them. Now, I'm looking at flats. They gave me quite a bit of money.'

'Who?'

'Them, I guess. The Quorum. It was an anonymous parcel of cash. Big bills. An offering of atonement.'

She was disgusted.

'I took their money too,' she said. 'I didn't give it back.'

'I should think not. That'd be bloody stupid.'

'*Can* they atone?'

He was thoughtful. 'I don't know. *I'm* not really ready to forgive them. I mean, philosophically is one thing, but it was *my* life that got demolished. It's not so much me, as the people who got in the crossfire. My Mum and Dad; they'll never understand what it was about. Anne; she's not had a happy decade. Dolar; he's landed with a criminal record, well, more of a criminal record. You.'

'Me?'

'Yes, you. You're stuck with Mark.'

'He's stuck with me. Not me, the idea of me.'

Sometimes he loitered outside the flat like a scarecrow. He was becoming more insubstantial. *The Shape* had interrupted publication, but the staff had bought out the title and a relaunch was announced. The Crush was continuing. She had looked into restraining orders, but the hassle was tailing off. She had the idea he could as easily obsess on her from afar as get close.

'Is it bad?'

'Not any more. Just embarrassing. How long can it go on?'

With chilling certainty, he said, 'Years.'

She'd tracked down Mark's ex and talked with her about the

problem. She said Mark was the world's champion at denial. He could ignore anything that contradicted his vision of his life.

Oddly, she had walked past Mark in the street in Wood Green and he had not recognised her. She realised the Crush was an abstract. Mark's 'Sally Rhodes' was not real. The connections with her were fading.

'What about the others?' she asked.

'Michael is moving to Basildon. He has most money left, but it's rupturing away rapidly. His wife baled out and his show was cancelled. He's involved in some labyrinthine lawsuit. *Private Eye* says he wanders the streets harassing people with white hair. Mickey's working in Planet Janet. My old job, I suppose. No one's heard of him, not even comics fans. I don't know if he remembers his other life or thinks it was a dream. I was in there the other day, and we had a talk about comics. Neither of us reckon much to this whizzkid Farhad Z-Rowe.'

'So it goes on?'

'I can't do anything about it,' he said. 'It's not a punishment, it's a sacrifice. It's part of the process they initiated, not a reaction to it. I'm thinking of writing about the mechanics of modern magic. In the Device, I learned a lot of things. Majorly millennial things.'

Derek Leech had announced an ambitious development in the Docklands. The Prime Minister hailed the scheme as a sign of imminent economic recovery and government subsidies were being made available. Constant Drache's designs were already controversial enough to be condemned by the Prince of Wales. It was hard to connect what Sally knew of the spiritual groundbreaking with the prosaic business of throwing up geodesic skyscrapers. A feature of Leech's mall-like entertainment complex would be the United Kingdom's first Virtual Reality chambers. He also promised a sporting arena, an IMAX cinema, galleries, museums, theatres, a concert space, retail outlets, a theme park.

'The future will be a party,' Leech announced, 'and you're all invited.'

For a price.

In sunlight, Neil's long, odd face was peaceful. He was funny-enthusiastic where he had been funny-cynical. He'd be hard not to like. In odd, almost creepy ways, he reminded her of Mark before the Crush, even of Connor in the Good Minutes.

'What are you going to *do*?' she asked.

He shrugged. 'Anything I want to. I have no past to anchor me. There's nothing to stop me. *No one* to stop me.'

'It's not going to be that easy.'

'I know,' he said, 'believe me, I know. I might go back and finish my degree.'

Fifteen years, she thought. Jesus Christ, what a waste!

'Then there's this book. I thought I might interview you for it. We're the experts.'

She'd been allowed to see how the machine worked. Just a glimpse. She'd never be able to watch TV or read a newspaper without remembering Derek Leech was more than just a media magnate. She'd never see an *Amazon Queen* comic without recalling the sidetracked stretch of her career when a phantom named Mickey Yeo tried to suck her out of existence. She'd never flirt without remembering that 'Sally, I love you' can be the scariest sentence in the English language. In remainder bookshops, in old magazines, in trivia quizzes, the Quorum had left marks. They might be gone, but the scars would remain.

Of all the world, only she and Neil knew the truth behind the comet-like crashes of three burning lights. And Leech, if he counted. If they never shared anything again, Sally and Neil were bound by what they knew.

After their pub lunch, Sally wanted to trundle Jerome through the park. If Neil wanted to come along, maybe put his back into the stroller, that was fine by her. It was still cold, but it would get warmer.

...AND OTHER STORIES

Although 'Organ Donors' is intended as a curtain-raiser to *The Quorum*, the other short stories included here aren't quite in continuity with the novel. However, they afford a look at other aspects of its protagonists, private detective Sally Rhodes and media magnate Derek Leech. Both reappear in 'Seven Stars' (which does include a brief catch-up on what happened after *The Quorum*) and Derek pops up in some of the Diogenes Club series, which will feature in later Titan Books editions. Thanks to the various editors of the stories and to Neil Gaiman, Phil Nutman and Stefan Jaworzyn for input into 'Mother Hen' (more on this debt in the forthcoming Titan Books reissue of *Bad Dreams*). Thanks also to Martin Fletcher, the original editor of *The Quorum*, and Eugene Byrne, who provided helpful commentary.

SALLY RHODES
MOTHER HEN

When the client came, Sally was scraping her scruples off the door. She had left RHODES CONFIDENTIAL INVESTIGATIONS, but the NO DIVORCE WORK footnote was going. She had lived with the Raymond Chandler Code of Chivalry for three years. And no thanks to an irregular procession of worried spinsters, she had never yet earned enough to make her accountant's elaborate tax avoidance schemes worth the effort.

The spinsters were uniformly faded. They had lost pets, or imagined prowlers, or wanted to trace long-ago school sweethearts. Recently, Sally had protected a tycoon's eminently kidnappable daughter during a weekend party. The girl had vomited liebfraumilch-flavoured porridge on her only decent dress, and Daddy still hadn't settled the expenses claim.

She would have been able to coast through the quarter; but she had run her Cortina through a red light and into a parked Porsche. The repairs, the insurance, and the fine had vacuum-cleaned both her bank accounts. At this stage in her career, Sally would welcome a nice, messy, protracted divorce commission.

The client, who had come unannounced and without an appointment, was a pot-bellied skeleton. He had a well-dressed, briefcase-carrying shadow with him.

'Ms Rhodes?' asked the client.

'It's miss,' she said, silently biting off her instinctual 'and proud of it, creepo!' What she said was: 'please go inside and get comfortable. I'll be with you in a sec.'

The two men passed into her office. She brushed some gold dust off her skirt, and wrapped the gilt flakes in yesterday's *Guardian*. The sign read ORCE WORK, but she'd fix that later. Inside, she basketed the newspaper and sat in the wonky swivel chair. The room was tidy through inaction rather than inclination.

She had recently given up smoking for economic reasons, so she picked up a biro with which to gesture. 'Gentlemen, how can I help?'

The opening question had been carefully calculated by the Sunderland Agency, her former employer, to have the maximum tongue-loosening effect on the sort of people who needed confidential investigations. That is, people in trouble. The client wasn't having any of it. He remained as smooth and confident as anyone who looks as if he has been lying dead in a bath for three weeks possibly can.

'I am Nigel Karabatsos,' he said. 'I am rich.'

'Congratulations.'

'I mention the fact in order to establish a basis for our relationship, not out of any undue pride. I am rich through inheritance, and can thus claim no honour from my wealth. My great-grandfather invented the sticking plaster.'

'I always wondered who'd done that.'

Karabatsos twitched a smile. He cradled his waistcoated stomach like a pregnancy. Aside from that swelling, there was scarcely a pocket of flesh on him. It took no morbid turn of the imagination to see the skull beneath his skin.

Sally realised the shadow was looking at her legs, and sat up straight. She had already pegged Karabatsos as a fruitcake, but knew she would have to bear with him. There weren't all that many people willing to entrust their affairs to a private detective who looked more like Connie Francis than Alan Ladd.

'I want you to see something. Mr Derewicz.' The shadow gave Karabatsos an expensive black case. With fingers like refrigerated sausages, Karabatsos opened the case and took out a cloth-wrapped bundle which he gave to Sally. 'It's a statuette. Please examine it.'

She unwound the faintly scented cloth, and held the cool dark marble thing in her bare hands. It was a black bird, with human legs, hair and breasts. It had ruby eyes and diamond talons. A golden shaft, slightly bent, pierced its torso, wedged immovably in the stone.

'Very pretty,' she said, trying not to sound impressed. Actually, she felt an extraordinary desire to possess the statuette. As a child, she used to disconcert her parents whenever she saw a toy or sweet that took her fancy by shouting 'I want it!'

'Yes,' purred Karabatsos. 'Of course, it's quite priceless. Nobody knows who made it, or when, where and why. The subject is classical, but there is something Germanic about the execution. Not exactly Gothic, but a chilly touch of the monasteries nevertheless...'

'What is it? An angel? A harpy? Foghorn Leghorn's sister?'

'There's a problem there. It first became known to history in 1520, when it was listed as one of the treasures of the Vatican. It is named as "Mythwrhn", which sounds slightly Welsh. Don't try to pronounce it. The best you'll be able to do is "Mother Hen".'

'Mother Hen?'

'That's it. Its passage around Europe becomes obscure until 1839, when an English adventurer named Fleetwood stole it from a minor Russian princeling. He was colourfully flogged to death by Cossacks, but the booty was smuggled into this country and came into the possession of his family. At about the turn of the century, it became a kitsch object much prized by certain mystic-minded crackpots. Edwin Arthur Waite swears in a memoir that the sight of the Mythwrhn sent him into a three-day fugue. W.B.

Yeats, the poet, is believed to have written "Leda and the Swan" in an attempt to exorcise the nightmares he suffered after examining the statuette...'

Sally resented being told who W.B. Yeats was. 'There are a lot of crazies about,' she interjected.

'As you say. Roger Fleetwood died recently. He had wanted to go into the Church like his father, but eventually decided instead to become a heroin addict. As Fleetwood's closest friend, I am executor of what remains of the estate. The Mythwrhn is a special bequest. It is to go to Roger's cousin, Joel Silliphant. Maybe you have heard of him. He once had some inexplicable success as a popular musician. I would like to see you deliver the statuette into his hands.'

Sally stroked the marble feathers. The hole in the story was obvious. 'I don't want to talk myself out of a commission, but wouldn't it be a lot simpler for you to give Silliphant his heirloom yourself?'

'There are problems,' sighed Karabatsos. 'I am afraid that Silliphant and I are not on civil terms. A dispute remains unsettled. The prospect of being in his company disgusts and appals me. At our last meeting, he attempted to bite off my lower lip...'

'He's a scratcher, Miss Rhodes,' said Derewicz, touching white scars on his cheek. He had a Halifax accent.

'Do not be alarmed. Silliphant is not violent at random. He simply feels he has cause not to love Mr Derewicz and myself. You should be in no danger. Besides, someone in your profession must surely expect to run some risks. You are, I trust, competent in the arts of dirty fighting?'

'Oh yes, in California these hands would have to be licensed as deadly weapons. But potential violence costs extra.'

'Would £500 cover your requirements?'

'Unless this Silliphant lives in Honolulu.'

'As a matter of fact, he can be found in Camden. Mr Derewicz has all the details.'

Sally was given a slim white envelope.

'There is a cheque inside,' said Karabatsos. 'Will you take the job?'

She was going to regret it, but...

'I don't see why not. I have a couple of other ongoing investigations, but nothing that can't wait. I should be able to deal with Mother Hen this evening.'

'Excellent. Incidentally, I'd advise you against telephoning Silliphant to tell him you're coming. That would give him time to work up an irrational rage. There will be no need to inform me once you have discharged your duties. Good day.'

Karabatsos stood up, steadied his wobbling stomach, and left. Before shutting the door behind him, Derewicz said 'you know you look just like that girl who sang "Where the Boys Are".'

Sally gave him her zero degree smile. She shuddered as if her grave had been spat on. With an unnerving spasm of strength, she snapped the biro in two.

She could have sworn, for a moment, that Mother Hen had blinked.

Sally knew from experience and *The Rockford Files* that nothing was as simple as the commission she had accepted. She was being followed.

Although most of her backstreet scuffles had been with prodigal pussies, she was not unprepared for the occasional dangerous game of midnight hide-and-seek.

One of the imaginary plague of peeping toms in Highgate had turned out to be real. A borderline psychotic with a greasy quiff and a pair of boltcutters had found her watching him watching women in a garage toilet. He had dragged her into a petrol-stinking workshop, used the shears as a bludgeon, and tried to rape her. She had used the tool for a purpose related to that which it was intended for and neatly snipped off one of her assailant's nuts. He had got a sociology degree in Pentonville, and she had been bound over to keep the peace.

There was an anonymous car tailing the 134 down the Archway Road. The bus stopped frequently, but the driver ignored all the opportunities to overtake it. Aside from the conductor, Sally shared the bus only with a pair of gibbering pensioners. The tail had to be on her.

The little Astra she sometimes carried for effect was locked up in a desk drawer back in Muswell Hill. Anyway, it didn't have a firing pin. If it came to physical violence, she thought she could hand out a fairly punitive whack with Mother Hen. Holding tightly the cloth-wrapped statuette, she got off a couple of stops early and dodged into a crowded kebab place.

The windows were misted over, but she discerned the blobby shape of the car as it drove by. She couldn't name the make but knew it was one of the common ones. Red tangles of dead cow turned over a weakly infernal light behind the counter. A loiterer with gorilla forearms and a 'Feed the World' T-shirt tried accidentally to touch her bottom. She deliberately stamped on his sandals, and stepped cautiously onto the crud-covered pavement.

Over the road, a giant chicken with a red and green chef's hat clucked out special prices for its barbequed brothers in a Tennessee Williams accent.

The roar of a civil aircraft drowned the beating of Mother Hen's wings. Drops of red fell hundreds of feet to splash in the streets.

The anonymous address in Camden turned out to be a club, Fly-By-Nite's. The pursuit car was cruising around looking for an inconspicuous but convenient parking space. Karabatsos's northern Polack was driving. He had on leather gloves and an SAS balaclava. Shit, thought Sally.

To get into Fly-by-Nite's, Sally had to squeeze through a dingy corridor beside a licensed sex shop, negotiate a rat-eaten bead curtain, and descend a creaky spiral staircase. The strains of that perennially popular heavy punk standard 'I Wanna Fuck a Pig' could be heard over the amp feedback. There was a heady whiff of drugs in the air.

She found herself in an overpoweringly loud environment, an economy-size cavern with wall-to-wall beefcake. The near-naked Conan clone on the door pointed to a sign. NO UNACCOMPANIED WOMEN. He had SUPER STEVE written on one of his pectorals. He mouthed a discreet 'naff off'.

She stuffed a five-pound note into his leather codpiece, not expecting any change. With a ball Pentel, she wrote on her hand: I'M A MAN IN DRAG. Super Steve wasn't satisfied, and put on an impressive display of brow-flexing. She smeared her palm clean on his oiled shoulder, and shouted 'where's Silliphant?'

Super Steve changed his attitude as promptly as a foreign waiter confronted with a television-advertised credit card. He signalled, and an understudy, smartly dressed as Robin the Boy Wonder, took his place as he led Sally through the flesh-jammed dance floor to a quieter room. Unsurprisingly, no one tried to touch her up.

'Would you mind waiting here?' asked Super Steve in a reassuringly Balham-shaded voice. 'I'll fetch Joel.'

'Thank you,' she said. 'By the way, a friend of mine will be coming in soon. He's a nice boy, just down from the North. He likes muscle guys.'

'There's a lot of that about,' he said, striking an Adonis pose that threatened to burst his black leather studded armlet. 'I'll see he has a good time.'

'I'm sure you will.'

Left alone, Sally sat in a low chair covered in crinkly plastic. She rested Mother Hen on a glasstop table. The cloth slipped, and an elegant head poked out. She smiled at the statuette, cheered by its unruffled confidence.

...as a little girl, Sally had liked Superman comics, and Chitty Chitty Bang Bang, and Biggles, and pterodactyls, and

Dumbo, and astronauts, and 'Snoopy and the Red Baron', and zeppelins, and…

Her upper arms ached a little. She should have found a carrier bag for Mother Hen rather than clutching it like a baby. She stretched, and flapped her arms from the shoulders.

Silliphant walked into the room and she froze in a stupid position. It couldn't be anybody else. His longish black hair was thinning, and his kabuki makeup was inexpertly applied, but he still looked like the king and queen of rock 'n' roll, from his plastic horns down to his symbol-edged black robe.

He strutted in like a born performer, almost reaching for an invisible microphone. He turned to throw his combined sneer and pout at her, and caught sight of Mother Hen. He flew backwards and flattened against a wall as if tugged by a fishing line.

'Get that fucking bird out of here,' he shrieked, his two-inch nails raking the furry wall, 'or I'll have you fucking disembowelled here and now!'

She thought he was going to attack her, but Silliphant burned out like a flashbulb. His fury expired in an instant and he fell sobbing on the floor. He chewed the carpet and kicked the wall. His back arched. He could have been undergoing shock therapy.

In the cavern, the band segued into a thrash version of an old Beach boys number. 'She'll have fun, fun, fun, fun, fun, fun, fun, til her Daddy takes her T-bird away!'

Sally stood up, a little embarrassed. She pointed to Mother Hen. 'I think this is yours,' she said.

Silliphant twisted on the floor and looked up at her. He had a snot moustache and tear-track scars in his white pancake. He was almost cried out.

'No,' he whimpered. 'I won't touch it. Karabatsos has no power over me. She can't have me. I repudiate the Thirteen.'

Silliphant reached into a rubber plant and grabbed it by the stem, close to the pot. Waxy leaves writhed as he swung the heavy ceramic pot above his head. He hit the table, cracked the glass.

The pot broke, clods of earth scattered.

Unsatisfied with the partial destruction, Silliphant threw himself onto the table, landing with all his weight. Chrome-plated tubes buckled, and the sheet glass exploded. Sally snatched Mother Hen out of the wreckage.

Silliphant grovelled in the earth and pottery and plant and glass until he found a jagged shard large enough to open his throat. He stopped screaming, and sawed roughly through his windpipe and a major artery.

His neck in ruins, he stood up. A Niagara of splatter fountained from beneath his jawline. He cried out almost triumphantly. Sally sidestepped and put a chair between herself and the dying man. She still got warm stains on her tights.

Silliphant fell into his mess and shut up. The pseudo-mouth in his neck kept gurgitating long after the rest of him had stopped kicking.

At last, glitter rock was dead.

Mother Hen crouched on a crumbling windowsill, talons sunk into the concrete, wings spread against red brick. She had been cheated of the prey ordained for her by the First Among Thirteen. The wound in her breast ached.

She remembered other red nights, and the statuette, and the Thirteen. Little else made sense. Her brain pan wasn't large enough for acute self-consciousness, but the fuzziness was clearing up. Her mind was still mostly mists, but a few pains and joys stood out as hard-edged tangibles.

Her talons twitched. She needed the red stuff. The killing frenzy rose in her. She pushed herself forward and caught the prevailing wind. Flapping occasionally against the complex cross-currents, she glided silently downwards.

She could feel the pull of the shaft from the statuette.

* * *

The alley was badly lit and unpopulated. Sally easily found the car. Like everyone remotely connected with crime, Derewicz evidently considered himself immune to it. The car was unlocked, and the keys were in the starter. Sally squeezed into the back, and crouched on the floor.

Derewicz came back, bruised and pissed off. He had lost his balaclava. He had a gun, which made things serious.

He saw her a moment after he had tossed his weapon into the front passenger seat. He grabbed for it, but she tipped the seat savagely forward. The gun fell into the clutter of old cigarette packets and porno magazines under the dashboard.

She grabbed his wrist and tugged hard. He was pulled off balance, and banged his head heavily on the metal jamb. He swore unimaginatively at her. She threw herself back and kicked the driving seat with both feet. He was scrunched against the steering wheel.

Derewicz pulled out, and angrily hammered the roof. Sally scrabbled for the gun, but couldn't reach. She heard the click of a switchblade.

A gun and a knife. Evidently Karabatsos favoured belt and braces methods.

A murderous black duvet swooped out of the sky and fell on Derewicz. Sally saw him lifted out of her field of view. There was a sound like someone beating the dust out of a fleshy carpet; then the more identifiable noise of a man being turned inside-out.

Through the Panavision oblong of the widescreen, Sally could see that it was raining entrails and scraps of expensive tailoring. She clambered awkwardly into the front seat, and shut the door. She strapped on the seatbelt, picked up the gun, and felt stupidly safe.

When dropped from even a moderate height on asphalt, the human body resembles nothing so much as a dustbin liner filled with watermelons. Derewicz thumped into the ground. In order to get out of the parking space, Sally would have to drive over him. She knew it would hardly make a difference.

She drove at random, scarcely aware of the red-eyed stone thing in the back seat. She found a packet of camels in the glove compartment and gave up giving up smoking. She felt tight inside, as she always did after witnessing unspeakable horror.

She turned on the radio and found a hippie show. The Holy Modal Rounders sang, 'It don't take much to get you up there, but when you come down, you land on your fee-ee-ee-ee-eet!'

The licence was in Karabatsos's name. His Swiss Cottage address was on the back of a crumpled envelope she found in the ashtray. So much for backbreaking detective work. She looked the street up in the car's tatty *A to Z*, and whiled away the short drive by thinking up the right hardboiled questions to ask.

It was an unobtrusively expensive house, a lot like all the others in sight but with obscene stained glass panels on either side of the front door.

The key was on Derewicz's ring, so she let herself in without making a fuss about it. The hallway was tastefully furnished with antiques in nice little niches. None of the pieces were as striking as Mother Hen.

Only one doorway off the hall showed a light. She opened it. The room was a study, and Karabatsos was in it.

He was stark naked, and lying in a circle of chalked symbols on the uncarpeted floor. His ribs looked like something from a Chinese takeaway, and his scrawny shanks were tattooed with a delicate tracery of ideographs.

As before, his stomach was the most notable thing about his person. It was purple with unhealthy yellow mottles, and rippled as it shifted on the countless cilia which affixed it to his abdomen. Vestigial hands clutched well-worn ridges under Karabatsos's armpits. Beautiful, long-lashed eyes stared out of the mass, just below his sternum.

'Miss Rhodes,' he said, not turning his head to her, 'you've not met my wife.'

He sat up carefully, cradling the flesh of his flesh, and pulled on a Sorcerer's Apprentice dressing gown. His schlong hadn't been anything to write home about.

'Joanna is quite ardent, I'm afraid. I pledged to give her my body, but I never thought it would come to this. Soon, I fear, I shan't have enough body left.'

'Mother Hen…' She held out the statue.

'Pretty, isn't she?' He didn't seem all that interested. 'I must say I'm surprised to see you. In her last killing frenzy, back in '68. she didn't stop until Henry Fleetwood put the retarding spell on her. He was the First Among Thirteen then, not that there were thirteen of us left. After the mess was cleared up there were only five: myself, Henry, my wife, Mr Derewicz and the odious Silliphant. My wife having long since disqualified herself from consideration as a human being, I suppose I am the only one. That rather devalues my position as the First, but never mind…'

'You're forgetting me, aren't you?'

Karabatsos decanted something red, and sipped it.

'No, my dear, of course not. You aren't easy to forget, believe me. It's just that you don't count. You've held on to the statuette long enough to catch whatever it is that upsets Mythwrhn so much. We never did quite work it out, but Fleetwood got the incantations down pat. You might have the temporary use of your limbs, Miss Rhodes, but you are as dead as Julius Caesar, Jacob Marley and silent pictures.'

'…and you?'

'Ah, I was careful. I am thrice protected. There was not a little pain involved, but the Mythwrhn cannot so much as touch me. It's not really magic, just transcendental arithmetic. It's quite fascinating once you get through the brand of patronising mumbo-jumbo the late Joel Silliphant was so keen on. Of course, you don't have time to make a thorough study of the subject…'

He poured a little liqueur into a slurping orifice between his wife's eyes.

'There there, Joanna. We'll be finished soon. Miss Rhodes, if you wouldn't mind leaving. My wife has had a tiring day.'

'Why me, conjure man?' She asked. 'How did I come into your game?'

'You have such a nice advertisement in the Thomson Local Directory. Now, I would appreciate not having to watch the Mythwrhn play with you...'

A rush of air blew the door behind Sally open. Mother Hen crowded into the hall.

'Oh well, I suppose my stomach can stand it. Try not to scream too much. The neighbours are liable to complain.'

Mother Hen brushed walls with her wings, uncomfortable without a sky above her. She brushed a heavy bronze mask to the floor, and closed her talons about the heavy metal, crushing it like a coke can. Her wound bled a little.

She drew her wings in and crouched as she came into the study. Once in the spacious room, she stretched. Sally saw the shifting, multi-coloured highlights in her superficially black feathers. Her flat stomach gleamed with honeyed perspiration. She was terribly beautiful.

'She doesn't want to kill you,' said Karabatsos. 'She wants to kill me. But, just now, she can't. We all have to obey laws. Obviously, my tattoos were worth the momentary discomfort. She has a very presentable bum, don't you think?'

Sally backed away. Mother Hen towered over Karabatsos, clacking her beak with rage. She turned her head on a swan neck and looked at Sally with kindly eyes.

Sally realised that she had left Derewicz's gun in the car, but assumed that it wouldn't have made much difference.

Karabatsos tried to look nonchalant, but his hands were quivering in voluminous sleeves. Mrs Karabatsos was chirruping something.

Mother Hen draped her wings around Karabatsos and hugged him. She dipped her head to his stomach, and gripped the squealing jelly with her razor-edged beak. Blue mucus sloshed loudly on herringbone tiles.

Karabatsos screamed like a man being partially castrated with a pair of boltcutters. He realised too late how close he was to his wife, and that he should have protected her too.

Mother Hen shook her head, and Karabatsos flew into a wall-sized bookcase. Delicately, she dropped the wriggling wife. The thing that had loved Nigel Karabatsos rolled like an upended louse. Its tubes waved feebly as it shrivelled and died.

Karabatsos leaked into a pile of broken-backed books. From nipples to pubes, he was an open wound. The neatly punctured bowels flopped loosely between his legs. He gulped deep breaths, but his lungs were as functional as a pair of ruptured balloons.

He had nothing courteous or acidic or witty or waspish to say as his contents spilled.

Sally looked at the feathered murderess, and could find no disgust for such a magnificent creature. The assassin tucked her head under her wing, and scratched feebly at her sundered breast. Sally knew what she had to do.

She took the statuette, and got a firm grip on the golden arrow. The shaft came free as smoothly as the sword-in-the-stone for the once and future king. Sally easily snapped the impertinent needle in two.

Unbloodied, Mother Hen stretched her wings and shattered the French windows. A light rain blew in from the walled garden. Her wound irised shut, leaving a negligible scar. She was no longer bound. She sang gently.

Sally was wrapped up in Mother Hen's feathery embrace. She closed her eyes and felt the great heart beating close by her ear. Her body thrilled as she was swept off her feet.

'Up, up, and away,' she whispered.

THE MAN WHO
COLLECTED BARKER

Sally Rhodes let Wringhim pick her up in the Dealer's Room, and willingly accompanied him back to the house in Lodovico Street. He matched perfectly the description the Australian's people had given her, down to the sharkskin suit, watery eyes and William Powell moustache. She spotted him straight off, flicking through a stack of *Spicy Mystery Stories* magazines at one of the stalls. She had done enough research in the past week to pass herself off as one of these bizarros, and engaged him in conversation. He was only too keen to brag. She had the impression he hadn't ever talked with a real, live girl before. That gave her an advantage. He was too pleased with her interest in him to question it. She dropped a few names, and he stooped for them.

'Dennis Etchison? Now, there's a thing. I have every story he ever wrote, in the magazines they originally appeared in. Men's magazines, mostly, if you get my drift...'

Sally smiled. 'That must give you an unbeatable pick-up line.' He didn't get it. 'You know, "come up and see my Etchisons"?'

He still didn't get it. She decided to abandon irony as a tool in this case.

Wringhim started to tell her about the three issues of *Vault of the Strangler* missing from his collection. He seemed to take their absence personally. His eyes glowed like neons, and his voice took on the exact lascivious tone of the husband in *Gaslight* talking about the hidden rubies. He recited the names of obscure pulp writers in an unholy litany, 'Seabury Quinn, Arthur Leo Zagat, Justin Case, Otis Adelbert Kline, Robert Blake...' His long fingers played over the yellowed edges of the stack of pulp magazines in front of him, curving into claws as he flicked an issue open to scan a contents list. He all but slobbered over a faded cover picture of a voluptuous girl, clad in two cobwebs, being consumed whole by a hungry plant. Unmarried, the file had said, no personal ties. It was easy to see how he had sublimated his procreative urges.

Later, in Lodovico Street, Wringhim produced a huge keyring and dealt with the triple locks on the door of the Collection Suite. She expected a dusty morgue with piles of ancient, rotting books, and skeletons of long-missing persons scattered on stone floors. She got a striplit, modern library, with free-standing shelves of bright-spined paperbacks arranged alphabetically by author, while the more dour hardbacks were behind glass against the walls. Many of the spines had embossed skulls, ghosts, severed hands, full moons behind clouds, bats. Titles were written in dripping blood, or green slime, or monkish gothic script.

'I have every book Arkham House ever put out, all personally signed to me by the authors.'

She thought that wasn't possible, but merely nodded, trying to look interested.

'And here, Miss Rhodes, I have a complete set of Ramsey Campbell's works.'

'The books look a bit... well, scruffy,' she said.

'Yes. I've coated them with dirt from the gutters of the streets in Liverpool where Campbell was living when he wrote the books. It's personalised touches like that that make any given item unique. You notice the red smudges on the binding of that American *Incarnate*?'

Indeed, she had. 'Yes, is that...?'

'Strawberry jam. Smeared by Tamsin Campbell, the author's own daughter. That would nearly triple the worth of the volume, of course. As I was saying, the personalised touches always add to the value.'

'Hmmn, interesting,' she murmured. The profile the Australian had put together didn't quite convey how many cowboys short of a posse Wringhim was. He had no record, but that didn't make him clean. He had independent means, which covered a multiplicity of indulgences. She was beginning to get a feeling about this lead. Not a nice feeling, but a useful one. Perhaps she would be able to report back to the Australian tomorrow after all.

'What's through here?' she asked, indicating another multiple-locked door.

'Ah, that's the centrepiece of my collection. That's where I keep my Barkers.'

'Clive Barkers?'

'Of course. He's the most collectible of the moderns, you know. There are so many special editions, so many variants...'

'And your collection is complete?'

He smiled, and she noticed his ratty little foreteeth poking out from under his double-slash of a moustache. 'But of course, Miss Rhodes. You must come and see.'

More keys ground, and the door was unsealed. The windowless room beyond lit up automatically, like a fridge. The light was ghostly, slightly glimmering.

'Special conditions operate in here. The lighting is calculated not to fade the dustjackets. All my Barkers are mint, Miss Rhodes, mint.'

It was cold. Doubtless, another preservative measure. Three walls were a neutral battleship grey, the fourth consisted of a ceiling-high set of bookshelves. Neon strips hummed on the ceiling. Opposite, the shelves was a divan. She got the impression that he spent a lot of time on the divan, just looking at his collection.

'Come in, come in.' She followed him into the Barker room.

He stood by the shelves, and indicated a set of books apart from the rest, on a shelf by themselves.

'Here I have all the editions of the *Books of Blood*. The first three volumes, of course. The others are down there. To a true collector, volumes four to six are immeasurably less interesting. I have them, but they aren't quite the thing… aren't quite special, if you get my drift. The first three books are where the action is. And I have all the action in the field, all the action.'

He was evidently proud of the accomplishment.

'Surely, there can't be that many,' she prompted.

'Ahh, but there are, Miss Rhodes, there certainly are. These are the original 1984 Sphere paperbacks with the twisted photographs on the cover. The first United Kingdom edition. Signed, of course, in red ink, inscribed personally to me, and dated before the official publication. As it happens, these are the first three copies to roll off the press…'

Gently, he pulled one off the shelf, and opened it to display the inscription. 'To Dave, thanks for your enthusiasm, Clive Barker,' it said. There was a picture of a zombie with a pencil moustache and no eyes under it.

'What's that smudge?'

He looked again. 'Ahh, an interesting story. When he was signing, Clive used my pen. I have an antique fountain pen, and the nib slipped a little. He cut his finger and bled onto the page. You've no idea how much more collectible that makes this book. No idea at all.'

Sally could have sworn she heard subliminal organ music under the eternal whirring of the extractor fan. This room didn't feel like a tomb, it felt like a morgue. And Wringhim was displaying his books as one necrophile coroner might show off his latest conquest to another, pulling out the gurney and throwing back the stained green sheet with a magician's flourish.

'And here are the reprint paperback editions, with Clive's own covers. And the Sphere library hardbacks, and the Weidenfeld and Nicolson general issue hardback. This is a set of the 1985 Weidenfeld and Nicolson limited edition, boxed and signed naturally. And the American Berkley editions, paperback and hardback, with variant covers. This is the Berkley uncorrected proof of Volume II, with the plain spine, put out in April 1986. This is the 1988 Sphere trade paperback omnibus volume, and the 1988 Ace/Putnam American equivalent. These are the two variant cover Scream/Press editions, 1985 and 1986. And, of course, there's Libros Sangrientos from Spain, Das Erste, Das Zweite and Das Dritte Buch des Blutes from Germany, Tunnel van de Dood and Prins van de Duisternis from Holland, Livre de Sang from France, and the ideographed Japanese editions. The one in the can is a special German edition with a warning sign.'

'And those books to one side?'

'Ah-hah, my special prizes,' his eyes shone again, with all the fervour of a scientologist describing the earthly manifestation of L. Ron Hubbard. 'These are all the special signed, numbered, limited 1985 Scream/Press edition, illustrated by J.K. Potter, bound by Kristina Anderson. Soon after, something horrible happened to the bookbinder and she hasn't been heard from since. The edition is in full leather red Niger Oasis Goatskin and embossed with gold, signed and dated, with zombie doodle and personalised dead baby joke inscription. The underspine is veined manuscript calf vellum from Germany, dyed red. The signatures are sewn in red linen thread. The endpapers are hand-painted with a Roman horse and English carnival motif, the top edge is stained yellow and painted with a Grand Guignol clown's head, the endbands are handsewn in red, yellow and black silk on linen cores, there are tissue overlays on all illustrations, and the title and copyright pages are splatted in human blood and red acrylic paint.'

'Very nice.'

'But there's more. Look, here…'

He pulled out yet another copy of the first *Book of Blood*, also leather bound, also embossed, presumably signed, dated, doodled and dead babied.

'Something must have gone wrong there,' she said. 'It looks a little rough.'

'Ah yes,' he said, his eyes shining again, spittle clinging to the ends of his moustache. 'This is a special special edition. It's bound in human skin.'

'Human skin? Isn't that illegal?'

'Not in Tijuana. The publishers found a doctor who could recommend locals who, although young enough to have unblemished skin, were dying of incurable diseases. By offering to pay a sum to the survivors of these poverty-stricken unfortunates, they were able to convince the patients to have the title, author's name and publication information tattooed on their chests and backs while they were still alive. Then, after the inevitable took its course, the grateful families handed over the corpses for a surgical flaying, and a skilled bookbinder was brought in to prepare a special special edition of five sets of the *Books of Blood*.'

This was beginning to sound both unhealthy and suggestive. He opened up the book at random, and she saw red printing on thick pages.

'They found several reams of unmarked papyrus from the Museum of Antiquities in Cairo. They were reckoned to come from the tomb of a High Priest of Seth who was expected to write his memoirs in the afterlife. There's supposed to be a curse on anyone who defiles its whiteness, but Clive Barker is a notorious iconoclast and the reams were used in the preparation of these volumes. The tooling is done in gold melted down from an Aztec sacrificial idol that miraculously survived the conquistadores. The top edge is stained with the hymenal blood of an Arab princess, kept fresh in a phial after her seduction by Sir Richard Burton, and traced with blasphemies in Sanskrit, Hebrew, Coptic script and Pig Latin. It's signed, inscribed, and doodled on, of course...'

'For the text, did they use...?'

'Human blood? No, it clots too quickly. This, sadly, is just red ink. Although, funnily enough, by some strange coincidence, when he was signing his zombie drawing…'

He turned to the page with the picture, and Sally saw the familiar stain.

'Would you care…?'

He handed the book to her. Gingerly, feeling it in the soft meat of her fingertips, she took it. The unique binding gave slightly as she squeezed. It was deeply tanned, and she saw a scattering of moles. The title and author's name stood out. She expected it to smell, somehow, but it was perfectly cured.

'The bookbinder unfortunately had his eyes put out shortly before the volumes were complete, and was therefore unable to appreciate the wonder he had created. One of life's tragedies, Miss Rhodes.'

'You have all five sets?'

'No,' he replied, 'only three. The other two are in the hands of…' he spat unconsciously, 'another collector. Thus far, he has resisted all my offers. But I am certain that I shall eventually prevail on him to part with them.'

'But I see five sets in that section.'

'Ahh, yes. These two are different. An even more special special special edition.'

She saw now that these two sets, three uniform volumes each, were lighter in colour.

'What could be more special than human skin?'

'Blood, Miss Rhodes, blood…'

She remembered her research. '"Everybody is a book of blood; wherever we're opened, we're red."'

'I beg your pardon?' Wringhim looked astonished.

'The epigraph. The epigraph of the *Books of Blood*. Remember?'

He looked faintly irritated. 'Oh, yes, of course, I was forgetting.'

'I'd have thought you would have known the books backwards by heart by now.'

'No,' he said, 'sadly not. I have no reading copies of the *Books of Blood*. Each of these is unique, a collectible. I couldn't risk reading them, turning the pages, breaking the spines. Ugh! I took the books out of the library once, and read most of the stories. Very good, I thought.'

His fingers strayed along the shelves to the lighter volumes.

'Blood,' he whispered. 'Blood.'

Sally was shivering in the cold now. Even the dead skin of the book in her hand had gooseflesh. Being Mexican, the former owner probably wasn't used to the chill. That organ she couldn't hear was playing Tequila now.

'This set, Miss Rhodes, is a unique prize, unique by virtue of blood.'

'Go on,' she said, knowing she couldn't stop him, 'tell me about it.'

'A cousin of Clive's, a distant connection, of course, but related by blood. I happened upon this fellow in a Cardiff pub one night. Evidently, he was something of a black sheep of the family. Always cadging drinks by the virtue of his name, and trying to impress barmaids with his relationship to a distinguished author. Clyde Barker, he was called. In his cups, he made the mistake of falling from a dock. He drowned.'

'Drowned?'

'From my point of view, most fortunate. If he had walked under a bus, he would have been no use at all, don't you see?'

'The skin...'

'Would have been irreparably damaged, yes. Clyde Barker died without means, and so I took the liberty of arranging for his funeral. I had to settle outstanding bills with several bookmakers and drinking establishments. I saw to it that he went to his grave in as good a suit of clothes he could hope for. Of course, I wanted something in exchange. But the skin is perishable. It goes first. A good suit will outlast the skin in the ground, any week of the year. So, this edition is bound in the skin of a blood relative of the author's, printed on the palimpsest parchment of a twelfth century black magician's grimoire, signed in red ink, with a watercolour self-portrait of the author as a rotting zombie on the inside front cover, personally inscribed to me, an original still-unpublished sixty-line poem called 'Rotting Love' scribbled on the title page, endbands handsewn in hemp thread pulled from the noose used in the execution of Dr Crippen, a spine of weapons-grade plutonium sealed in lead, a book-lock that was once part of the famous Iron Maiden of Nuremberg and finally bled on in a Rorschach pattern by Clive Barker himself. The bookbinder accidentally had his hands severed in an accident with a printer's guillotine, and will sadly never work again.'

Sally had to take charge of the situation now. Wringhim was raving, too far gone for the police to deal with. She produced her licence. 'I'm a private investigator,' she said. 'The Australian hired me. He's expecting four more books and three movies...'

He turned at last to the final set of the *Books of Blood*, edged in gold, bound in what she knew to be human skin.

'...a lot of people want to know where Clive Barker is, Mr Wringhim...'

He pulled out the first volume, and presented the cover to her. The nose was flattened, the lips and eyelids sewn shut with thick black thread, but the face was still recognisable.

'And this, is the special special special edition of the *Books of Blood*.'

She pointed her little ladylike gun at him. He ignored it and opened the book to the redly blotched title page.

'The hard part, Miss Rhodes,' he said, 'came after the books were bound. The hard part was getting the author to sign them.'

GARGANTUABOTS VERSUS THE NICE MICE

'A thousand a day,' she told them. 'And my train fare down from Victoria. Where else are you going to find a private detective with qualifications in child psychiatry?'

They didn't really have a choice. She leaned back in the hotel's idea of an easy chair, and took a few tactical sips of Perrier water. They looked at each other. General Jones wanted to tough her price down, but R.J. Woolavington was more than ready to cave in.

'Miss Rhodes, do you mind if we confer?' snapped the General, waving a wet-end cigar. He still sounded like a US Marine Drill Instructor, although his gut would strain a dress uniform more than it was straining his lightweight tropical suit. He had never been more than a non-com in the service, but now he was in charge of the largest, most diversified private army in the world.

'Not at all. Take your time. This meeting will be included in my bill. And there's a wasting-my-time fee to cover even if you don't want to hire me.'

The General glared at her, and dragged Woolavington into the suite's bathroom for a final browbeating. Sally looked at the glossy brochures on the coffee table. Gung-Ho Jones had an undersea outfit now, complete with spring-loaded speargun and an octopus whose arms could constrict automatically. On the cover of his pamphlet, Gung-Ho ($14.99) was grappling with the octopus ($19.99) in a sunken Spanish galleon ($74.99), grinning his one-sided grin (free, but copyrighted) and posing dramatically. Actually, thanks to the awkwardness of his hips and shoulder-joints, Gung-Ho could barely stand up straight, let alone assume a dramatic pose.

Sally was more intrigued by the Woolavington Train Set she had seen downstairs. It was an idealised lay-out modelled on the Home Counties in the thirties, complete with genuine miniature steam engines, an entire village, a tunnel through a hill and over three miles of tracks. As a child, she would rather have had one of Woolavington's trains, but her parents had given her a Sandie Doll (one of the General's products) instead.

The General and Woolavington were back, an agreement reached. Neither of them were happy: the General because he was going to have to accede to Sally's terms, and Woolavington because the General was going to screw him into putting up more than half her fee.

'One K is okay,' growled the General, 'but we'll want results quickly. Before the convention is over.'

'That gives me a week? Easy.'

'Don't be so sure, we've had our best men on it for a year. Nada.'

'I'm better than most. Now, why don't you and Mr Woolavington tell me your troubles.'

'Well,' grunted the General, 'it's...'

'Mr Woolavington, you start.'

The spinsterish English tycoon hadn't been able to get out a complete sentence all afternoon. Sally thought she owed him a chance to say his piece.

'Um, as you must know, General Jones and I are veterans of the trade. I inherited my business from my father, who had it from his father. We've been making model trains – not toy trains – for over one hundred years. Because we believe in craftsmanship, our prices are, um, high. In recent years, our market has mainly been among adult collectors. Still, we've been badly hit...'

'Not as badly as some, Woolavington.'

'Let him speak, General.'

'The businesss changes, fluctuates, evolves. Woolavington and Company has stayed in business by staying the same. I've long been reconciled to the fact that our trains will never again be a majority force in the market, but I had thought we would be able to retain our grip on the customers we do have, but...'

'But the Japs and the freaks are creaming us is what!' shouted the General, fat face reddening, cigar ash falling unheeded on his lapels. 'I ain't like him, Miss Rhodes. I came into toys – toys, that's what I call 'em, and I'm proud of 'em – when I was invalided out of the Corps. I got some extra bits and pieces in my leg on Iwo Jima. I put out the first Gung-Ho Jones in '47. He was a Clean Marine then, like me. But I didn't stick with that like Woolavington with his choo-choos. Gung-Ho Jones has kept up with the times. He's been through all the services, plus he's been a super-secret agent, an astronaut, a SWAT cop, counter-terrorist, you name it. A couple of years back, Gung-Ho was a barbarian swordsman on an alternate world. Now he's a Blastmaster with the Universe Corps. Don't ask me what that means. As far as I can tell, it's a lot like being a Marine. Our strategy has been to stay in fashion, and, of course, to sell more and more units as the range of Gung-Ho Jones accessories, sidekicks and adversaries expands. It worked for thirty years, but these last couple of quarters, it's been shot to shit...'

The General picked up a handful of leaflets and shook them. He obviously took his business personally. Sally wondered what an adult psychiatrist would have made of his obvious identification with his nine-inch tall product. Had he left his guts on Iwo Jima, and built up his toy empire to make himself into a hero by proxy, the victor of a million bedroom-floor battles?

'Last year, I did three million in deals on the first day of this show, Miss Rhodes. Yesterday, I barely managed to get five K and change from a few individual orders. The main chains don't want to know. I believe in market forces, supply and demand, competition, all that stuff. But this isn't capitalism, it's genocide.'

Sally wondered if the General realised that when he lost control his hands contorted like Gung-Ho Jones' – one with an extended finger and a grip to (shakily) hold a gun, the other a tight fist with fingers fused like a deformity. The leaflets crumpled tight in the fist.

'We're not the only people affected,' said Woolavington. 'There are, um, over three hundred stands and displays in the halls downstairs. At this show, only two of them have been busy. And they've been very busy. They're burying us.'

'The Japs and the Freaks.'

'So you said, General. Could you be more specific?'

'The Gargantuabots and the Nice Mice. Take a look.' The General took a boxed robot and a cuddly toy from the suite's dressing table, and handed them to her. 'They have TV shows, too.'

The cuddly toy was a fat mouse, the size of a teddy bear. It had heart-shaped eyes, a perky little smile and adorable whiskers. Still in its cellophane, it looked as if it was in cryogenesis until someone found a cure for terminal cuteness. Sally found the robot more appealing, marginally. She'd been like that as a child, too. She wondered how much her Thunderbirds models would be worth if she hadn't set fire to them with lighter fluid when she was eleven.

'Oh, these are the robots that turn into different things, right? They look like dinosaurs, but twist into tanks or aeroplanes. I've seen kids with them. They must be popular.'

'Unnaturally popular, Miss Rhodes. And the Nice Mice are equally successful. This year, the toy business is a duopoly.'

'Are you sure you're not overreacting to bad sales? I can see the appeal of both lines. I did my thesis on Playthings and Society. The Gargantuabots combine many aspects which would appeal to the stereotypical small boy: prehistoric monsters, giant robots, motor-vehicles, martial imagery. The transformation aspect is undeniably ingenious, and probably helps kids develop hand-eye coordination. Most popular toys have some subliminal educational value, I suppose. Even Gung-Ho Jones. And the Nice Mice are innocuous, almost calculatedly so. They aren't to my taste, certainly, but pre-school children need fantasies of reassurance, not of mass destruction. What with the backlash against war toys, something like the Nice Mice was bound to come along eventually. I expect you only wish you'd thought of it first.'

'We know all that, Miss Rhodes. Our toys are designed by shrinks too. Gung-Ho Jones and Sandie cover the whole range of socio-economic and psycho-behavioural classes. We offer something for every kid there is. Every kid whose parents have $14.99, that is. Until AIDS, we were even going to give Sandie a homo best friend who could wear all her dresses. The demographics were right for it. We were doing great, then these crazies came on like gangbusters and kicked our asses. We had the same thing with computer games, but that fad boomed and bust over three seasons, and even at its height it never came close to hurting us as bad as we're hurting now.'

He balled the useless leaflets, and threw them in the general direction of a waste-paper basket. He missed. Woolavington fidgeted, cleaning his nails with an eyetooth. Sally wasn't convinced these men were sane, but she could tell they were genuinely worried.

'Okay, I'll look into it,' she said. 'What can you tell me about the parent companies? And who they have here?'

'Gargantuabots come out of Japan. The Sphere Corporation. Their top man is two floors down, in the Royal Suite. His name is Baron Toru Ghidrah. And the Nice Mice are headquartered in California, somewhere in Silicon Valley. They're Buddhists or hippies or some shit. The parent company is registered as Cloud Incorporated. They don't have executives or presidents, but the delegate who seems to be sort of in charge is called something stupid. Rainbow? Sunshine? Moonbeam? What is it, Woolavington?'

'Cornfield. Cornfield Zwingli. I think he used to be Swiss.'

Sally took it all in. 'Ghidrah and Zwingli. I'll look them up. Of course, if I unearth any unethical or illegal business practices you'll want full details before you decide whether to blow the whistle on them or copy them, right?'

'Very funny, Miss Rhodes. Did you have a Sandie when you were a little girl?'

Sally said yes. The General leaned over the table and stubbed his cigar out on the perky smile of the mouse toy. Its cellophane crackled and hissed. 'Then, get these bastards for her.'

Sally started on the floor, mingling with the buyers. The Exhibition Hall was the size of a dirigible hangar. It was easy to see who was doing business. At opposite ends crowds were gathered beneath two towering figures. The Gargantuabot was frozen mid-way between being a cyborg Tyrannosaurus Rex and a snarling bulldozer-cum-car crusher. Its eyes lit up like furnaces, its metallic limbs moved jerkily, its claw-catchers tore at the air and recorded growls filled the hall. Twin video projection screens stood either side of the robot. A trailer for the *Gargantuabots: The Motion Picture* was running on both screens, one weirdly about three seconds ahead of the other. The Nice Mouse (was that the singular form of Nice Mice?) was quieter, floating serene and chubby above a worshipping multitude, its heart-shaped eyes closed in blissful sleep, its perky smile beaming out, its adorable whiskers twitching in time to a happy tune. Large, cloud-shaped balloons lazily drifted upwards past the giant and gathered like a clump of unhealthy fruit under the ceiling.

There were other stands, but they were drab by comparison. Many were unmanned, their owners having drifted off to be where the action was. One or two were being gloomily dismantled by workmen under the direction of sad-eyed, shiny-suited executives who knew when to quit. At the Woolavington table, a couple of reps were playing Chinese checkers. A miniature fork-lift truck was removing a large, still-sealed block of imitation Trivial Pursuit games.

'It's so nice,' gushed a middle-aged woman, whose lapel was infected with a rash of membership badges, to no one in particular. Sally decided to cultivate her as a source of information and nodded vigorously. From the badges, Sally gathered the woman's name was Tilly Barnes, and that she was from the Happie Chappie toy shop in Slough. 'They're extending the Nice Mice line to include the Nice Mice Uncles! And they're taking orders round-the-clock!'

Sally wondered if Tilly Barnes was on something. She'd have examined the buyer's eyeballs, but her eyes were screwed almost shut in ecstasy. Her smile was uncannily familiar. Tilly Barnes' nose twitched as if possessed of adorable whiskers. What a strange day: first Gung-Ho Jones in the flabby flesh, now an ageing Nice Mouse in dungarees.

'I've had a simply super idea for a window display for the Uncles! I'm going to just fill the whole expanse of frontage with pink and pale blue fur, and have a big poster up with a list of Nice Things Children Can Do For Each Other. And every time I hear that a child has done one of those Nice Things I'll have his or her name put up on another poster, with lots of Nice Mice Uncles standing around and cheering and applauding. Won't that be nice?'

Once, Sally had been stopped in the street and told how wonderful the Church of Scientology was. And, on another occasion, at a party, a young tycoon in a blue jump suit had tried to get off with her while explaining at unmerciful length just how EST had changed his life. She had even heard out a lady client who claimed opting for privatised medicine was the best decision she'd ever made. This was worse.

'Are you ordering anything from Woolavington this year?' Sally asked.

The buyer's face went blank, as if someone had just ejected the software out of a slit in her back. Her eyes stared blind as shoebuttons – clear but empty – and then scrunched up again. She resumed her flow.

'And I'm organising a Niceness drive with all the other toy shops in my area. It'll coincide with the new film, *The Nice Mice in the Land of the Kuddlekats*, and the video release of *The Nice Mice Cheer Up the Prime Minister of Nastiness*. We're making children who do Nice Things for OAPs into Honorary Nice Mice Little Ones. And giving out Nice Mice ears to the grannies and grandads. Won't that be nice?'

Sally had a sudden urge to indulge in fantasies of massive violence. She excused herself, and headed for the Gargantuabots Stand. Four Japanese girls in Noh make-up and traditional dress were solemnly demonstrating the various transformations of the latest generation of Killatrons, who were apparently the Militant Tendency of the Gargantuabots. Admiring buyers stood in awed silence as the girls' origami gestures reshaped stegosauri and dimetreodons into cybernetic samurai and robot crusaders. Nobody spoke, nobody moved from their place.

'Ladies and gentlemen,' began a hawk-faced Japanese, 'this season, the Gargantuabots will be moving forward again. We are introducing a line of quadruple-change figures, the Quadroids.' There was a collective intake of breath. 'All of you who increase your orders will be rewarded. All of you who do not will… let us say, be inconvenienced.'

The man, whom Sally had pegged as Baron Ghidrah himself, paused and looked around the crowd, making eye-contact with a dozen individuals. A tall young man standing near Sally looked down, and covered his face with his hands. Sally realised he was silently crying, his shoulders heaving with suppressed sobs. As he slid away, the others avoided his touch like a leper's.

'More! I'll take more!' shouted a very fat, very sweaty man. 'As many as you can spare! I'll discontinue all other brands. Just, let me carry the Quadroids, that's all I ask. Let me carry the Quadroids!'

Japanese girls in conservative business suits calmed the fat man down, cooing reassurances Sally couldn't hear into his ears. He stopped sweating. Baron Ghidrah momentarily did something with his face that might have counted as a smile, then resumed his speech.

'But enough of such things. We are all aware of the situation. And of the importance of increasing sales and orders. I am pleased to report that the Quadroids are battle-ready as of this moment, and will be deployed in all outlets before the week is out. There can be no compromise. That is all.'

Baron Ghidrah bowed without a trace of humility and left the stand. The Japanese girls led polite applause, which was noisily and enthusiastically joined by the rest of the throng. There was a mighty creaking from above, as the Tyrannosaurus/bulldozer-crusher slowly stretched itself into a pterodactyl-winged space shuttle and then contracted into the figure of an armoured giant out of a gothic nightmare. As the monster changed, fire belched from its joints and metal strained noisily against metal. Sally wondered if the transformations were supposed to be painful.

There wasn't much more she could pick up in the public section of the convention, but she dutifully double-checked her findings to date by dropping into the bar and striking up conversations with the buyers. She found that opening gambits like 'well, are you going for the Gung-Ho Jones Undersea Adventurer line?' or 'what do you think of Sandie's new pop star image?' were liable to yield very, very short exchanges. However, the simple mention of the Quadroids or the Nice Mice Uncles was enough to have her pinned down for a quarter of an hour by either a simpering fanatic or a grim-faced yuppie zombie with a calculator for a heart. Didn't anyone play with Lego any more?

A party of Arabs in sunglasses and burnouses in the hotel for a political negotiation had somehow got mixed in with the toy people. Not a few were clutching Nice Mice or Gargantuabots to be taken back to the Emirates. Sally wandered through the crowds drifting about the lower levels of the hotel, at something of a loss. This wasn't the sort of case where her usual, highly ethical methods – footwork, meticulous questioning, library research, applied intelligence – were all that useful. Obviously, it was time to bring unusual, slightly unethical, methods to bear. She had her picklocks with her.

The Royal Suite was guarded by two three-piece suit samurai. They weren't apparently armed, but something about their frozen faces told Sally they could kill in any one of twenty-five different ways with each individual finger. She kept on walking past them. They didn't look at her, which was what tipped her off. Any male human being will take at least a glance at any female human being between the ages of 12 and 45 who happens to walk past. She paused at the turn of the corridor, and pulled out her compact to check her eyebrows. She wouldn't wear make-up if it didn't give her an excuse to carry around a mirror she could use for looking at people behind her. Baron Ghidrah and attendants came out of the lift. The samurai let them into the suite without a word. Double doors were quietly shut behind them. There was no way in from the front. She decided to try the Nice Mice first.

Cloud Incorporated had a drinks party going in their suite, and there was nobody on the door to check her ID. Which was a shame, since it was very convincing. Unbearably happy music burbled out of the loudspeakers – Mantovani Plays Nauseating Vomit or something – and brightly dressed children and adults were congregated around several chubby people in realistic, man-size Nice Mice costumes. The Nice Mice tended to come in colours Sally found offensive – dayglo pink, lemon yellow and eggshell blue, apricot white. Children laughed as their adorable whiskers twitched.

'Shall we do our special Niceness Dance, children,' squeaked a thinner-than-usual Nice Mouse who was striped like a barber's pole, 'and don't forget to hum the Niceness Hum and smile the Niceness Smile.'

Some children cheered. Sally assumed they must be robots. No real kid would put up with this icky crap. But the children joined in, imitating the Nice Mouse's epileptic gestures and humming like demented bees through risus sardonicus grins.

'Oh hello, isn't this fun?' It was Tilly Barnes again. There was no escape. Perhaps she should have tried to get past the Godzilla Brothers. It could have been less painful. 'You must meet my children. They've just been made into Honorary Nice Mice Little Ones. They're so excited.'

Three little replicas of Tilly Barnes in pastel overalls grinned perkily up at Sally. Their names were sewn across already-prominent tummies – Jake, Jonquil and Dylan. They each had an armful of Nice Mice and were practically levitating with glee. Jonquil looked as if he was about to have an accident.

Sally guessed there must be a marijuana session going on in the back room. With all these hippies around, that would make sense. She sniffed the air. Nothing. Tilly Barnes handed her a paper cup full of thick cherry goo. There were no alcoholic drinks on offer. No wonder Cloud Incorporated didn't need bouncers.

'You must meet Cornfield, he's so real.'

'Gosh, I wish I were real.'

'No, really. Here he is…'

Sally looked around, expecting some kind of executive longhair mutation. She only saw parents and children. And Nice Mice. One of the costumed characters – the stripey bastard – came over, its adorable whiskers erect with glee, and hugged Tilly Barnes until she went oomph.

'Hi Sally,' said the mouse through its perky grin, looking at her name-tag. 'My handle is Cornfield Zwingli. What's your starsign?'

'You see. Real.'

The mask was very good, and the costume didn't bag at all. Somehow, Sally thought that was obscene. She saw sharp little teeth in the mask's snout, and no amount of adorableness around the whiskers could disguise the rattiness of the tail.

'I'm new in the toy racket,' Sally said. 'I hear you run a very profitable business.'

'It's more than a business, Sally,' squeaked Zwingli, 'it's a children's crusade. We at Cloud Incorporated truly believe we're doing something important, educating a generation for tomorrow. Who knows, Sally, if today's world leaders had been Honorary Nice Mice Little Ones as children, perhaps the planet wouldn't be the Bad Vibes Zone it is.'

Sally hated the indiscriminate use of her first name. She put on her hard, businesslike face. 'That's fine, but my shop has to stay going. What are your profit margins like?'

A faraway twinkle came into Zwingli's eyes. 'Negotiable, Sally. Whatever you can lay out is in harmony by us. We have no trouble scoring bread. I guess it's because we've got Niceness on our side, Sally.'

'How do you stack up against the Gargantuabots?'

Sally fancied a dark cloud passed over Zwingli's gleam. The adorable whiskers trembled with a hint of indignation. 'Well, Sally, far be it from me to badmouth our colleagues but I hardly think a dinosaur that turns into a nuclear weapon is the sort of bag future world leaders should be playing with. Pardon me, I see some really important people I have to rap with...'

Zwingli bent down, and wriggled his snout. 'Hi, children. Jake, Jonquil, Dylan, what Nice Things have you done today?'

'Isn't he...?' gasped Tilly Barnes, evidently near some sort of sexual climax, groping for an adjective.

'Real? Maybe.'

Sally made the mistake of sipping her cherry goo, and quickly dumped the drink. She wasn't sure she could take any more of this. Looking at Zwingli, she realised just how detailed his costume was. Under his tail, she thought she could see a tiny, pristine asterisk of asshole. And she couldn't work out how his human head fit inside his rodent one allowing his moist and cheery eyes to be so prominent. Those heart-shaped patches of darker fur around the eyes were particularly creepy. She shivered, despite the heat of the party, and made a getaway. Mercifully, no one stopped to check her ID as she tried to get out of the suite.

The samurai were still on duty. For symmetry's sake, Sally had to get into the Sphere Corporation suite and look around. So far, the whole set-up had only been strange. There was no evidence of actual brain-washing – unless there was something chemical in the goo. It was possible that an epidemic of appalling taste among parents and children could have turned the toy business into a two-horse race. But not likely.

'Hi, Sally Rhodes, hotel security,' she said, waving her bus pass at the samurai. 'You got a bomb threat. Some ecology nuts complaining about your country's animal rights record.'

The samurai didn't look at her. They stood still as wooden Indians. She continued, 'Me, I think if whales are so intelligent they should stop swimming near Japan, right? It's probably a hoax. We get one every week. Have you let anyone in wearing a duffel coat, eating yoghurt and carrying a big ticking black ball with "BOMB" written on it?'

Neither moved a muscle, but the door opened. When she got through alive, Sally assumed her routine had worked.

'Thanks fellas. Like I say, it's bound to be a mix-up. But ever since Norman Tebbit got his wake-up call, the management has been jumpy.'

There was an army of Gargantuabots arrayed on the floor, ranked according to size, ferociousness, adaptability and kill-count. Baron Ghidrah sat in a throne-sized chair, surveying the formation. Executives were prostrate before him, foreheads to the carpet, bums in the air. No one took any notice of her.

Baron Ghidrah took out a sales chart from a folder on his lap and held it up like a magician demonstrating a trick. The graph line rose steadily, but was marred by a minuscule dip near the top. With great deliberation, Baron Ghidrah tore the chart in four and handed it to an executive. The man rose to his knees and took the paper. He balled it and put it into his mouth, gulping manfully. Baron Ghidrah clapped once, a sound as sharp as a pistol shot. The executive reached for his stomach and pulled his shirt open. From the back, Sally couldn't see anything, but she heard burst buttons skittering on the polished wood floor.

'Excuse me,' she said, 'where's the bomb?'

The executive on the point of seppuku froze, and Baron Ghidrah finally paid her some attention. He glared, his eyes red, and rose from his throne. His clothes creaked like cast iron. The head of the Sphere Corporation stepped past his executives, and walked slowly, lumbering like a copper giant, down the aisle. Multitudes of Gargantuabots turned. Sally smiled, but her patter seized up in the back of her throat.

The Baron's eyes burned, making him look like the Shogun of Castle Dracula. The kimono slid from his shoulders. She saw where the skin joined the plastic, and where the plastic joined the metal. Lights went on and off behind a transparent plate in his chest. His shoulders heaved as the spiked epaulettes slid out of the flesh. His head raised six inches as he came apart at the waist, and his entire torso spun round. A tail snaked out. A new head, that of a bejewelled dragon, shot out of his former back. Steam gushed from holes in his body.

Shit, Baron Ghidrah was a Gargantuabot!

'Never mind,' Sally said, 'wrong room number. It happens all the time. I'm a hooker. Some big shot wants me to dress up like a Sandie Doll and do it with some Nice Mice.'

The Dragon Ghidrah stalked towards her, its massive feet denting the floor. The executives were undergoing lesser transformations of their own. Sally saw four sets of claws extended. The upper set clacked wickedly, the others just dripped venom.

'Uhhh,' she tried to think of something to say, 'Klaatu barada nikto?' The dragon kept coming. 'Don't know that one, eh? Pax. Uncle.'

A set of claws lodged in her pullover, scrunching it tight around her spine. She was lifted up, wool biting into her armpits. Her jeans were dripping with hot water. She searched in vain for some trace of humanity in the creature's face.

'Hey, chill out, Baron babe,' came a mellow voice from behind her. 'Remember, you haven't done your Nice Thing today.'

The dragon snarled, and dropped her. She landed painfully on one knee. Zwingli was in the room with them. He was still dressed up. Or, rather, he was still a Nice Mouse.

The dragon roared, and spat a gobbet of flame onto the carpet near her.

'So, let me get this straight,' the General began, 'you two are representatives of, what did you call them, galactic empires? Like in Star Wars? Great toys, lousy movie, by the way. And you thought that rather than zap each other to spacedust in some border dispute, you'd all just beam on down to Earth and see who could sell the most toys?' No one contradicted him. 'Not only is that crazy, it's immoral. Didn't you think of the business ecology you'd be pissing all over? God, I hate extra-terrestrial know-it-all show-offs. Kick their alien asses back into orbit, that's what I say.'

Baron Ghidrah, who had been prevailed upon to revert to his human disguise, grunted, and spat a hissing coal into an ashtray. Zwingli twitched his adorable whiskers, but nobody bothered with him.

'Tell me, why did you have this war in the first place?'

'Don't lay that Bring Down City Jazz on me, dude,' Zwingli squeaked. 'They started it. We just want to live in peace and oneness with tolerance for all creeds and colours, and a respect for a wide variety of spiritual beliefs and ways of life.'

'Then what was the war about?'

'Them,' croaked Baron Ghidrah. 'Look at them. How do they make you feel… inside? Be honest.'

'Nice Mice? They make me sick.'

'Then how do you think we feel? Can you imagine the sheer pleasure of wiping out millions of these vermin with a single blast?'

'Now you come to mention it,' said the General, 'I reckon I can.'

Everyone looked at Zwingli. He grinned perkily and hummed his Niceness Hum. His stripes revolved in serene contentment.

'So, in conclusion, you guys want to piss off back to the stars and finish slugging it out, and you're prepared to leave us alone?'

Baron Ghidrah cleared his throat in assent. Zwingli chirruped, 'This isn't settling anything. We've saturated the market, and no clear top dog has come out of it. Those are the breaks. Sorry, guys.'

'Terrific. Miss Rhodes, here's your thou. Although you didn't do much to earn it, since these bozos were leaving anyway.'

Sally caught the envelope. 'So that's everything?'

'Um, not quite.' It was Woolavington. He'd been quiet since the meeting began, as usual. 'Miss Rhodes, when you get home you'll find a Woolavington Train Set waiting for you. It's a vintage model from the thirties. I wish you every happiness with it. If you ever have children, please let them play with it. And, um, I have a little announcement. Miss Rhodes, General Jones, you'll be pleased to know I've been talking with our friends here and it looks as if Woolavington and Company will be trading high again. I've secured the sole and exclusive rights to the manufacture, sale and exploitation of the Nice Mice and the Gargantuabots and, um, all related merchandise, including books, films, videos, cartoons, T-shirts, lunch-boxes, posters, and so on…'

The General's cigar hit the floor before his jaw. 'But…'

'Yes, General. That means we will be competing in the modern market again. I'll still make the trains, but I think the company will need such stronger products if it is to regain its pre-eminence in the field. And while the enterprises of Mr Zwingli and Baron Ghidrah might have failed to resolve their differences, they must be judged highly successful as business ventures. I've, um, spoken with your board of directors and we've agreed – as of now, I'm a majority shareholder in your firm, by the way – to turn over most of your factories to the production of, um, Gargantuabots and Nice Mice. We feel it's time for Gung-Ho Jones to retire. Now, isn't that, um, nice?'

General Jones' cigar lay on the carpet, a burning circle radiating from it. Sally stepped on the fire before it could spread.

'Settled?' she asked. They all looked at each other. 'Good. Let's go home.'

Imperial High War Deathlord Ghidrah, First Exalted Killbastard of the Doomfleet, glared in fury at the screenspeaker. The rodent regatta stretched as far as the eye could see, the great pastel hulls of the starships twinkling with sticky glitter graffiti. The flagship Have a Nice Day was targeted dead centre, and the Niceness Hums of a myriad mice filled the airwaves.

Ghidrah's metal chest swelled with steam as he recalled the victories of the Gargantuan Omnisphere. He remembered the Fall of the Perpetuum Dynasty, the degradation of the Pain Princes of Stagwald Carnasson, the humiliation of the 709 Warrior Popes of the Planet Shit, the extinction of the Eternity Pirates of Zeugma III.

On the bridge of the Doomship, the Lesser Deathspitters assumed the respectful position, bifurcate tails in the air, forehorns to the manure-clogged deck. An Inferior Scumjumper handed Ghidrah a Cancer Sceptre. He flicked its head, and thick smoke poured from its end. His lieutenants began to transform. The Sacred Gargantuan Killing Cry rose in competition with the Hum.

'May The Great Devastaticon feast on the entrails of our enemy this day,' roared Ghidrah. 'Begin the attack!'

'Aye-aye,' snapped Provisional Humanoid Blastmaster General 'Gung Ho-Jones, saluting smartly as he brought his mailed fist down on the activation control of the ship's main battery of termination tasers. Instant death sprang from the Doomfleet.

The cathedral arches of the ship rang with the din of battle.

DEREK LEECH
THE ORIGINAL DR SHADE

Like a shark breaking inky waters, the big black car surfaced out of the night, its searchlight headlamps freezing the Bolsheviks en tableau as they huddled over their dynamite. Cohen, their vile leader, tried to control his raging emotions, realising that yet again his schemings to bring about the ruination of the British Empire were undone. Borzoff, his hands shaking uncontrollably, fell to his ragged-trousered knees and tried one last prayer to the God whose icons he had spat upon that day in the mother country when he had taken his rifle butt to the princess' eggshell-delicate skull. Petrofsky drooled into his stringy beard, his one diseased eye shrinking in the light like a slug exposed to salt, and uselessly thumb-cocked his revolver.

The canvas top of the Rolls Royce 'Shadowshark' raised like a hawk's eyelid, and a dark shape seemed to grow out of the driver's seat, cloak billowing in the strong wind, twin moons reflected in the insectlike dark goggles, wide-brimmed hat at a jaunty angle.

Petrofsky raised his shaking pistol, and slammed back against the iron globe of the chemical tank, cut down by another silent dart from the doctor's famous airgun. In the distance, the conspirators could hear police sirens, but they knew they would not be taken into custody. The shadowman would not allow them to live out the night to further sully the green and fruitful soil of sacred England with their foul presence.

As the doctor advanced, the headlamps threw his expanding shadow on the Bolsheviks.

Israel Cohen, the Mad Genius of the Revolution, trembled, his flabby chins slapping against his chest, sweat pouring from his ape-like forehead down his protruberant nose to his fleshy, sensual lips. He raised a ham-sized fist against the doctor, sneering insane defiance to the last:

'Curse you, Shade!'

REX CASH, *Dr Shade Vs the Dynamite Boys* (1936)

They ate an expensively minimalist meal at Alastair Little's in Frith Street, and Basil Crosbie, Leech's Art Editor, picked up the bill with his company card. Throughout, Tamara, his agent, kept reminding Crosbie of the *Eagle* awards Greg had picked up for *Fat Chance*, not mentioning that that was two years ago. As with most restaurants, there was nowhere that could safely accommodate his yardsquare artwork folder, and he was worried the sample strips would get scrunched or warped. He would have brought copies, but wanted to put himself over as sharply as possible. Besides, the ink wasn't dry on the pieces he had finished this morning. As usual, there hadn't been time to cover himself.

Whenever there was dead air in the conversation, Tamara filled it with more selected highlights from Greg's career. Greg guessed she had invited herself to this lunch to keep him under control. She remembered, but was carefully avoiding mention of, his scratchy beginnings in the '70s – spiky strips and singletons for punk fanzines like *Sheep Worrying*, *Brainrape* and *Kill Your Pet Puppy* – and knew exactly how he felt about the Derek Leech organisation. She probably thought he was going to turn up in a ripped rubbish bag, with lots of black eyeliner and safety-pins through his earlobes, then go for Crosbie with a screwdriver. Actually, while the Sex Pistols were swearing on live television and gobbing at gigs, he had been a neatly dressed, normal-haired art student. It was only at the easel, where he used to assemble police brutality collages with ransom note captions, that he had embodied the spirit of '77.

If Tamara would shut up, he thought he could get on with Crosbie. Greg knew the man had started out on the *Eagle*, and filled in on *Garth* once in a while. He had been a genuine minor talent in his day. Still, he worked for Leech, and if there was one artefact that summed up everything Greg loathed about Britain under late Thatcherism, it was Leech's *Daily Comet*. The paper was known for its Boobs 'n' Pubes, its multi-million Giveaway Grids, its unflinching support of the diamond-hard right, its lawsuit-fuelled muckraking, and prose that read like a football hooligan's attempt to imitate the *Janet and John* books. It was Britain's fastest-growing newspaper, and the hub of a communications empire that was putting Leech in the Murdoch-Maxwell bracket. In Madame Tussaud's last annual poll, the statue of Derek Leech had ranked eighth on the Most Admired list, between Gorbachev and Prince Charles, and second on the Most Hated and Feared chart, after Margaret Thatcher but before Adolf Hitler, Colonel Gaddafi, Count Dracula and the Yorkshire Ripper.

Crosbie didn't start talking business until eyedropper-sized cups of coffee arrived. With the plates taken away, the Art Editor opened his folder on the table, and brought out a neatly paperclipped set of notes. Tamara was still picking at her fruit salad, five pieces of pale apple and/or pear floating in a steel bowl of water with a solitary grape. She and Crosbie had been drinking dry white wine with the meal, but Greg stuck to mineral water. The gritty coffee gave him quite a punch, and he felt his heart tighten like an angry fist. Since *Fat Chance*, he hadn't done anything notable. This was an important meeting for him. Tamara might not dump him if it didn't come out right, but she might shift him from her A-list to her B-list.

'As you probably know,' Crosbie began, 'Leech United

Kingdom is expanding at the moment. I don't know if you keep up with the trades, but Derek has recently bought up the rights to a lot of defunct titles with a view to relaunch. It's a lot easier to sell something familiar than something new. Just now, Derek's special baby is the *Evening Argus*.'

'The Brighton paper?' Greg asked.

'No, a national. It folded in 1953, but it was very big from the '20s through to the War. Lord Badgerfield ran it.'

'I have heard of it,' Greg said. 'It's always an *Argus* headline in those old films about Dunkirk.'

'That's right. The paper had what they used to call "a good War". Churchill called it "the voice of true democracy". Like Churchill, it was never quite the same after the War... but now, what with the interest in the 50th anniversary of the Battle of Britain and all that, we think the time is right to bring it back. It'll be nostalgia, but it'll be new too...'

'Gasmasks and rationing and the spirit of the Blitz, eh?'

'That sort of thing. It'll come out in the Autumn, and we'll build up to it with a massive campaign. "The voice is back." We'll cut from this ovaltine-type '40s look to an aggressive '90s feel, yuppies on carphones, designer style, full-colour pages. It'll be a harder newspaper than the *Comet*, but it'll still be a Leech UK product, populist and commercial. We aim to be the turn-of-the-century newspaper.'

'And you want a cartoonist?'

Crosbie smiled. 'I liked your *Fat Chance* work a lot, Greg. The script was a bit manky for my taste, but you draw with clean lines, good solid blocks of black. Your private eye was a thug, but he looked like a real strip hero. There was a bit of *Jeff Hawke* there. It was just what we want for the *Argus*, the feel of the past but the content of the present.'

'So you'll be wanting Greg to do a *Fat Chance* strip for the new paper?'

Greg had made the connection, and was cracking a smile.

'No, Tamara, that's not what he wants. I've remembered the other thing I know about the *Argus*. I should have recognised the name straight off. It's a by-word...'

Crosbie cut in, 'That's right. The *Mirror* had *Jane* and *Garth*, but the *Argus* had...'

Greg was actually excited. He thought he had grown up, but there was still a pulp heart in him. As a child, he had pored through second- and third-hand books and magazines. Before *Brainrape* and *Fat Chance* and *PC Rozzerblade*, he had tried to draw his other heroes: Bulldog Drummond, the Saint, Sexton Blake, Biggles, and...

'Dr Shade.'

'You may haff caught me, *Herr Doktor Schatten*, but ze glory off ze Sird Reich vill roll over zis passetic country like a tchuggernaucht. I die for ze greater glory off Tchermany, off ze Nazi party and off Adolf Hitler...'

'That's where you're wrong, Von Spielsdorf. I wouldn't dirty my hands by killing you, even if it is what you so richly deserve.'

'Ain't we gonna ice the lousy stinkin' rat, Doc?' asked Hank the Yank. The American loomed over the German mastermind, a snub-nosed automatic in his meaty fist.

'Yours is a young country, Henry,' said Dr Shade gently, laying a black-gloved hand of restraint upon his comrade's arm. 'That's not how we do things in England. Von Spielsdorf here may be shot as a spy, but that decision is not ours to make. We have courts and laws and justice. That's what this whole war's about, my friend. The right of the people to have courts and laws and justice. Even you, Von Spielsdorf. We're fighting for your rights too.'

'Pah, decadent *Englische schweinhund*!'

Hank tapped the German on the forehead with his pistol-grip, and the saboteur sat down suddenly, his eyes rolling upwards.

'That showed him, eh, Doc?'

Dr Shade's thin, normally inexpressive lips, curled in a slight smile.

'Indubitably, Henry. Indubitably.'

Dr Shade Monthly No 111, (May, 1943)

The heart of Leech UK was a chrome and glass pyramid in London docklands, squatting by the Thames like a recently arrived flying saucer. Greg felt a little queasy as the minicab they had sent for him slipped through the pickets. It was a chilly Spring day, and there weren't many of them about. Crosbie had warned him of 'the Union Luddites' and their stance against the new technology that enabled Leech to put out the *Comet* and its other papers with a bare minimum of production staff. Greg hoped none of the placard-carriers would recognise him. Last year, there had been quite a bit of violence as the pickets, augmented by busloads of radicals as annoyed by Leech's editorials as his industrial relations policies, came up against the police and a contingent of the *Comet*-reading skinheads who were the backbone of Leech's support. Now, the dispute dragged on but was almost forgotten. Leech papers had never mentioned it much, and the rest of the press had fresher strikes, revolutions and outrages to cover.

The minicab drove right into the pyramid, into an enclosed reception area where the vehicle was checked by security guards. Greg was allowed out and issued with a blue day pass that a smiling girl in a smart uniform pinned on his lapel.

Behind her desk were framed colour shots of smiling girls without uniforms, smart or otherwise, their nipples like squashed cherries, their faces cleanly unexpressive. The *Comet* Knock-Outs were supposed to be a national institution. But so, according to the *Comet*, were corporal punishment in schools, capital punishment for supporters of Sinn Fein, and the right to tell lies about the sexual preferences of soap opera performers.

446   KIM NEWMAN

Greg wondered what Penny Stamp – Girl Reporter, Dr Shade's sidekick in the old strip, would have made of a *Comet* Knock-Out. Penny had always been rowing with the editor who wanted her to cover fashion shows and garden parties when she would rather be chasing crime scoops for the front page; perhaps her modern equivalent should be a pin-up girl who wants to keep her clothes on and become Roger Cook or Woodward and Bernstein?

He rode up to the 23rd floor, which was where Crosbie had arranged to meet him. The girl downstairs had telephoned up, and her clone was waiting for him in the thickly carpeted lobby outside the lift. She smiled and escorted him through an open-plan office where telephones and computers were being installed by a cadre of workmen. At the far end were a series of glassed-off cubicles. She eased him into one of these and asked if he wanted tea or coffee. She brought him instant coffee, the granules floating near the bottom of a paper cupful of hot brown water. There was a dummy edition of the *Evening Argus* on the desk. The headline was IT'S WAR! Greg didn't have time to look at it.

Crosbie came in with a tall, slightly stooped man and ordered more coffee. The newcomer was in his seventies but looked fit for his age. He wore comfortable old trousers and a cardigan under a new sports jacket. Greg knew who he was.

'Rex Cash?' he asked, his hand out.

The man's grip was firm. 'One of him,' he said. 'Not the original.'

'This is Harry Lipman, Greg.'

'Harry,' Harry said.

'Greg. Greg Daniels.'

'*Fat Chance*?'

Greg nodded. He was surprised Harry had kept up with the business. He had been retired for a long time, he knew.

'Mr Crosbie told me. I've been looking your stuff out. I don't know much about the drawing side. Words are my line. But you're a talented young man.'

'Thanks.'

'Can we work together?' Harry was being direct. Greg didn't have an answer.

'I hope so.'

'So do I. It's been a long time. I'll need someone to snip the extra words out of the panels.'

Harry Lipman had been Rex Cash from 1939 to 1952, taking over the name from Donald Moncrieff, the creator of Dr Shade. He had filled 58 Dr Shade books with words, 42 novels and 135 short stories, and he had scripted the newspaper strip all the while, juggling storylines. Several of the best-known names in British adventure comics had worked on the Dr Shade strip: Mack Bullivant, who would create *Andy of the Arsenal* for *British Pluck*, Tommy Wrathall, highly regarded for his commando and paratroop stories in *Boys' War*, and, greatest of all, Frank FitzGerald, who had, for six years, made Dr Shade dark, funny and almost magical. They were all dead now. Harry was the last survivor of those days. And so the *Argus* was calling in Greg to fill the footprints.

'Harry has been working up some storylines,' said Crosbie. 'I'll leave you to talk them through. If you need more coffee, give Nicola a buzz. I'll be back in a few hours to see how you're doing.'

Crosbie left. Harry and Greg looked at each other and, for no reason, started laughing like members of a family sharing a joke they could never explain to an outsider.

'Considering Dr Shade must be about 150 by now,' Harry began, 'I thought we'd start the strip with him trying to get the DHSS to up his heating allowance for the winter...'

SHADE, DOCTOR Scientific vigilante of mysterious origins, usually hidden behind a cloak and goggle-like dark glasses, although also a master of disguise with many other identities. Operating out of an outwardly dilapidated but inwardly luxurious retreat in London's East End, he employs a group of semi-criminal bully boys in his neverending war against foreign elements importing evil into the heart of the British Empire. Originally introduced (under the name 'Dr Jonathan Shadow') as a minor character in *The Cur of Limehouse* (1929), a novel by Rex Cash (Donald Moncrieff), in which he turns up in the final chapters to help the aristocratic pugilist hero Reggie Brandon defeat the East End opium warlord Baron Quon. The character was so popular with the readers of *Wendover's Magazine*, the monthly publication in which the novel was serialised, that Moncrieff wrote several series of short adventures, later collected in the volumes *Dr Shadow and the Poison Goddess* (1931) and *Dr Shadow's Nigger Trouble* (1932). In 1934, alleging plagiarism of their character, THE SHADOW, Street and Smith threatened to sue Badgerfield, publishers of Wendover's and of the collections, and, to appease the American firm, the character was renamed Dr Shade.

A semi-supernatural, ultra-patriotic avenger whose politics would seem to be somewhat to the right of those of Sapper's Bulldog DRUMMOND or the real-life Oswald Mosley (of whom Moncrieff was reputed to be a great admirer), Dr Shade is much given to executing minor villains with his airgun or gruesomely torturing them for information. He appeared in nearly 100 short novels, all credited to Rex Cash, written for *Dr Shade Monthly*, a pulp periodical issued by Badgerfield from 1934 until 1947. The house pseudonym was also used by a few other writers, mostly for back-up stories in the 1930s, when the prolific Moncrieff's inspiration flagged. The character became even more popular when featured in a daily strip in the *Evening Argus*, most famously drawn by Frank FitzGerald, from 1935 to 1952. Moncrieff, after a bitter dispute with Lord Badgerfield, stopped writing Dr Shade in 1939, and the strip was taken over by Harry Lipman, a writer who had done a few Dr Shade stories for the magazine. By the outbreak of war, Lipman had effectively become Rex Cash, and was producing stories and novels for the magazine as well as scripting the strip.

Lipman's Dr Shade is a less frightening figure than Moncrieff's. Although his uniform and gadgets are unchanged, Lipman's hero is an official agent of the British government who refrained from sadistically mistreating his enemies the way Moncrieff's had. It was revealed that Dr Shade is really Dr Jonathan Chambers, an honest and dedicated general practitioner, and the supernatural elements of the strip were toned down. During WWII, Dr Shade's politics changed; as written by Moncrieff, he is an implacable foe of the non-white races and international communism, but Lipman's hero is a straightforward defender of democracy in the face of the Nazi menace. Moncrieff's Moriarty figure, introduced in *Dr Shade and the Whooping Horror* (1934), is Israel Cohen, a stereotypically Jewish master criminal in league with Russian anarchists and Indian Thuggees in a plot to destroy Britain's naval superiority. During the War, Cohen was retired (although he returned in the late 1940s as a comic East End nightclub owner and *friend* of Dr Shade) and the penumbral adventurer, joined by two-fisted American OSS agent Henry Hemingway and peppy girl reporter Penny Stamp, concentrated exclusively on licking Hitler.

Moncrieff's Dr Shade novels include *Dr Shade Vs the Dynamite Boys* (1936), *A Yellow Man's Treachery* (1936), *Dr Shade's Balkan Affair* (1937), *To the Last Drop of Our British Blood* (1937), *The Bulldog Bites Back* (1937), *The International Conspirators* (1938) and *Dr Shade in Suez* (1939), while Lipman's are *Dr Shade's Home Front* (1940), *Underground in France* (1941), *Dr Shade Takes Over* (1943), *Dr Shade in Tokyo* (1945), *Dr Shade Buries the Hatchet* (1948) and *The Piccadilly Gestapo* (1951). The character also featured in films, beginning with *Dr Shade's Phantom Taxi Mystery* (1936; dir. Michael Powell), in which he was played by Raymond Massey, while Francis L. Sullivan was a decidedly non-Semitic Israel Cohen, renamed 'Idris Kobon'. Valentine Dyall took the role in a BBC Radio serial from 1943 to 1946, and Ronald Howard wore the cloak in a 1963 Rediffusion

TV serial, *Introducing Dr Shade...*, with Elizabeth Shepherd as Penny Stamp and Alfie Bass as Israel Cohen.

See also: Dr Shade's associates: Reggie BRANDON, Lord Highbury and Islington; Henry HEMINGWAY (Hank the Yank); Penny STAMP, Girl Reporter; and his enemies: Israel COHEN, the Mad Genius of the Revolution; ACHMET the Almost-Human; Melchior Umberto GASPARD, Prince of Forgers; Professor IZAN, the Führer's Favourite.

DAVID PRINGLE, *Imaginary People: A Who's Who of Modern Fictional Characters* (1987)

Greg and Harry Lipman met several times over the next few weeks, mainly away from the Leech building. In Soho pubs and cheap restaurants, they discussed the direction of the new Dr Shade strip. Greg had liked Harry immediately, and came to admire his still-quick storyteller's mind. He knew he could work with this man. Having taken Dr Shade over from Donald Moncrieff, he didn't have a creator's obsessive attachment to the property, and was open to suggestions that would change the frame of the strip. Harry agreed that there was no point in producing a '40s pastiche. Their Dr Shade had to be different from all the character's previous incarnations, but still maintain some of the continuity. Gradually, their ideas came together.

In keeping with the *Argus'* stated old-but-new approach, they decided to set the strip in the near future. Everybody was already talking about the turn of the century. They would have Dr Shade come out of retirement, disenchanted with the post-war world he fought for back in the old days, and assembling a new team of adventurers to tackle up-to-the-moment villains against a backdrop of urban decay and injustice. Greg suggested pitting the avenging shadowman against rapacious property speculators laying waste to his old East End stamping grounds, a crack cartel posing as a fundamentalist religious sect, corporate despoilers of the environment, or unethical stockbrokers with mafia connections.

'You know,' Harry said one afternoon in The Posts, sipping his pint, 'if Donald were writing these stories, Dr Shade would be on the side of those fellers. He died thinking he'd lost everything and here we are, half a century later, with a country the original Dr Shade would have been proud of.'

Nearby, a bored mid-afternoon drinker, swallows tattooed on his neck, zapped spaceships, his beeping deathrays cutting into the piped jazz. Greg pulled open his bag of salt and vinegar crisps. 'I don't know much about Moncrieff. Even the reference books are pretty sketchy. What was he like?'

'I didn't really know the man, Greg. To him, Lipmans were like Cohens… not people you talked to.'

'Was he really a fascist?'

'Oh yes,' Harry's eyes got a little larger. 'Nobody had a shirt blacker than Donald Moncrieff. The whole kit and kaboodle, he had: glassy eyes, toothbrush moustache, thin blond hair. Marched through Brixton with Mosley a couple of times. Smashed up my brother's newsagent's shop, they did. And he went on goodwill jaunts to Spain and Germany. I believe he wrote pamphlets for the British Union of Fascists and he certainly conned poor old Frank into designing a recruiting poster for the Cause.'

'Frank FitzGerald?'

'Yes, your predecessor with the pencils. Frank never forgave Donald for that. During the War, the intelligence people kept interrogating Frank whenever there was a bit of suspected sabotage. You know the line in *Casablanca*? "Round up the usual suspects." Well, Donald put Frank on the list of "usual suspects".'

The space cadet burned out. He swore and thumped the machine as it flashed its 'Game Over' sneer at him.

'Were you brought in specifically to change Dr Shade?'

'Oh yes. Badgerfield was an appeasement man right up until Munich but he was a smart newspaper boy and saw the change in the wind. He dumped a lot of people – not just fascists, lots of pacifists got tarred with the same brush – and about-faced his editorial policy. You'd think he'd overlook the comic strip, but he didn't. He knew it was as much a part of the *Argus* as the editorial pages and his own "Honest Opinion" column. My orders when I took over were quite blunt. He told me to "de-Nazify" Dr Shade.'

'What happened to Moncrieff?'

'Oh, he sued and sued and sued, but Badgerfield owned the character and could do what he wanted. When the War started, he became very unpopular, of course. He spent some time in one of those holiday camps they set up for Germans and Italians and sympathisers. They didn't have much concrete on him and he came back to London. He wrote some books, I think, but couldn't get them published. I heard he had a stack of Dr Shade stories he was never able to use because only His Lordship had the right to exploit the character. Then, he died...'

'He was young, wasn't he?'

'Younger than me. It was the blitz. They tried to say he was waving a torch in the blackout for the *lüftwaffe*, but I reckon he was just under the wrong bomb at the wrong time. I saw him near the end and he was pretty cracked. Not at all the privileged smoothie he'd been in the '30s. I didn't like the feller, of course, but you had to feel sorry for him. He thought Hitler was Jesus Christ and the War just drove him off his head. Lots of Englishmen like that, there were. You don't hear much about them these days.'

'I don't know. They all seem to be in parliament now.'

Harry chuckled. 'Too right, but Dr Shade'll see to 'em, you bet, eh?'

They raised their drinks and toasted the avenging shadow, the implacable enemy of injustice, intolerance and ill-will.

* * *

IN PRAISE OF BRITISH HERO'S

Those of us PROUD TO BE BRITISH know that in this nations HOUR OF DIREST NEED, the True Blue BRITISH HERO'S will appear and STAND TALL TOGETHER to WIPE FROM THE FACE OF THIS FAIR FLOWER OF A LAND those who BESMERCH IT'S PURITY. With the WHITE BRITON'S in danger of drowning under the tidal wave of COLOUREDS, and the dedicated and law-upholding BRITISH POLICE going unarmed against the SEMITEX BOMBS, OOZY MACHINE GUNS and ROCKET LAUNCHERS of the KINK-HAIRED NIGGER'S, MONEY-GRUBBING YIDS, ARSE-BANDIT AID'S-SPREADERS, SLANT-EYED KUNGFU CHINKIE'S, LONG-HAIRED HIPPY RABBLE, LOONY LEFT LESBIONS, and RAGHEADED MUSSULMEN, the time has come for KING ARTHUR to return from under the hill, for the CROSS OF ST GEORGE to fly from the banners of the CRUSADERS OF CHRISTENDOM, for ROBIN HOOD to come back from the greenwood of Avalon, for the archers of CRECY to notch up their arrows on the orders of GOOD KING HENRY THE FIFTH, for ADMIRAL HORATIO NELSON to take command of the STOUT-HEARTED FLEET, for RAJAH BROOKE OF SARAWAK to show the coons and gooks and spooks and poofs whats what, for the MURDER of GENERAL GORDON to be avenged with the blood of AY-RAB troublemakers, for DICK TURPIN to rob the JEW-INFESTED coffers of the INVADING IMMIGRANT VERMIN AND FILTH, for DR SHADE to use his airgun on the enemies of WHITE LIBERTY

The time will come soon when all GOOD BRITISH MEN will have to dip their FISTS in PAKKYNIGGERYIDCHINKAY-RAB BLOOD to make clean for the healthy WHITE babies of our women this sacred island. The STINKING SCUM with their DOG-EATING, their DISGUSTING UNCHRISTIAN RITUAL PRACTICES, their PIG-SCREWING, CHILD-RAPING,

MARRIAGE-ARRANGING, DISEASE-SPREADING habits will be thrown off the WHITE cliffs of Dover and swept out to sea as we, THE TRUE INHABITANTS OF GREAT BRITAIN, reclame the homes, the jobs, the lands and the women that are ours by DIVINE RIGHT.

KING ARTHUR! ST GEORGE! DR SHADE!

Today, go out and glassbottle a chinkie waiter, rapefuck a stinking coon bitch, piss burning petrol in a pakky newsagent, stick the boot to a raghead, hang a queer, shit in a sinnagog, puke on a lesbion. ITS YOUR LEGAL RIGHT! ITS YOUR DUTY! ITS YOUR DESTINY!

ARTHUR is COMING BACK! DR SHADE WILL RETURN!

Our's is the RIGHT, our's is the GLORY, our's is the ONLY TRUE JUSTICE! We shall PREVALE!

We are the SONS OF DR SHADE!

'JOHNNY BRITISH MAN', *Britannia Rules* fanzine,

Issue 37, June 1991

(Confiscated by police at a South London football fixture.)

Harry had given him a map of the estate, but Greg still got lost. The place was one of those '60s wastelands, concrete slabs now disfigured by layers of spray-painted hatred, odd little depressions clogged with rubbish, more than a few burned-out or derelict houses. There was loud Heavy Metal coming from somewhere, and teenagers hung about in menacing gaggles, looking at him with empty, hostile eyes as they compared tattoos or passed bottles. One group were inhaling something – glue? – from a brown paper bag. He looked at them a moment or two longer than he should have and they stared defiance. A girl whose skin haircut showed the odd bumps of her skull flashed him the V sign.

He kept his eyes on the ground and got more lost. The numbering system of the houses was irregular and contradictory and Greg had to go round in circles for a while. He asked for directions from a pair of henna-redheaded teenage girls sitting on a wall and they just shrugged their shoulders and went back to chewing gum. One of the girls was pregnant, her swollen belly pushing through her torn T-shirt, bursting the buttons of her jeans fly.

Greg was conscious that even his old overcoat was several degrees smarter than the norm in this area and that that might mark him as a mugging target. He also knew he had less than ten pounds on him and that frustrated muggers usually make up the difference between their expectations and their acquisitions with bare-knuckle beatings and loose teeth.

It was a Summer evening and quite warm, but the estate had a chill all of its own. The block-shaped tiers of council flats cast odd shadows that slipped across alleyways in a manner that struck Greg as being subtly wrong, like an illustration where the perspective is off or the light sources contradictory. The graffiti wasn't the '80s hip-hop style he knew from his own area, elaborate signatures to absent works of art, but was bluntly, boldly blatant, embroidered only by the occasional swastika (invariably drawn the wrong way round), football club symbol or Union Jack scratch.

CHELSEA FC FOREVER. KILL THE COONS! NF NOW. GAS THE YIDS! UP THE GUNNERS. FUCK THE IRISH MURDERERS! HELP STAMP OUT AIDS: SHOOT A POOF TODAY. And the names of bands he had read about in *Searchlight*, the anti-fascist paper: SKREWDRIVER, BRITISH BOYS, WHITEWASH, CRÜSADERS. There was a song lyric, magic markered on a bus stop in neat primary school writing, 'Jump down, turn around, kick a fucking nigger. Jump down, turn around, kick him in the head. Jump down, turn around, kick a fucking nigger. Jump down, turn around, kick him till he's dead.'

You would have thought that the Nazis had won the War and installed a puppet Tory government. The estate could easily be a '30s science-fiction writer's idea of the ghetto of the future, clean-lined and featureless buildings trashed by the bubble-helmeted brownshirts of some interplanetary axis, Jews, blacks and Martians despatched to some concentration camp asteroid. This wasn't the Jubilee Year. Nobody was even angry any more, just numbed with the endless, grinding misery of it all.

Eventually, more or less by wandering at random, he found Harry Lipman's flat. The bell button had been wrenched off, leaving a tuft of multi-coloured wires, and there was a reversed swastika carved into the door. Greg knocked and a light went on in the hall. Harry admitted him into the neat, small flat. Greg realised the place was fortified like a command bunker, a row of locks on the door, multiple catches on the reinforced glass windows, a burglar alarm fixed up on the wall between the gas and electricity meters. Otherwise, it was what he had expected: bookshelves everywhere, including the toilet, and a pleasantly musty clutter.

'I've not had many people here since Becky died' – Greg had known that Harry was a widower – 'you must excuse the fearful mess.'

Harry showed Greg through to the kitchen. There was an Amstrad PCW 8256 set up on the small vinyl-topped table, a stack of continuous paper in a tray on the floor feeding the printer. The room smelled slightly of fried food.

'I'm afraid this is where I write. It's the only room with enough natural light for me. Besides, I like to be near the kettle and the Earl Grey.'

'Don't worry about it, Harry. You should see what my studio looks like. I think it used to be a coal cellar.'

He put down his art folder and Harry made a pot of tea.

'So, how's Dr Shade coming along? I've made some drawings.'

'Swimmingly. I've done a month's worth of scripts, giving us our introductory serial. In the end, I went with the East End story as the strongest to bring the doctor back...'

The East End Story was an idea Harry and Greg had developed in which Dr Jonathan Chambers, miraculously not a day older than he was in 1952 when he was last seen (or 1929, come to that), returns from a spell in a Tibetan Monastery (or somewhere) studying the mystic healing arts (or something) to discover that the area where he used to make his home is being taken over by Dominick Dalmas, a sinister tycoon whose sharp-suited thugs are using violence and intimidation to evict the long-time residents, among whom are several of the doctor's old friends. Penelope Stamp, formerly a girl reporter but now a feisty old woman, is head of the Residents' Protection Committee, and she appeals to Chambers to resume his old crime-fighting alias and to investigate Dalmas. At first reluctant, Chambers is convinced by a botched assassination attempt to put on the cloak and goggles, and it emerges that Dalmas is the head of a mysterious secret society whose nefarious schemes would provide limitless future plotlines. Dalmas would be hoping to build up a substantial powerbase in London with the long-term intention of taking over the country, if not the world. Of course, Dr Shade would thwart his plots time and again, although not without a supreme effort.

'Maybe I'm just old, Greg,' Harry said after he had shown him the scripts, 'but this Dr Shade feels different. People said that when I took over from Donald, the strip became more appealing, with more comedy and thrills than horror and violence, but I can't see much to laugh about in this story. It's almost as if someone were trying to force Dr Shade to be Donald's character, by creating a world where his monster vigilante makes more sense than my straight-arrow hero. Everything's turned around.'

'Don't worry about it. Our Dr Shade is still fighting for justice. He's on the side of Penny Stamp, not Dominick Dalmas.'

'What I want to know is whether he'll be on the side of Derek Leech?'

Greg really hadn't thought of that. The proprietor of the *Argus* would, of course, have the power of veto over the adventures of his cartoon character. He might not care for the direction Greg and Harry wanted to take Dr Shade in.

'Leech is on the side of money. We just have to make the strip so good it sells well, then it won't matter to him what it says.'

'I hope you're right, Greg, I really do. More tea?'

Outside, it got dark, and they worked through the scripts, making minor changes. Beyond the kitchen windows, shadows crept across the tiny garden towards the flat, their fingers reaching slowly for the concrete and tile. There were many small noises in the night, and it would have been easy to mistake the soft hiss of an aerosol paintspray for the popping of a high-powered airgun.

AUSSIE SOAP STAR GOT ME ON CRACK: Doomed schoolgirl's story – EXCLUSIVE – begins in the *Comet* today.

THE *COMET* LAW AND ORDER PULL-OUT. We ask top coppers, MPs, criminals and ordinary people what's to be done about rising crime?

BRIXTON YOBS SLASH WAR HERO PENSIONER: Is the birch the only language they understand? 'Have-a-Go' Tommy Barraclough, 76, thinks so. A special *Comet* poll shows that so do 69% of you readers.

DEREK LEECH TALKS STRAIGHT: Today: IMMIGRATION, CRIME, UNEMPLOYMENT. 'No matter what the whingers and moaners say, the simple fact is that Britain is an island. We are a small country and we only have room for the British. Everybody knows about the chronic housing shortage and the lack of jobs. The pro-open door partisans can't argue with the facts and figures.

'British citizenship is a privilege not a universal right. This simple man thinks we should start thinking twice before we give it away to any old Tom, Dick or Pandit who comes, turban in hand, to our country, hoping to make a fortune off the dole...'

WIN! WIN! WIN! LURVERLY DOSH! THE *COMET* GIVEAWAY GRID DISHES OUT THREE MILLION KNICKER! THEY SAID WE'D NEVER DO IT, BUT WE DID! MILLIONS MORE IN LURVERLY PRIZES MUST GO!

This is BRANDI ALEXANDER, 17, and she'll be seen without the football scarf in our ADULTS ONLY Sunday edition. BRANDI has just left school. Already, she has landed a part in a film, *Fiona Does the Falklands*. The part may be small, but hers aren't...

CATS TORTURED BY CURRYHOUSE KING?: What's really in that vindaloo, Mr Patel?

DID ELVIS DIE OF AIDS?: Our psychic reveals the truth!

GUARDIAN ANGEL KILLINGS CONTINUE: Scotland Yard Insiders Condemn Vigilante Justice.

The bodies of Malcolm Williams, 19, and Barry Tozer, 22, were identified yesterday by the Reverend Kenneth Hood, a spokesman for the West Indian community. The dead men were dumped in an underpass on the South London Attlee Estate. Both were shot at close range with a small-bore gun, execution-style. Inspector Mark Davey of the Metropolitan Police believes that the weapon used might be an airgun. This incident follows the identical killings of five black and Asian youths in recent months.

Williams and Tozer, like the other victims, had extensive police records. Williams served three months in prison last year for breaking and entering, and Tozer had a history of mugging, statutory rape, petty thieving and violence. It is possible that they were killed shortly after committing an assault. A woman's handbag was found nearby, it's contents scattered. Witnesses report that Williams and Tozer left The Flask, their local, when they couldn't pay for more drinks, and yet they had money on them when they were found.

The police are appealing for any witnesses to come forward. In particular, they would like to question the owner of the bag, who might well be able to identify the 'Guardian Angel' executioner. Previous appeals have not produced any useful leads.

A local resident who wishes to remain anonymous told our reporter, 'I hope they never catch the Guardian Angel. There are a lot more nigger b*st*rds with knives out there. I hope the Angel gets them all. Then maybe I can cash my pension at the post-office without fearing for my life.'

Coming Soon: BRITAIN'S NEW-OLD NEWSPAPER. CHURCHILL'S FAVOURITE READING IS BACK. DR SHADE *WILL* RETURN. At last, the EVENING has a HERO.

From the *Daily Comet*, Monday July the 1st, 1991

Saturday mornings were always quiet at comic conventions. Every time Greg went into the main hall there was a panel. All of them featured three quiet people nodding and chuckling while Neil Gaiman told all the jokes from his works-in-progress. He had heard them all in the bar the night before, and kept leaving for yet another turn around the dealers' room. They had him on a panel in the evening about reviving old characters: they were bringing back Tarzan, Grimly Feendish and Dan Dare, so Dr Shade would be in good company. At the charity auction, his first attempts at designing a new-look Dr Shade had fetched over £50, which must mean something.

He drifted away from the cardboard boxes full of overpriced American comic books in plastic bags to the more eccentric stalls which offered old movie stills, general interest magazines from the '40s and '50s (and, he realised with a chill, the '60s and '70s), odd items like *Stingray* jigsaws (only three pieces missing, £12.00) and *Rawhide* boardgames (£5.00), and digest-sized pulp magazines.

A dealer recognised him, probably from an earlier con, and said he might have something that would interest him. He had precisely the smugly discreet tone of a pimp. Bending down below his trestle table, which made him breath hard, he reached for a tied bundle of pulps and brought them up.

'You don't see these very often…'

Greg looked at the cover of the topmost magazine. *Dr Shade Monthly*. The illustration, a faded FitzGerald, showed the goggled and cloaked doctor struggling with an eight-foot neanderthal in the uniform of an SS officer, while the blonde Penny Stamp, dressed only in flimsy '40s foundation garments and chains, lay helpless on an operating table. INSIDE: 'Master of the Mutants' a complete novel by REX CASH. Also, 'Flaming Torture', 'The Laughter of Dr Shade' and 'Hank the Yank and the Hangman of Heidelberg'. April, 1945. A Badgerfield Publication.

Greg had asked Harry Lipman to come along to the con but the writer had had a few bad experiences at events like this and said he didn't want to 'mix with the looneys'. He knew Harry didn't have many of the old mags with his stuff in and that he had to buy these for him. Who knows, there might be a few ideas in them that could be re-used.

'Ten quid the lot?'

He handed over two fives and took the bundle, checking the spines to see that the dealer hadn't slipped in some *Reader's Digests* to bulk out the package. No, they were all *Dr Shades*, all from the '40s. He had an urge to sit down and read the lot.

Back in the hall, someone was lecturing an intently interested but pimple-plagued audience about adolescent angst in *The Teen Titans* and *X-Men*, and Greg wondered where he could get a cup of tea or coffee and a biscuit. Neil Gaiman, surrounded by acolytes, grinned at him and waved from across the room, signalling. Greg gestured his thanks. Neil had alerted him to the presence of

Hunt Sealey, a British comics entrepreneur he had once taken to court over some financial irregularities. Greg did not want to go through that old argument again. Avoiding the spherical Sealey, he stepped into a darkened room where a handful of white-faced young men with thick glasses were watching a Mexican horror-wrestling movie on a projection video. The tape was a third- or fourth-generation dupe, and the picture looked as if it were being screened at a tropical drive-in during the monsoon.

'Come, Julio,' said a deep American voice dubbed over the lip movements of a swarthy mad doctor, 'help me carry the cadaver of the gorilla to the incinerator.'

Nobody laughed. The video room smelled of stale cigarette smoke and spilled beer. The kids who couldn't afford a room in the hotel crashed out in here, undisturbed by the non-stop Z-movie festival. The only film Greg wanted to see (a French print of Georges Franju's *Les Yeux sans Visage*) was scheduled at the same time as his panel. Typical.

On the assumption that Sealey, who was known for the length of time he could hold a grudge, would be loitering in the hall harassing Neil, Greg sat on a chair and watched the movie. The mad doctor was transplanting gorilla hearts and a monster was terrorising the city, ripping the dresses off hefty *senoritas*. The heroine was a sensitive lady wrestler who wanted to quit the ring because she had put her latest opponent in a coma.

Greg got bored with the autopsy footage and the jumpy images, and looked around to see if anyone he knew was there. The audience were gazing at the screen like communicants at mass, the video mirrored in their spectacles, providing starlike pinpoints in the darkness.

He had been drawing a lot of darkness recently, filling in the shadows around Dr Shade, only the white of his lower face and the highlights of his goggles showing in the night as he stalked Dominick Dalmas through the mean streets of East London. His hand got tired after inking in the solid blacks of the strip.

Occasionally you saw Dr Chambers in the daytime, but 95 per cent of the panels were night scenes.

There was a glitch on the videotape and the film vanished for a few seconds, replaced by Nanette Newman waving a bottle of washing-up liquid. Nobody hooted or complained and the mad doctor's gorilla-man came back in an instant. A tomato-like eyeball was fished out, gravyish blood coursing down the contorted face of a bad actor with a worse toupee. Stock music as old as talking pictures thundered on the soundtrack. If it weren't for the violence, this could easily have been made in the '30s, when Donald Moncrieff's Dr Shade was in the hero business, tossing mad scientists out of tenth-storey windows and putting explosive airgun darts into Bolshies and rebellious natives.

Although his eyes were used to the dark, Greg thought he wasn't seeing properly. A corner of the room, behind the video, was as thickly black as any of his panels. To one side of the screen, he could dimly see the walls with their movie posters and fan announcements, a fire extinguisher hung next to a notice. But the other side of the room was just an impenetrable night.

He had a headache and there were dots in front of his eyes. He looked away from the dark corner and back again. It didn't disappear. But it did seem to move, easing itself away from the wall and expanding towards him. A row of seats disappeared. The screen shone brighter, dingy colours becoming as vivid as a comic book cover.

Greg clutched his *Dr Shades*, telling himself this was what came of too much beer, not enough food and too many late nights in the convention bar. Suddenly, it was very hot in the video room, as if the darkness were burning up, suffocating him...

A pair of glasses glinted in the dark. There was someone inside the shadow, someone wearing thick sunglasses. No, not glasses. Goggles.

He stood up, knocking his chair over. Somebody grumbled at the noise. On the screen, the Mexico City cops had shot the gorilla man dead and the mad doctor – his father – was being emotional about his loss.

The darkness took manshape, but not mansize. Its shadow head, topped by the shape of a widebrimmed hat, scraped the ceiling, its arms reached from wall to wall.

Only Greg took any notice. Everyone else was upset about the gorilla man and the mad doctor. Somewhere under the goggles, up near the light fixtures, a phantom white nose and chin were forming around the black gash of a humourless mouth.

Greg opened the door and stepped out of the video room, his heart spasming in its cage. Slamming the door on the darkness, he pushed himself into the corridor and collided with a tall, cloaked figure.

Suddenly angry, he was about to lash out verbally when he realised he knew who the man was. The recognition was like an ECT jolt.

He was standing in front of Dr Shade.

The Jew fled through the burning city, feeling a clench of dread each time a shadow fell over his heart. There was nowhere he could hide. Not in the underground railway stations that doubled as bomb shelters, not in the sewers with the other rats, not in the cells of the traitor police. The doctor was coming for him, coming to avenge the lies he had told, and there was nothing that could be done.

The all-clear had sounded, the drone of the planes was gone from the sky, and the streets were busy with firemen and panicking Londoners. Their homes were destroyed, their lilywhite lives ground into the mud. The Jew found it in his heart to laugh bitterly as he saw a mother in a nightdress, calling for her children outside the pile of smoking bricks that had been her house. His insidious kind had done their job too well, setting the Aryan races at each other's throats while they plotted with the

Soviet Russians and the heathen Chinee to dominate the grim world that would come out of this struggle. Germans dropped bombs on Englishmen, and the Jew smiled.

But, in this moment, he knew that success of the Conspiracy would mean nothing to him. Not while the night still had shadows. Not while there was a Dr Shade…

He leaned, exhausted, against a soot-grimed wall. The mark of Dr Shade was on him, a black handprint on his camelhair coat. The doctor's East End associates were dogging him, relaying messages back to their master, driving him away from the light, keeping him running through the night. There was no one to call him 'friend'.

A cloth-capped young man looked into the alley, ice-blue eyes penetrating the dark. He put his thumb and forefinger to his mouth and gave a shrill whistle.

'Ere, mateys, we gots us a Yid! Call fer the doc!'

There was a stampede of heavy boots. Almost reluctant to keep on the move, wishing for it all to be over, the murdering filth shoved himself away from the wall and made a run for the end of the alley. The wall was low, and he hauled himself up it onto a sloping roof. The East End boys were after him, broken bottles and shivs in their hands, but he made it ahead of them. He strode up the tiles, feeling them shift under his feet. Some came loose and fell behind him, into the faces of Shade's men.

Using chimneys to steady himself, the stinking guttershite ran across the rooftops. He had his revolver out, and fired blindly into the darkness behind him, panic tearing him apart from the inside. Then, he came to the end of his run.

He stood calmly, arms folded, his cloak flapping in the breeze, silhouetted sharply against the fiery skyline. The thin lips formed a smile, and the child-raping libellous Israelite scum knew he was justly dead.

'Hello Harry,' said Dr Shade.

DONALD MONCRIEFF, 'Dr Shade, Jew Killer'
(unpublished, 1942)

*　*　*

'Hello, Harry,' said Greg, jiggling the phone in the regulation hopeless attempt to improve a bad connection, 'I thought we'd been cut off...'

Harry sounded as if he were in Jakarta, not three stops away on the District Line. 'So there I was, face to goggles with Dr Shade.'

He could make it sound funny now, hours later.

'The guy was on his way to the masquerade. There are always people in weird outfits at these things. He had all the details right, airgun and all.'

Greg had called Harry from his hotel room to tell him about all the excitement the Return of Dr Shade was generating with the fans. Kids whose *parents* hadn't been born when the *Argus* went out of business were eagerly awaiting the comeback of the cloaked crimefighter.

'Obviously, the doc has percolated into our folk memory, Harry. Or maybe Leech is right. It's just time to have him back.'

His panel had gone well. The questions from the audience had almost all been directed to him, and he had had to field some to the other panelists so as not to hog the whole platform. The fans had been soliciting for information. Yes, Penny Stamp would be back, but she wouldn't be a girl reporter any more. Yes, the doctor's Rolls Royce 'Shadowshark' would be coming out of the garage, with more hidden tricks than ever. Yes, the doctor would be dealing with the contemporary problems of East London. When someone asked if the proprietor of the paper would be exerting any influence over the content of the strip, Greg replied 'well, he hasn't so far,' and got cheers by claiming, 'I don't think Dr Shade is a *Comet* reader, somehow.' Somebody even knew enough to ask him to compare the Donald Moncrieff Rex Cash with the Harry Lipman Rex Cash. He had conveyed best wishes to the con from Harry and praised the writer's still-active imagination.

At the other end of the line, Harry sounded tired. Sometimes,

Greg had to remind himself how old the man was. He wondered whether the call had woken him up.

'We've even had some American interest, maybe in republishing the whole thing as a monthly book, staggered behind the newspaper series. I'm having Tamara investigate. She thinks we can do it without tithing off too much of the money to Derek Leech, but rights deals are tricky. Also, Condé Nast, the corporate heirs of Street and Smith, have a long memory and still think Moncrieff ripped off The Shadow in the '30s. Still, it's worth going into.'

Harry tried to sound enthusiastic.

'Are you okay, Harry?'

He said so, but somehow Greg didn't believe him. Greg checked his watch. He had agreed to meet Neil and a few other friends in the bar in ten minutes. He said goodnight to Harry, and hung up.

Wanting to change his panelist's jacket for a drinker's pullover, Greg delved through the suitcase perched on the regulation anonymous armchair. He found the jumper he needed, and transferred his convention badge from lapel to epaulette. Under the suitcase, he found the bundle of *Dr Shade Monthly*s he had bought for Harry. He hadn't mentioned them on the phone.

Harry couldn't have got back to bed yet. He'd barely be in the hall. Greg stabbed the REDIAL button and listened to the clicking of the exchange. Harry's phone rang again.

The shadows in the room seemed longer. When Harry didn't pick up immediately, Greg's first thought was that something was wrong. He imagined coronaries, nasty falls, fainting spells, the infirmities of the aged. The telephone rang. Ten, twenty, thirty times.

Harry couldn't have got back to bed and fallen into a deep sleep in twenty seconds.

You also couldn't get a wrong number on a phone with a redial facility.

The phone was picked up at the other end.

'Hello,' said a female voice, young and hard, 'who's this then?'

'Harry,' Greg said. 'Where's Harry?'

''E's got a bit of a problem, mate,' the girl said. 'But we'll see to 'im.'

Greg was feeling very bad about this. The girl on the phone didn't sound like a concerned neighbour. 'Is Harry ill?'

A pause. Greg imagined silent laughter. There was music in the background. Not Harry Lipman music but tinny Metal, distorted by a cheap boombox and the telephone. Suddenly, Greg was down from his high, the good feeling and the alcohol washed out of his system.

'Hello?'

'Still here,' the girl said.

'Is Harry ill?'

'Well, I'll put it this way,' she said, 'we've sent for the doctor.'

Evidence has come to light linking Derek Leech, the man at the top of the pyramid, with a linked chain of dubious right-wing organisations here and abroad. A source inside the Leech organisation, currently gearing up to launch a new national evening paper, revealed to our reporter, DUNCAN EYLES, that while other press barons diversify into the electronic media and publishing, Derek Leech has his eye on a more direct manner of influencing the shape of the nation.

'Derek has been underwriting the election campaigns of parliamentary candidates in the last few by-elections,' the source told us. 'They mostly lost their deposits. Patrick Massinghame, the Britain First chairman who later rejoined the Tories, was one. The idea was not to take a seat but to use the campaigns to disseminate propaganda. The *Comet* has always been anti-immigration, pro-law-and-order, anti-anything-socialist, pro-hanging-and-flogging, pro-military spending, pro-political-censorship. But the campaigns were able to be rabidly so.'

Leech, who has regularly dismissed similar allegations as 'lunatic conspiracy theories', refused to comment on documents leaked to us which give facts and figures. In addition to funding Patrick Massinghame and others of his political stripe, Leech has contributed heavily to such bizarre causes as the White Freedom Crusade, which channels funds from British and American big business into South Africa, the English Liberation Front, who claim that immigrants from the Indian Sub-Continent and the Caribbean constitute 'an army of occupation' and should be driven out through armed struggle, the Revive Capital Punishment lobby, and even Caucasian supremacist thrash metal band Whitewash, whose single 'Blood, Iron and St George' was banned by the BBC and commercial radio stations but still managed to reach Number 5 in the independent charts.

Even more disturbing in the light of these allegations, is the paramilitary nature of the security force Leech is employing to guard the pyramid that is at the heart of his empire. Recruiting directly from right-wing youth gangs, often through advertisements placed in illiterate but suspiciously well produced and printed fanzines distributed at football matches, the Leech organisation has been assembling what can only be described as an army of yobs to break the still-continuing print union pickets in docklands. Our source informs us that the pyramid contains a well-stocked armoury, as if the proprietor of the *Comet* and the forthcoming *Argus* were expecting a siege. Rumour has it that Leech has even invested in a custom-made Rolls Royce featuring such unusual extras as bullet-proof bodywork, James Bond-style concealed rocket launchers, a teargas cannon and bonnet-mounted stilettos.

Derek Leech can afford all the toys he wants. But perhaps it's about time we started to get worried about the games he wants to play...

Searchlight, August 1991

* * *

The minicab driver wouldn't take him onto the estate no matter what he offered to pay and left him stranded him at the kerb. At night, the place was even less inviting than by day. There were wire-mesh protected lights embedded in concrete walls every so often, but skilled vandals had got through to them. Greg knew that dashing into the dark maze would do no good, and forced himself to study the battered, graffiti-covered map of the estate that stood by the road. He found Harry's house on the map easily. By it, someone had drawn a stickman hanging from a gallows. It was impossible to read a real resemblance into the infants' scrawl of a face, but Greg knew it was supposed to represent Harry.

He walked towards the house, so concerned for Harry Lipman that he forgot to be scared for himself. That was a mistake.

They came from an underpass and surrounded him. He got an impression of Union Jack T-shirts and shaven heads. Studded leather straps wrapped around knuckles. They only seemed to hit him four or five times, but it was enough.

He turned his head with the first blow and felt his nose flatten into his cheek. Blood was seeping out of his instantly swollen nostrils and he was cut inside his mouth. He shook his head, trying to dislodge the pain. They stood back, and watched him yelp blood onto his chest. He was still wearing his convention tag.

Then one of them came in close, breathed foully in his face, and put a knee into his groin. He sagged, crying out, and felt his knees going. They kicked his legs, and he was on the ground. His ribs hurt.

'Come on, P,' one of them said, ''e's 'ad 'is. Let's scarper.'

'Nahh,' said a girl – the one he had talked to on the telephone? – as she stepped forwards, ''es not properly done yet.'

Greg pressed his nostrils together to stanch the blood and

realised his nose wasn't broken. There was a lump rising on his cheek, though. He looked into the girl's face.

She was young, maybe fifteen or sixteen, and there was blonde fur on her skull. Her head was lumpy and the skinhead cut made her child's face seem small, as if painted on an easter egg. He had seen her the last time he was here. She wore Britannia earrings, and had a rare right-way-round swastika tattooed in blue on her temple.

'Come on…'

P smiled at him and licked her lips like a cat. 'Do you need telling any more, Mr Artist?'

The others were bunched behind her. She was small and wiry, but they were like hulks in the shadows.

'Do you get the picture?'

Greg nodded. Anything, just so long as they let him alone. He had to get to Harry.

'Good. Draw well, 'cause we'll be watching over you.'

Lights came on in a house opposite and he got a clearer look at their faces. Apart from P, they weren't kids. They were in the full skinhead gear, but on them it looked like a disguise. There were muffled voices from the house, and the lights went off again.

'Kick 'im, Penelope,' said someone.

P smiled again. 'Nahh, Bazzo. 'E knows what's what, now. We don't want to hurt 'im. 'E's important. Ain't ya, Mr Artist?'

Greg was standing up again. There was nothing broken inside his head, but he was still jarred. His teeth hurt and he spat out a mouthful of blood.

'Dirty beast.'

His vision was wobbling. P was double-exposed, a bubble fringe shimmering around her outline.

'Goodnight,' said P. 'Be good.'

Then they were gone, leaving only shadows behind them. Greg ran across the walkway, vinegar-stained pages of the *Comet* swirling about his ankles. Harry's front door was hanging open, the chain broken, and the hallway was lit up.

Greg found him in his kitchen, lying on the floor, his word processor slowly pouring a long manuscript onto him. The machine rasped as it printed out.

He helped Harry sit up, and got him a teacup of water from the tap. They hadn't hurt him too badly, although there was a bruise on his forehead. Harry was badly shaken. Greg had never seen him without his teeth in and he was drooling like a baby, unconsciously wiping his mouth on his cardigan sleeve. He was trying to talk but couldn't get the words out.

The phone was ripped out of the wall. The printer was scratching Greg's nerves. He sat at the desk and tried to work out how to shut it off without losing anything. He wasn't familiar with this model.

Then he looked at the continuous paper. It was printing out a draft of the first month of new Dr Shade scripts. Greg couldn't help but read what was coming out of the machine.

It wasn't what he had been working on. It wasn't even in script form. But Harry had written it and he would be expected to draw it.

Unable to control his shaking, Greg read on.

'I'm sorry,' said Harry. 'It was Him. They brought Him here. He was here before Donald started writing Him. He'll always be here.'

Greg turned to look at the old man. Harry was standing over him, laying a hand on his shoulder. Greg shook his head and Harry sadly nodded.

'It's true. We've always known, really.'

Beyond Harry was his hallway. Beyond that, the open door allowed Greg to see into the night. The shadowman was out there, laughing…

…the laughter faded into the noise of the printer.

Greg read on.

* * *

He thought for a moment before selecting the face he would wear tonight. The Chambers identity was wearing thin, limiting him too much. These were troubled times and stricter methods were required. He considered all the people he had been, listed the names, paged through their faces.

Sitting behind the desk at the tip of the glass and steel pyramid, he felt the thrill of power. Out there in the night cowered the crack dealers and the anarchists, the blacks and the yellows, the traitors and the slackers. Tonight they would know he was back.

The press baron was a useful face. It had helped him gain a purchase on these new times, given him a perspective on the sorry state of the nation.

He thought of the true patriots who had been rejected. Oswald Mosley, Unity Mitford, William Joyce, Donald Moncrieff. And the false creatures who had succeeded them. This time, things would be different. There would be no bowing to foreign interests.

He fastened his cloak at his throat, and peeled off the latest mask. Smiling at the thin-lipped reflection in the dark mirror of the glass, he pulled on the goggles.

The private lift was ready to take him to the Shadowshark. He holstered his trusty airgun.

Plunging towards his destiny, he exulted in the thrill of the chase. He was back.

Accept no pale imitations. Avoid the lesser men, the men of wavering resolves, of dangerous weaknesses.

He was the original.

REX CASH, *The Return of Dr Shade* (1991)

Greg was at his easel, drawing. There was nothing else he could do. No matter how much he hated the commission, he had to splash the black ink, had to fill out the sketches. It was all he had left of himself. In the panel, Dr Shade was breaking up a meeting of the conspirators. African communists were infiltrating

London, foully plotting to sabotage British business by blowing up the Stock Exchange. But the doctor would stop them. Greg filled in the thick lips of Papa Dominick, the voodoo commissar, and tried to get the fear in the villain's eyes as the shadowman raised his airgun.

'Did you hear,' P said, 'they're giving me a chance to write for the *Argus*. The Stamp of Truth, they'll call my column. I can write about music or politics or fashion or anything. I'll be a proper little girl reporter.'

Crosbie told him Derek Leech was delighted at the way the strip was going. Dr Shade was really taking off. There was Dr Shade graffiti all over town, and he had started seeing youths with Dr Shade goggles tattooed around their eyes. A comics reviewer who had acclaimed *Fat Chance* as a masterpiece described the strip as 'racist drivel'. He hadn't been invited to any conventions recently, and a lot of his old friends would cross the street to avoid him. Greg's telephone rang rarely, now. It was always Crosbie. To his surprise, Tamara had cut herself out of the 10 per cent after the first week of the *Argus* and told him to find other representation. He never heard from Harry, just received the scripts by special messenger. Greg could imagine the writer disconsolately tapping out stories in Donald Moncrieff's style at his Amstrad. He knew exactly how the other man felt.

He had the radio on. The riots were still flaring up. The police were concerned by a rash of airgun killings but didn't seem to be doing much about them. It appeared that the victims were mainly rabble-rousing ringleaders, although not a few West Indian and Asian community figures had been killed or wounded. Kenneth Hood, a popular vicar, had tried to calm down the rioters and been shot in the head. He wasn't expected to live and two policemen plus seven 'rioters' had died in the violent outburst that followed the attempt on his life. Greg imagined the shadowman on the rooftops, taking aim, hat pulled low, cloak streaming like demon wings.

Greg drew the Shadowshark, sliding through the city night, hurling aside the petrol-bomb-throwing minions of Papa Dominick. 'The sun has shone for too long on the open schemes of the traitors,' Harry had written, 'but night must fall… and with the night comes Shade.'

Early on, Greg had tried to leave the city but they were waiting for him at the station. The girl called P and some of the others. They had escorted him home. They called themselves Shadeheads now, and wore hats and cloaks like the doctor, tattered black over torn T-shirts, drainpipe jeans and steel-toed Doc Martens.

P was with him most of the time now. At first, she had just been in the corner of his vision, watching over him. Finally, he'd given in and called her over. Now, she was in the flat, making her calls to the doctor, preparing his meals, warming his single bed. They'd pushed him enough and now he had to be reassured, cajoled. He worked better that way.

Derek Leech was on the radio now, defending the record of his security staff during the riots. He had pitched in to help the police, using his news helicopters to direct the action and sending his people into the fighting like troops. The police were obviously not happy, but public opinion was forcing them to accept the tycoon's assistance. Leech made a remark about 'the spirit of Dr Shade' and Greg's hand jumped, squirting ink across the paper.

'Careful, careful,' said P, dipping in with a tissue and delicately wiping away the blot, saving the artwork. Her hair was growing out. She'd never be a *Comet* Knock-Out but she was turning into a surprisingly housewifely, almost maternal, girl. In the end, Shadeheads believed a woman's place was with her legs spread and her hands in dishwater.

In the final panel, Dr Shade was standing over his vanquished enemies, holding up his fist in a defiant salute. White fire was reflected in his goggles.

The news was over, and the new Crüsaders single came on.

'There'll Always Be an England.' It was climbing the charts.

Greg looked out of the window. He imagined fires on the horizon.

He took a finer pen and bent to do some detail work. He wished he had held out longer. He wished he'd taken more than one beating. Sometimes, he told himself he was doing it for Harry, to protect the old man. But that was bullshit. They hadn't been Reggie Barton and Hank Hemingway. Imaginative torture hadn't been necessary and they hadn't sworn never to give in, never to break down, never to knuckle under. A few plain old thumps and the promise of a few more had been enough. Plus more money a month than either of them had earned in any given three years of their career.

Next week, the doctor would execute Papa Dominick. Then, he would do something about the strikers, the scroungers, the slackers, the scum…

A shadow fell over the easel, cloak spreading around it. Greg turned to look up at the goggled face of his true master.

Dr Shade was pleased with him.

GOING TO SERIES

MEMO
From: **Tiny Chiselhurst, producer/creator**
To: **April Treece, junior researcher**
Re: **Untiled Docusoap/Gameshow Pilot**

Here's the final draft of the flyer. Every word approved by Dr
Wendel and Miss Lark as calculated to reach the cross-section of
personality types we need.

EVERYDAY MEGASTARS WANTED
Is this you? 18-45, sexy, extrovert, killer body, unconventional,
tagged 'difficult' by lesser mortals, ambitious, unattached,
competitive, 'bonkers', up for anything?
Apply: Mythwrhn Productions
Box 101, Leech Pyramid Plaza, London Docklands.

As a classified ad, this is to go into the following periodicals:
Big Bazookas, the *Sunday Comet*, the *Nazi Atrocities* part-work,
Young Offender, *Pop Hitz* and *Shy Girl Monthly*. As a flyer, it is to
be distributed via inner-city clubs, comic shops, student union
buildings, social security offices and police stations. We agree that we
should target especially the waiting rooms of probation officers and

court-approved psycho-therapists, the business places of drugs and weapons dealers, abortion and VD clinics, all-night casualty wards, Young Conservative meetings, and pubs that cater to the motorcycle, rugby football, slag-on-the-pull and stockbroking communities. Word from the top of the Pyramid is that Cloud 9 (Derek Leech!) is really hyped on this project, so let's get things moving.

[NB: this is for sending to the applicants only, and should under no circumstances be confused with the real series proposal, which is available on an eyes only need-to-know basis to security-cleared insiders at mythwrhn and cloud 9 – Tiny]

SERIES PROPOSAL

This seven-part (initial run) series combines three of the most popular (and, let's face it, economical) TV formats of the last ten years: fly-on-the-wall docusoap, slags-on-holiday mock doc and sci-fi/adventure gameshow. A group of charismatic, sexy young chicks and chaps, strangers to each other, are brought together in a luxurious, Bond-style environment (country estate, mountaintop hunting lodge, beach house) and have to spend a week together. Cut off from civilisation, the contestants (subjects, stars?) are in contact with a host – we think we can get US smartmouth obonxio-comic Barry Gatlin, but other options are Ruby Wax or someone off *Star Trek* – who communicates via video-link each evening and sets tasks and competitions, which range from puzzle-solving exercises through treasure hunting on the grounds of the luxury retreat and harmless combat games to how-low-can-you-go? gross-out or endurance dares. Meanwhile, the stars are on camera day and night; we trust that days of strenuous competition will be followed by evenings of unwinding in wild, entertaining and provocative manners. Over the course of the week, we will see how each contestant scores, in every imaginable way.

Tiny Chiselhurst, Creator and Owner

* * *

Dear Potential Megastar,

Thank you for your interest. Please fill in the attached form and
return it to me at Mythwrhn Productions.

This isn't an exam: the answers you give aren't right or wrong, but
will help us determine whether you are the type of person for our
show. Don't think too hard or try to give answers you think we
want. Be yourself.

All forms are confidential.

Best wishes,
April Treece, Researcher

....

ARE YOU A MEGASTAR?

1: Please write your name, age, contact details, next of kin,
and rough annual income.

2: Sex?
... male.
... female.
... yes, please!
... don't know.

3: How many jobs have you had since leaving school?

4: Do you feel yourself to be...
... attractive to the opposite sex.
... unattractive to the opposite sex.
... attractive to the same sex.
... horny.

... a love god/goddess in the flesh.

5: How many sex partners have you had per year, on average, since the age of twelve?

6: Do you feel yourself to be...
... more intelligent than the average.
... less intelligent than the average.
... of average intelligence.
... too intelligent to be measured by this stupid question.
... a real Brainiac.
... a spoon.

7: If attacked in your home, what household items would you use to defend yourself?

8: Which of these describes you?
... a conformist.
... a maverick.
... a team-player.
... scary.
... a tosser.
... a leader.
... a nurturer.
... a bitch.
... the best there is at what you do.
... a disappointment.

9: Have you ever broken a law and not been caught? If so, please give details.

10: Would you be willing to do severe harm to...
... an enemy soldier on a battlefield.
... a violent criminal threatening your mother.

... a member of parliament.

... a spastic.

... your mother.

... a wounded animal.

... a stranger.

... no one at all, under any circumstances.

... a television personality.

... a former boy or girlfriend who treated you badly.

11: Would you have sex with someone unappealing just because they were famous, notorious, physically unusual, or on television? If you have, please give details.

12: When Bambi's mother was shot, what was your reaction?

... it was very tragic and sad.

... the bitch got what she deserved.

... venison pies, yum!

... Bambi ought to avenge his family.

... Who's Bambi?

13: Have you ever written an anonymous letter or made a prank phone call? If so, please give details.

14: When you broke up with your last boy or girlfriend, was it...

... just one of those things.

... all for the best, really.

... your fault.

... their fault.

... a prelude to revenge.

... one more fucking thing on your plate.

... never had a boy or girlfriend, and don't much like the sound of it.

15: Would you play a computer game called *Dunblane Massacre*?

16: Have you ever…

… performed in a karaoke pub.

… had sex with two or more partners simultaneously.

… experienced memory loss after alcohol or drug intake.

… been on television.

… considered joining the armed forces.

… had sex in a public place.

… used terms of racial ('nigger', 'chink') or sexual ('cunt', 'queer') abuse in general conversation.

… deliberately botched a job interview?

… stalked a celebrity.

… got your own back on someone who had done you a wrong.

17: Which of the Spice Girls would you most like to rape?

18: Do you believe in…

… UFO abductions.

… Our Lord, Jesus Christ.

… other people's pain.

… microwaves.

… ghosts.

… an eye for an eye.

… Swedish Sin.

… yourself.

… turning the other cheek.

… capital punishment.

19: When was the last time you were really happy? Please give details. If never, please give details.

20: Could you take a week off from your life/work/family to star in a television series? Please answer honestly, to save time later.

* * *

PRODUCTION SUB-MEETING, No. 19
PRESENT, for MYTHWRHN PRODUCTIONS: **April Treece (Featured Researcher), Claire Bates (Minion), Davinda Paquignet (Recording Angel).**

BATES: Can I just say, off the record, how much I *hate* this proposal.

TREECE: Get in the queue, Claire. Tiny's got this bonnet bee that they love it at the top of the Pyramid. It's all the things Derek Leech, our ultimate lord and master at Cloud 9 Television, is supposed to be keen on. Cheap, crass, cruel and compulsive.

BATES: And crap!

TREECE: You might say that. I couldn't possibly comment.

BATES: Dav, stop writing this down!

PAQUIGNET: Sorry, force of habit.

BATES: Ape, have you sorted through the completed forms?

TREECE: God, yes.

BATES: Where did we find these sickos?

TREECE: Milling about in general population.

BATES: 'Which of the Spice Girls would you most like to rape?' What sort of question is that. A bit sex-specific, surely.

TREECE: The responses are 75 per-cent male.

BATES: Sur-prise.

TREECE: So far as we can tell. Those who ticked 'yes, please' for 'sex?' are sometimes hard to work out. And those are our pass applicants.

BATES: They'll be men. Or really dim tarts.

TREECE: A frightening number of women responded. Some skipped the Spice question. Some didn't. A few nominated male equivalents. You wouldn't think anyone could have those fantasies about Frank Dobson or...

BATES: Ugh! Don't say any more! I don't want to know!

PAQUIGNET: I didn't think it was possible to have the amount of sex most of these people say they have.

TREECE: Not if you work in television, it isn't.

BATES: Too bloody right.

TREECE: Dr Wendel says to divide that answer by ten to get a proper figure. Except for the ones who claim to be virgins. Half of them aren't lying.

PAQUIGNET: What about the lad who gave names and addresses? Are we supposed to phone the victims up to check him out?

TREECE: No wonder he can't keep a steady girlfriend.

BATES: If you had a party, would you want any of these people to come?

TREECE: God, no. But this is Tiny's baby, and we have to carry it to term, no matter how we feel. Look, Claire, it's a looney idea and even Derek Leech wouldn't seriously consider putting it out. We're more likely to see live bullfighting on British TV than this horror, so we won't get hurt. Let's go as far with it as we have to before Tiny, inevitably, changes his mind.

BATES: I don't want my name on any of the documentation, or a credit on any proposal or pilot. I'm serious. I don't want a paper trail connecting me to this... this atrocity. Dav, stop bloody writing!

....

Dear Loser

Thank you for your interest. Unfortunately, you are not the person we – or anyone else – are looking for at this time.

We wish you joy in your continued obscurity.

Sincerely,
April Treece, Rejecter-in-Chief

* * *

MEMO
From: **April Treece, senior researcher**
To: **Tiny Chiselhurst, producer/creator**
Re: **Horrible People Pilot**

We sent out entry forms to the first 5,000 people who responded to the ad or the flyer and got 2,389 completed returns. I passed on the 968 papers with 'yes, please!' ticked for Question Two – the famous 'trigger signal' – to Dr Wendel and Miss Lark, who have evaluated them all and selected 178 'possibles'. I'm astonished not only at the number of people out there who have sent anonymous letters but are proud enough of the fact to boast about it at enormous length, continuing onto the other side of the paper, to strangers. As requested, I've sent a curt rejection letter to all 178 and ignored the rest.

I still don't believe this is going to fly, or that even Cloud 9 will broadcast it if it does. That said, reading over the completed forms, I'm starting to understand why audiences might actually enjoy watching the show. Are real people really this awful? The runners have stuck up their favourite forms on the message board. At the moment, the champion is the Sporty Spice fan who would see off an attacker by taking a mouthful of bleach and offering a blow-job, though my clear winner is the 'nurturer' guy or girl (ambiguous name and no helpful answer to Q2) who claims to have shagged seven of Dr Who's companions (not including K-9, I trust). Do we have a title yet?

....

MEMO
From: **Tiny Chiselhurst, producer/creator**
To: **April Treece, chief researcher**
Re: **Bedlam Unplugged**

Any of the 'possibles' who get back to us to complain about the 'Dear Loser' letters should be invited for interview. Please note whether applicants complain via e-mail, telephone or the post, and pass print-outs, recordings and photocopies to Dr Wendel and Miss Lark. Anyone not classed as a 'possible' who complains we haven't got back to them should also be considered for interview if the complaint shows the proper character type. Taking the usual wastage into account, we only need a dozen or so strong candidates.

I know the troops have their doubts about this, Ape, but I've got a gut feeling that it is going to be a winner! At present, Cloud 9 inclining towards a neutral title like *A Week Off* or *Microcosm*, though I'm all for something as blunt as *It's Madhouse!* or *The Pit* and cleverclogs Bender has voted for *The Raft of the Medusa*. How does one go about offering someone a blow-job if one has a mouthful of bleach? Sign language. And if you threw a brick in the Soho House, you'd be lucky to hit someone who *hadn't* shagged seven of Dr Who's companions. Onwards and upwards!

....

INTERVIEW TRANSCRIPT, NO. 17.
APPLICANT: Harry 'Donger' Bennett, 32.
FOR MYTHWRHN: Tiny Chiselhurst, Dr Vernon Wendel, Myra Lark, April Treece.

LARK: Harry…
BENNETT: Everyone calls me 'Donger'. Ever since school.
LARK: Ah, Donger… first, we must apologise for the mix-up with the letter.
BENNETT: So you should. Nearly missed your chance there, didn't you?
LARK: Indeed.
BENNETT: But I like your whole approach, really. 'Dear Loser'.

No poncing about there. Puts the losers right in their place. The real losers. I like to see that.

LARK: You describe yourself as competitive?

BENNETT: No. I would describe myself as a winner. It's just a fact of life. Ever since school.

LARK: You did well in school?

BENNETT: Too right. Fighting them off, I was. Had half the Sixth Form, and a couple of the younger teachers. The beginning of a great career.

LARK: And academically?

BENNETT: Rugby, football, basketball. Everything. Except cricket. That's for poofs.

LARK: You don't like, uh, homosexuals?

BENNETT: Show me a bloke who says he does and I'll show you a poof. It's not a natural thing, is it? Whatever they say these days.

LARK: You've never been married?

BENNETT: I've been engaged a couple of times, if that's what it takes to get the cork to pop.

LARK: It's important that you be unattached, for the show. Do you have a girlfriend?

BENNETT: A couple, actually. But no one I can't chuck if something tasty comes along.

LARK: You understand, then, that there's a certain standard of, ah, wildness expected on shows like this.

BENNETT: I've seen my share. Holidays in the sun. Drunken tarts gagging for it. Is this like that?

LARK: There's an element of that format, but there's also a game aspect, a competitive streak. Physical competition.

BENNETT: *Blind Date* meets *Gladiators*?

LARK: You might say that. You look as if you could look after yourself.

BENNETT: I've had my share of scrapes. I come out on top. By any means necessary, if you know what I mean and I think you do.

LARK: You work for an estate agent?

BENNETT: I work *as* an estate agent. It's just what I do in the days. History is made at night.

LARK: Do you like your job?

BENNETT: I like helping people. Setting families on the road to home-ownership.

LARK: Really. Really?

BENNETT: Well, no. You're sharp. That's what we're supposed to say. I like the push and the commission. There are so many ways to make something work to your advantage. That side of it is fun, but there's always a problem with the pillocks.

LARK: The pillocks?

BENNETT: Buyers, sellers, the lot of them. Pillocks. Always pulling out at the last minute, or screaming that they've been rooked, that they weren't told something it was their business to find out. You know the sort. Pillocks.

CHISELHURST: Donger, do you find April attractive?

BENNETT: Phwoarr!

TREECE: Really, Tiny.

BENNETT: No, fair question. You look very good for your age, Miss Treece. April. Smart. Good clothes. I like that. Not like some of the shag-slags. Some women put on a suit and look dikey, but not you.

CHISELHURST: If Dr Wendel came at you in a pub with a knife, could you take him?

BENNETT: No offence, but yes.

WENDEL: You might be surprised.

BENNETT: Like I said, I'm a winner. If he had a knife and I didn't, I'd bottle him. End of story. It's not even that he's older and smaller, but it's that he hasn't got the heart. Most people haven't. Too squeamish.

CHISELHURST: Thank you, Harry... ah, Donger. We'll be in touch.

BENNETT: Have I passed? Is there anyone behind the mirror?

CHISELHURST: We have enjoyed this interview.

BENNETT: I'm in, aren't I? I bloody knew it. You won't regret this. You need me. I'm a natural for your show, what's it called?

TREECE: Provisionally, *It's a Madhouse!* It may change.

BENNETT: *It's a Madhouse!*, yeah. I like that. Anything can happen in the next half hour. Anything.

CHISELHURST: April will show you out, ah, 'Donger'.

BENNETT: Excellent. I'll be back. Ka-poww!

....

INTERVIEW TRANSCRIPT, NO. 34.
APPLICANT: **Shona Murtaugh, 24**
FOR MYTHWRHN: **Tiny Chiselhurst, Dr Vernon Wendel, Myra Lark, April Treece.**

WENDEL: So, Shona…

MURTAUGH: [high-pitched giggles]

WENDEL: I beg your pardon.

MURTAUGH: 'So, Shona'. Sounds funny like that. [high-pitched giggles] Are you all right. Look like you've swallowed a lemon, you do.

WENDEL: It'll pass.

MURTAUGH: [high-pitched giggles]

[noise of glasses and bottles rattling on table]

WENDEL: I beg your pardon.

MURTAUGH: You're funny, you are. You've got to have a laugh, haven't you, though. [high-pitched giggles]

WENDEL: It's not actually a physiological necessity, but there may be some psychological explanation.

MURTAUGH: You what? You talk mental, you do. [high-pitched giggles]

CHISELHURST: We were interested in your sexual history.

MURTAUGH: [extremely high-pitched giggles]

CHISELHURST: Well, Shona, we were. You seem to have been an unusually busy girl.

MURTAUGH: I just like… [high-pitched giggles]

WENDEL: We're not here to judge you.

MURTAUGH: Yes, you are. To see if I'm right for your show.

[noise of bracelets clattering]

WENDEL: Well, of course, in that sense, you're right.

MURTAUGH: You should watch what you say. People might think you were taking liberties. People might not like that. People might not like that at all, thank you very much indeed. I should cocoa.

[thump on table]

WENDEL: I apologise.

MURTAUGH: So you should, so you should. [high-pitched giggles] I can't help it. It's your face. You look like a bearded collie. I think I'll wet my knickers. I'm mad, me. You must think I'm dreadful. Sorry.

[faint grinding of teeth]

LARK: Others have noted the, ah, resemblance between Dr Wendel and a dog.

MURTAUGH: [high-pitched giggles] I'll do myself an injury at this rate. You're a funny mob, aren't you. Not outright funny like Jim Davidson, but it's the way you say things, all sly and clever but with hidden meanings. It's all there, isn't it? You must have enough cleverness to get to the moon in this room, eh? All to get to the bottom of me. It don't seem right. I should be trying to get to the bottom of you.

TREECE: You're not working at the moment.

MURTAUGH: I was sacked from my last place, at the DSS. Went from one side of the counter to the other. Something will come along. It always does. I'm good at getting jobs, not so good at keeping them. [high-pitched giggles] This is like a job interview, isn't it?

WENDEL: There are similarities. But there are differences.

MURTAUGH: That sounds cryptic. [high-pitched giggles] So, do I get it?

CHISELHURST: You're short-listed, certainly.

MURTAUGH: [high-pitched giggles]

CHISELHURST: April will show you out.

MURTAUGH: Ta ta for now.

[noise of leaving]

TREECE: What was that girl on? Laughing gas?

LARK: Every time she went off, I felt it in my fillings. It's quite extraordinary.

TREECE: All the dogs in the area have gone mad.

CHISELHURST: I think she's a natural for *It's a Madhouse!*.

TREECE: You can't put Shona on television, Tiny. There'd be bomb threats.

CHISELHURST: Ape, that girl is a star. Her funeral will be bigger than Diana's.

....

EXTRACT FROM INTERVIEW TRANSCRIPT, NO. 41.
APPLICANT: **MARTIN LEIGH, 39**
FOR MYTHWRHN: **Tiny Chiselhurst, Dr Vernon Wendel, Myra Lark, April Treece.**

LEIGH: Prison's not so bad, once you've made your mark. You just have to let them know where you are on the totem pole. You pick out some old villain, some big nob from years ago who still thinks he's got it, and you take him apart. Mark his face, put him in the infirmary, get the boot in. Then you take what was his, make it yours. Earn some respect. You can come out ahead, if you've got good currency. Fags and smack, mostly, but you can build an empire on a good source of chocolate.

TREECE: You have a lot of tattoos.

LEIGH: More than you can see. Turns you on, does it? All the birds like ink. And, inside, some of the fellers. You'd think it'd make a difference, but after a while. Well, one hole's as good as another.

WENDEL: And so, how long were you a warder?

LEIGH: About five years. After the Paras and the SAS wouldn't have me, it seemed a decent option. You wouldn't think the Paras and the SAS would be soft, would you? I've had ex-Paras on my block and made them whine and beg. Shows you how much tests and interviews count for anything.

....

EXTRACT FROM INTERVIEW TRANSCRIPT, NO. 72.
APPLICANT: ANDREA D'ARBANVILLIERS-HOLMES, 19
FOR MYTHWRHN: **Tiny Chiselhurst, Dr Vernon Wendel, Myra Lark, April Treece.**

LARK: What are you looking for in a man, Andrea?
D'ARBANVILLIERS-HOLMES: Good shoes are a sign.
LARK: Of what?
D'ARBANVILLIERS-HOLMES: Status, you might call it. There are other giveaways. Like, if he has a good post code but only owns a flat. I mean, if he hasn't got enough to buy a house by now, things are hardly likely to get better.
LARK: Do you believe in romance?
D'ARBANVILLIERS-HOLMES: Yes, of course. But it's easy to come by, isn't it. There are always blokes falling over their willies to get to you. After a while, you have to impose stricter criteria. It's not money in and of itself, it's the things that come with it.
LARK: Do you believe in marriage?
D'ARBANVILLIERS-HOLMES: Absolutely. That's why I'm so careful about who I get married to. And about who I hop into bed with. It can't be just anybody, you know.
TREECE: Andrea, why do you want to be on television?
D'ARBANVILLIERS-HOLMES: Well, it's advertising, isn't it? I hope to make an impression on the right people.

* * *

EXTRACT FROM INTERVIEW TRANSCRIPT, NO. 108.
APPLICANT: **DONOVAN WYKE, 27**
FOR MYTHWRHN: **Tiny Chiselhurst, Dr Vernon Wendel, Myra Lark, April Treece.**

WENDEL: I put it to you, Donovan, that you are a habitual fantasist, a chancer who drifts through life dreaming of the big scores but inevitably botches even the petty scams, a bloodsucker who has exploited and betrayed every human connection you have ever made, a man unable to understand even the concepts of honour and fidelity, a compulsive liar with no conscience about wild promises made and broken, a congenital screw-up who is lucky not to have been knifed in an alley or wound up living on the streets begging for spare change to feed your crack habit.

WYKE: Well, I suppose if you were being hardcore about it, but there are explanations.

CHISELHURST: Welcome to *It's a Madhouse!*, Donny.

WYKE: You won't regret this. I can promise you that.

....

EXTRACT FROM INTERVIEW TRANSCRIPT, NO. 125.
APPLICANT: **PETRA KIDNER, 22**
FOR MYTHWRHN: **Tiny Chiselhurst, Dr Vernon Wendel, Myra Lark, April Treece.**

KIDNER: There's just something sexy about fire. I feel it in my clit, in my nipples, in the scar tissue on my inner thigh and upper back. I love everything about fire. The smoke, the flames, the heat, the crackle. Every month, I take off my eyebrows. See. The pain is there, a part of it, but very minor. I just like to see things burn.

LARK: Things?

KIDNER: Things, *mostly*. But there's nothing like it, you know. The smell, the texture, the taste. Burning flesh. It gets to me. Does that make me weird? I'm not, you know. I like a cup of tea and *EastEnders* and always send my Mum a box of chocs on Mother's Day. Some girls love one particular pop group or a particular type of bloke. With me, it's different. It's fire.

LARK: So what is your favourite pop song?

KIDNER: [laughs] What else? Jose Feliciano, 'Come on Baby, Light My Fire'.

....

EXTRACT FROM INTERVIEW TRANSCRIPT, NO. 128.
APPLICANT: **JOSHUA BREW, 22**
FOR MYTHWRHN: **Tiny Chiselhurst, Dr Vernon Wendel, Myra Lark, April Treece.**

CHISELHURST: You complained that we hadn't responded to your entry form?

BREW: IT'S NOT *RIGHT* THAT PEOPLE SHOULD BE TREATED THAT WAY.

CHISELHURST: We explained that your form was lost in the post.

BREW: YES, I ACCEPT THAT *NOW*.

CHISELHURST: But when you phoned the duty officer, you made quite an impression. That's a distinctive voice you've got there.

BREW: WHEN YOU'RE USED TO PREACHING THE *WORD OF OUR LORD JESUS CHRIST* AT *HEATHEN POP FESTIVALS*, YOU NEED A BIT OF *LUNG POWER*. I DO BREATHING *EXERCISES*.

CHISELHURST: You'll forgive me for saying this, but you don't seem like the normal type of young person we've been seeing for this show.

BREW: JUST BECAUSE I'M A *CHRISTIAN* DOESN'T MEAN I DON'T LIKE A '*GOOD TIME*' AS MUCH AS THE NEXT YOUTH. I OWN MANY *CLIFF RICHARD* COMPACT DISCS. I CAN JIVE WITH THE BEST OF THEM. SOME OF OUR

CHRISTIAN YOUTH MOVEMENT EVENINGS ARE EVERY BIT AS *WILD* AS A RAVE. WE PLAY CHARADES AND DRINK *CIDER*.

TREECE: Kickin'.

BREW: OH YES. BUT MY MAIN INTEREST IS BATTLING *THE DEVIL* WHEREVER I FIND HIS *EVIL WORKS*. I WON'T TOLERATE *SATAN* IN ANY OF HIS MANY FORMS. THAT I CAN *GUARANTEE*.

....

MEMO
From: **April Treece, production associate.**
To: **Tiny Chiselhurst, producer/creator**
Re: *It's a Madhouse!*

Disaster! Donger Bennett, our prize plonker, the man we most want to see on *It's a Madhouse!*, has found 'true lurve' and wants to back out. Apparently, there's someone out there blind stupid enough to marry him. One Maxine Evenson, another estate agent. They'll probably breed! It's too horrible! We have a contract, we could sue, but that could lead to publicity, which might lead to Derek the Antichrist having us killed. NB: that last bit was a joke! Please advise.

....

MEMO
From: **Tiny Chiselhurst, producer/creator**
To: **April Treece, assistant producer**
Re: *It's a Madhouse!*

Make an appointment for a house viewing with Miss Evenson, and claim to be Donger's last fiancée – I know that's going to be disgusting for you, but maximum brownie points are involved – with only her best interests at heart. Play her a snippet of the initial interview tape, to wit:

LARK: You've never been married?

BENNETT: I've been engaged a couple of times, if that's what it takes to get the cork to pop.

Then present her with the background check dossier we assembled before offering him the contract. You might highlight in pink the more significant sentences. Tell her you had the dossier done when he proposed, like a survey before buying a house. If she's another bloody estate agent, she'll understand. If this is handled quickly, the crisis will fizzle. Trust me.

....

MEMO
From: **April Treece, co-associate producer.**
To: **Tiny Chiselhurst, producer/creator**
Re: *It's a Madhouse!*

Maxine Evenson is out of Donger Bennett's life, lucky girl. On my own initiative, I ordered Claire to call on the Donger for a follow-up interview, which means we owe her hazard pay. While fighting him off and, we trust, not lying back and thinking of television, she let him see suitably cropped and doctored photographs of Andrea Double-Barrel, Miss Giggly and Petra the Pyro. Donger is extremely keen to climb back into the Madhouse. It's my hope he gets on especially well with Martin 'Lockdown' Leigh.

....

PRODUCTION MEETING, No. 54
PRESENT, for MYTHWRHN PRODUCTIONS: **Tiny Chiselhurst (Producer), Phil Bender (Director), Barry Gatlin**

(Presenter), **Constant Drache (Designer)**, **April Treece (Production Assistant)**, **Claire Bates (Researcher)**, **Davinda Paquignet (Researcher)**.

PRESENT, for CLOUD 9 TELEVISION: **Derek Leech (Supremo)**, **Heather Wilding (Executive Expediter)**, **Basil Quilbert (Security)**

CHISELHURST: You've all seen the highlights reel we put together of the video interviews. Incidentally, you'll notice we got coverage of the room from three angles. The traditional behind-the-mirror shot was augmented by prototypes of the secret cams we'll be using for *Madhouse!* None of the interviewees spotted either gadget, and here we had to install the equipment in an existing environment rather than being able to dress the set from the ground up as we will on location.

WILDING: One is in the light fitting. As for the other, I give up.

CHISELHURST: Behind the fire regulations notice.

WILDING: You're recording now?

CHISELHURST: No. Davinda is taking minutes.

WILDING: Derek?

LEECH: That is acceptable.

CHISELHURST: So, how did you all like the tape? Do you see the potential.

GATLIN: MY FAVOURITE IS THE *CHRISTIAN*!

PAQUIGNET: Ouch, my ears!

WILDING: We see potential, Tiny. The tape represents your best prospects for *Madhouse*?

CHISELHURST: We have a couple in back-up, but yes. Dr Wendel?

WENDEL: It's not just a matter of getting the right people, but of getting the right mix. They can't all be too samey. There has to be a demographic spread of class, age and sex types among the subjects.

WILDING: But, ugh, no oldies, right? This is yoof you're giving us.

WENDEL: No one over thirty-five, indeed. And eighty per-cent under twenty-five. We built that early into the parameters of the experiment.

WILDING: Experiment?

CHISELHURST: It's how Biffo the Boffin thinks. Heth, believe me, this is Light Entertainment, not Heavy Educational.

WILDING: Educational worries me. It's a zapper prod. And so, frankly, are a lot of these people. Where did you get them?

CHISELHURST: They're real people, Heth. They came in of their own accord.

WILDING: You must have recruited the prison guard... what was his name?

TREECE: Martin Leigh. Lockdown Leigh.

WILDING: Yeah, him. He's a Central Casting Psycho.

CHISELHURST: He's our borderline choice, actually. Miss Lark thinks he's a bit obvious. Those tattoos might scare off some of the others too early.

LEECH: I like Leigh. He'll be a leader. For a while.

CHISELHURST: My thoughts exactly, Derek. He's a star in the making.

BATES: The one I hate most is Arabella Thingy-Thingy. The gold-digging posh bird.

BENDER: She's my favourite. That voice. It's not on a level with the LOUD CHRISTIAN or Miss Giggle, but there's something awful about it. Almost Thatchery.

GATLIN: Looks like a horse, though. I don't want to fuck her.

BENDER: Enough people will. You're a Yank, Barry. You don't understand this nanny thing we Brits have.

GATLIN: I don't want to fuck her. But I do want to hit her.

BATES: Is that how you divide them. Into ones you want to, uh, have sex with, and ones you want to hit?

GATLIN: Them? People in general?

BATES: Contestants, participants, subjects, victims, whatever we call them.

GATLIN: It's a fair enough system. Now, the Flame-On Chick. I *definitely* want to fuck her. I could light her fire, baby-cakes. You can take that to the bank and cash it!

TREECE: You're a sick man!

GATLIN: That's why you hired me, cherry-bee. You ain't gonna get Alastair Cooke to present *It's a Madhouse!*

TREECE: There's still Craig Charles.

GATLIN: [laughs] Get the fuck outta here!

CHISELHURST: We're off-topic, space kiddettes. Back to our mad people, please.

PAQUIGNET: I don't think they're mad.

CHISELHURST: What do you mean, Davinda?

PAQUIGNET: They're just… ordinary. Even the pyromaniac girl. I don't see them as any worse than the people I meet in clubs every night of the week.

WENDEL: Miss Paquignet, you are a junior assistant minion, I am a senior forensic psychologist. I assure you every one of these subjects is suffering from a severe, probably incurable personality disorder.

LEECH: Incurable?

WENDEL: By conventional means.

CHISELHURST: It's possible that *Madhouse!* will have some therapeutic effect.

WILDING: Oh, give us a break, Tiny. This is docusoap shit, not *On the Psychiatrist's Couch*. If we even thought you were sneaking something with content past us, you'd be off the air faster than a Girl Guides *Tribute to Gary Glitter* concert. We're not funding this for therapy. The point is that the people you've selected don't *deserve* help. Right?

TREECE: I certainly don't want to see 'Donger' Bennett get in touch with his inner self and accept it.

BATES/PAQUIGNET: Donger the Plonker!

TREECE: He made a big impression on the girls in the office.

WILDING: And our office too. And we only saw the tape.

TREECE: You should meet him in person, get the full-strength

Donger. Someone must have died and made him Bumgroper General. And he has this… smell. I think he uses rhino semen as an aftershave.

BATES: If nothing else, *Madhouse!* is the show that will tell the world Donger Bennetts are no longer acceptable.

GATLIN: So, none of you wanted to fuck him?

BATES/PAQUIGNET/TREECE: [retching noises]

GATLIN: Just asking, kittens. I thought he made some solid points, myself.

TREECE: [laughs] Are you sure you don't want to be a contestant rather than the presenter?

GATLIN: [laughs and shivers] No way, Ape.

WILDING: As ever, we're concerned with costs. How have you been coming along with the location?

CHISELHURST: That's Constant's department. Care to report?

DRACHE: Clearly we need isolation, and also a certain ambience of luxury. There's a lifestyle element to the series, a subliminal trace of *Fantasy Island* or the 007 films, so we want a touch of class to set off the anticipated behaviour of the participants. First, we looked for country houses within the United Kingdom, but that proved impractical. Besides the liabilities of renting somewhere we all expect to sustain quite a bit of damage during the recording, our mainland is too small, too crowded. There's nowhere, even in the wilds of Scotland, more than half a day's hike from civilisation. It's important that the players not have the option of just quitting and walking off. In the end, we've settled on an island. Several possibilities in British waters have come to light, but we favour the Med.

WILDING: That'll cost.

DRACHE: Not in the end. We think the climate, the traditional association of the Mediterranean with 'fun in the sun', will significantly add to the show's appeal. Never make the mistake of underestimating the fuck factor.

BENDER: *Baywatch* was a joke in the States, but a huge ratings hit here. That's not all down to tits. If you live in Bolton and it's drizzling over the gas-works, you want to switch on the telly and see sun-drenched beaches, azure seas, drinks with a mess of fruit in them and skimpy bathing suits. It's a can't-miss proposition.

CHISELHURST: And international waters will help with some of the legalities. That's always been a concern for Cloud 9, I know.

LEECH: It makes sense.

WILDING: Then it'll be authorised. But we've worked with you before, Constant. I want no overruns on this. Don't kit the set up with so much fucking decor that the animals get lost. This is a people programme, remember.

DRACHE: We have definite ideas on the look of the show.

TREECE: Abstract sculptures. Lots of sharp metal edges. Heavy candlesticks. Agricultural implements as ornaments.

CHISELHURST: You see the possibilities, Derek.

WILDING: No need to spell it out, Tiny. Now, our other concern. Clearly, we're in a cutthroat business and the competition can't get wind of this. The format'd be too easy to clone.

CHISELHURST: We're already thinking of licensing it to the States. Look how *Who Wants to Be a Millionaire?* took off. And it's a natural for the Japanese market.

WILDING: Our main concern isn't plagiarism, though. It's backlash. You all know Mr Quilbert?

CHISELHURST: Basil, hi.

WILDING: He'll be heading up our security operation. As of now, he owns you. Understand.

QUILBERT: Good morning, Mr Chiselhurst, Miss Treece. And those I haven't met. We'll have one-to-one sessions scheduled soon. It is a condition of the involvement of Cloud 9 in this project that all matters concerning security be channelled through me. There will be no exceptions. We have prepared acceptable cover stories as to the nature of the programme, based on the mock proposal you sent out to the applicants, and these will be leaked steadily to the trades. We're building the cover stories around Mr Gatlin's track record in extreme stand-up and the well-established 'adventure game' style of show. The truly radical nature of *It's a Madhouse!* should not become evident until we are ready to broadcast. I have prepared various strategies for dealing with the cries for suppression we envision as inevitable. Cloud 9 will preface the premiere with a week of anti-censorship programming, with our tame 'intellectuals' debating the less coherent and attractive members of various censorious or regulatory bodies. The purpose of this is to defang those most likely to object to a show which we consider will have the widest possible audience. If columnists have just spent an hour on Cloud 9 crying for freedom of speech and expression, they can hardly turn round and say we should not broadcast a show they consider to be objectionable. We used this basic strategy very successfully last year with the launch of the Lolita Channel and a variant is currently in play to pave the way for our 24-hour War and Gore strand.

CHISELHURST: So, I take it, you're giving us a go. Derek?

WILDING: Cloud 9 will take *Madhouse!* to series. Make us television history, Tiny.

....

THE FINAL SELECTION
Harry Bennett
Joshua Brew
Andrea D'Arbanvilliers-Holmes
Petra Kidner
Martin Leigh
Shona Murtaugh
Donovan Wyke

NOTES, by MYRA LARK
The optimum number of participants was set at seven early in the planning stages. An odd number ensures that, in the event of factionalisation, there will be an uneven split, with shifting

loyalties or connections making for an unstable, potentially eventful series of relationship storms. In the event of heterosexual liaisons forming, one of the men will be left out. The most obvious candidate would be Mr Brew, because of his religious persuasions. More interesting from our purposes would be Mr Bennett, whose self-image is constructed entirely around his ability to coerce sex from females. It has been a subject for concern that Mr Leigh is too obviously dominant among the group, being habitually used to attaining his personal objectives through violence, but Dr Wendel and I have conferred and we see avenues around this 'problem'. If a blunt solution is required, Mr Leigh could be handicapped in some manner and forced to a great extent to rely on the goodwill of the others for his continued comfort. A subtler way out would be to arrange matters so that, from the outset, Mr Wyke is in a more commanding position. His record suggests that he can for a short while at least project the image of a confident, born leader.

After running simulations and role-play scenarios with fully-briefed substitutes, these eventualities occur in every single variation of the basic situation.

a) After three days, multiple sexual exchanges will have taken place. There will also have been betrayals, extensive verbal and minor physical abuse and the development of very deep, though shifting, attachments and dislikes within the group.

b) At the six-day stage, a danger point is reached as the group turn against the experiment. We believe they will make an effort to destroy all recording devices in sight, and repeat our suggestion that these be dummies. Some of the 'hidden' cameras should be easily discoverable and disablable too. It is vital that we keep the subjects' attentions on each other and not foster a group paranoia directed at external bodies (eg: the production company), so we must insert into the scenario the idea that one or more of the subjects are in fact 'plants' working for us. You will recall that an early stage of development, we rejected the idea of actually having a 'mole' in the group as unnecessary and unsatisfying. We believe these subjects are capable of creating and starring in their own paranoia/entertainment scenario with very little help from us.

c) Once the imaginary 'plants' have been dealt with, the programme will continue as before. Food, sexual favours, soft drugs and basic services will become currency. It is to be stressed that we should not go out of our way to make things difficult for the subjects – by withdrawing or tampering with the food supply, for instance – since the purpose of the show is to let them be themselves. Their own personality types are what is at issue here, are the factors that will make them stars. We have every confidence in them.

d) Most of the variables become extreme on the eighth day, when the subjects realise the experiment is not limited to the week they thought they had committed themselves to. Then, the communications from Mr Gatlin should become more cryptic or mocking, playing on the knowledge of the survivor personalities we have gained in the course of the first week. It is possible that the group will forge together to attempt escape, but the inherent instabilities of the personality mix make this a highly unlikely and unworkable venture.

NB: Our amended psych profiles and the medical details of the subjects are attached. Note especially Mr Bennett's asthma, Miss Kidner's understandable high degree of tolerance for searing pain and Mr Wyke's clinical sociopathy.

....

MEMO
From: **Tiny Chiselhurst, producer/creator**
To: **April Treece, co-associate producer**
Re: *It's a Madhouse!*

We have our madhouse! It's three miles or so from St. Helena, and we've bought it outright so it's our own country (what should we call it?) and we can write the law-book. It was a refuge for the idle rich in the 1920s, and comes complete with a villa Drache is having restored to its original condition at great expense to Cloud 9. From the snaps I've seen, it's very Agatha Christie. The hidden cams are being installed as I write. We're taking advantage of the restoration to build a lot of versatility into the cams. There will be no blind spots on this island, though the stars will be told that there is one room set aside for privacy. Naturally, that's where we expect a great deal of the action to take place, so it's bugged from here to there and gone.

Just in case our stars take too long to find out about each other, we're planting scrapbooks about each of them in the villa library. For the first week, Barry will transmit instructions nightly via a two-way TV hook-up to set out games and contests we've designed to be uneven and unfair, to sow discontent among the stars, and string them along the game aspect. Dr Wendel and Miss Lark disagree about when or if they will tumble to the 'real' nature of the show, but both are sure it won't come until well after we have got the good stuff going. I sense Satellite Awards in the making.

....

MEMO
From: **April Treece, associate producer**
To: **Tiny Chiselhurst, producer/creator**
Re: *It's a Madhouse!*

Mr Q reports Shona Murtaugh is really Judy Burke, a freelance journalist for *Scam* magazine. The bitch is undercover doing an exposé on rigged docusoaps. She must be imagining headlines along the lines of TV TEAM FORCED ME TO HAVE SEX WITH PLONKER.

* * *

MEMO
From: **Tiny Chiselhurst, producer/creator**
To: **April Treece, co-executive producer**
Re: *It's a Madhouse!*

Shona or Judy? It doesn't matter. What I want to know is whether the meltdown giggle is real or fake?

. . . .

MEMO
From: **April Treece, executive producer**
To: **Tiny Chiselhurst, producer/creator**
Re: *It's a Madhouse!*

The shriek is real. I've got that from three sources. Probably why she got the assignment. No one can stand to have her in the office.

. . . .

MEMO
From: **Tiny Chiselhurst, producer/creator**
To: **April Treece, co-producer**
Re: *It's a Madhouse!*

If the giggle's real, the girl's in. Have Mr Q disable any mobile phone or computer up-link she might contrive to get to our island (that goes for the others too, BTW). Miss Lark considers someone genuinely hiding her name will be a shoo-in to get tagged as the 'plant'. If the scenario runs as expected, I doubt Judy the Journo will ever file copy.

* * *

REQUEST FORM No. 69
Re: *It's a Madhouse!*
From: **Constant Drache, Production Designer**
To: **April Treece, producer**

It is vital that my team be supplied with the following as soon as possible.

1: A set of Sabatier kitchen knives. The sharpest in the world, and the most stylish. The full set runs to eighty-five pieces, and includes special blades for paring apricots, shelling crabs, etc.

2: Traditional tools for the shed. Nothing electric or rubber-gripped, just plain old wooden-handled hammers, screwdrivers, saws, awls and axes. I want that rough, honest-work, *Waltons* feel for this location.

3: Matches (books, boxes, art deco containers), cigarette lighters, flints, candles, magnifying glasses, tapers. Every room, almost every surface, will be fully equipped with little temptations. Also: fire-lighters, paraffin, brandy.

4: Paintings. We're concealing the video com-link behind a print of Edvard Munch's *The Scream*. It's a cliché touch, perhaps, but effective. Miss Lark and Dr Wendel have come up with a list of artworks appropriate for every participant, and we can make sure their rooms are designed to reflect, intensify or provoke their particular quirks. Bennett's room, for instance, will be furnished with erotic prints of male nudes.

5: Ill-hanging doors. The villa is being refitted from the ground up. It is appropriate, given the title and the intent of the show, that none of the doors or windows be fitted properly. Every angle will be a few degrees out of right, every oblong almost imperceptibly a parallelogram. The house is almost an eighth player in our game, and it gets billing on the title so I'm sure even the tightwads at the top of the Pyramid will be pleased to allow the expenditure.

* * *

think I could resist it. You're still an anti, though?

BATES: No. I cracked when you sent me after Donger. I hate myself for this, but I wouldn't miss it for the world.

PAQUIGNET: It's going to be very popular. I think we're all going to do very well out of it.

TREECE: So, Claire, do you want to change your mind about the credit? After the Donger Affair, Tiny said you could go from Senior Researcher to Junior Producer if you want. It's a Hell of a way to get it, but…

BATES: Ape, I'll take it. Where do I sign, and in what?

....

CONTINUITY ANNOUNCER SCRIPT,
CLOUD 9 TELEVISION.

Seven very special people. One very unusual house. An island paradise.

What happens?

You can find out *tonight*, exclusively on Cloud 9 TV, the Derek Leech Channel. To subscribe to this pay-per-view premiere, call our numbers now!

The show everyone will be talking about tomorrow!

It's people. It's real. It's raw. It's struggle. It's surprise. It's life. It's Something Else.

It's a Madhouse!

Coming up next…

JAGO

by KIM NEWMAN

In the tiny English village of Alder, dreams and nightmares are beginning to come true. Creatures from local legend, science fiction and the dark side of the human mind prowl the town.

Paul, a young academic composing a thesis about the end of the world, and his girlfriend Hazel, a potter, have come to Alder for the summer. Their idea of a rural retreat gradually sours as the laws of nature begin to break down around them. Paul and Hazel are soon drawn into a vortex of fear as violent chaos engulfs the community and the village prepares to reap a harvest of horror.

A brand-new edition of the critically acclaimed novel. This edition also contains the short stories 'Ratting', 'Great Western' and 'The Man on the Clapham Omnibus'.

"A roaring good read." *The Times*

"Newman's prose is sophisticated and his narrative drive irresistible." *Publishers Weekly*